SOFT BURIAL

WEATHERHEAD BOOKS ON ASIA

**WEATHERHEAD EAST ASIAN INSTITUTE,
COLUMBIA UNIVERSITY**

For a complete list of books in the series, please see the Columbia University Press website.

SOFT BURIAL

A NOVEL

FANG FANG

TRANSLATED BY

MICHAEL BERRY

Columbia University Press   *New York*

This publication has been supported by the Richard W. Weatherhead Publication Fund of the Weatherhead East Asian Institute, Columbia University.

Columbia University Press wishes to express its appreciation for assistance given by the Pushkin Fund in the publication of this book.

Columbia University Press
Publishers Since 1893
New York   Chichester, West Sussex
cup.columbia.edu

Ruanmai copyright © 2016 Fang Fang

Translation copyright © 2025 Michael Berry
All rights reserved

Library of Congress Cataloging-in-Publication Data
Names: Fang, Fang, 1955– author. | Berry, Michael, 1974– translator.
Title: Soft burial : a novel / Fang Fang ; translated by Michael Berry.
Other titles: Ruan mai. English
Description: New York : Columbia University Press, 2024. |
Series: Weatherhead books on Asia | Identifiers: LCCN 2024015986 (print) | LCCN 2024015987 (ebook) | ISBN 9780231214988 (hardback) | ISBN 9780231214995 (trade paperback) | ISBN 9780231560566 (ebook)
Subjects: LCSH: Land reform—China—History—20th century—Fiction. | China—History—1949-1976—Fiction. | LCGFT: Historical fiction. | Novels.
Classification: LCC PL2857.A6352 R8313 2024 (print) | LCC PL2857.A6352 (ebook) | DDC 895.13/52—dc23/eng/20240525
LC record available at https://lccn.loc.gov/2024015986
LC ebook record available at https://lccn.loc.gov/2024015987

Printed and bound by CPI Group (UK) Ltd, Croydon, CR0 4YY

Cover design: Chang Jae Lee
Cover image: Fang Fang

CONTENTS

Translator's Introduction *vii*

Soft Burial 1

Coda 383
Afterword: We Don't Want a Soft Burial 387

TRANSLATOR'S INTRODUCTION

To be put into the earth without a coffin and have your body placed directly into the dirt is one kind of soft burial; but when the living insist on consciously or unconsciously cutting themselves off from what happened, covering up the past, abandoning history, and refusing to remember, this is another form of soft burial committed over the passage of time. And once the past has been committed to a soft burial, it will likely lie there generation after generation, forgotten for all eternity.

—Fang Fang

*S*oft Burial is a remarkable novel in the canon of contemporary Chinese literature. Part of what sets the book apart is its innovative literary form, which employs diary entries, shifting settings (Wuhan, Shenzhen, and Eastern Sichuan) and temporal spaces (from the late 1940s to the 1990s), experimental leanings (such as the use of a series of flashback-like sequences that run in reverse chronological order), and alternating character perspectives. But the novel also stands out for its unique fate after publication, going from being honored with a major

Chinese literary award to being attacked and banned in China within the span of a few days.

First published in 2016, *Soft Burial* was written by the prolific Chinese author Fang Fang. Born in 1955, Fang Fang (pen name of Wang Fang) moved with her family to Wuhan at the age of two and went on to become the award-winning author of dozens of volumes of essays and fiction. Wuhan is also the city where the majority of her later stories are set. Fang Fang began writing in the mid-1970s and published her first novel in 1982; during the early phase of her career she was best known for the novella *The Scenery* (*Fengjing*, 1987), which has been included as required reading in Chinese high school textbooks. Several of Fang Fang's stories have been adapted for film and television, included the well-regarded 2012 film *Feng Shui*, which was based on her novel *A Thousand Arrows Through the Heart* (*Wanjian chuanxin*, 2007). She also served as the chair of the Hubei Writers Association, a position that attests to the prestige that Fang Fang enjoyed within official circles in China. With the publication of *Soft Burial*, however, her standing in China would begin to change.

Soft Burial can be read on several levels: it is a work of historical fiction (depicting the late 1940s); a portrait of contemporary Chinese society (during the economic boom of the 1990s); a mystery or historical thriller that resists providing clean and predictable answers; and most importantly, it is a novel that prods readers to face deep ethical questions about historical trauma and the moral imperative to remember. It is this latter category that seems to target the long-entrenched ethical stance of *mingzhe baoshen*, which is sometimes translated as "put your own safety before matters of principle" but often amounts to "keep your mouth shut and stay out of trouble." Over the course of the historical vicissitudes of the early years of the People's Republic of China, which included political campaigns like the

Anti-Rightist Campaign (1957–1959), the Great Leap Forward (1958–1962), and the Cultural Revolution (1966–1976), a culture of silence gradually began to set in. For millions of Chinese, *mingzhe baoshen* became one of the most important maxims to follow in their everyday lives; it was about protecting their families, it was about survival. But it also brought forth a culture of secrecy and silence, passed on from one generation to another; its accumulated impact is one of historical erasure.

Suffering from amnesia, the female protagonist of *Soft Burial*, who remains nameless for the first several chapters of the book, is a potent avatar for the broader historical erasure at play. However, it is ultimately her son who, several decades later, must belatedly bear the weight of long-suppressed trauma. While narratives of historical trauma (even those employing literary tropes like amnesia to address unspeakable acts of past violence) may seem fairly common in world literature today, *Soft Burial* stands out not only for the literary dexterity with which Fang Fang executes her project but also for the complex ways she pushes the belated effects of suppressed trauma decades into the future, projecting its impact on later generations. *Soft Burial* is also notable for articulating that which in China, even at the time of its publication in 2016, could not (and still cannot) be spoken.

Upon initial publication, *Soft Burial* was lauded by critics in China and even awarded the coveted Lu Yao Literature Award, named for the beloved author of such humanistic novels as *Life* (*Rensheng*) and *The Ordinary World* (*Pingfan de shijie*). However, just a few months after being released by the prestigious People's Literature Publishing House, *Soft Burial* itself came under attack. A series of scathing essays and denunciations appeared in periodicals and on websites like Red Culture (Hongse wenhua), and a conference was held in Wuhan (the very day Fang Fang was given the award) against *Soft Burial*. Like a strange political specter returning from the Cultural Revolution era, the conference had all the features of political denunciation meetings from the 1960s, including a large poster stating "*Soft Burial* is a terrible poisonous weed!" More online attacks followed, and by the end of May 2017, *Soft Burial* had been taken off the shelves of bookstores throughout China. A novel that had dared to challenge the code of silence regarding modern Chinese history had been silenced. Over the years a series of other novels have explored some of the more controversial periods of early People's Republic of China (PRC) history, so why was this narrative deemed so particularly damaging?

There were two factors at play. The publication of *Soft Burial* happened during a new period of tightening controls over fiction, film, and other cultural works. President Xi Jinping introduced the concept of "telling the good China story" (or "telling the China story well") as early as 2013; this political stance would quickly have major implications for the kinds of narratives that were acceptable and how they should be told. The impact and further development of this policy can be seen in Xi's 2014 talks at the Beijing Forum on Literature and Art (which revisited many of Mao's cultural policies from the 1940s) and the 2018 shift of oversight of the film industry to the Ministry of Propaganda. It was against this backdrop of more heavily regulated cultural policies that *Soft Burial* appeared. The other factor is tied to the historical backdrop of the novel: the Land Reform Campaign of the late 1940s. During the early years of the PRC, the government launched a series of massive political campaigns, the vast majority of which (including the aforementioned Anti-Rightist Campaign, the Great Leap Forward, and the Cultural Revolution) were later deemed to be largely failures, unleashing economic instability, political chaos, famine, and the persecution of countless individuals. Historiography in the PRC has continued to view the Land Reform Campaign as a necessity intricately tied to the legitimacy of the Chinese Communist Party's rule. Even if the latter political movements were riddled with chaos and violence, the Land Reform Campaign is seen as the one thing the CCP "got right," a cornerstone movement in the founding of the People's Republic, existing in sacred historical space beyond reproach and criticism.

Soft Burial is not a work of historiography but a work of historical fiction set, in part, against the Land Reform Campaign that takes a sympathetic stance in portraying members of the landowning class. Fang Fang was already challenging deeply entrenched stereotypes (like the "evil landlords" that appeared in countless socialist narratives), how "class struggle" functions, and unspoken literary rules about how Chinese writers portray the past. That said, the version of history that emerges in *Soft Burial* is certainly not a one-sided "revisionist" account of official PRC history; it is a complex and nuanced vision of the past riddled with ethical dilemmas and unanswered questions. None of the characters stands beyond moral reproach, but through Fang Fang's pen, all of them are rendered in human terms, unlike the deeply entrenched black-and-white portrayals of landlords as villains and the peasant revolutionaries who led the movement as heroes. Readers of *Soft Burial* are repeatedly prodded to ponder the actions of the revolutionaries, the landlords, and even their descendants decades later as the novel strips this historical moment of its revolutionary myths and reframes it from a human perspective. But in 2016, even that was enough to elicit claims that Fang Fang was using the work to refute the historical place of the Land Reform Campaign, challenge the political legitimacy of the Chinese Communist Party, or bring about a "color revolution." *Soft Burial*, a novel about the social, political, and ethical structures that result in the silencing of history, was itself given a soft burial, unceremoniously removed from bookstores and swiped from the Chinese internet.

At the heart of *Soft Burial* is a series of diary entries written by Qinglin's father from the late 1940s through the mid-1950s. Those entries provide a skeleton key for unlocking the mysteries of the past, but they remain concealed and unread, locked away in an old leather trunk for the majority of the book. Even the main protagonist remains deeply ambivalent about whether to read the diaries and what to do with the information they contain. But lurking beneath this question is a deeper quandary that should resonate with all readers: What do we do with *our* diaries? Do we remain complicit through silence and complacency, continue to *mingzhe baoshen*, to keep our mouths shut and stay out of trouble? Or do we interrogate the past, record our present, provide testimony to history, and speak truth to power? Fang Fang gave her own answer not only through the writing of this book but also in 2020 when she wrote her own diary. *Wuhan Diary* was one of the first long-form narrative records of the COVID-19 global health crisis and a day-to-day account of the first citywide lockdown in response to the novel coronavirus. And unlike the diary in *Soft Burial* that was locked away for decades and filled with exhortations that the author's son *not* stir up the past, Fang Fang's personal story took a very different approach. Published online and uploaded in real time each day to an army of tens of millions of readers, Fang Fang's dispatches pointed to a new ethical engagement with the act of writing, recording, and speaking truth through literature. In the words of one of her protagonists from *Soft Burial*, "When it comes to history, someone needs to preserve the truth about what happened."

My translation of this novel began in 2019 and was temporarily interrupted by *Wuhan Diary*, which I worked on from

February through April 2020. Thanks go first to Fang Fang for her patience and support throughout the translation process, and for the model of moral courage that she continues to inspire me with. I am indebted to the National Endowment for the Arts for a Translation Grant to support this novel. Thanks to Hongling Zhang, who first introduced me to Fang Fang and suggested this project. My deep appreciation and thanks to Jennifer Lyons for championing this work; Jennifer Crewe, Christine Dunbar, Leslie Kriesel, and the editorial team at Columbia University Press; the two anonymous external readers, who provided helpful suggestions; and my family. I dedicate this translation to the memory of Michael Henry Heim (1943–2012), an old friend who knew a thing or two about the ethics and practice of translation.

SOFT BURIAL

1

INNER STRUGGLE

She is someone in a state of constant inner struggle.

She is old. Her saggy skin is so loose that it doesn't even wrinkle anymore. Instead, her face and neck are covered with thin lines. Her pale complexion makes those lines appear as if they were carefully etched onto her face, one stroke at a time; they don't at all resemble a series of marks haphazardly left behind by the blade of time. Her eyes are cloudy, yet when she opens them you can still catch a sudden spark of brilliance shining through.

Her gaze often locks onto a particular object, as if she is lost in deep thought, but sometimes it simply looks as if she is just staring into space. Occasionally, when this happens, pedestrians passing by will stop out of curiosity and ask, "Hey Granny, you okay? You got something on your mind?"

During those moments she looks dazed and usually stares back blankly at the passerby, mumbling some indistinct words. Not even *she* realizes what she is saying. In those moments even she herself wouldn't be able to explain what was going through her mind. It just felt as if all kinds of queer things were tugging at her memory, trying to leap out of her head. Those were things she had spent a lifetime trying to avoid. She tried to resist them. Her resistance was like a thick, tight net, enveloping the army of demons that were constantly trying to break out. For her entire life she had carried that net with her, always ready to face down those demons.

When her husband was still alive, he would occasionally urge her to think hard and maybe she would be able to figure out what was going on inside her; perhaps then she could find some kind of inner peace. She took her husband's advice, and there were many times when she tried so hard to find a quiet place inside herself and bring those memories forth. But whenever she tried, she would suddenly be struck by some terrible sensation: It felt as if her entire body were being pierced by countless needles. It was as if her body were being ripped apart from the inside. During those moments the pain and exhaustion made her feel as if she could barely breathe.

Filled with desperation, she told her husband, "Don't force me. I can't do it. As soon as I go to that place in my mind I feel like I'm going to die." Her husband was rendered silent by her strong reaction. After a brief pause, he told her, "Then perhaps you should just let it go. Try keeping yourself busy with something else. That should take your mind off those other things."

She ended up taking her husband's advice and busied herself with all kinds of daily tasks. She'd never had a real career; taking care of the household was her only real job. She worked hard cleaning and straightening up, keeping the house spotless. Whenever people came over, they would compliment her on how impossibly clean and tidy the house was. Her husband was a physician, so he also took particular pride in her cleaning habits.

And so her life gradually settled into a normal routine.

Many years went by and things didn't change much for her. Yet each year it was as if there were a thin, dense membrane growing around her, tightly sealing in that thing lurking beyond her memories. Year after year that thin membrane grew thicker, congealing into a wall that sealed away all those demons that had been hidden deep in her unconscious.

But as for what that thing was, she had no idea.

She first developed amnesia during spring 1952.

It wasn't until many years later when her husband one day returned from the hospital with a stern expression and began to tell her about the "Cultural Revolution." The hospital was holding political meetings on a daily basis and people were starting to put up "big character posters" accusing him of having a "problematic history." She was beside herself with anxiety but couldn't grasp the full significance of what her husband was telling her. Then her husband suddenly told her, *You'll be okay. I will protect you. Just don't ever bring up those things that happened in the past. Your greatest enemies aren't those people out there, it's those things you no longer remember. If anyone ever asks you about those things in the past, you just tell them you don't know anything and you'll be fine.*

She didn't realize that this was not just her husband's way of consoling her—it was also his gentle way of reminding her about what to do in case things ever got bad. Instead, his words struck an uncomfortable chord deep within her. It was as if those old ghosts, hidden deep down for so long that they had virtually disappeared, not only had been awakened but also were now right there in her husband's hands. *What does this mean? How could he possibly know all these details about things that even I can't remember?* As those thoughts raced through her mind, she could feel a terrifying atmosphere closing in. That feeling of terror now remained right there beside her, every minute, every day.

And so she realized that her husband, this man she so deeply loved for so many years, was also someone to be deeply feared.

Why? Why would she ever have such feelings? She didn't understand why she would be struck by this sense of fear and apprehension. But it was always there.

SOUNDS OF THE RIVER

She was completely naked when they pulled her out from the rushing river. Her entire body was covered with bruises. Those injuries were caused by the river rocks pounding against her skin under the heavy current. One of the people who saved her said she had been in the water so long that except for her black hair, her entire body had turned so pale that they had trouble figuring out exactly where all the bruises were. It was a good thing that the day they found her there happened to be a few military doctors seeing patients at a nearby village; the villagers rushed her straight to those visiting doctors. After administering emergency life-saving treatment, the doctors had her admitted to the hospital.

She remained in a coma for more than two weeks before waking up. When she finally came to and tried to answer the doctors' questions, she suddenly found herself at a complete and utter loss.

Where are you from? Which village? How old are you? Who else do you live with? How did you fall into the river? Did your boat capsize, or did a bad person throw you in? Were you the only one who fell into the water? The doctors took turns asking questions, and even though they spoke softly, their voices were like sharp nails scraping against sandpaper. She couldn't take it anymore—it was too painful. She curled herself into a ball on her hospital bed. *That's right, who am I? Where do I live? What's my name? How did I fall into the river?* But she had no answer to any of those questions. *Why can't I remember? How could I not even know who I am?* She started to cry. "I can't remember," she said.

She really couldn't remember.

Then they said, *Think hard, try to remember. Someone pulled you out of the river. Try to go back to that moment when you were pulled out of the river. See if you can piece things together from there.*

She did as they suggested and tried hard to remember what happened, but as soon as she thought of the river, the rushing sound of the water exploded like a bolt of lightning inside her. And with the sound of the river came a strange unspeakable fear. It was as if a demon were hiding in the river's waves; although she couldn't see it or touch it, it was there ruthlessly lashing out against her body and soul. For a second she lost control of herself and broke out in a hysterical fit of tears and screams.

That was when a certain Dr. Wu stepped in to put an end to all the questions. "She is likely in a state of shock," he explained. "Stop forcing her to remember, just let her concentrate on her recovery."

With those words, everyone put the matter to rest. As time went by, though, you could still tell by the way those doctors talked to her that they all felt great pity for her.

The weather that spring was gorgeous.

The pink flowers on the peach tree outside the window were in full bloom. A row of white apricot flowers lined the walls of the courtyard, though they were hard to make out from a distance because of the way they blended into the white courtyard walls. Farther off the dark green leaves on a group of thick and sturdy gingko trees were gently swaying in the wind; it was hard to tell just how old the trees were. And even farther off in the distance the shadows of the mountains gently danced up and down, their outlines resembling flower petals. In the corner of the courtyard the white jasmine had already come into full bloom; its petals were on the verge of falling. But those glowing chrysanthemums were still bursting with color. This rich array of colors came into her field of vision. All the birds that had returned with the spring seemed reborn with a new vitality. Even though the wind still carried a slight winter chill, the birds fluttered about singing their songs. The scenery and the sounds gradually helped her settle down.

As far as her new life was concerned, this was where her memories began—here in a small town east of the river.

It was only later that the doctors and nurses told her all kinds of stories about how she had been saved. They said that when Dr. Wu and the others first brought her to the hospital, nobody thought she would make it. There was one day early on where three different doctors almost pronounced her dead; they even summoned the undertaker to pick up her body from the hospital. It was a good thing Dr. Wu was so meticulous in his care: it was only after he noticed her middle finger slightly twitch that he insisted they keep her admitted for further observation. She woke up a few days after that. Hearing those stories allowed her to reconstruct how she had escaped from death's door and made it back.

There was one person in particular who played a crucial role in this story. That was none other than Dr. Wu, the man responsible for saving her life. Living through this near-death experience allowed her to gradually appreciate what she had been through and what Dr. Wu had done for her. Although her memories were limited to this short time in the hospital, contained within them were all the emotions of a complete human experience. As far as she was concerned, that was all she needed to begin anew.

That is how she learned to take all those painful, lost memories and let them go. And that is how she carried on . . . all the way until now.

Forgetting is not always a form a betrayal. Sometimes forgetting is a form of survival. But that was something that Dr. Wu taught her.

SHE LIKED TO BE ALONE

Compared with those elderly people you see in the parks dancing and going for long leisurely strolls, time seemed to have had a particularly harsh impact on her. According to the age listed on her official residence card, she was only in her early seventies—but her age was based on Dr. Wu's estimate of her age at the time they found her in the river. They used the date they discovered her as her birthday. That date was filled in by hand by Dr. Wu—it would stay with her for the rest of her life.

She looked much older than other women supposedly her age. When she looked in the mirror, she always assumed that excessive work and exhaustion had prematurely aged her. She never went to those community dances and didn't like interacting with people she didn't know. She liked to be alone. Loneliness never bothered her; she just preferred to spend time with herself. She didn't have any relatives or friends. Occasionally the old lady next door would come by to invite her out for a walk. The neighbor would try to coax her out of the house by saying, "Staying active is the secret to a long life." But still she'd refuse to go.

It wasn't that she didn't want to live a long life, just that she had a heavy heart. It weighed on her to the point that she didn't even want to go out; she preferred to just sit quietly by herself. On sunny days she would always go out to sit on the steps across from the Park Hill Church. She would raise her head and gaze at the large gray building standing before her. Although the large sign for "Church" was bathed in sunlight, she didn't see its luminescence. Instead she felt as if each day she were witnessing its gradual decay, then at other times it felt as if she were seeing its rejuvenation, but then, upon further study, she would again see the decay. She found this process quite interesting. Her husband used to enjoy going for walks with her, and they would often pass this road on their way to the historical neighborhood of Tanhualin.

During their walks her husband would often tell her all kinds of strange stories. This is the story he told her about that Catholic church: The Qing court forbade the construction of churches in China, yet those foreign priests still traveled all the way to China intent on building them. Those desperate priests were on the verge of giving up when a Chinese helped them figure out a solution. He suggested that they write a formal request to the court to build a *da wang tang* (大王堂), a "Hall of the Great King," and once the request was approved, they could add a stroke to the character *da* (大), transforming it to *tian* (天), or "Hall of the Heavenly King," making it a church. The foreigners thought this a superb idea and sent in the formal request as suggested. As soon as the court realized it was not an application to build a church, they immediately approved it. Then the foreigners not only added a stroke to turn the character *da* (大) into *tian* (天) but also turned *wang* (王) into *zhu* (主), which effectively transformed the name from *da wang tang* (大王堂), or "Hall of the Great King," into *tian zhu tang* (天主堂), "Hall of the Heavenly Lord," which is how the Catholic church is referred to in Chinese. When the local officials came to inspect the church, they discovered that the official application, which even had the court's seal, was to open a "Hall of the Heavenly Lord." The officials couldn't understand what had happened, but since all the approvals seemed to be in order, they let it go. After all, they had been hoodwinked before and weren't terribly concerned about this one application.

This story left a deep impression on her; she even laughed out loud the first time she heard it.

But her sitting there now had nothing to do with that story. She was there to enjoy the row of green foliage in the courtyard wrapping around Our Lady's Hill. At the base of the hill was a statue of Our Lady of Lourdes. Her face appeared adorned for all eternity with a smile of purity and peace. They would always see her on their strolls and stop to admire her. The first time they passed the statue she asked, "Who is she?" Her husband responded by saying that there used to be a time when people would approach the statue and ask, "Who are you?" Our Lady would respond, "I am the Immaculate Conception." She didn't understand what "Immaculate Conception" meant. Her husband wrote the words out on the palm of her hand to make it clearer. "What does it mean?" she asked. "What it means," her husband explained, "is that she is untainted by original sin."

She still didn't quite understand what he was trying to explain, but she could feel her heart racing. Her husband continued his explanation as they left the church and continued on their leisurely walk: "This is something we should both remember. In this world, we all come forth from the Immaculate Conception. You and I too."

She still wasn't quite sure what he was saying. Finally her husband said, "Just remember Our Lady of Lourdes. She will always help you find that place of inner peace."

She still didn't understand all the things her husband was trying to explain, but from that point forward, just laying eyes on the statue of Our Lady of Lourdes indeed gave her a sense of peace. Not only that, but seeing Our Lady provided her with a feeling of comfort that permeated her entire being. Yet still she wondered, *What does "Immaculate Conception" mean?*

There was a hemp-colored cat that lived on that street near the church; he had a face that resembled one of those animal spirits you read about in fairy tales. When she sat there on the steps across from the church, the cat would often silently stroll over and squat down beside her. The cat loved to gaze up at her with his big, wide eyes, and sometimes he would even extend his paw toward her. The cat looking at her somehow made her feel so at home. She would often reach out to rub his back, which seemed to calm him. But then one day the cat was gone. She looked all over for him and even called out to him. "Sparrow! Sparrow! Where'd you go?" The hemp-colored cat heard her call and rushed over. As she sat down beside him, she suddenly thought, *Why did I just call him Sparrow?*

She is now sitting on the curb under the bright sun, at her feet a wicker basket filled with shoe pads. She had embroidered them by hand with lotus flower and mandarin duck patterns. She wasn't quite sure why she was able to embroider them, as she had no recollection of ever having learned embroidery. But whenever she picked up a shoe pad, she instinctively seemed to know what to do with it. There was a period of time when she worked as a nanny for the family of Professor Ma. One winter's day, Mrs. Ma gave her an old pair of cotton shoes. She thought they were too big, so she turned them into shoe pads. And then, without even really paying attention, she picked up a needle and embroidered a begonia. Mrs. Ma carefully admired her handiwork: "You're really talented. Have you studied embroidery before? It's really got a nice artistic feel to it!"

But Mrs. Ma's compliment didn't have the desired effect; instead, it was as if a rock suddenly crashed down on her, disturbing something deep inside her. She felt a kind of terror, a terror that came from some unknown deep place. It was as if some unseen danger were descending on her. Every strange face or sound she encountered made her shudder. This went on for several months until, finally, she decided to give up embroidery. She worked for the Ma family for many years, until the time Mrs. Ma passed away. Then, when Professor Ma got remarried to a much younger wife, her son called her back home.

Her son's name was Qinglin.

THOSE THINGS SHE NEVER GIVES UP

She originally lived with Qinglin in an apartment off a narrow alley in the Hanhualin neighborhood in Wuchang. It was a subsidized rental that had been allocated to them back when her husband was still alive. They had lived there for many years. Her husband was Dr. Wu—the same doctor who had saved her during a trip to the countryside to treat patients. Her love for him was forged not only through marriage but also by the fact that he was the man who had saved her life. When she came out of her coma at the hospital, Dr. Wu was the first person she laid eyes on. Her new collection of memories also began with him.

She would often wonder, *When did I first fall in love with him? Was it the first time I laid eyes on him? Or that time I visited him in his office?* She couldn't even remember what it was that brought her to Dr. Wu's office. All she remembered was seeing a copy of *Dream of the Red Chamber* on his desk and being unable to resist picking it up to flip through its pages. Her lips unconsciously uttered the name of the book's protagonist, "Daiyu," which somehow sent a wave of uneasiness through her heart. It was also precisely at that moment that Dr. Wu stepped into his office. He looked surprised to see her flipping through his book and took it from her hand. He flashed her a hard look and hesitated for a few seconds before saying, "I think you might be better off if you don't tell anyone you know how to read." She gazed back at him, puzzled. He continued, "Please don't misunderstand what I'm trying to say. I'm just concerned that if people know you are educated, they might start getting suspicious. After all, your background is a mystery, and it could lead people to make certain . . . assumptions. Do you know what I mean?"

She actually *didn't* know what he meant, but she nevertheless followed his advice. Somehow his words made that uneasiness immediately disappear, replacing it with a blanket of comfort and warmth.

A few days after that, Dr. Wu recommended her for a housekeeping job at the home of Political Commissar Liu, who lived in the military compound. Political Commissar Liu was a veteran cadre from the old days of the revolution; his wife was also a cadre. Dr. Wu explained why he recommended her for the job as he walked her outside toward the intersection, and as he spoke his words seemed to be hinting at all kinds of meanings: "I think you will find things to be much less complicated once you start working there, which long term will be better for your life going forward." Again she felt that blanket of warmth filling her heart and was suddenly struck with a kind of revelation, for she somehow knew that Dr. Wu's words were extremely important for her. Hidden inside her, though, was also a trace of fear.

But all of that took place long before they had fallen in love.

Many years passed, yet she always remembered this man and the sound of his voice. Commissar Liu continued to work his way up the political ladder and was eventually transferred to another city; she followed his family when they moved to Wuhan. Everyone referred to the commissar's wife as "Sister Peng," and that is also how she addressed her. Sister Peng was quite good to her, always referring to her as the best nanny they ever hired. She was responsible for taking care of the Liu children, cooking, and cleaning; it was a quiet and secure life without a lot of drama. The thought of applying for another job or moving somewhere else never even crossed her mind, and she never thought of getting married. She just stayed with the Liu family wherever they went. She assumed that was how things would continue for the rest of her life.

Then one year Dr. Wu got transferred to Wuhan and made a special trip to visit his old supervisor, Commissar Liu. It was a pleasant surprise when he laid eyes on her again at the Liu house and immediately asked, "You've been here with them all these years? How have you been?"

She was quite excited and wasn't sure where that enthusiasm came from. Her voice quivered as she responded, "I've been wonderful. It's all thanks to you that I've been doing so well." He gazed deeply into her eyes. That look spoke of some kind of secret between them. She didn't know what that secret was, but in that moment she could feel her heart skip a beat.

That night Dr. Wu had dinner at Commissar Liu's house, where the table was filled with dishes she had carefully prepared. Everyone caught up over dinner, and it was only from that conversation that she realized that Dr. Wu's wife had passed away. Dr. Wu's wife had been especially close with Sister Peng; they had been through a lot together over the years. As soon as Sister Peng learned of Mrs. Wu's passing, she immediately set down her chopsticks and began to wipe away her tears. The woman Dr. Wu had saved all those years ago was standing beside the table and could feel her heart drop.

Commissar Liu heaved a long, deep sigh before asking Dr. Liu, "So how have you been holding up? Are you still single?"

"That's right," Dr. Wu responded. "It's just me."

"And you haven't considered remarrying?" asked Commissar Liu.

"A few friends have tried to set me up, but I haven't found the right one," answered Dr. Wu.

"I don't know how a grown man like you manages all alone!" As he spoke, Commissar Liu's eyes fell on her. "Why don't I play the role of matchmaker?" He gestured toward her. "After all, you two are old friends!"

Dr. Wu's gaze followed the line drawn by Commissar Liu's finger, and he turned his head toward her. She felt extremely uncomfortable and didn't know how to respond. But he flashed her a smile, and from that smile she could tell that he liked the idea.

That ended up being her last year at Commissar Liu's house. She had singlehandedly raised all three of the Liu children, and when she left they all stood at the front door watching her silhouette retreat into the distance. The youngest child was even crying.

She didn't look back and instead just clung firmly to Dr. Wu's arm and walked into her new life. Once they arrived at Dr. Wu's house, the first words out of her mouth were "Why did you want to marry me?"

He flashed her a smile. "I don't think I'd ever be able to truly rest at ease if you married someone else."

She seemed to partially understand what he was trying to say, but she wasn't entirely sure. Then she gave a strange response: "That's right, I don't think I'd ever be able to rest easy with anyone but you!"

As soon as the words escaped her lips, she was overcome with a strange, indiscernible fear. Night was descending and the sky was turning from gray to black. As the sky darkened, that sense of fear gripping her seemed to tighten, though she had no idea what it was that so terrified her. When Dr. Wu embraced her and pulled her close, her entire body began to tremble in fear. Through his caresses, Dr. Wu gently whispered, "It's okay, I know, I know. I'm here for you. Don't be scared, it's going to be okay."

There in his arms she asked herself, *What does all this mean? What does he know? What is it that he understands that I don't understand? What is it that's going to be okay?*

That night she had a terrible nightmare that woke her up. That next morning Dr. Wu looked at her and said, "Try not to be so anxious and think too much. I will be here to protect you. I married you because I know about what happened when you were first saved. I'm the only person in the world who really understands what you are going through. But there is nothing for you to be afraid of now."

Those words left her in tears and she fell into his arms. At the same time she had the sensation that a sharp, poisonous needle was about to stab her in the back. She could feel that needle following her at close range wherever she went. She unconsciously put up her defenses, mentally preparing herself that one day that needle would finally pierce her flesh.

From that point on she had her own family. Married life was good to her; she felt happy and content, even though that uncomfortable feeling followed her wherever she went. But she was no longer someone else's servant—she was now the proper wife of a respected man. That was enough to give her a sense of contentment.

Her life settled into a predictable, everyday routine. Each morning she would wake up and prepare breakfast for her husband and see him off to work; by the time he came home in the afternoon for lunch, his meal would already be waiting for him on the table; and after he returned to work, she would gradually start getting dinner ready and would wait for him to come home. She took special care in attending to him and made sure he didn't have to fret over any of the little household affairs.

Over time, she gradually began to feel a new kind of happiness growing in her heart. That happiness managed to push aside that unsettled feeling inside her. *Perhaps this is how my life will be from now on*, she thought.

It wasn't too long before she got pregnant. Dr. Wu was ecstatic and she was also quite excited. But she discovered that whenever she was alone that indescribable sense of fear would return and wrap itself around her. That feeling would come at her from all sides, just like those demons from the river all those years ago—it was as if they had quietly returned and were now lying in wait. They were just waiting for the right moment to launch their fatal attack. During her pregnancy that feeling of terror had grown to be almost unbearable. She started seeing things: she was afraid something was lurking behind the walls; she would see strange shapes in the clouds; when she looked up at the trees, she thought there were things hidden among the leaves; when she turned off the lights, she thought something would appear. Sudden noises would immediately put her on edge, but she could never figure out the source of the terror and paranoia that followed her. What she did know was that this thing inside her was always there, as if it had been with her since birth.

Dr. Wu brought her to the church every day, and standing before the statue of Our Lady of Lourdes, he would tell her, "Look at the Holy Mother's eyes. She is telling you, Don't be afraid. Don't worry. Everything will be okay."

Standing before the statue, she was deeply moved by the look in the Holy Mother's eyes, which brought her a true sense of inner peace. But then as soon as she got home, everything would start up all over again. Without any other options, Dr. Wu decided to take her to see a psychologist and told the doctor all about her amnesia. The psychologist suspected that whatever had happened in the past must have been extremely traumatic.

He thought the only way to get to the bottom of what was wrong was to face the past; he thought that her remembering what had happened might be the key to finally expel her demons.

But her instinctive reaction was always to resist. Whenever she would try to recall old memories, her entire body would immediately be assaulted by an all-consuming pain—she couldn't take it. Dr. Wu would try to encourage her, saying, "Just try to bear it. If you can remember what happened, you might be able to finally find peace." But she would retort, "And what if once I remember I find myself in even more pain? What should I do then?"

Dr. Wu fell silent; he didn't say another word for the rest of the night. She knew that he had been up all night pondering what to do. The next morning Dr. Wu said, "Just let it go. Erasing it from your memory is probably the best option for you."

It was during this series of incessant panic attacks that she gave birth to her son. On the day she gave birth she really thought that the demon hiding within her for all those years was finally going to show its face. She couldn't stop shuddering. Even the nurse assigned to her lost patience with her and called in Dr. Wu to help. Although spouses are not normally allowed into the delivery room, when she went into labor an exception was made to allow Dr. Wu to sit beside her. In her state of confusion she suddenly started to think that the demon that had been after her was none other than Dr. Wu. The feeling of terror inside her began to take over. She screamed at Dr. Wu, "Get out! Get the hell out!" Dr. Wu raised his voice: "Don't be afraid! I love you and we can get through this together." But it was as if she couldn't hear anything he said—she just kept hysterically screaming. The obstetrician and the maternity nurses didn't understand what was happening. One of the nurses even said, "What's going on? A few minutes ago she was begging us to let her husband sit next to her." But just moments later she was panting for breath and completely ignoring the nurses.

It was only when Dr. Wu finally left the delivery room that she calmed down and was able to deliver a healthy baby boy.

Dr. Wu was quite excited when he returned to the delivery room. His eyes filled with tears as he caressed her face. "Our son is so beautiful. Thank you. Thank you for giving us a son to carry on the family line. Don't worry. No matter what happens, there is nothing to be scared of."

She was too exhausted to respond. Dr. Wu continued, "I hope you can understand that when I married you, my only wish was for you to have a stable, peaceful life."

Perhaps those words really did help to calm her down, because that demon she so feared never truly showed its face. Instead, she had a son, and he gradually started to grow up. Her son's bright eyes and innocent laughter would provide her with the greatest comfort she could ever have hoped for. She wanted to have a second child, a daughter, but suffered a miscarriage during her first trimester. Dr. Wu tried to console her by telling her, "It's okay. We should be content with just a son. As long as he grows up healthy, everything else will be okay."

Much time passed. That internal feeling of fear seemed to be gone, and the demon lurking inside her appeared to gradually fade away.

THE POISON THORN HAS BEEN REMOVED

But then something completely unexpected occurred: her beloved Dr. Wu, who she always thought would be by her side until the end, left her a widow. An accident took his life while he was out running errands.

That year a public bus in Hankou was hit head-on by a train passing through the city. When the accident occurred, the entire intersection became a river of blood. Her beloved Dr. Wu was on that bus. When she heard the news, she and her son, Qinglin, rushed to the scene; they had to transfer several times to get there via public bus. In the chaos of people screaming and crying, she caught sight of the disheveled bodies strewn along the blood-soaked street. Her head began to buzz, and suddenly she was struck by a strange feeling of déjà vu. And in that moment the demons that she thought had released her from their grip seemed to arch their backs, poised to come at her again. Her entire body began to tremble and her legs grew weak as she dropped to her knees.

Qinglin started to cry and pulled at his mother's clothes. "Mom! Get up! Stand up!"

Startled, she got to her feet and started yelling at the emergency medical workers on the scene: "No soft burial! I don't want him to have a soft burial!" As the words left her mouth, she could sense that something was wrong with this world.

Qinglin tightly grasped his mother's hand; he didn't understand what she was yelling. It was only after the funeral that he finally got up the nerve to carefully ask his mother, "Mom, what's a soft burial?" His question only left her confused: "Soft burial? What soft burial are you talking about?" She was at a complete loss as to what he meant.

Those words—soft burial—seemed to come out of nowhere, descending as if from heaven. They seemed to be so very close to her while also so very distant. From far away she could hear someone speaking loudly, the voice heavy and old. The second she heard that voice in her ear she was struck by the feeling that her entire body was being pierced by thorns, the pain so terrible that she couldn't even respond to Qinglin.

In just the span of a few short days her beloved Dr. Wu, Qinglin's father, a man who had been brimming with life, was cremated, burned to ash, his remains placed in a porcelain urn and buried on a mountain. From that point forward their life together consisted only of that photo hanging on the wall. In the photo Dr. Wu looked over them with a warm smile, just as he had in life. Whenever her son went out, she made it a habit to frequently wipe down the photo; she would caress Dr. Wu's face through the glass frame and mumble indistinctly to herself.

Then one day as she was wiping down the photo she suddenly realized that the terror that had been lurking inside her was gone. Those old demons that had been lying in wait for so long had been driven away by that man who had brought her so much comfort and support; he had removed the poison thorn that had been embedded so deeply into her life. Dr. Wu's death was like a hurricane that had swept away all the things that had left her afraid; what remained was a feeling of peace and calm—the once-raging seas were now as placid as the face of a mirror. From that point forward her life would be filled with scenes of expansive peace.

Yet she clearly felt confused: she didn't understand why the death of the man she had been so deeply in love with would leave her with this sense of such utter serenity.

IN HER EMPTY HEART NOTHING WAS LEFT BUT TIME ITSELF

After the death of her husband she slept for three days straight. It was a deep and satisfying sleep; she had not slept like that in a long, long time. When she finally awoke, it was high noon and she pulled the curtains back to let in the brilliant sunlight. The bright rays of the sun pierced through the window and shone directly into her heart. It hit her suddenly, like an explosion that lit her up inside. From that point forward she began to feel that life was more stable. That sense of stability was much more tangible than anything she had ever felt when Dr. Wu was by her side.

Qinglin was still quite little and they had a long road ahead. So starting that year she decided to go back to work and took a new job as a caretaker. It was the only thing she had ever really learned how to do. She got a job as an attendant at her husband's former hospital, where she took care of the inpatients. The first patient she was assigned to was none other than Professor Ma's wife. At the time, Professor Ma wasn't even a professor yet and his wife was in the hospital about to give birth. She took care of Mrs. Ma with the same care she had shown Dr. Wu. Her quiet, gentle manner really won over Mrs. Ma. When Mrs. Ma was released from the hospital, she was still quite weak and didn't know how to properly care for a newborn, and so she offered her a job as a live-in caretaker. She accepted Mrs. Ma's offer. She wasn't fond of social interactions and disliked all the noise and chaos in the hospital. And, just like that, she started her new job; she would stay with the Ma family for many years. There she raised Professor Ma's child alongside her own son, Qinglin.

Eventually Qinglin went off to college in Shanghai, where he studied architectural design. Since her salary wasn't enough to support Qinglin's tuition fees, she decided to rent out her house. By pooling together her salary and the rental income, she was able to ensure that Qinglin's life in college wouldn't be too bad. Qinglin realized how much emphasis his mother had placed on making sure he got a good education, and so he worked hard. He would write her letters promising her that one day he would make a lot of money and buy her a great big house. She was delighted that her son thought about doing something nice for her, but she didn't care about ever having a great big house; all that mattered was for Qinglin to have a good life.

Qinglin didn't return home to live with his mother after graduation because by that time their house had been torn down. There would have been nowhere for him to stay, and besides, he was more interested in making money. So he instead decided to head south, as everyone had been saying that there were more opportunities down in southern China. Every sentence Qinglin uttered meant so much to his mother. She would always tell him, *Don't worry about me. I feel terrible that I can't take care of you anymore. You need to find a good life for yourself on your own now.*

During those years when Qinglin was trying to make it in the world, he was forever busy and rarely had a chance to visit his mother. He kept jumping between different jobs, and only after working for four different companies did he finally find a boss who seemed to appreciate what he could bring to the table. Like Qinglin, his boss hailed from Wuhan. His boss opened up all kinds of new doors for Qinglin, which quickly began to turn his life around. Over time, Qinglin began to settle down; he bought a house in the south and got married. He and his wife didn't have a formal wedding ceremony but instead opted to take a trip abroad. Just before they left, Qinglin brought his wife back to Wuhan so that his mother could meet her. At the time his mother still didn't have a place of her own, so they just went out to eat at a fancy restaurant in a hotel; they even invited Professor Ma and his wife to join them. Qinglin's wife was quite beautiful; she was extremely warm toward Professor Ma and his wife but treated her new mother-in-law with a polite distance. She figured that her mother-in-law was, after all, nothing but a housekeeper, so what power could she possibly wield over her?

Eventually, Professor Ma died from cancer. She helped Mrs. Ma get through what was the most difficult phase in her life and, eventually, was the one who was there for Mrs. Ma during her end-of-life journey. Qinglin rushed home for Mrs. Ma's funeral. He rented a small room on Huayuan Mountain and told his mother, "Mom, you don't need to work anymore. I'll take care of you from now on. Things might be a little tight for the next few years; I don't quite have enough to buy you that house we talked about, but you can stay here for the time being." Then he added, "Once I make it big, I promise I will buy you the best house out there!"

She couldn't care less about whether Qinglin made it big; but she saw how dark his complexion had grown, how skinny he had become, and how the wrinkles were beginning to appear on his forehead. He was starting to really resemble his father, which left her somewhat depressed.

Qinglin didn't stay long before leaving again. The reality of life forced him to be practical.

She was left alone in that little room. When the wind blew, the windows would rattle. In the middle of the night she could hear her neighbors snoring and talking in their sleep, sounds that came right through the paper-thin walls. And each day the morning sunrise would sweep away the feeling of silent loneliness that had encapsulated the room overnight. When she ate, her chewing sounded as loud as a car rumbling by. The utter quiet there seemed to exponentially increase her boredom. She barely uttered a single word on most days. Her world was consumed by such utter peace and quiet that it was as if she were the only one left in the world. In her empty heart nothing was left but time itself.

I HAVE NO NEED FOR MEMORIES

One day while on her way to buy groceries, she was struck by a bicycle speeding down the street. As she fell to the ground, her head slammed against a telephone pole and blood immediately started dripping from her forehead. The blood clouded her vision, but she could make out a row of canna lilies lining the street. Beside the lilies a street hawker had set up a collection of items for sale, among which was a pair of hand-embroidered children's shoe soles. The crimson soles were adorned with a pair of goldfish. The second she caught sight of those soles, her heart immediately tightened up.

It was a good thing her injury wasn't serious. She needed only three stitches, and after getting bandaged up she was escorted home. But Qinglin was quite shaken by the accident; as soon as he received the phone call from his mother's landlord telling him about what happened, he rushed back to Wuhan. For some reason, however, she couldn't get those two embroidered goldfish out of her head. She just kept mumbling, *Those fish, those fish.* Qinglin thought his mother was in the mood for fish, so he went to the market the next morning to pick up a few live crucian carp.

By that time she was already starting to come around. Her son's thoughtfulness even seemed to make her head feel better; ultimately, *she* was the one who ended up preparing a dish of watercress carp for her son. That was Qinglin's favorite dish.

After Qinglin had sufficiently lectured her on all the things she needed to be careful about, he rushed back to where he was living in southern China to get back to work. As Qinglin left, she gazed at his retreating silhouette, and in that moment those goldfish reappeared before her eyes. She didn't understand where this was coming from, but she felt a strange impulse come over her. Ignoring that her head was still bandaged, she went out and purchased needles, thread, and some pieces of cloth. She remembered that she had once embroidered shoes, back when she was still living with Professor Ma's family. Tracing the shape of her own feet, she quickly cut out two sole-sized pieces of cloth.

The sun was still quite bright that day, so she sat before the window, picked up a piece of cloth, and embroidered her first stitch. It wasn't as if she really needed a new pair of soles; then again, perhaps she was just trying to find an antidote to her boredom. It took her only a few days to embroider a pair of soles with a double-goldfish design. The act of embroidery seemed to bring her a sense of unprecedented peace and serenity. The feeling was so intense that it felt as if the heavens had suddenly bestowed on her a great gift of happiness. It was as if she were born to do this. Once she completed that first pair of soles, she embroidered a second pair, and by then she was hooked—there was no stopping her.

She embroidered peonies, mandarin ducks, and even the mythical chimera-like creature the *qilin*. Time slipped by on the tip of her embroidery needle. She lost track of how many soles she had embroidered. But on the side of her bed, which was adjacent to the wall, there were already several layers of soles piled up. Even her thin pillow was propped up high by all the soles on her bed. Only after she ran out of space did she finally break down and buy a wicker basket. She decided she ought to try selling some of the soles.

That is what finally got her out of the house. She began selling her embroidered soles out on the street across from the Catholic church. It wasn't that she was short of money; she'd managed to put some cash away from her time as a caregiver, and Qinglin would always send money home during the holidays. Qinglin always sent generous amounts of money home to her, and she made sure to deposit it all into her savings account. She figured that Qinglin would one day need that money when he was ready to buy a house.

She was able to sell one or two pairs of soles each day, a pace that suited her perfectly. She went out to sell her soles only when the weather was good. Sitting under the warm sun, she would occasionally gaze across the street at the statue of Our Lady of Lourdes, which was surrounded by a circle of greenery. She often felt as if she were gazing directly into the eyes of Our Lady, which gave her a sense of deep comfort.

The only problem was that whenever this feeling of comfort welled up inside her, some other painful things would also rise up and wouldn't let go—they would come and go, encircling her very being. This was especially the case when the canna lilies were in bloom, for whenever those red flowers appeared, things from her past would reappear and chase her down. She did everything she could to avoid them, but they were always there following her. She could feel them floating and moving, teasing her, trying to entice her to turn back and try to catch them. She recalled the sense of terror she'd once felt, which made her close her eyes and say to herself, *Don't look back. I don't need to know where I came from, I don't need to know my name, and I don't need to remember who my family was. I don't need any of that. All I need to remember is what happened after I met Dr. Wu. As long as I have my son, Qinglin, in my life, that's enough. There is a reason people forget,* which was something Dr. Wu once told her.

Dr. Wu was still quite young when he first spoke those words to her; they had become her mantra.

THE WORD "DING ZI"

For many years she lived her life as if nothing really mattered to her. She knew very few people, and very few people knew her. Her name was Ding Zitao.

That was the name Dr. Wu gave her. Dr. Wu told her that back when they first found her and she was semiconscious with a high fever, she would occasionally scream out "Ding Zi!" which meant "nails." No one could figure out what this signified. When she finally came to, Dr. Wu asked her what her name was so that he could fill out her medical chart. But she just shook her head and said she couldn't remember.

That was during the height of spring, and the first flower on the peach tree outside the hospital had just appeared. Dr. Wu wrote the words "Ding Zi" on her chart. As he was about to commit the third character in her name to paper, he looked over at her and caught a glimpse of the peach blossoms outside the window. He added the word *tao*, or "peach," to her name. He told her, "You need to remember the words 'Ding Zi.' Perhaps, one day, they will help jog your memory about what occurred in the past."

Ding Zitao gazed at Dr. Wu and thought, *You are my past. Do I really need anything else?*

2

LET ME BRING YOU HOME

It was an overcast day. Qinglin had rushed back to Wuhan to share some good news with his mother—he wanted to surprise her.

He asked the driver to pull over to a supermarket not far from where his mother lived. He wanted to pick up some fruit to bring his mother because he knew she was never willing to spend her own money buying things like fruit.

But when Qinglin arrived, he was surprised to discover that his mother wasn't home. Ever since he was a child, he had known that his mother kept to herself and rarely went out. A few neighbors were sitting outside playing mah-jongg; they were all clamoring to tell Qinglin, *Go look for her down over by the Catholic church. Your mom hangs around there all day selling those shoe pads she makes!*

Puzzled, Qinglin thought she had ample money to get by. He immediately set out for the church to find her. He scanned the area and, indeed, there was his mother sitting across the street from the Catholic church. He also saw the wicker basket filled with embroidered shoe pads. One look and he immediately became annoyed. He bounded over to his mother to admonish her. "Mom, what are you doing selling stuff on the street? You . . . you . . . you . . . If you're short on money, you should have told me!"

Ding Zitao was absolutely dumbfounded to see her son, Qinglin, unexpectedly standing before her; after her initial shock she immediately felt as if the world had turned brighter. That's because as far as Ding Zitao was concerned, Qinglin was always like the sun: anytime, anyplace, he could always light up her heart.

"I'm not short on money," she hurriedly responded. "I'm just bored, and this is a way for me to kill the time. It's a hobby I do for fun. And I'm able to get some sun while enjoying myself. Look, I embroidered all these myself!"

Qinglin picked up one of the embroidered soles, carefully admiring the patterns and the handiwork. So shocked was he by the superior level of craftsmanship that his annoyance promptly abated. "Mom, where were you hiding this talent? You did all this all by yourself? Wow, it's really amazing. How come I never saw you embroider like this before?"

Ding Zitao was delighted. "I also embroidered several pairs for you, but I feared you would think they were too tacky, so I didn't dare to give them to you."

"How can you say that?" Qinglin responded. "From now on when I buy new shoes, I'll be sure to buy a size larger so that I can always insert your soles."

Ding Zitao smiled. "You always say the right thing to make me happy."

Qinglin picked up the wicker basket. "Mom, let's go home. No need to sell any more of these."

Qinglin led his mother a few steps forward to where a black sedan was waiting for them. When the driver saw Qinglin approaching, he rushed over to open the door for him. Qinglin gestured toward the car and told Ding Zitao, "Mom, get in!"

Somewhat bemused, Ding Zitao countered, "I live just a few steps away; we don't need to drive. Whose car is this anyway?"

"It's our car!" Qinglin proudly responded. "Just come with me, Mom."

Ding Zitao got into the car, and within a few minutes they were driving through the endless stream of traffic. A bit dizzy, Ding Zitao asked, "Where are we going? Are you taking me out to eat again?"

Every time Qinglin came home to visit, he would take his mother out to dinner. He would always say that he wanted his mother to have a chance to catch up with the tastes of the new era. But this time was different; instead, he said, "We're going home. I'm taking you home."

Again bemused, Ding Zitao asked, "Whose home are you talking about?"

"Our home." Qinglin smiled. "The home where you will be able to enjoy life from now on. You won't be staying in that room on Huayuan Mountain any longer."

Ding Zitao appeared shocked. "What about my clothes? And all the shoe soles I made? And our lease with the landlord isn't up until the end of the year . . ."

"Mom, you don't need to worry about any of that. I'll take care of everything. I'll have someone move all your things to the new house tomorrow. I'll even have them bring all the dust if you want it!" Qinglin laughed heartily. "That's right; I'll even have them bring all the leftover food in your refrigerator, your broom, and all your kitchen rags! I'll tell them not to leave a single thing behind!"

Ding Zitao also laughed. She thought, *He's my son after all!* Even though he was always repeating himself, it was all music to her ears. And no matter what he asked her to do, she was always all too happy to comply.

Their car turned off the thoroughfare onto a small road that ran adjacent to a lake. You could see waterbirds soaring through the open sky above the lake. In the distance stood a series of erect trees that looked like a row of curtains pulled across the horizon. As Ding Zitao gazed out over the water, another body of water slipped into her mind. That too was a place where waterbirds soared. It was a lake surrounded by thick and dense reeds. A small rowboat drifted along; a large osprey stood upright on the hull. She tried to compose herself . . . the thick bed of reeds and the small rowboat all disappeared. There above the lake before her eyes the waterbirds continued to soar. Ding Zitao needed a momentary mental break; it was as if something in her mind had been thrown into a state of disorder, and that feeling left her nauseated. That thing that had once haunted her seemed to be circling her again.

It wasn't long before their car veered away from the lake and onto another main road. Again they found themselves in a sea of heavy traffic.

Ding Zitao flung her head a few times as if trying to shake something off her body. "Where are we going?" she asked.

"Jiangxia. It's in the South Lake region," responded Qinglin. "The environment there is really gorgeous. The air quality there is also much better than in other parts of the city. It's a great place for you to spend the rest of your retirement."

But Ding Zitao responded mournfully, "If you're not there with me, it really doesn't matter where I spend my retirement."

"My company is developing a new area in Jiangxia, and I've been transferred to oversee this project," said Qinglin. "From now on I'll be living with you."

Ding Zitao was elated. "Really? Your wife is okay with this?"

"She also agreed to move here," said Qinglin. "But she is going to wait until Baobao starts college before moving."

"That's wonderful news. I can't tell you how much I miss Baobao!" exclaimed Ding Zitao.

"He is quite a handful these days! I hope he doesn't annoy you too much!"

Ding Zitao laughed. "Don't be silly! That dear grandson of mine could never do anything to get on my nerves!"

Qinglin broke out in laughter. "There is one other thing I must mention. I hope you don't mind, but from now on I plan to eat dinner at home, and what I'm most looking forward to are your home-cooked meals! We should alternate: meat one day and fish the next!"

That also made Ding Zitao laugh. Qinglin had a voracious appetite as a child; all he wanted to eat was meat and fish. One day at school his teacher asked the class, "What is the meaning of a happy life?" Qinglin raised his hand to respond, "Eating meat one day and fish the next!" The entire class broke out in laughter. Later the teacher sought out Ding Zitao to tell her, "Don't be too frugal when it comes to meals; give the kid whatever he wants." Back then, supporting herself on her salary as a caregiver, Ding Zitao really didn't have enough money to buy expensive food; instead, she promised Qinglin, "One day when you grow up and start making money, I'll cook for you every day: meat one day and fish the next! That's a promise!"

Once their laughter had died down, Ding Zitao declared, "That's a given. Your mom made you a promise: meat one day and fish the next!"

Qinglin laughed again. "I knew that was what would make you most happy."

IS THIS QIERENLU OR SANZHITANG?

Their car finally pulled into a fancy upscale neighborhood. Qinglin pointed out to his mother all the places they drove by: "This is the neighborhood park, where you can go for walk. This is the association clubhouse, where you can borrow books, play Chinese chess and mah-jongg; they even have an exercise room." Their car drove around an engineered lake with a small island pavilion in the middle. Qinglin continued his tour: "This waterside pavilion is really nice. And the hardwood walkways are really well done. If you like to be by the water, you can come here for walks. But you should come here only during the day, as the lighting isn't so good at night, so it's not that safe."

Eventually they pulled up to a yard filled with blooming flowers. Qinglin slipped out of the car and ran around the rear of the vehicle to open the door for his mother. Extending his right hand to help her out of the car, he bowed slightly and said, "This way please, my queen."

Ding Zitao patted him on the shoulder as she climbed out of the car. "Look at you, a grown man and you're just as naughty as ever!" she said with a laugh.

Perhaps because the drive had been so long, or perhaps because she was unaccustomed to being in a car, Ding Zitao was overcome by a terrible spell of dizziness. Right after she patted her son, she momentarily lost her footing. But Qinglin caught her in his arms, scolding her gently, "Mom, don't scare me! The good days are still ahead of us; you've got to take care of yourself!"

Ding Zitao pulled herself together and, regaining her balance, chuckled. "I think I just got a little carsick."

Qinglin helped Ding Zitao as they walked across the yard to arrive at a red, two-story building. He pointed to the house. "Take a look! What do you think?"

"Not bad. But it is fairly small for a dormitory. How many families can live here? Most companies build great big tall dormitories for their employees."

Qinglin laughed. "This isn't a dormitory. It's a single-family house: it's our home; it's *your* home."

Ding Zitao was left virtually speechless. "My house? Is this Qierenlu or Sanzhitang?"

"What? What do you mean by this *lu* or *tang* business?" asked Qinglin, but Ding Zitao looked rather dumbfounded.

"What do I mean by *lu* or *tang*?" responded Ding Zitao. "Well, the entrance looks different from Qierenlu; nor does it resemble Sanzhitang."

Qinglin was mystified. "Qierenlu? Tang-whatever? Where are these places? What are you talking about?"

Ding Zitao didn't respond to his questions. Instead, she just said, "Doesn't this resemble the house of a rich landowner? Aren't you afraid they will confiscate your property? They'll be coming for you."

Qinglin chuckled; he could barely contain his laughter. Even the driver, who was helping Qinglin with his luggage, couldn't help laughing. The driver said, "Madame, Mr. Wu is indeed a big-time landowning capitalist!"

Qinglin laughed. "Mom, don't worry about whether I'm a landowner or a capitalist. From now on you're the owner of this villa! But your only responsibility is to live here and enjoy life! Right now, in the year 2003, you, Mrs. Ding Zitao, are the proud owner of your very own villa! We are living in a new era; no one is ever going to bother you. And I, Wu Qinglin, hereby promise to make you the happiest and most pampered mother in the world!"

Qinglin spoke with an air of pride. He was sure his mother would get a kick out of his joke, but she did not laugh or look at all pleased. In fact, she appeared rather scared. Her gaze gravitated to a patch of bamboo growing just to the right of the front door. New branches were beginning to sprout on the bamboo tree. The leaves on those new branches were a pale green. Suddenly Ding Zitao heard a voice in her head: *A row of bamboo before my window, I marvel at the emerald green*. It was a male voice, and she could almost make out the speaker's face, which seemed to appear before her eyes. Without thinking, Ding Zitao blurted out, "It's a poem by Xie Tiao."

"Mom," Qinglin responded, "what are you talking about?"

Ding Zitao looked uncertain. "I didn't say anything," she said. As she spoke, though, she realized that she did actually say something . . . but what exactly did she just say?

"You said the name of someone named Xie-something . . ." Qinglin said. "But I couldn't make out exactly what you said."

"I was looking at the bamboo and thinking how beautiful it looked," explained Ding Zitao, "and then I suddenly remembered a line of poetry: *A row of bamboo before my window, I marvel at the emerald green.*"

Qinglin had never before heard his mother recite a single line of poetry. He couldn't help but be surprised. "Mom, that's pretty impressive! Who wrote that?"

Ding Zitao seemed to be seized by a fit of anxiety. She didn't respond. Instead, she silently wondered, *Who did write that poem? Where did I read it?*

I REMEMBER RED

It was a large open room. In the center was a leather couch, behind which stood a dark brown wooden sofa table with intricately carved floral patterns and curves like those of a woman's body. Those curves affected Ding Zitao like the strings of a zither, resonating through her heart. "This is our living room," said Qinglin.

In the eastern corner of the room stood a potted tree. Ding Zitao recognized it as a Guiana chestnut tree, referred to in

Chinese as a money tree. Professor Ma used to have one in his house. Along the wall on the western side of the room could be seen a large shoulder-high porcelain vessel adorned with an ornate painting. "A friend of mine from Taiwan gave this to me," Qinglin explained. "He's really into Chinese antiques."

The pattern on the porcelain was classically inspired, and when Ding Zitao saw it, she suffered yet another, even more severe blow to her heart. "Isn't that a pattern from 'Guiguzi Descends the Mountain'?" As the words left her lips, her voice began to tremble. But she couldn't understand why she would be gripped by this sense of fear.

Qinglin was taken aback. "Wow, you know even that!"

Ding Zitao's responded automatically. "Of course. My father always used to paint that pattern."

Qinglin had never heard his mother mention anything about his maternal grandfather, so her comment piqued his curiosity. "Are you talking about my grandfather? Mom, what was his profession?"

That question caught Ding Zitao off guard. *That's right, what did her father do? Where did he go?* Somehow those questions seemed to be connected. Just thinking about them felt like a needle pricking her heart, and she broke into a cold sweat.

Qinglin instantly sensed that something was off about his mom. He hesitated for a few seconds before he said, "Mom, I think you must be tired. You can tell me about Grandfather some other time. Let's go upstairs so that you can rest. I'll give you a tour of the rest of the house later on after we eat. Without a tour, you'll get lost in this house!" He laughed.

Qinglin wasn't a person who usually laughed at minor jokes. In that moment he realized that his laughter was forced and exaggerated, but he wasn't quite sure why he was behaving like that.

Ding Zitao's bedroom was located upstairs, positioned in the best spot in the entire villa. The room faced south and had a large full-length window. Hanging on both sides of the window were gray velvet curtains in a light floral pattern. During the winter months the entire room would be bathed in sunlight, according to Qinglin, and as he told his mother, "It will be so bright that you'll be able to do your embroidery without even wearing your reading glasses!"

Standing at the window afforded Ding Zitao a bird's-eye view of the entire yard. The yard was like a garden, filled with tall camphor trees, magnolias, and two ginkgo trees; also visible were several small camellias, Chinese roses, and cape jasmines, along with an open plot of land. Qinglin proudly pointed to the open plot and explained that it was for his mother to plant whatever she wanted. "You can plant whatever flowers or vegetables your heart desires. Gardening is a great hobby and also a good form of exercise." As Qinglin stood at the window pointing out all the different trees and plants, Ding Zitao felt so overwhelmed that her head began to spin.

The room was fitted with a large bed and a six-drawer dresser. The comforter on the bed had a soft cover made from silk with a satin weave. Qinglin knew that his mother disliked duvet covers; she preferred traditional-style blankets quilted on both sides, even if this meant she had to quilt her blanket each month. The fabric's light purple satin weave was the same color as the peonies in bloom embroidered on the comforter, making it feel quite luxurious—so much so that Ding Zitao couldn't help reaching out to touch the fabric. "It's perfect. Peonies are my favorite," she exclaimed. "But why are they purple? I thought they were red."

Qinglin laughed. "When did we ever have a comforter like this in our house? This one is brand new; I picked it out just for you, Mom." He could tell that Ding Zitao was again taken off guard by what he had said.

Ding Zitao started mumbling to herself. "They're coming. They will take all our property away. They are going to take my blanket. They took away everything that my mom ever gave me. I don't want to let it all go, but I have no choice."

Qinglin laughed. "Don't worry, Mom! If you're worried about the evil landlord Hu Hansan from the movie *Sparkling Red Star*, he is gone and never coming back! It's all my fault! I just wanted to surprise you, but I never imagined you had grown so accustomed to living in poverty that all this would scare you." He continued, "Mom, don't worry. Every penny I made was on the up-and-up. This villa is my way of expressing my filial respect to you. I just want you to be happy during your golden years. There is absolutely nothing for you to worry about. This is your home now; it's our home. You and I are the masters of this house."

Ding Zitao nodded her head in confusion. She had no idea what she had been saying. But she finally began to understand that from the moment she stepped into this house, it was hers.

From this point forward, she would again have a place of her own. Her son, Qinglin, gave her this house. She had such a kind and filial son, and she was a happy mother.

STRUCK BY THE BUTTSTOCK

That night Qinglin presented an entire table full of tasty dishes, and he even brought out the good liquor. For this meal he insisted that his mother not lift a finger; instead, he had the housekeeper do all the cooking. Although the housekeeper prepared all the food, it was Qinglin who prepared the menu. He gestured to the housekeeper as he introduced her to Ding Zitao: "This is

Donghong. From now on she'll be taking care of you." He then turned to the housekeeper to say, "Donghong, from this day forward my mother will be the boss around here. If you are unclear about anything, please ask her for instructions."

Ding Zitao smirked and blurted out, "You're crazy! I'm no boss!"

"Mom, once upon a time you were *my* boss!" Qingling asserted. "Now you've got two of us to boss around!" He made himself laugh again with that and continued, "Mom, if you feel like resting and doing nothing, that's what you should do! If you feel like doing some work, you do it! But you call the shots from now on!"

Both Ding Zitao and Donghong giggled at Qinglin's little speech.

That night mother and son enjoyed a full range of delicious food. The plates and bowls were all light yellow and seemed to emanate a gentle warmth. This was the kind of life Ding Zitao had always dreamed of; all she had really ever wanted was to sit down and have a nice quiet meal with her beloved son.

Qinglin took out a bottle of spirits from the cabinet. "This is a good bottle of Luzhou wine, aged many years; it was one of Dad's favorites. Today I would like to use one of Dad's beloved spirits to toast my dear mother! It will be as if Dad and I are toasting you together! Mom, can I pour you a cup?"

Thinking about how mature her son now was, Ding Zitao was filled with a sense of gratitude. She laughed. "When your dad used to drink, I never took a single sip. Alcohol was pricy back then. Even when your dad had a bottle, he was usually too frugal to actually drink it. Only during the Chinese New Year or on special holidays would he sneak a little taste."

Qinglin was quite moved. "I just wish Dad were still here with us. It would have been so nice for us all to be together now. I put out a set of plates and utensils for Dad. This is, after all, our home; there should be place for Dad here too."

Dr. Wu's face flashed before Ding Zitao's eyes . . . but then came the image of dead bodies strewn on the ground. She suddenly realized that these bodies were not alongside the train tracks; they were under a group of trees. Beside those trees could be seen a large pit next to a tall mound of dirt. The position and clothing of those bodies looked oh so familiar to her, but she didn't recognize Qinglin's father among the dead. She shook her head, trying to snap out of her reverie.

Distracted pouring the wine, Qinglin didn't notice his mother's reaction. "Mom, what do you say? Can I pour you a cup? Shall we get a little drunk? I suspect you've never been drunk in your life. Shall we give it a try? We haven't had our own place to call home in decades, but today we do. There is a lot to celebrate."

Qinglin smiled as he poured his mother a cup of wine. Ding Zitao came to and took the cup her son had handed her; it felt so small. "Okay then. Today I will drink with my son."

Qinglin clapped his hands in delight. "Mom, if you're willing to drink with me, I swear I'll come home every night for dinner! That will be the best way to train you how to hold your liquor!"

"That's right, you'll make me into a granny alcoholic!" Ding Zitao laughed.

With that back-and-forth banter, mother and son began drinking and eating. Qinglin toasted his mother, saying, "To you, Mom! With gratitude for raising me. I know it wasn't easy for you. I know you put me first all these years. And that is why my greatest aim in life is to ensure that you are happy in your retirement. I think I have finally almost achieved my goal."

Ding Zitao smiled contently as she accepted her son's toast. Qinglin emptied his cup. "Mom, why don't you have a sip?"

Ding Zitao lifted the small drinking cup to her lips, but as soon as she got a whiff of the alcohol, a familiar scent enveloped her. It was a tiny spark that set the fire inside her ablaze. She could hear a stern, admonishing voice yell, "Drink! Drink it! Drink three cups if you want to have energy! Show us you've got the guts!" The face behind that voice gradually became clear: it was a man. His face was that of someone who had lived through a lot and was brimming with an imposing authority.

Ding Zitao's hands began to shake uncontrollably; but still caught up in the excitement of the moment, Qinglin did not yet notice. Instead, he urged his mother, "Mom, have a taste! Liquor is such an amazing thing; it is such a shame that you still haven't experienced the taste of a good spirit! Mom, I'd rather drink with you than with anyone else in the world!"

Ding Zitao pulled herself together and took a good look at Qinglin. His face was glowing with happiness and excitement. His happiness was also Ding Zitao's happiness, and so Ding Zitao raised her cup and downed the wine in one sip.

"Way to go, Mom! You're amazing," Qinglin cried out. "But pace yourself! Don't drink too quickly. This isn't water you're drinking!"

It was such a familiar taste and smell: a mixture of dirt and vegetation combined with a sweaty, fishy stench. The sounds of muffled cries and screams also made their way to Ding Zitao's her ears. She felt an intense pain assault her back.

Noticing her unusual expression, Qinglin anxiously asked, "Mom, what's wrong?"

"My back is in terrible pain," replied Ding Zitao. "He struck me with the buttstock of his rifle. He didn't hold back. It hurts so much."

"What are you saying?" Qinglin asked. "Did someone hit you? With a buttstock? Mom, are you okay?"

But Ding Zitao kept mumbling, "My back hurts . . . it hurts so much."

Qinglin rushed over to his mother and, standing behind her, began to gently massage her back. *Perhaps she drank too fast*, Qinglin thought. He blurted out, "It's my fault. Mom, don't drink anymore. You'll feel better once you get some food in your system. I'm just so happy to be here with you having dinner together in our own home."

Ding Zitao was also filled with happiness. She stopped drinking and tried to forget the taste and smell the liquor triggered. All she wanted was to have a nice meal with her son; she wanted to hear how her grandson and her daughter-in-law were doing and learn all about her son's new project at work.

During their long conversation, the pain in her back gradually abated and began to disappear.

THIS IS THE ABYSS OF DARKNESS

That night, Qinglin accompanied Ding Zitao to her room. Everything in the bathroom was a new marvel for her. Donghong had already run the bathwater for her, and the water temperature was just right. Ding Zitao undressed and climbed into the tub to soak in the hot water. She couldn't remember ever having taken a bath like that before. In fact, she still hadn't quite figured out how to control the hot and cold water. But Donghong took meticulous care of her, even helping her into a set of soft pajamas.

Ding Zitao was feeling disoriented, as if it were not her own life anymore. Even the slippers were so soft that she felt as if her feet were not touching the ground. When Ding Zitao expressed her misgivings, Donghong just laughed heartily and explained that Mr. Wu was an important boss, and this was how all those people lived.

Donghong helped her get to the bed, supported her as she climbed in, and tucked her in with the brand-new comforter. But as the purple underside of the quilt pressed against Ding Zitao's body, she again began to feel uncomfortable.

Qinglin dropped by her room to tell her that in the morning he needed to make a quick trip back south. Once he had completed all the necessary paperwork, he would be back, but it would be a few days. In the meantime Donghong would be here to take care of her. The driver, Old Zhang, would also be here to move all her belongings from the old place. Other than having a much bigger house and people to take care of her, she would find everything else the same and should feel free to do whatever she wanted.

Ding Zitao nodded her head. She knew that her son had an important job and that was the priority. Qinglin wished his mother goodnight before leaving her room.

Ding Zitao indeed felt tired. Donghong placed a glass of water beside her bed and, with a gentle smile, told her, "Madame, I hope you have a good rest."

"Did you add the honey? Little Tea," responded Ding Zitao.

Donghong smiled. "Did you want honey water? Or tea? I'll pick some up for you tomorrow. Madame, my name is Donghong. Please try to remember."

"Of course you're Little Tea!" insisted Ding Zitao. "I brought you with me from my parents' house. You've been with me ever since you were a child."

Donghong laughed. "Little Tea? Madame, I'm afraid you had too much to drink. I just starting working here for the Wu family today."

Ding Zitao was too confused to respond. She lay down in bed and felt overcome by an intense feeling of exhaustion. She couldn't even open her eyes.

Her new bed was quite large and extremely comfortable. The comforter had a fragrant smell and was so soft that it made her entire body feel as light as a feather; indeed, she felt as if she could float off to the heavens. She felt as if she could walk on the clouds, which seemed to be right under her feet. She couldn't resist stepping out onto them and climbing up their billowing layers as if she were ascending a staircase. As she ascended the never-ending staircase of clouds, the sky turned a deep blue. Filled with curiosity, she ran compulsively toward that azure-blue patch of heaven. In her trancelike state, she seemed to return to her youth. Back then she loved to run, and she loved to effortlessly run up the staircase, which was made of green, semitransparent flagstones that shone. And there standing before her was someone waving her on. Suddenly she caught sight of those hands that, so many years ago, always extended to her as he called her name. It was such a familiar scene. She laughed and ran even faster toward him. What a marvelous feeling!

But then, all of a sudden, the staircase disappeared. With no time to stop herself, she stepped onto a patch of nothingness and began to fall. She fell at a much faster pace than the speed at which she had climbed. She couldn't help crying out, "Lu Zhongwen, catch me! Lu Zhongwen . . ."

But she couldn't find his hands. She couldn't even see her own hands. Everything had been encapsulated in a blanket of thick, white clouds. You couldn't see a thing. She reached out and kept trying to find something to grab onto. Her hands franticly grasped for something, anything; but all she could grab was emptiness. Then a sentence unexpectedly popped into her head: *Falling upon the vast white void of the earth, it was so pure*. She figured that the vast white void referred to in *Dream of the Red Chamber* was likely something like this. And so she decided to stop struggling and surrender. She would just let herself land wherever this vision took her. In the end, she had but one sensation left: the sense of falling, falling . . .

And just like that, she fell from atop the bright clouds and dropped down, down, down. The great white void around her eventually turned gray, and then darker until she was enshrouded in a deep black. This blackness was bottomless, endless, boundless.

And then a face slowly arose from the depths of the darkness. Ding Zitao covered her face and opened her mouth to scream, "You will go to hell! Yama, the King of Hell, will have his way with you!"

Against this sea of darkness, that face came into focus. She recognized her. It was her second mother, her father's concubine. Ding Zitao couldn't help crying out, "Second Mother, that's not what happened! No!"

No one could hear her.

But she now knew that *this* was the abyss of darkness from which there was no escape.

3

A CHANCE MEETING AT THE NOODLE SHOP

Liu Jinyuan went for walks at Hongshan Park every morning.

His hair, his beard, and even his eyebrows were completely white, yet his face was a deep red. The stark juxtaposition between red and white was enough to leave a lasting impression on most people. When he was out walking along the main road, people would constantly stop him to say hello; they all came over to greet a familiar face. Ever since the park opened its gates to the public and stopped charging for admission, strolls in the park had been part of his daily routine. He used to come here with his wife and they went for countless walks together in the park; but she eventually passed on. She died of a sudden heart attack. She was sitting on the sofa watching television when she died. She had been watching *Romance of the Three Kingdoms*, and when it got to the part where Liu Bei made his three visits to the thatched cottage and Zhuge Liang slipped into his eternal slumber, she heaved a deep sigh; no one noticed just how long that sigh lasted.

Liu Jinyuan was sitting on an adjoining sofa, his eyes glued to the television as he commented on the show to his wife. He told her that back when he was trying to help Wu Jiaming remain at the hospital, he had to make four separate trips to the military zone. He kept going on about it, but his was wife wasn't responding. He was on the verge of getting upset with her for ignoring him: "Did you forget that it was Wu Jiaming who saved your life?" He turned to look at her and realized something was wrong. He checked her breathing and realized that she was already gone.

Liu Jinyuan and his wife didn't exactly have what you would call a perfect marriage, but they had spent most of their lives together and had grown accustomed to having each other around. Even though he had long known about her heart condition, the reality was still hard to accept. The tears poured down his face. That night there were two separate calls for emergency vehicles to come to their house—one to the hospital and one to the funeral home. They had two sons: the older son went with his mother to the funeral home, and the younger son accompanied his father to the emergency room. Later, Liu Jinyuan couldn't even remember how he ended up in the hospital or the details surrounding his discharge. All he knew was that he resumed his walks in the park the very day he returned home.

It was the first time he was truly alone and the first time he tasted true loneliness. It was also on that very same day that a young person briskly walking down the street approached him and smiled. There was something familiar about his smile; it gave Liu Jinyuan the warm feeling you get when you see an old friend. He tried to figure out where he had seen a smile like that before. He could almost place that person's face but just couldn't quite pin it down. Before that moment he had never really paid much attention to the pedestrians he passed on the street, let alone the expressions on their faces. But now he found himself suddenly noticing a stranger smiling at him. He couldn't help but reciprocate with a smile.

That single smile was enough to dispel the feeling of loneliness festering inside him.

Liu Jinyuan didn't even remember how long he had lived in this area. In his mind, time was like long rope that over the years began to form knots. Those knots turned into messy balls that were difficult to unwind. This was especially true after he had retired; with so much free time on his hands, all those little tasks he needed to take care of started popping up. First of all, his two children were already grown up; what were once two naughty little bastards that he was dying to give a good whipping to ended up becoming two young men who looked respectable on the outside but, deep down, were still dogs on the inside. When they first came back home in their fancy cars with their new wives, both sons were quite cocky. And the younger son, Liu Xiaochuan, really put on airs. Whenever he would visit home, without speaking he would throw a few expensive cartons of cigarettes on the table or carry in a few cases of expensive Maotai spirits. His employees who accompanied him under the pretext of paying their respects to his parents would practically line up. Liu Jinyuan loathed all this, and yet he couldn't reject it. After all, it is always nice when someone pays their respects to you. Once he retired and had no more power at work, none of those people from his former work unit came around to kiss up to him anymore. Although employees from his son's company kissing his ass still qualified as ass-kissing, it was actually very different. Another thing that was different was that all the buildings and roads around his house had completely changed. The buildings were now much taller and the roads much wider than before; there was also much more traffic on the street. Everything that had once been so familiar now felt quite strange. And all those people he had known for so long were gradually beginning to disappear. Of course, Liu Jinyuan knew where they had gone, for it was the same place he too would sooner or later visit. Perhaps it was a good thing that he had close friends already there; that way, things would be easier for him when he finally arrived. He wasn't sad, but after those familiar points of reference he had grown accustomed to over the years began to gradually transform and disappear, he did feel the changes taking their toll; it felt as if someone were chopping his memories into little pieces with a pair of scissors. Those remaining memories he still clung to were also gradually being lost with each snip of the scissors. That's how people are: if they don't have tokens from the past to remind them of things, many of their memories just disappear; it is as if the things never happened. His former employee Wu Jiaming always used to say, *The greatest thing that we are innately equipped with as humans is the ability to forget.*

That morning as Liu Jinyuan left the park on his walk, he was overcome with the sudden urge to have a bowl of Shanxi-style shaved noodles. After having left his hometown many years ago, he had long grown accustomed to southern food; he loved both the mild and the spicy dishes. His son Liu Xiaochuan always used to say that his father's stomach was able to handle both northern and southern cuisine, all food east and west; he had an open and magnanimous appetite that was perfectly suited to the direction of the reform era. Liu Jinyuan loved that quote of his son's. But for some reason those shaved noodles from his hometown were like a hook that had suddenly grabbed hold of him.

He knew there was a Shanxi noodle house a block over and had even thought about eating there a few times, but since his wife was from Sichuan and had absolutely no interest in Shanxi noodles, she always refused to go. Liu Jinyuan called the shots when it came to most household affairs; however, when it came to eating, he always deferred to his wife. That's because she did all the cooking. So even though that noodle house was so close that he could practically smell the noodles from his doorstep, he never once ate there.

But now he decided to go.

The noodle shop was quite small; it had only a few beat-up old tables and stools. One look and he knew that this was the kind of restaurant someone could run for a lifetime and still never turn a major profit; it was instead the kind of place a family relied on to eke out a meager living and make their way through life. There was a ragged-looking old dog chained up near the entrance to the noodle house. Even that dog reminded Liu Jinyuan of his hometown of Liudong Village.

When he walked in, he heard the accent of the guy running the restaurant and immediately knew that they had grown up in the same area. When Liu Jinyuan began to speak, the noodle shop boss immediately lit up. He spoke in a boisterous, exaggerated tone. "Wow, what a thrill to see someone from my hometown!"

Liu Jinyuan laughed. "Not really. I haven't been back home in decades. But it feels so good to hear someone who speaks the same dialect."

"Look," said the noodle shop boss, "I've been saying this for a long time: no matter how far you wander from home or how long you've been away, when you meet someone from home, it's like family. The main thing is that in our hearts we all long for noodles from home."

"That's right," Liu Jinyuan quickly added, "I came here especially for your noodles!"

"Well, today's your lucky day," replied the boss. "You're the second customer of the day who is from our hometown! Just check out that old man squatting over there; one look at the way he is squatting and I can guarantee you that he is also from Shanxi!"

Liu Jinyuan looked over in the direction the boss had gestured and indeed saw an old man squatting on a wooden bench, his head practically buried in his bowl of noodles. Liu Jinyuan laughed. The old man's posture while squatting was identical to the way people back home used to eat. He hadn't seen anyone do that in years.

The old man seemed to sense that there were people talking about him. He turned to see Liu Jinyuan and the noodle boss smiling at him. He nodded his head slightly and adjusted his position, sitting down on the bench. Liu Jinyuan nodded back at him.

"Why don't you have a seat at the same table with him?" the boss suggested.

"Sounds good," replied Liu Jinyuan.

As they spoke, he walked over toward the old man. Before his wife's death he rarely struck up small talk with strangers. He simply never developed that habit; but now that his wife was gone, he suddenly had a strong urge to connect with other people.

Deep inside, he must have been quite lonely.

RIGHT NOW HIS JOB IS TO STAY ALIVE

The table was quite small, and even though the boss's wife had just wiped it down, it still looked all oily and sticky. Liu Jinyuan thought to himself, *It's a good thing I never brought my wife here. Given her pickiness, she would certainly have launched into another tirade about how dirty and unhygienic northerners are.* Heaven knows how many times they had gotten into arguments about that. He must have explained to her a thousand times that back in his hometown in northwest Shanxi province there simply wasn't enough water for people to wash themselves as frequently as people in the south did, but she still didn't seem to get it. If it hadn't been for the fact that transporting buckets of water every day was so exhausting, he would probably have been too lazy to ever join the revolution! His wife was from Sichuan, where there is water everywhere you look; there was no way for her to understand what life was like in a place like Shanxi. They also had a housekeeper from Sichuan who basically shared the same views as his wife; when it came to cleaning, the housekeeper was actually even pickier than his wife, making sure every corner of their house was spotless. They even made sure the kids changed their shorts and socks every day. She said she would rather do the wash every day than have any funny smells in the house. Living under the same roof as these two women made him particularly sensitive when it came to cleanliness.

The condiments tray on the table was also sticky and oily. It contained bottles of soy sauce, vinegar, and hot sauce, the caps of which were all disgusting. Liu Jinyuan was no longer used to squatting while he ate, so he sat down on a stool. The old man turned to him to assert, "The vinegar they use here is the best Shanxi vinegar you can find!"

Liu Jinyuan took a look at the bottle. "These days you can buy authentic Shanxi vinegar in all the stores . . ."

The shop boss came over with a bowl of piping-hot Shanxi shaved noodles. Before he even got to the table, that familiar fragrance had already reached Liu Jinyuan's nostrils, and his stomach immediately started to rumble. The boss explained, "This is actually home-fermented rice vinegar that we make in house; one taste and you'll know how good it is. What they sell in the stores is called Shanxi Extra-Aged Vinegar, but it still tastes different from the homemade stuff we brew. I'm not sure why."

The old man responded, "It takes only slightly inferior water or ingredients or even a minor change in the brewing time and temperature to result in a vinegar that doesn't taste authentic."

"That makes sense," said Liu Jinyuan. "Where are you from, my friend?"

"Northwest Shanxi," the old man replied. "A place called Hejiagou, 'He Family Ravine.' My name is He Quanqi. When I was a kid everyone used to call me Little Qi. Now that I'm an old man, everyone calls me Old Qi."

"That's a great name!" the boss added. "Old Qi, Old Qi. I like that. It also means 'always rising,' so they'll never knock you down!"

Liu Jinyuan and Old Qi both broke out in laughter.

"We indeed come from the same place," exclaimed Liu Jinyuan. "My surname is Liu and my given name actually has in it the character *Jin*, used as the abbreviation for Shanxi Province! When I was a kid everyone used to call me Little Jin, but as I got older nobody ever called me Old Jin—they all call me Old Liu! But we're from the same place, so please call me Old Jin!"

"You're also from northwest Shanxi?" Old Qi asked.

"Of course," replied Liu Jinyuan. "I come from a place called Liudong Village. I left right after the War of Resistance against Japan ended."

"Wow, your accent really changed after all these years!" Old Qi grew excited.

"Is that so?" said Liu Jinyuan. "I spent more than half my life here in the south. I never picked up any of these southern dialects, but my native tongue has changed a bit over the years."

The two of them sat there eating their noodles and chatting about random topics. They were indeed old; they had never met, and yet there were endless things for them to talk about as they slurped down their noodles.

Old Qi said that he was seventy-two years old, but back when he was eighteen he also wanted to leave Shanxi and see the world; unfortunately, his parents both fell ill and he never made it out. That day at the noodle shop he was celebrating his seventy-third birthday with a bowl of noodles. "You know what they say about Yama coming for you when you hit seventy-three, so I'm hoping to avoid that."

"Listen, old friend," said Liu Jinyuan, "don't think like that! They also say that Yama comes for you at the age of eighty-four, and I'm about to hit eighty-four!"

Old Qi quickly put down his chopsticks and offered a slight bow to apologize. But Liu Jinyuan just waved his hand and shook it off. "It's okay. Anyway, it is just a saying. Actually, when I think about this life I have lived, it's all been worth it. I've done all types of jobs. I've suffered and I've been able to experience what true happiness feels like. I've fought in wars, suppressed bandits, executed prisoners, served as a cadre member, been the target of political persecution, and even spent time in prison. I even visited North Korea. My friend, I hope this doesn't scare you, but a lot of people have died by my hand, if not a hundred, then at least eighty or so. Of course, there were also many times when I came very close to death myself."

"Wow, that is really quite something! I never fought in a real war, but . . ." he suddenly lowered his voice, "I did participate in the Land Reform Campaign. The terror I experienced during that time was probably no less than what you experienced during the war."

"I heard the elders talk about it," replied Liu Jinyuan. "I was hospitalized at that time. I had a close childhood friend who was dirt poor; he didn't even have enough money to marry a wife, but during the land reform he was given the former servant girl of a rich family in the village. She turned out to be a real beauty in the bud!"

"We shouldn't talk about it, but it's really one of those things that is just too difficult to mention," said Old Qi. "Just mentioning what happened during that time is enough to send cold shivers down your spine. My aunt's family was completely wiped out. Only their son survived. I hid him far away beyond the mountains and never went back to check on him. It has been decades and I have no idea if he even survived."

Liu Jinyuan heaved a deep sigh. "There are so many things that shouldn't be talked about. I fought in wars for half my life. I can't tell you how many times I've been fired at. My blood helped build this red nation. And yet during the Cultural Revolution they arrested me! They called me an antirevolutionary. Can you believe it? After being a revolutionary my entire life I suddenly became labeled as an antirevolutionary! Is that not evil? It was something I could never have imagined at the time. Something inside me died, but somehow I made it through. So when you said 'too difficult to mention'—that's exactly right. We shouldn't mention those things that are too painful. Do you live in the neighborhood?"

"That's right," replied Old Qi, "my residence card still lists Taiyuan as my home, but my daughter went to college here and met a guy from Hubei who she married. She didn't even ask for her parents' permission! She just eloped! I feel like these kids don't take their parents seriously these days. Everything we do for them is in vain. The only thing I can do is occasionally come down here to visit them and see my grandkids. But I can never get used to the weather here, and I still don't like the food! The locals can't understand me because of my accent; I can't understand them either. It's really frustrating."

"I was in the same boat when I first left Shanxi," responded Liu Jinyuan. "But now I'm more worried about whether I'd be able to adapt to Shanxi if I ever went back. I've been away too long. Both my wife and our longtime housekeeper were from Sichuan; after serving me their food for so many years, they completely trained my palate to appreciate only Sichuan food!"

"That's a shame," said Old Qi. "You must not mind the spicy food."

Liu Jinyuan snickered, "Oh, I've long gotten used to it!"

"Well, even if your palate has shifted, sooner or later everyone needs to return home. That's where your roots are," said Liu Jinyuan.

"I'm not sure. We live in a different era now. These days nobody talks about roots anymore. When we die, they just burn our bodies to ash and put the remains in a little ceramic urn—how can we still talk about roots? These days you're lucky if you even have a memorial tablet erected in your honor."

"That's right," agreed Old Qi, "if your children come to light incense for you each year during Tomb-Sweeping Festival, I suppose that means you had a damn good life."

Both men heaved a deep sigh.

As he wiped down the adjoining table, the noodle shop boss said, "What're you two sighing about? Just the fact that you two were able to find your way to this restaurant for a bowl of hometown noodles means you guys are way ahead of the game! What would those people from your generation who have already left us say if they were to hear you sighing? They'd be gritting their teeth in spite!"

Again, the boss's words made the two old men burst out laughing. Liu Jinyuan hastened to add, "You're right. We should be satisfied with what we have. There is something to be said for knowing contentment."

Liu Jinyuan burped several times as he made his way out of the noodle shop. There was something quite satisfying about the way he burped. He hadn't felt that kind of deep satisfaction in a long time.

As they reached the main road, he and Old Qi said goodbye. Neither of them exchanged contact information; they simply said they would meet again at the noodle shop. They both believed that as long as that noodle house was around, they would eventually run into each other there. But the last thing Liu Jinyuan said was, "Sichuan food is amazing; it's a great blessing to be able to eat spicy food." He missed his wife.

Liu Jinyuan leisurely strolled down the street toward home.

He didn't have a single care in the world. Right now his biggest job was simply to keep on living and figure out a way to pass the time.

GOING SOUTH

Liu Jinyuan came down with a cold as soon as he arrived home. He had a cough and was experiencing shortness of breath.

Just before Liu Jinyuan's wife passed away, his older son, Liu Xiao'an, had moved in with them. Liu Xiao'an used to work in a remote factory along the third line of defense but retired early. After retirement he joined his younger brother Liu Xiaochuan's business for a while, but his brother eventually sent him away, saying that without specialized training there was nothing he could really contribute to the company; he would be better off just going home and taking care of their parents full time. Knowing his brother was holding things down at home would allow Liu Xiaochuan to rest easy while away on business trips. Liu Xiaochuan paid his brother a salary of 200,000 yuan a year, along with a house and a car. Liu Xiao'an and his wife did the math and figured it was a good deal, so they came back home. They rented out their own house and moved in with Liu Xiao'an's parents. Liu Xiao'an's parents ended up footing the bill for all their food and daily expenses and even paid for the housekeeper's salary—that allowed Liu Xiao'an and his wife to use all their money for their own entertainment. Liu Jinyuan's wife once pulled her husband aside and asked him, "Didn't Xiaochuan give them a ton of money to take care of us? How come they don't even pitch in for food? They even ask our housekeeper to wash their clothes!" But Liu Jinyuan just downplayed his wife's concerns: "Don't make it into an issue. Just be happy we have our son here taking care of us. Anyway, our pension funds are more than enough to support four or five people. Money is meant to be spent. Even if we were to spend all our money, I'm sure Xiaochuan would step in to help." That speech from Liu Jinyuan won his wife over; she even handed all her money over to Xiao'an to manage it for them. "Just be sure to take care of us and feed us well. Spend whatever money is left however you want." With that they saved themselves a lot of hassle.

Every morning Liu Xiao'an and his wife would go out dancing in the park with people from the neighborhood and pick up groceries on their way home. Liu Xiao'an's wife never trusted the housekeeper when it came to buying groceries; she always suspected the housekeeper was skimming from the grocery money. That meant that Xiao'an and his wife ended up doing most of the shopping. Usually in the afternoon Liu Xiao'an's wife would either go to the beauty salon or play mah-jongg with her friends, leaving her husband at home to spend time with his parents. In actuality "spending time with his parents" amounted to Liu Xiao'an holed up in his own room playing Chinese chess online. In the evening they would all watch television together. Liu Jinyuan loved to watch war films. He would wave his finger at the screen complaining, "How can they fight like that? They're going to send those soldiers to an early grave!" He would continue, "That's not how that battle was fought! That never happened during that battle!" Liu Xiao'an would grumble, "What're you worrying about? It's not like there was an audience back when you went to war! People were happy just to come out of the battle alive. They've got tens of thousands of people watching these battles on TV; they've got to make them look good and have big battle scenes; it's not like anyone is dying for real!" There was nothing Liu Jinyuan could say to that. His son was right, and there was no use arguing.

That's how things carried on in his old age. Liu Jinyuan was okay with it. At least there were still people coming in and out of the house; there was still a feeling that the house was alive. That wasn't the case with the Zhang family next door. Their children had all gone abroad, and when the wife died, the husband was left all alone except for a caregiver to look after him. Their family had a lot of money, but what was the point if you couldn't spend it? You might be well off, but if your nice big house is cold and empty, you'd be better off being dirt poor and living in a tiny shack surrounded by your family.

Liu Jinyuan didn't go for his walk that day; he couldn't get out of bed. When Liu Xiao'an and his wife returned from their morning dancing routine, they noticed that Father still hadn't gone out and rushed to his bedroom to check on him. The moment they saw him lying in bed listless, they got scared. They immediately called for an ambulance and rushed him to the nearby military hospital, and the doctors there gave him a thorough examination. According to the hospital it was nothing serious, just a cold. The doctor explained that the rapidly fluctuating climate in Wuhan causes many elderly people to develop colds.

Liu Xiao'an called his little brother, Liu Xiaochuan, to update him on their father's condition. Although Liu Xiao'an was the older brother, Xiaochuan was his boss, which meant that Xiaochuan was the one who made all the family decisions. Liu Xiao'an told him, "Overall he seems okay. His fever has gone down a bit. When I hear him coughing, I feel terrible." Liu Xiaochuan immediately responded, "As soon as his fever goes down, let's bring Dad down to Shenzhen. He can go back to Wuhan when it warms up there."

Liu Jinyuan had a pretty strong constitution. After he spent three days on an IV drip, his fever went down and his energy started to return. But his cough lingered. He didn't want to stay in the hospital any longer and insisted on going home. He knew that there are some old-timers who, once admitted, start to rely on the hospital; it becomes a psychological crutch, and they never make it home. He didn't want to die in the hospital like them. There wasn't much in this life that scared him, but he was terrified of being hospitalized. The smell of formalin that pervaded the hospital made him dizzy. Many years ago he used to call Dr. Wu Jiaming from the military hospital over to his home for house calls whenever something was wrong. Wu Jiaming had been living in a remote mountainous region when Liu Jinyuan recruited him into the army; later Liu Jinyuan helped him become a doctor. Wu Jiaming had a kind and quiet disposition, but he always had a rational explanation for why a given medicine should be taken for a given aliment. The most important thing was that those explanations always won Liu Jinyuan over. Liu Jinyuan was lucky that after he was promoted and transferred to Wuhan, Wu Jiaming also ended up transferred there. Any ailment big or small, all Liu Jinyuan had to do was make a phone call and Wu Jiaming would come right over. He was always proud to get that special treatment. It was a shame, then, that Wu Jiaming died so very young. *Otherwise*, Liu Jinyuan thought, *I would never have needed to go to the hospital for a little thing like this. Would I have ever needed to be on an IV drip? Would I still be coughing after three days of IV infusions? Wu Jiaming would just have silently written out a prescription for some herbal medicine and I would have been fine.*

When Liu Xiaochuan called to check on his father, Liu Jinyuan was coughing so badly he could barely catch his breath.

Growing agitated, Liu Xiaochuan started yelling on the phone, demanding that Liu Jinyuan take a flight to Shenzhen the very next day. Liu Xiaochuan told his brother that one of his company managers was flying back to their headquarters and could accompany their father on the flight; all Liu Xiao'an needed to do was get their father to the airport.

Liu Xiao'an was only too willing to accommodate his brother's request. He and his wife had been itching to go to Taiwan on vacation but had been unable to get away because of his father. Now that his father was going south and would probably be there for at least a month, they would finally have ample time to take their trip. He immediately agreed to get his father on the plane.

That night they packed his bags; actually, there wasn't much to pack because Liu Xiaochuan had everything his father would need in Shenzhen. The only thing Liu Jinyuan packed himself was a portable transistor radio. He used that radio to listen to the news each morning. He knew there was no way Liu Xiaochuan had one of those in Shenzhen. Liu Xiaochuan would always tell his dad how much better the television was than the radio. But Liu Jinyuan was set in his ways; he liked his radio. *But how could he be expected to understand?* he thought. *When you watch TV, you have to just sit there and can't do a damn thing. But when you listen to the radio, you can brush your teeth, shave, brew tea, read the newspaper—you can do all kinds of things!* He knew, though, that his generation saw things differently than the younger generation. His grandchildren no longer watched television; as soon as they came home from school they were online surfing the internet.

These days Liu Jinyuan was increasingly unwilling to spend his time talking to young people. He felt that they were all totally ignorant. But the real killer was that they thought *he* was the one who was ignorant! One year during the family's Spring Festival dinner he told his grandchildren about how he had participated in the campaign to suppress the bandits in western Sichuan. He told them about a friend of his who got captured while attempting to deliver a crucial piece of intelligence and ended up dying a terrible death at the hands of the bandits. Liu Jinyuan wanted his grandchildren to realize that the happy life they were now enjoying didn't come easy. But he could never have imagined that his youngest grandson would reply, "Humph, Grampa, I really don't know how to describe your generation. You're all so conservative and stupid. I try to teach you how to use the internet, and you just can't get it. If your friend could have used the internet, he would have had all kinds of ways to send his secret message! Just one click and his message would have been sent! He really deserved what he got! What a waste!" Liu Jinyuan was so furious that he slammed his chopsticks down on the table, clanking against the dishes. He then yelled, "What the hell do you know?!" His grandson still had the gall to talk back. "It's you old people who don't know nothing! And you accuse me of not knowing anything!" All the younger people at the table couldn't stop laughing. Liu Xiaochuan, his younger son, laughed so hard that he almost fell off his chair. What else could Liu Jinyuan say? In that moment he felt he was fighting this battle alone. Even though the entire family was together during that Spring Festival holiday, he didn't enjoy it one bit. He felt that with the exception of agreeing on basic things like eating and sleeping, there was absolutely no way to see eye-to-eye with them.

The next morning Liu Jinyuan was off to Wuhan Tianhe International Airport. Liu Xiao'an knew the manager assigned to accompany his father on the trip quite well; they shook hands, and Xiao'an patted him on the back. "Qinglin, you look like you're getting younger all the time! You must have gotten a huge salary bump when they promoted you to manager of the new branch!"

Liu Jinyuan suddenly thought that this manager looked quite familiar. Had he met him somewhere before? Then he remembered that Liu Xiaochuan's employees often came to the house to drop off various things; perhaps that was where he had seen him? It was a strong possibility. When the manager saw Liu Jinyuan, he quickly greeted him politely, saying, "Uncle Liu, good to see you."

Since the man was a manager, Liu Jinyuan responded, "Nice to meet you, Manager."

Both Liu Xiao'an and Qinglin broke out in laughter. Liu Xiao'an said, "No need to be polite with him, Dad! Treat him like family! His name is Qinglin. Xiaochuan taught him everything he knows. Back when I was in charge of the office, I was his supervisor."

"That's right," Qinglin said with a laugh. "Uncle Liu, please just call me Qinglin. I promise to get you safely to your destination."

That last sentence immediately set Liu Jinyuan at ease and gave him a good impression of Qinglin. He liked it when people spoke formally like that.

Liu Jinyuan's face lit up with a smile. The name Qinglin sounded familiar, but he still couldn't put his finger on where he had heard it before. But then he figured that since both his sons knew him, they must have mentioned his name before around the house.

Liu Xiao'an rushed off as soon as his father was in Qinglin's capable hands. They had a lot of time to kill in the waiting area and an even longer flight ahead, but Qinglin was extremely thoughtful and took good care of Liu Jinyuan. He chatted with him the entire time and even brewed tea for him. Qinglin also prepared some sweets to go with the tea. Liu Jinyuan hadn't been this delighted to spend time with a young person in what felt like forever.

Liu Jinyuan asked Qinglin how he had first gotten a job at his son's company.

Qinglin explained how he had gone through several other jobs before being hired. When Qinglin showed up for his interview, Liu Xiaochuan detected his accent and immediately switched to Wuhan dialect for the rest of their interview. Mr. Liu even complimented Qinglin on his name, which he said had a poetic ring to it. He said his own family, in contrast, was quite lazy when it came to names, as he and all his siblings had simply been haphazardly named after the places where they were born: his older brother was born in Xi'an, so his name was Liu Xiao'an; he himself was born in Sichuan and so was named Liu Xiaochuan; and his sister was born in Wuhan and named Liu Xiaowu—their parents didn't care whether it sounded like a girl's name. After his little sister grew up and started working at the Public Security Bureau, she actually changed the last character in her name, *wu*, from "military" (武) to "dance" (舞). She loved to dance, and that new name actually suited her quite well.

Liu Jinyuan burst out laughing. He agreed completely with his son. Back then he was indeed quite frustrated by the prospect of choosing names for his children and just went by the cities in which they were born.

"At the time, I told Mr. Liu that it wasn't that his parents were lazy," explained Qinglin, "just that they just wanted to create a kind of record for their own lives. 'That way whenever they speak your names,' I explained, 'they will think back to what was happening in their lives when you were born. I think it is quite meaningful, actually. They don't want to forget the past.' Uncle Liu, did you know that that was the very comment that got me hired? Mr. Liu said that my remark showed my consideration for others, which was a quality he was looking for in his employees. So, in some sense, *you're* the one I should thank for getting me that job!"

Liu Jinyuan smiled and felt elated. Qinglin really knew how to move him with his words.

When the plane arrived in Shenzhen, Liu Xiaochuan was waiting at the airport to pick up his father. A few of the other passengers on the plane greeted Liu Xiaochuan when they saw him: "Good to see you, Mr. Liu!" "Mr. Liu, here to pick up a friend?"

Liu Jinyuan was perplexed by all the attention his son was getting. "How is it that everyone knows you?"

Liu Xiaochuan just laughed, but Qinglin took the time to explain. "There's not a person in the world who doesn't know Mr. Liu! And Mr. Liu knows them all too!"

Liu Jinyuan got into Liu Xiaochuan's private car and gestured for Qinglin to join them. Qinglin waved his hand. "Uncle Liu, this is where we say goodbye. I'm actually going in the opposite direction." With that, he stood there watching as Liu Xiaochuan's car drove off. He kept waving until the car was completely out of sight.

While in the car, Liu Jinyuan turned to his son and said, "Xiaochuan, you should have given Qinglin a lift."

Liu Xiaochuan laughed. "I would have been happy to! He's the one who always refuses!"

"What's the big deal about his accepting a ride? It's no big deal," Liu Jinyuan commented.

"Back when you were in the army, would an average platoon leader have dared to ride in the same car with you?" Liu Xiaochuan retorted.

Liu Jinyuan didn't respond, but he realized his son was right.

"The business world isn't that different from when you were in the military," added Liu Xiaochuan.

"I had a really good impression of that manager you sent to accompany me on the plane," Liu Jinyuan commented.

"When kids come up poor, they tend to be hardworking and know how to conduct themselves properly. Unlike my big brother, who's too lazy to even lift a finger!" said Liu Xiaochuan.

"Don't talk about your older brother like that. Things are difficult for him too. Anyway, since Qinglin comes from a poor family, you should be good to him," said Liu Jinyuan.

"Of course," responded Liu Xiaochuan. "Without my support, do you think he would ever have gotten this far? When I first met him, he had only a hundred yuan in his pocket. Now he's got enough cash to buy a private villa!"

"There you go bragging again!"

Liu Xiaochuan laughed. "I don't dare brag about many things, but this is one thing I'm allowed to brag about!"

Liu Jinyuan fell silent. He hated it when his son was cocky like that. Whenever he was with his son, there were always these uncomfortable moments. He felt more at ease with Qinglin, whom he had met just a few hours before. There was something so natural about their interaction. It was the kind of feeling that leaves you warm inside; he hadn't felt that sense of closeness in a long time. He couldn't even remember the last time someone had left him with that kind of impression.

Left over from the past were, in Liu Jinyuan's mind, just a few hazy impressions that no longer seemed connected to anything. He felt that his memory was like a suit of armor that had been stripped away after a long battle. He was getting old.

4

QINGLIN'S SHOCK

As soon as Qinglin got back to his company headquarters, he received a phone call from Donghong; he was so shocked by what she said that he almost dropped the phone.

Donghong told him that his mother had woken up late. At first she just thought that the old lady had slept in after staying up late the previous night, but later she realized that wasn't the case at all. Ding Zitao was completely out of it; she didn't respond to anyone around her and acted as if she couldn't hear anything. She was a completely different person than she was the night before. She just sat there staring off into space; it was hard to tell exactly what she was looking at. Occasionally her lips would move as if she were talking, but no sound came out of her mouth. If you put food in front of her, she would eat it; otherwise, you would never know she was hungry. At first she even seemed to forget how to use the bathroom and dirtied her pants. After a few accidents, Donghong finally figured out a system for taking her to the bathroom at regular intervals and sitting her down on the toilet. Donghong would have to yell in her ear, "Do you need to do number one or number two?" Ding Zitao finally got the hang of it, but she was behaving like a robot. Donghong and the driver, Mr. Zhang, took her to the hospital. But since she didn't have a cough, a fever, or any other symptoms of illness, the hospital couldn't figure out what was wrong with her. The doctor just told them to take her home and keep an eye on her.

Bewildered at first, Qinglin had no idea what might be going on with his mother. He asked Donghong to put the phone to Ding Zitao's ear—he thought that once his mother heard his voice, she would start to come around. He started calling out to his mother through the phone, but there was no response on the other end. Donghong took the phone back and commented, "She's behaving as if she can't even hear you."

Qinglin rushed to the airport and managed to make the last flight of the day to Wuhan. It was the middle of the night by the time he arrived home.

The house was so quiet that it felt as if no one were at home. Donghong stayed in her room with the door closed. Qinglin went straight up to his mother's room. There he saw Ding Zitao sitting upright on a rattan chair; she was completely motionless. Qinglin loudly announced his arrival: "Mom, I'm home!"

She still didn't respond. Normally Ding Zitao would have rushed over to greet him with a big smile. Qinglin wanted to cry. He threw himself before his mother and, half kneeling, said, "Mom, what's wrong? It's me, Qinglin. Don't scare me. Your new life is just getting started."

Ding Zitao didn't move and her eyes didn't even look at him. Donghong heard the commotion and silently entered the room, then she explained, "She's been like this all day long. She slept until five o'clock in the afternoon and would have kept on sleeping had I not woken her. I even had to spoon-feed her dinner—she wouldn't touch her food unless I fed her. I didn't try to put her to bed because I was hoping your return might snap her out of it."

Qinglin started to call out even louder to his mother, "Mom! Mom! It's me! I'm back. It's me, Qinglin!"

Ding Zitao remained unresponsive. Even though there were two people right next to her talking to her, it was as if they didn't exist. She just sat there staring blankly at the wall as if no one else were in the room. She appeared lost in her own world, unable to pull herself out.

Qinglin became anxious. "How did you discover she was like this?"

"It was past ten o'clock in the morning when I noticed that she still hadn't gotten up, so I went over to wake her. That's when I realized something was wrong. Her clothes and sheets were all soiled with urine. I tried to speak to her, but she was behaving as if I wasn't even there. That's when I called you, but you were probably already in the air, so I couldn't get through. I started to worry and quickly got her into a change of clothes and had Mr. Zhang drive us to the hospital. They said her blood pressure and heart were all fine; they couldn't find anything wrong. The doctor thought she may have experienced some sort of shock. But he didn't think she needed to be hospitalized. He thought she might get better on her own in a few days."

Qinglin felt his mother's forehead; her temperature was normal. He also checked her breathing, which seemed okay. Only then did he heave a sigh of relief. "Nothing happened that could have put her in a state of shock. What could have caused this? It couldn't be related to her moving into this new house, could it?"

"That's right. Mr. Zhang and I also couldn't think of anything that could have triggered this," replied Donghong. "The only thing was the move. The doctor thought that perhaps she was not used to the new house and this was her psychological response."

Qinglin thought about it and realized that it had indeed been several decades since his mother had a place to truly call home;

now, all of a sudden, she had this new house—in some way, it was a huge adjustment for her. Overexcitement can also trigger a state of shock. "I hope she gets better in a few days."

"Nothing else happened all day," said Donghong. "Except for being taken to the bathroom and fed at fixed times, she just sat there quietly for the entire day."

Qinglin was puzzled. "What the hell kind of an illness is this? Does she have dementia? Doesn't that usually come on slowly?"

"Exactly," replied Donghong. "My grandmother had dementia, and its progression was slow; it took a long time before it got to the point where she could no longer recognize us. But with your mother all this happened overnight."

"I really don't get it," said Qinglin.

"That's right," Donghong added. "Last night when I was putting your mother to bed, she said some strange things. At one point she called me Little Tea. She even said that she brought me with her from her parents' home and that I had grown up with her family."

That really surprised Qinglin. "What does that even mean?"

"I was also puzzled," replied Donghong. "At the time I just thought she had too much to drink and was just talking nonsense."

As she spoke, Donghong led Ding Zitao to the bathroom; after that she helped her change into her pajamas and got her into bed. She turned to Qinglin to assure him, saying, "Who knows, perhaps she'll wake up tomorrow morning and be back to normal? My grandmother always used to say, *Sometimes there are things you can't accomplish during the day that you can only do at night.*"

Qinglin agreed. "Yeah, my mom used say, *People change after night falls*. Let's hope they are both right."

Donghong pointed to a pile of cardboard boxes in the corner. "Sir, Mr. Zhang brought your mother's belongings over from her old place this afternoon. Everything is here."

Qinglin walked over and gently kicked one of the boxes with his foot. "I'd like you to go through these boxes tomorrow. You can put her clothes in the dresser, but just throw away all those other random items she has around her apartment. No need to keep that stuff. Be sure to hold on to those shoe soles she made. But right now you should get some rest."

Donghong nodded and left the room. Qinglin pulled a chair over and sat down beside the bed. He gazed at his mother and whispered, "Mom, whatever difficulties you might be facing, you've got to get through this. I'm sure you can pull through, am I right? Tomorrow morning I'll be waiting to see my mom's familiar, smiling face."

SOMEONE HIDING A SECRET

All night long Qinglin was unable to sleep. He kept seeing his mother's face appearing before his eyes. In his mind's eye he saw her transform from a young woman to an old lady. His memories of the past were like pages of a book flipping by.

For his entire life Qinglin always had the impression that his mother's sole purpose in life was her family. Early on she fully devoted herself to taking care of her husband and son, and when her husband passed, she was even busier as she single-handedly had to support herself and her son. Qinglin knew that because his mother had been working as a live-in caregiver, she didn't have any friends to speak of. He had only just started elementary school when his father died and had forgotten almost all his memories of him; one of the only things he held on to was the memory of his father's voice. When his father was alive, he used to talk to Qinglin all the time. His father would always say, *No matter what you do when you grow up, whether you are rich or poor, you have to take good care of your mom. She is a very special person, but she has had an especially tough life.*

Qinglin never really thought too much about those words his father uttered; he just thought his father wanted him to be a good filial son. But looking back now, he realized that his father's words harbored another layer of meaning. *What was it about her that was so special?*

There was something else about her that always left Qinglin with a strange feeling: he didn't have any relatives. In fact, he didn't have any close relatives or even distant relatives on either his father's side or his mother's side—not a single one. His residence card listed Wuhan as his ancestral home, and yet from their accents he knew that neither of his parents could have been Wuhan natives. His father had a pronounced northern accent, and his mother spoke with a southwestern inflection you could detect from the way she pronounced final particles. Once when he was in college he mentioned this to a classmate. His classmate just laughed. "You don't have any relatives? Don't tell me your parents popped out of a rock like the Monkey King?"

He had asked his mother where her family was originally from, and she just responded, "Right here in Wuhan." When he followed up by asking her, "Then how come you don't really speak Wuhan dialect so well?" she explained that she had spent her childhood years away from Wuhan and that later, when she began working as a housekeeper, all the families she worked for were northerners. He then asked, "So how come we don't have a single relative here in Wuhan?" She just responded, "You're the only relative I need." He pushed back, "But I'm not a relative, I'm your son!" To which his mother replied, "A hundred relatives can't measure up to a single son."

At that point there seemed nowhere for their conversation to go. Later on Qinglin became consumed with his own work and never had the time to go digging into their past.

And now, after all these years, his mother suddenly mentioned her father? And he was someone who liked to paint "Guiguzi Descends the Mountain" patterns? Qinglin realized if that was true, then at the very least his mother did not grow up in a poor family as she had always claimed. What were her childhood and teenage years like? If she wasn't born into a poor family, why didn't she ever get an education? How could it be that he never once heard his mother talk about her past? It was as if she never had a childhood.

Qinglin knew that his mother was only somewhat literate. She said she had picked up some basic reading skills at a school set up in the 1950s to eradicate illiteracy. So it was completely natural for her not to ever read books or the newspaper. But then how was it that she was able to recite lines from an elegant classical poem? Qinglin thought back to that line of poetry she had uttered, *A row of bamboo before my window*, and realized she had instinctively recited that line in response to the bamboo she saw outside the door of their new house.

Qinglin suddenly had an idea: he turned on his computer and typed in *A row of bamboo before my window*, and the search engine automatically displayed the second line of the verse: *I marvel at the emerald green*. This was precisely the line his mother had recited. Even more shocking was when he saw the name Xie Tiao listed as the author—he immediately remembered the sound of his mother saying, "It's a poem by Xie Tiao." A peculiar feeling came over him.

Somehow his mother knew who Xie Tiao was. Xie Tiao was a poet of the Northern and Southern Dynasties period. In the popular terminology of today, he was a largely neglected "lesser-known poet." Even someone like Qinglin, who had a college education, had never heard of Xie Tiao; yet somehow his mother, who was barely literate, not only knew his work but was able to freely recite his poem in response to the scenery around her.

Gradually Qinglin started to recall other peculiar things his mother had said. As when she first saw the new house, she said something about something-lu. Was it Qierenlu? And then something-tang? And then there was that moment when she saw the porcelain vessel and immediately recognized the pattern from "Guiguzi Descends the Mountain." When she saw the purple comforter on her bed, she said it should have been red. And then there was that strange comment about being in pain after someone hit her with a buttstock. But there was more, like what Donghong told him his mother had said about Little Tea. All this started to make him feel as if his mother was a stranger. Just the day before, he had been thinking that he didn't know her as well as he should, but now he felt as if something had caused his mother to undergo a shocking transformation. She had slipped into an oblivious state and was no longer the mother he once knew. She seemed to be a different person entirely, someone hiding a secret. This secret made him feel as if his mother were a massive book, but all he had ever seen was its cover. As for the contents of that book, he had never read even a single page.

HER SPIRIT IS NO LONGER OF THIS WORLD

Qinglin's sole wish was for his mother to snap out of her daze and get better. But every morning when he stepped into his mother's room, all he saw was her blank stare. She was incapable of tears or laughter; in fact, she remained utterly expressionless. The only difference between her being asleep and being awake was whether her eyes were open or closed; otherwise, everything else was exactly the same.

Qinglin's life was thrown into disarray. He spent all his time accompanying his mother to all kinds of doctor appointments. He also took her to see various Buddhist monks and Taoist priests; the monks recited magic incantations, and the priests performed their rituals. He even hired a venerable master priest to come to the house to perform an exorcism. Qinglin spent several hundred thousand yuan on all this, but at the end of the day, his mother showed absolutely no improvement.

Then one day Qinglin's former college classmate, Long Zhongyong, passed through Wuhan with his father on his way from Shanghai to Guizhou. He wanted to go to the Huangpi District to visit his aunt who had moved to Wuhan after marriage and was planning on staying a day or two. Qinglin insisted Long Zhongyong stay at his house. "No need to stand on ceremony," Qinglin said. "After all, just think of how many years we lived together as roommates! If you stay here, you can use our car whenever you need it. It'll also be good to catch up."

Long Zhongyong could tell that Qinglin was sincere and took him up on his offer. Long Zhongyong's father had been suffering from Alzheimer's disease for three or four years, and Long Zhongyong had to watch firsthand as his father slipped away, all the while knowing there was nothing he could do about it. He said, "To see such a wise man like him turn into this is really heartbreaking. There are really no words to describe it."

Qinglin sat in the living room with Long Zhongyong telling him about his mother's condition. He related how all he ever wanted was to make his mother happy, and yet the very night he moved her into this new house, she transformed into a completely different person. She became someone completely cut off from the real world. By the time he finished his story, Qinglin felt on the verge of crying, but he had no tears left. Then he said, "Perhaps it would have been easier to take if my mother's progression had been more like your father's. At least then I would have had more time to process the sadness."

Long Zhongyong's father was sitting quietly beside them the whole time, staring at the floor, but then he suddenly spoke: "Her spirit is no longer of this world."

He was still staring at the floor and never once glanced at Qinglin, and yet his words rang out clear as a bell. It was as if the sound of those eight words bounced off the floor and into the air, echoing throughout the room.

Qinglin and Long Zhongyong were both utterly shocked. Long Zhongyong explained that it had been a very long time since his father had said anything other than a three-word sentence. He also said that when his father first started to develop symptoms of Alzheimer's, he would often say that he was in the process of leaving this world and heading to another place; he also said he would take his time on this journey. Long Zhongyong explained, "Their way of understanding things is probably quite different from that of normal people. Perhaps, in some weird way, this condition is something they want for themselves and isn't an illness at all."

What Long Zhongyong and his father had said really struck a deep chord with Qinglin. He thought, *Probably, perhaps, in fact . . . she isn't sick at all; she's just letting her spirit wander off to another world for a while, letting it have a chance to look around at the people and things on the other side. Perhaps when she is done she will come back. Otherwise, how else are we to understand her ignoring the people around her and instead getting lost in her own world, especially since she doesn't have any other symptoms? She is still able to carry out all her other basic functions like eating, drinking, going to the bathroom, and sleeping.*

Qinglin felt a sense of relief. He figured the only path forward was to follow the course of nature. He decided to go back to his normal work routine and try as best he could to enjoy life. He figured that was what his mother would have wanted him to do.

And so he indeed returned to his old way of life. He was as busy as ever, like a top that never stops spinning.

He left his mother's care completely in Donghong's hands. Donghong's job was actually quite simple. Besides straightening up the house and tending the garden, all she had to do to care for Ding Zitao was to feed her, take her to the bathroom at regular intervals, and change her clothes every day or two; otherwise, there really wasn't much to be done.

AN OLD LEATHER TRUNK

One day when Qinglin came home, he noticed an old leather trunk left outside by the front door; the trunk was dark brown with rusty metal rivets around the corners. Something about the trunk looked familiar to Qinglin, but whatever it was that gave him that sense of familiarity felt so very distant—for the time being he simply couldn't put his finger on where he had seen it. He summoned Donghong so that he could ask her about the trunk.

Donghong responded, "Today I was going through your mother's things and found that trunk packed up in a large cardboard box. Inside were also a quilt and some other things. I wanted to throw everything in the box in the trash, but then Old Zhang insisted on opening up each item and properly tying them all up before disposing of them. It was only then that

I discovered that leather trunk. The old man said that the trunk was worthless and asked me to give it to him, but I didn't. The trunk is actually still locked."

Qinglin now remembered seeing that trunk up on top of his mother's dresser, where she had carefully placed it after the death of his father. He remembered his mother telling him, "This was once your father's. He always kept it locked, so I don't know what's inside. He told me to give it to you after he dies. But you had better wait until after *I* die before you open it."

After not having a place of their own for so many years, Qinglin completely forgot about that trunk. At that moment, though, the image of his mother talking to him while standing on a stool holding the trunk over her head as she put it away on top of the dresser flashed clearly before his eyes. He was struck by a feeling that was at once intimate and uncanny. Qinglin told Donghong, "This trunk belonged to my father. Please bring it to my bedroom."

That night Qinglin went online and wrote several work emails before calling his son to check in. After that he went into his mother's room and, sitting beside her bed, shared with her everything that had happened at work that day. One of his colleagues had told him about someone who was in a vegetative state but suddenly woke up one day after one of his family members kept coming by every day to talk to him. Qinglin thought that his mother might also snap out of her comatose state if he kept talking to her every day. Perhaps when she saw Qinglin, she would say, "Hi, Qinglin! I'm so happy to be able to open my eyes and see you standing there."

Qinglin went on and on with his mother before he finally remembered the trunk. He hurried over to his room and dragged the trunk over, setting it down in front of his mother. The trunk was fairly heavy. Lifting it up, Qinglin said, "Mom, can you see this? It's Dad's leather trunk. I just found it. Do you know what's inside? Do you still have the key?"

But the only response Qinglin got was his mother's steady breathing. It was as if nothing in the world had anything to do with her—and that included the two people she loved most in life, her husband and her son.

Qinglin decided to open the trunk. He found a screwdriver and pried open the lock. The first thing he saw was a few worn-out old medical books; he figured they must have been his father's old textbooks. But beneath those textbooks lay a stack of journals. Qinglin thought the whole thing seemed strange. He thumbed through them and realized that some of them were his father's medical journals and his notes from when he later worked at the hospital. The rest of them were records of his father's life: they were like diaries, but not really. Some of them were dated, but others were labeled only with a year or a season. He could tell from the faded handwriting that they were quite old.

Suddenly Qinglin grew excited. He wondered if these journals might contain the answer to whatever secrets his mother had been hiding. He grew increasingly curious and, sitting down on the floor, began to put the journals in chronological order based on the numbers written on the upper right-hand corner of each one.

The journals began in autumn 1948 and went until 1966. His father must have stopped writing after the start of the Cultural Revolution.

Qinglin reached out and opened the first notebook; he wanted to start at the beginning. As his gaze fell on those rows of faded Chinese characters written in pen, he felt a sudden sense of anxiety. He didn't know what these notebooks contained. He wondered if contained within those pages was a side of his parents that he never knew. And if so, how might that affect his life?

A strange fear welled up inside him. Why did his mother ask him to wait until after she was dead before opening the trunk?

Qinglin's heart began to pound. He hesitated for a moment before putting the notebooks back in the trunk. He thought, *I'm probably not ready yet.*

5

THE STAIRCASE UNDER THE GRAY LIGHT

As she fell, Ding Zitao could feel her body growing heavier and heavier. Her heart felt as if it were being squeezed, strangled by countless strands of fine silk; her breathing became strained. She no longer had the strength to fight and was preparing to take one final breath and then let go. It was precisely at that moment that she heard a loud explosion. That was followed by the sound of all the bones in her body cracking; for a second she felt as if her entire body were being ripped apart.

It took a long time for her to come to and realize that she had stopped falling. She was worried that she had fallen all the way to the bottom. It was pitch-black all around her, and she didn't know where she was or even if she was dead or alive. She couldn't help asking herself, *Am I dead? Am I already dead?*

As she asked herself these questions, she remembered what her mother had once told her: "As long as you are alive, there will be pain and suffering. But all that pain will end when you die." The entire scene from that moment seemed to materialize before her eyes: She was so young back then, just a little girl sitting in the sewing room, learning how to embroider the feathered patterns of a peacock's tail, when a needle suddenly pricked her hand. She began to wail the second she saw the fresh blood begin to drip from her fingertip. Her mother walked over, took a cursory look, and began reprimanding her. She used the same words her own father had used to admonish her when she was little. Her mother's family ran an embroidery business on Kejia Alley in Chengdu, and her father was renowned near and far for his incredible embroidery skills. Their family specialty was embroidering silk renditions of famous Song dynasty paintings, which were prized among wealthy collectors. Her mother had been refining her embroidery skills since she was a child. When she agreed to marriage, it was only under the condition that her husband's family set aside a special room for her to practice her embroidery. They immediately agreed. At that moment the embroidery room and the silk embroideries hanging on the loom flashed before Ding Zitao's eyes. Her mother was standing beside the loom arranging the edges of one of the embroideries with one hand while gently caressing the embroidered pattern with the fingers of her other hand. Her mother lowered her head and said, "But there is another way. If you can erase your memory, you'll never know that you were once in pain."

Ding Zitao adjusted her position; her entire body felt wracked with pain. She thought, *If that is true, then I am still alive. I can still feel the pain . . . and I still remember.*

Her ears became more sensitive and seemed able to hear a faint whistling coming, it seemed, from some faraway place. From this boundless distance this sound encircled her and, one layer after another, encased her as if tightly wrapping her up like a mummy. She felt as if she were now part of that distant abyss; at the same time, it was as if that abyss were a million miles away. Yet she was not afraid; she just felt a sense of overwhelming exhaustion. She closed her eyes, but she couldn't tell if she was sleeping or awake.

Meanwhile, time continued to move forward according to its own rules. Perhaps it had been a day or perhaps a year; perhaps it had been one hundred days, or perhaps an entire century had slipped by. The density of the darkness began to give way. A gentle gray light began to appear from above, and in that light could be seen a soft layer of fabric. It was through that layer of fabric that Ding Zitao gazed upward; row after row of lines gradually followed the gray light upward as if ascending a staircase. She began to count the levels going up; she got up to eighteen before she could no longer see clearly.

She wondered, *Eighteen. Why were there exactly eighteen? What does it mean?*

NO, THAT'S NOT TRUE!

A cold wind suddenly rushed in; it lasted only for a moment, yet it sent a chill straight through her bones. She shuddered, and as her body trembled, she suddenly remembered something from a long time before. She was sitting beside a lake in a small bamboo pavilion and gazing at the ripples forming in the autumn water as the gulls flew overhead. In response to the chilly air, she recited a poem to herself: *The evening drizzle conjures dreams of the distant fortress where battles once raged. The melody of the reed pipe from atop the tower sends a cold chill through my heart.*

Someone placed a jacket over her shoulders. That gesture warmed not only her body but also her heart.

Who was it? Ding Zitao wondered. *Who was it that placed this jacket over her shoulders?* She couldn't remember. "Who was it? Who are you?" she couldn't help but ask out loud. A deep male voice responded, "It's me, Lu Zhongwen. I was afraid you might catch a chill."

"Lu Zhongwen," said Ding Zitao, "where have you been? I haven't seen you in so long."

"I was going to ask you the same thing," replied Lu Zhongwen. "Where have you been? What about my parents? And my grandmother, my aunt? What about my brother? And Sister Huiyuan? Where have you all been? My Little Ding Zi . . . how come I haven't been able to find you?"

Ding Zitao was dumbfounded. Where *did* they all go? She looked around in every direction to see if the people he had mentioned were anywhere to be seen. All were members of Lu Zhongwen's family, her family.

They were in a wide open space, but it was enveloped in what appeared to be a thick foglike mist; she couldn't even see Lu Zhongwen. She called out, "Where are you? Lu Zhongwen, where did you go?"

Lu Zhongwen's voice sounded as if coming from some faraway place. Ding Zitao couldn't even tell from which direction the voice came. But she heard him calling out to her: "I'm looking for you! Where are you?"

Indeed, where am I? Ding Zitao wondered. *What is this place?*

Through the gray mist she again caught sight of that eighteen-floor staircase. Then she was struck by a sudden thought: *Am I in hell?* It was just like Second Mother's curse: You should go to hell!

Ding Zitao looked at her hand to see if there was any blood, but she couldn't see anything. She could feel that her hand was still there, but her eyes were blind. She suddenly became disgusted by her own hands; they seemed such dirty, disgusting things—she hated them for existing.

Why? Ding Zitao thought. *What happened?* She raised her hands and began alternately slapping someone with each of her hands. That crisp sound of hands slapping skin rang in her ears. The sound startled her. She could hear what sounded like trumpets ringing in her ears, yet her hands were now frozen. Through the nonstop brassy notes of those trumpetlike horns a series of faces began to materialize before her. Her hands were slapping those faces. These were faces she knew all too well—they gazed at her with blank stares as the cold palms of her hands slapped them mercilessly.

Sounds of happiness and celebration surrounded her, and then there was the clanking noise of metal. And then came a sharp voice crying out, "You're going to hell! Yama will never release you!"

Ding Zitao instantly cried out, "No! That's not true!"

She told herself, *No, that's not true! I shouldn't be sent to hell. I can't be stuck in hell. I need to get out! Tell Zhongwen, tell Second Mother, tell everyone! That's not what happened! What they say happened isn't true. It's not what they think!*

It was then that she suddenly had an idea: She needed to get out. She must escape. She needed to tell everyone, even those people who had been staring at her with a look of cold intensity. She needed to tell them that no one had planned what eventually happened. It had nothing to do with her. Even if she had to go to hell itself, she needed to set things straight.

And so . . . she began to pull herself up.

HELL I: SCREAMS FROM THE RIVER

Little by little she crawled her way up. Ding Zitao couldn't tell how long she had been crawling before she finally dragged herself to the first step of that staircase. She got to her feet and raised her head to look up. She thought, *For me, this is already the eighteenth floor.* But she asked herself, *What do I want to tell them? Where do I even start?*

She discovered that although she was filled with stories she wanted to get out, she didn't know how to begin.

It was then that the river water rose up to submerge her. Large rocks surrounded her. The surging flow of the water pushed her from one rock to another. She struggled with all her might, trying to cling to one of the rocks. But the surfaces of the river rocks were all incredibly slippery, and every time she tried to grab onto one of them, another wave would quickly knock her down.

She kept screaming until her voice grew hoarse, "Ding Zi! Ding Zi!"

Ding Zi was still on the boat. He was bundled up in a floral-patterned blue cloth. He was asleep. She could still remember the look on his little face as he slept soundly. There was even the trace of a smile. His little legs had kicked open part of the cloth he had been swaddled in, allowing one of his tiny embroidered shoes to poke out. She had personally embroidered those shoes, which were adorned with a pair of goldfish.

The night before he left, Lu Zhongwen kept hugging Ding Zi. Father and son laughed and played together all evening. Lu Zhongwen said, "Can you say Baba?"

Ding Zi repeated, "Ba . . . Ba."

Lu Zhongwen was smiling from ear to ear. He laughed as he lifted his son high into the air. And just as Ding Zi was high above his father, he peed. Ding Zi peed right into Lu Zhongwen's face. In his surprise, Lu Zhongwen let out a wild scream and quickly handed Ding Zi to her. As he rushed out of the room to wash his face, he could hear everyone laughing. After washing his face and changing his clothes, Lu Zhongwen went back in to give Ding Zi a gentle spanking. "You rotten little egg! Is that your going-away present for Baba?"

She laughed. "Of course it is. That's our little Ding Zi marking his territory!"

Lu Zhongwen was heading to Hong Kong. Before he left he told her, "I'm going to miss you and our little Ding Zi. But I'll be back as soon as I can. Please take good care of him. My parents shouldn't need any special help, but should something happen while I'm gone, please be sure to lend them a hand."

"Don't worry," she responded. "I've got everything covered. I've also got Little Tea and Ritchie to help out."

"Did you know that Ritchie has a crush on Little Tea?" Lu Zhongwen asked. "He wants to marry her. You wouldn't object, would you?"

"How could I?" she laughed. "I'm only too happy for them! Ritchie has been with you since he was a child, and Little Tea has grown up with me; it's a perfect match. One day their baby can play with Ding Zi."

Lu Zhongwen gave Ding Zi another hug before he left. They followed him as far as they could as he rode off in the family's horse-drawn cart.

But what about now? Where had Ding Zi gone? Where was that boat? Where did it go?

Meanwhile she was caught in the rapids. Like a living rock, her body was knocked around by the will of the current. This was a strange rock indeed. It seemed to resist the relentless waves that buffeted her. It would alternately tumble and remain still, choosing a chaotic, unpredictable path through the waters. There was no trace of any sounds made by humans coming from either side of the river; in fact, even the sound of leaves rustling in the wind was barely audible. The water crashing down on the rocks obliterated all other sounds, so nothing else could be heard. At this point she was still conscious. From time to time there would be a slight break before the next onrush of water crashed down on her; in these moments she opened her mouth to catch some air, but each time she ended up choking on the water. Those voices rushed into her heart, but all that was left were her cries of "Ding Zi! Ding Zi!" Her crazed screams almost made her heart explode. Even the mountains that surrounded the river on both sides seemed to tremble at the sound of her screams.

The rushing water quickly pushed her downstream. The clamorous sound of the water crashing against rocks grew more intense. She thought what she was hearing was the sound of her own screams. She couldn't even tell the sky apart from the water. Her dear son, Ding Zi, where did he go? She used every last bit of strength in her body to look for him but couldn't see him anywhere.

She was chaotically flipping around in the water when her finger touched something floating. Only after grabbing hold of it did she discover it was a plank of wood. As she hugged that plank of wood, she suddenly recognized it—it was a piece of her family's boat, the same boat that Ritchie had been paddling. She instantly realized the implications: Did the boat hit a rock and split apart? Then . . . what happened to her Ding Zi? He had been bundled up on that boat . . . what happened to him? The moment those questions came to mind, she sensed her will to live fading. And so . . . she released her grip and let everything go.

If Ding Zi is gone, what's the point of living? That was the last thought that crossed her mind as the current swept her away.

HELL II: A BOAT LOST ON THE WATER

Every ounce of energy in Ding Zitao's body was used up. She no longer knew what she was doing. All that consumed her was the desperate feeling of trying to gasp for breath.

In the darkness she caught a whiff of a refreshing scent—the smell of the water. She wondered if she had already reached the river's edge.

Then she caught sight of Ritchie. He jumped down from the boat and started running toward her. She was already standing up in the water when he rushed over to hold her back. "What are doing?" he asked. "Sister Daiyun, where are you going?"

She stared at him blankly but didn't respond. Ritchie pulled her over to the boat. He climbed aboard and reached out to pull her up. "How come you're coming so late?" Ritchie asked. "Master Lu told us we have to arrive at Gulfway Village by dawn; Cousin Song will be waiting to pick us up at the mouth of the river. Is Ding Zi okay? Looks like he is having a good nap. Where's Huiyuan? Master Lu said you were coming together. Is she on her way? Shall we wait for her? If we wait too long, someone will catch us."

Still not thinking straight, she just whispered, "There isn't anyone else."

With Ding Zi in her arms, she sat down in the boat. She looked confused and no longer had full control of herself. It was as if she had only just enough energy to follow instructions from others.

The boat quickly left the riverbank. When they realized that no one was pursuing them, Ritchie heaved a sigh of relief. As he rowed the boat, he said, "Yesterday afternoon Master Lu asked me to moor the boat here. I followed the secret tunnel beneath the watchtower to get here. Is that the same route you took? Nobody knows about that tunnel. Master Lu said his grandfather had constructed it, but it was only for use in times of emergency. Master Lu also asked me to accompany you to find Brother Zhongwen; that way I could look after you along the way. But how come it's just you and the baby? If Miss Huiyuan stays home, they might also drag her out to be struggled against. What would we do then?"

She merely grunted a response but didn't feel like talking. There was so much she had bottled up inside her that she felt as if something were pressing against her internal organs, making them twist and turn. She was broken and felt like throwing up, but nothing was coming out.

"Then again," Ritchie continued, "I heard that Jindian is now the section head of the work division. He always had a great relationship with Mistress Huiyuan. I'm sure he wouldn't give her any trouble."

"Don't mention him!" she instantly yelled.

Ritchie was so taken aback by her response that the entire boat rocked. He quietly grumbled, "What's wrong with you?" After which he started to go on again. "I grew up with Brother Zhongwen. I used to accompany him to school every day, and later when he went to study at the master's house, I would sit outside waiting for him. On our way home Brother Zhongwen would always teach me the characters he learned that day."

She was becoming deeply annoyed. She really didn't feel like talking. Nor was she in the mood to listen to his yapping. All she wanted was some quiet time to settle down.

As the current strengthened, it began to carry their small boat away with the river; all of a sudden they found themselves in a part of the river surrounded by mountains. As the peaks around them soared into the sky, the river became increasingly narrow and turbulent, its current fluctuating between patches of calm and violent waves. It was a good thing that Ritchie was quite familiar with this stretch of the river; he knew where all the rocks were and how the path of the river flowed. He deftly wielded the boat pole through the section of the river straddled by cliffs and, with his skills, was able to navigate the perilous waters and keep the boat moving forward.

Ding Zi remained fast asleep in her arms, as if he understood what had happened the previous night and knew to keep quiet and not make a fuss. She wasn't wearing enough to keep herself warm; her back was frozen, and it was only that toasty baby in her arms that kept her chest area warm.

"Ding Zi's being such a good baby!" said Ritchie. "Tomorrow we'll have to tell him that he got to ride in Uncle Ritchie's boat all night!"

She still didn't respond. Ritchie was an orphan adopted by her husband's parents. They had also adopted another orphan—his name was Jindian. He was a bit older and worked for the family alongside their other long-term laborers. Since Ritchie was younger, he was always spending time with her husband, Lu Zhongwen. The two of them had grown up together and were as close as brothers.

Ritchie didn't seem to mind that she wasn't responding to anything he said; he just kept on talking. "Master Lu said that Brother Zhongwen will be staying in Hong Kong. He asked me to come right back after I get you safely to him. Sister Daiyun, do you think I should bring Little Tea anything back from Hong Kong?"

In her confusion, the words "Little Tea" seemed to tear something open, allowing the light to shine in. She unconsciously repeated, "Little Tea?"

"That's right," said Ritchie. "Little Tea likes those scarves with the floral patterns that you always wear. Perhaps I should buy her one of those?"

It was already starting to grow light out. The sun still hid behind the mountains, though, and as the river surged between the mountains, its water flowed into their dark shadows. The wind picked up, and she immediately felt a damp chill.

Abruptly, she broke out crying. "They're dead," she cried. "They are all dead." Her anguished cries seemed to drown out the sound of the rushing water and reverberated throughout the mountains.

"Dead?" Ritchie asked. "Who is dead?"

"All of them," she answered through her tears.

The boat began to rock more violently in the waves as Ritchie cried out, "What happened? How did they die? Who did it? Who killed them? The main gate should have been locked! No one should have been able to get into the compound!"

She buried her head against Ding Zi. Crying, she said, "Ding Zi's grandfather wanted everyone to die together. Someone passed a message from the village saying that come dawn, the villagers were coming to launch a struggle session against the Lu family. The struggle was to last three days. After that, they were going to divide up the family's laborers and property. Jindian was the one who made the call."

Ritchie froze in utter shock. He steered the boat silently and, after a long pause, cried out, "What does any of this have to do with Little Tea? Little Tea is penniless—she's not part of a landlord's family. Her last name isn't even Lu! Why would they need to kill her?"

Finally beginning to calm down a bit, she raised her head and responded, "Little Tea made the decision for herself. They were going to force her to marry Uncle Ma's second son. Little Tea wasn't willing to do that, but she knew that there was no saying no to them. Once they had made their decision, it was final. To resist them would mean death."

Ritchie stopped steering the boat, and it immediately began to rock back and forth. Ritchie screamed, "Little Tea was mine! She promised to marry me. I'm also a poor man! Uncle Ma even has his own room; I don't even have a place of my own! Sister Daiyun, please don't joke with me!"

Choking on her tears, Daiyun told him, "I buried her with my own two hands. I buried her under the palm tree near the western wall of the compound. She is buried together with Ziping. They are lying together, shoulder to shoulder." As she spoke, she broke into another wave of cries. "As I put her in the ground, I kept thinking that Little Tea was still breathing . . ."

"How could you let her die?" Ritchie demanded. "How could you bury her?"

"What was I supposed to do?" she said through her tears. "Just leave her there for the sun to sear her face the next morning?"

Ritchie began to scream at her. "How could you do that? Weren't you supposed to be responsible for taking care of Little Tea? She treated you like her own flesh-and-blood sister—why didn't you save her? Why couldn't you have taken her with you when you ran away? We have plenty of room on the boat for another person. Why didn't you take her with you?"

She had never seen Ritchie act this way before. Deep down she was thinking, *How dare a servant speak to me like that!* But instead of retorting in anger, she just coldly said, "And what would have been the difference if I hadn't buried her? She's dead. It's not as if she'd have been able to marry you anyway!"

Ritchie cried out even more violently, "Sister Daiyun, I always treated you and Little Tea like my own sisters. How could you do that? How could you be so cruel?"

She was on the verge of yelling at him for speaking to her with such insolence, but before she could say a word she heard a massive splash. She looked up to discover that Ritchie was gone. The boat began to rock even more violently in the current. She screamed, "Ritchie! Ritchie!"

She could hear Ritchie's voice gliding over the water. "Please don't blame me, but I can't take care of you. I've got to go back to find Little Tea."

The boat continued on its wild journey to the rapids, occasionally crashing into the slimy rocks. She let out a terrified scream, but the only response came from her own voice. She quickly put Ding Zi down and picked up the pole to steer the boat. No longer able to hear Ritchie's voice—all she heard was the roaring of the water—she frantically did whatever she could to try to stabilize the rocking boat. But she had never spent any time on the water before and had no idea how to steer a boat.

Meanwhile the current picked up, pushing the boat into one rock after another. Then she lost her balance, falling down into the bed of the boat. Before she could even react, the entire boat capsized. As she fell into the water she screamed, "Ding Zi!"

From that moment on, the only thing on her mind was Ding Zi.

HELL III: FRANTICALLY RUNNING DOWN A MOUNTAIN PATH

Ding Zitao could see a mountain path. She could see herself running down that path.

The path was winding and surrounded on both sides by short bushes and shrubs, and occasionally there were large rocks blocking it. Looking down the zig-zagging path, you'd think someone had haphazardly laid it down like a belt thrown carelessly on the floor; the path continued all the way deep into the forest. Someone kept whispering orders into her ear: *Daiyun, you must . . . you must . . .* That voice made her heart tremble.

Only now did she finally begin to realize that *she* was this woman named Daiyun.

Her father was an avid reader of *Dream of the Red Chamber* and loved the characters Lin Daiyu and Shi Xiangyun. He said, "If my daughter could have both Daiyu's intellect and Xiangyun's charm, she would certainly have a life filled with good fortune." And so he took one Chinese character from each of their names and gave his daughter the name Daiyun. Her father was a book collector who was always practicing calligraphy and painting. In the east wing of their compound were three large rooms that basically served as her father's private library and study. One room he reserved for painting and calligraphy. While writing his calligraphy, her father would often call her over, elongating the second syllable in her name: "Yun . . . come over and help me prepare the ink." Daiyun liked playing with her father's inkstone, which had a dark tint somewhere between brown and green and was engraved with the image of two men playing Chinese chess. It was cold and smooth to the touch. But she didn't like the process of preparing the ink. The process of rubbing the stone made her hand sore, and it always made her shirt dirty. Daiyun's mother also hated it when he summoned their daughter to help with the ink. She always thought that should be the job of her husband's concubine, and she wanted to keep Daiyun with her in the embroidery room. What Daiyun's mother wanted most was to pass on all her embroidery techniques to her daughter. Yet Daiyun's father still liked to summon her to help him. He would say, "My little girl Daiyun is so good at preparing the ink! The way she grinds the inkstone produces just the right thickness and texture. Whenever she prepares the ink, my calligraphy and painting reach another level!" And then he would add, "I think we should use that same famous Cao Sugong ink from last time!"

But as she was running, the voice speaking in her ear was not that of her father. Father's voice was always soft and easygoing; this voice had a stern harshness to it.

It was pitch-black along the mountain path; there was not only no moon but also not even a single star visible in the sky.

The dark clouds above were so thick and expansive that you couldn't see how far they went or how many layers there were. Daiyun carried her child on her back, alternately walking and running. She didn't seem to need to actually see that path, for her feet instinctively knew the way.

Yet on this dark night when nothing seemed to exist, there was someone whose voice was continuously speaking to her through the air; it was as if the voice were directing her through this maze: *Enter the watchtower. Beneath the staircase is a pile of broken wooden window panels with engraved floral patterns; move them aside and behind them you will see a small door—this is the gateway to the secret tunnel that Grandfather constructed. The tunnel leads all the way out behind the mountain. When you crawl out from the tunnel, you will see a pile of thatched grass covering a hole; beyond that you will find a tea farm. Pass through the tea farm and look for two old camphor trees. Behind the trees is a bamboo fence. Climb over that fence and walk south for ten steps and you will see a stone path. The path will twist its way up a small hill. Just follow the path, but be careful not to hurt your feet on the rocks. The path will take you down the mountain. Just keep running down that path. Follow all its twists and turns into the forest, and when it starts to ascend, just keep following the path up. Just be sure not to stray from the path; take it to the very end. At the end of the path you will arrive at the river, and there you will find Ritchie waiting for you. Get there as fast as you can. If dawn arrives and they catch you, I'm afraid they will kill both you and your son.*

That voice was her father-in-law, Lu Ziqiao, speaking to her. His directions were firm and resolute and left no room for negotiation.

It wasn't exactly quiet up in the mountains, where myriad sounds surrounded her. As she ran down the path, she would occasionally hear flocks of startled birds taking flight. The sound of their wings flapping rang out into the night. But those sounds no longer frightened her, for stranger things that were much larger and more terrifying drowned them out.

And so she ran. She ran like mad. She ran as if her very life depended on it. She knew that if they caught her, it would be the end. The terrified faces of her parents and other family members, their pleading cries, their screams of terror, and the details the other villagers described about the terrible way in which her family had died were all like a whip driving her to run faster. Just a few months earlier she had been eating with her parents at a restaurant in Qierenlu. By then the family had already turned over all their assets to the state and sent all the servants back home to their families; virtually all their wealth was gone. That day the family drank together and made a bowl of longevity noodles to celebrate her mother's birthday. Her father said that the fact that they were able to sit together in Qierenlu and enjoy a meal as a family was already a blessing they should treasure. Qierenlu had been built by her grandfather. Back when it was being built, a distant uncle who lived next door got upset that the building was too high and kept coming over to argue with them about the construction. Each time he came over to complain, her grandfather would cut one roof beam off his project's height, and that happened three times in a row. Everyone else in the family was furious, and all were ready to unite around her grandfather to show their support. But her grandfather just said, "We must learn tolerance and understanding; we cannot make enemies of our neighbors, especially over the little things." After the building was complete, he named it Qierenlu, or "Cottage of Tolerance." And though the height of the building ended up being much lower than others, the family continued to prosper. Meanwhile, that distant uncle living in that large tall house next door ended up having three sons who constantly argued over their family's wealth; their bitter fights went on for years and ended up bringing the entire family to financial ruin. Her father would say, "You see, tolerance is itself a form of good fortune." Almost ten members of their family lived in Qierenlu. She lived there throughout her childhood, right up to the time she left for the city to attend school. She always felt more attached to that place than anywhere else in the world.

But who could ever have imaged that just a few days after they'd had that meal together, she and her family would be torn apart. She thought, *Daddy, you followed Grandfather's instructions all these years and tolerated everything your entire life, but what was the result of putting up with all that? You did everything you could, and in the end they still executed you. Not only that, but your actions brought down the entire family—Mom, Second Mother, Sister-in-Law—they all died for your lofty ideal of tolerance. What did this tolerance get you in the end?*

The pain inside left her completely shattered.

Gradually, she began to hear the faint sound of flowing water. Before long she thought she could smell the water in the air. She saw the river. And then, there was Ritchie.

By then she was completely and utterly exhausted, yet she still couldn't allow herself to slow down. It was as if she were born to run. When she saw the water, she knew she had made it and knew she should stop, and yet her legs just kept on walking. She staggered forward, running straight for the water.

Ritchie had to stop her. "What are doing?" he asked. "Sister Daiyun, where are you going?"

6

EVEN A LIFE THAT ISN'T BUSY IS STILL DEEPLY EXHAUSTING

Qinglin's period of intense work had passed. His company's real estate project in the Jiangxia District had a clear path forward. They were able to purchase the land they needed for a reasonable price, and the design plan for the area was already complete. All parties involved had discussed the plan and everyone was on board. Their development project was slated for an area referred to as Sakyamuni Ridge.

Before they broke ground on the new development, Liu Xiaochuan came to personally inspect the site. He was clearly quite pleased with the work Qinglin had done. During his tour of the site he kept nodding his head in approval as he listened to Qinglin describe the project. Occasionally he would even put his arm around Qinglin's shoulder to signal an even more intimate form of approval, which actually made Qinglin feel a bit uneasy.

That afternoon they had fish balls at a restaurant on the shore of Tangxun Lake. The tender fish balls were boiled in a white broth and were absolutely delicious. After finishing an entire bowl of fish balls, Liu Xiaochuan was in a great mood and started to open up about stories from his childhood. He said that he and his buddies used to secretly drive off in one of the military jeeps to go bird hunting. "Throughout much of Chinese history this entire area had been completely undeveloped and devoid of people. That was especially the case for the area referred to as Sakyamuni Ridge. It wasn't until sometime during the Ming or Qing dynasty that villages started appearing in the area. It was said that after a massive flood one year, residents who were unprepared packed up and fled. When they ended up in Sakyamuni Ridge, the floodwaters suddenly began to retreat—actually, that was because the altitude here is higher. But people back then weren't the brightest and instead took it as a sign that they had discovered a blessed land. And so they decided to stay behind and laid down their roots here in Sakyamuni Ridge. People in Wuhan never much differentiated between 'blessed sites' and 'Buddhist sites,' and so the place eventually earned the name Sakyamuni Ridge. It was of course great to have the Buddhist master Sakyamuni protecting this place. But even more important was for everything to work out in the end, so the fact that this is a 'blessed site' is more important than the fact that it is a Buddhist site."

All nodded their heads in agreement as Liu Xiaochuan spoke. Qinglin nodded along with them, but deep down he was thinking it was all a load of bullshit. Qinglin knew what kind of person Liu Xiaochuan was—having grown up in a military compound in Wuhan, he enjoyed a privileged upbringing that had left him with an unwavering sense of entitlement. Bragging and bullshitting were an innate pastime for people like Liu Xiaochuan. Qinglin knew that as long as he lived, he would never be able to assume such an attitude with such natural ease.

But Qinglin did start to feel more comfortable.

He took the flight back to Shenzhen with Liu Xiaochuan. As he was waiting for the flight to take off, Qinglin kept thinking about his wife and son. Because of his work obligations and his mother's condition, he was unable to spend as much time with his family as he would have liked, which was a constant source of guilt. Liu Xiaochuan seemed to be able to read Qinglin's mind and laughed. "Don't worry! You've still got a long road ahead of you. My dad retired when he was sixty; he came home after filling out all the retirement paperwork and said, 'Now I can finally spend some quality time with my wife.' They spent the next twenty years together, just the two of them. And later he thought that period of his life was completely devoid of excitement. He even said it was a good thing that they spent a lot of time apart early on; otherwise, just the thought of spending fifty or sixty years of your life with the same person is enough to make you feel life isn't worth living! What do you say to that? And those pearls of wisdom were coming from someone who had been through it all and come out on the other side."

Qinglin laughed. He thought that Uncle Liu was really one interesting old fellow.

Qinglin spent a week at home. Each morning he would show his face at the office, but since he didn't have any projects he was responsible for at that office, he would spend most of his time just catching up with his work buddies before heading back home. He spent the rest of his days helping his son with his homework, and in the evening he would go out shopping or to the movies with his wife. Both his wife and son couldn't have been happier, and Qinglin felt that his life was more carefree than it had been in a long time. For his mother in Wuhan, though, one day lying in bed might as well have been a hundred days, and so, gradually, the depression and anxiety he had been feeling about his mother's condition began to dissipate. His mother no longer had any future to speak of. Perhaps the only thing he could do to express his filial duty to his mother was to keep her alive and wait patiently.

Qinglin had always been an extremely practical man. He was able to see the way society worked; thus he knew that a man like him, without any money or connections, would have to be practical if he wanted to make it in this world. It was precisely that practical approach to living that had allowed him to arrive at his current place of contentment.

Only occasionally did he think about what Liu Xiaochuan had said about his father's views on whether life was worth living. He thought there was indeed some logic behind the notion that even a life that isn't busy can also be extremely exhausting.

That happened to be just around the time that Qinglin's former classmate Long Zhongyong called to tell him about the unique residence of a former landlord that had just been discovered in western Hubei. Long Zhongyong told him he was conducting an architectural survey of buildings constructed by wealthy private families in China; he was taking three of his graduate students to check out this new site and asked Qinglin if he was free to tag along.

Qinglin's classmates had all ended up working in the same profession as his, eventually taking jobs at various companies and design schools. A few of his former classmates went on to graduate school and eventually founds jobs teaching at universities. Long Zhongyong was one of them. After he finished his PhD, his alma mater invited him to stay on as a professor. When working on projects, Qinglin and his classmates would often give each other ideas and turn each other on to the work of famous international designers; they all kept in frequent touch. But since Qinglin and Long Zhongyong were roommates for a full four years, they stayed even closer in touch. Whenever Qinglin had a new project, he would call Long Zhongyong to get his input.

Since Qinglin not only had some free time but was, frankly, feeling a bit bored, he immediately responded to Long Zhongyong's invitation: "Count me in! And since we're going to Hubei, let me pick up all the expenses on the road." Qinglin figured that he was in much better economic shape as compared with a college professor.

They arranged to meet at Xujiaping Airport in Enshizhou, which is in western Hubei. Because he liked to be prepared, Qinglin made sure to arrive at Enshizhou half a day early. When he found out that the property they were going to visit was in Lichuan County, he was quite surprised. He had always had the impression that Lichuan was one of the most impoverished places in the region. The older boy from next door to him growing up had actually been sent to Lichuan as an educated youth during the rustication movement. That neighbor had told him all about that area: the main staple there was potatoes, and people there lived very difficult lives. *How could there have been a rich family living in this impoverished area? And how could they have built a luxurious mansion compound there?* He couldn't help thinking that there was something strange about the whole thing.

Qinglin looked up an old friend living in Enshizhou, from whom he borrowed a jeep; then he made a long-distance call to the guesthouse in Lichuan to book a few rooms. He then asked around for directions on how to get to the mountains where the site was located. He even sketched out a map. It was only after all this preparation that he drove the jeep back to the airport to pick up Long Zhongyong and his graduate students.

The flight was delayed, and Long Zhongyong and his students didn't arrive until nearly eight o'clock that evening. When Long Zhongyong learned not only that a jeep was there to pick them up but also that they would able to use it for their entire trip and that their hotel was already booked, he exclaimed,

"I knew it! As long as you're here, I won't have to worry about flying blind and bumping into walls everywhere! Whenever things go wrong, you always find a way to make it right."

Qinglin was pleased to hear his friend's compliment. As he asked everyone to hop in the jeep, he smiled and explained, "Well . . . we're not there yet! This is a mountainous region and there are several layers of mountains we have to drive through to get there. We still need to go pretty far into the mountains. If the road conditions are good, we may be able to get there in time for a late dinner; but if the roads are tricky, we might not get there until the middle of the night."

The students were speechless when they learned just how far it was.

It was a bumpy road, and looking out the car windows, they could see only an expansive darkness. Occasionally they would pass one or two houses, the lights like little glowing beans in the distance. And the only thing revealed in the jeep's headlights was the shadow of the mountains. Their little off-road jeep was bumping along as if rocked by a surge of massive, billowing waves.

One of the students became scared and asked, "Professor Long, are you sure a rich family once lived out here? Could someone have really built a luxury residence out here in the middle of nowhere?"

Long Zhongyong responded, "In this world, when it comes to the affairs of humans, there is truly nothing that lies outside the realm of what's possible."

Qinglin agreed.

GREAT WATER WELL AT CYPRESS DAM

Only when they stepped out of the jeep the next morning were they finally able to see clearly. The previous night they had felt as if they were driving down an endless road through wave after wave in a sea of endless mountains. But now that it was light, they realized that because none of the peaks were very high, they didn't feel as if they were deep in the mountains. Looking around in all directions, they saw a landscape that actually felt quite open. Scattered around were plots of farmland and houses, and a sense of peace and tranquility infused the land: this was probably the kind of rural scene that people imagined when they heard those pastoral songs.

Once they left town, they saw hardly any people on the road. At the foot of the mountain several fields of crops shone bright green under the early summer light. After a while they passed an earthen house beside which they saw a vegetable garden and a few trees. The trees spread out unevenly around the house as if they had randomly found a place to set down their roots.

They pulled over for a smoke break, and after standing by the road for a while, Qinglin said, "After all these years busting my ass at work, I've seen countless types of scenery. I'm usually quite numb to it all, but today there is something about this place that moves me."

Long Zhongyong agreed, "You're right. There is something so pure and primal about this place. It is as if it hasn't changed in a thousand years."

The same student who had raised the question the previous night added, "Professor, this is the countryside—these places look the same no matter where you go! Don't tell me you don't know that? Since these places are so primitive and impoverished, they become one with nature. Why would anyone with money ever want to live in a place like this?"

"Well, you don't know until you see it; but once you lay eyes on a place like this, it's hard not to be excited," said Long Zhongyong. "This place really gives me a special feeling. It is precisely the kind of place where the rich would want to build a big house. You have to realize that Chinese people with money don't like to show off their wealth. They prefer to put down deep roots, and they usually choose their ancestral hometown as the place to plant those roots. Of course they wouldn't build a big compound in a place that is too poor or where there are frequent droughts and large patches of barren land; that would be too inconvenient. But this place was perfect. It had the protection provided by those mountains and enjoyed plenty of accessible water sources. The only issue was its remoteness. But that is not something the wealthy are usually concerned about. In fact, they tend to prefer a remote location, since that makes it easier for them to conceal their wealth. At the same time, the locals tend to be mostly sincere and honest; they put family rules before the laws of the land, they fear the local clan rules more than the government authorities, and they are easy to deal to with. Each clan has its own militia to protect its members. And even if enemies are afoot, it is not easy to find them in the mountainous terrain. Come to think of it, this place is really like a true *jianghu*—a land of outlaws that operates according to its own rules."

The students were still confused and didn't entirely believe what their professor had told them. But Qinglin thought that everything Long Zhongyong had said made perfect sense. At the same time, he also assumed that the only thing waiting for them would be a big house, the kind you often see in the countryside—he himself had seen his fair share of those country estates in Hubei—but he really didn't expect much else.

Their destination for this trip was a place called Cypress Dam, where stood a mansion referred to as Great Water Well. It was an unusual name. It is said that the family that once lived here had been the target of bandits, but the lack of any nearby water source eventually forced the bandits to give up. After the bandits left, the family dug a deep well beside their compound and expanded their courtyard wall to include the well. The family clan leader then inscribed three words on that wall: "Great Water Well." And from that point forward everyone referred to their compound as Great Water Well.

While in the car on the way there the group had been chatting about the architectural differences between private mansions in northern China versus those in southern China, how the true foundation of state wealth was built on the resources of these rich residents who had gone to such lengths to conceal their wealth, how traditional Chinese homes had mastered the art of blending in with the natural environment, and how the design of these traditional homes reflected wide-ranging cultural symbolism. Long Zhongyong commented, "All these things are completely gone now. The only thing you can see in those old designs, created in a time before we had architects, is a reverence for nature. Only buildings able to meld with their environment and become one with nature can stand a chance of being preserved over time, whereas these days almost all the architecture you see in the countryside seems to adopt a threatening posture toward nature. It is as if those buildings are saying, 'Look at me! I'm better than you! I'm more eye-catching and attractive!' But in the end, I don't think a single one of these buildings will stand the test of time. You can never win when you are up against the power of nature."

Qinglin was so impressed by Long Zhongyong's rather novel comments that he added, "That's exactly what our former teacher always used to emphasize. When it comes to everyday living spaces, you need to start with a low-key design and then take it down another notch. Actually, that goes not only for people's homes but also for life in general. If you want to play the long game, you need to keep things low key and follow nature's lead."

"Mr. Wu, when you say 'the long game,' are you referring to how long we live?" one of the students asked.

Qinglin was a bit taken aback by the question and, after an extended pause, responded, "I suppose so."

All three students laughed. But Qinglin silently wondered what that laughter really meant.

The dilapidated site of Great Water Well finally appeared before them. Qinglin pulled over by the side of the road, and everyone got out and started approaching this rather inconspicuous mansion. From a distance none of them noticed anything special about the place. The main gate to the compound was left open at a forty-five-degree angle. "These residences in the south all pay a lot of attention to *feng shui*," explained Long Zhongyong. "This main gate must be situated away from the mountains so that it opens toward the nearest body of water."

Above the main gate was a large horizontal plaque inscribed with the characters *qinglian meiyin*, or "The blue lotus in the gorgeous shade." When Qinglin saw those words he immediately identified the line from a famous poem by Li Bai and surmised, "I'll bet the family that built this compound was named Li."

Long Zhongyong laughed. "Look at the way they emphasize their connection to the literati instead of the imperial lineage. You can tell right away how cultured this family was."

One of the students joked, "Do you know how long ago the dynastic reign of the Li family during the Tang dynasty was? Even if they wanted to link their family to that imperial reign, I'm afraid they would be stretching things!"

Another student chimed in, "This just shows that the poet Li Bai was more famous than the reign of Emperor Li; the family could gain more honor and respect by associating themselves with the poet than with the emperor."

They all laughed as they strolled inside the compound. They could immediately tell from the layer of dust on the handrails and the stale smell inside the house that no one had lived there in a long time. A old watchman remained there to keep an eye on the property; they greeted him on their way in, explaining that they were all architecture students from the university who had come with their professor to look at the grounds. The old man said nothing; he just offered a simple smile and let them in. It seemed that nobody normally visited, but when tourists occasionally showed up, he was more than happy to let them in to look around.

Once inside the compound, they realized that there were layers upon layers of structures separated by a series of inner courtyards. Their surprise grew as they ventured deeper inside. After walking around the property a bit, Long Zhongyong exclaimed, "This is no simple hundred-year-old residence. It is the villa compound of a longtime landowning family. From the shifts in architectural style among the structures, this place must be at least a few hundred years old. You can also see traces of different dynasties in the architectural design work."

Qinglin was also quite surprised by what he was seeing. But when he stepped into the ancestral hall, his surprise immediately turned to shock. The Huizhou-style design used for the garden walls perfectly matched the towering mountain peaks in the distance. The scale of the ancestral hall made them realize that this southern villa was truly a priceless site. The entire design was uniformly conceived, and you could see how much care was put into every detail of the construction—from the eaves to the veranda and from the doors to the windows, each feature seemed to support the overall design. Through these meticulous details one could sense how this rich southern Chinese family was expressing their respect toward their own cultural heritage.

The three graduate students counted the inner courtyards—they had already counted twenty of them! But that was nothing compared with the number of structures and rooms. Although all around them they could see that the ravages of time had left their indelible impact, reminders of the extravagant elegance of the past could be seen in the meticulously rendered floral patterns carved into the window panes and the colorful designs painted on the eaves. One of the students exclaimed, "My God, look at the way they carved a head of cabbage into the column cap! Who would even attempt a design so bold? They were really quite daring in terms of how they combined elements of Chinese and Western architectural style."

But Long Zhongyong explained, "Actually, it isn't that rare to see something like this. One of the things the architecture of these private homes placed the most attention on were symbols of good luck. Since the Chinese word for cabbage, *baicai*, is a homophone for "a hundred riches," it is actually quite common to see images of cabbage in buildings like this. However, later during the Republican era these attempts to combine Western and Chinese design became much more clunky, as you started to get the nouveau riche to copy Western-style column-head designs while holding on to their traditional Chinese roots. So you would start to see them just slapping cabbage designs right on top of Western-style columns."

Outside the ancestral hall, one layer of mountains seemed to retreat into the distance while another layer seemed to be closing in.

Qinglin was left utterly speechless—he never imagined he would get so much out of this visit. But what left him with the biggest sense of amazement were the large Chinese characters carved deep into the two screens flanking either side of the villa's garden. They were the largest characters that appeared anywhere on the estate, and there was only one character on each side— *ren* and *nai*, "tolerance" and "restraint." *What kind of experiences had this family been through that they would choose these two words to represent the true essence of life?*

Those words seemed to strike a deep chord with Qinglin, but it wasn't something tangible he could put his finger on. Instead, his hands felt buried in a sea of thick clouds—he clearly had grasped something but still didn't know what that was.

Long Zhongyong decided to stay in town for a few days. He and his students were going to conduct a major survey of the compound. The plan was to catalog the entire site, starting with the overall layout and going down to the most minuscule of details, from the doors and windows to the murals, couplets, and inscriptions. From there they would draw up sketches, survey the grounds, and analyze all the architectural and cultural components of this compound.

Long Zhongyong noted, "The Chinese people have always known about these villa manors in the Jiangnan region just south of the Yangtze, but most people are unfamiliar with these southern villas. I want to devote my next book to the architecture of these private southern villa estates."

"You're right," said Qinglin, "especially when it comes to the south-central region of China. I don't think many people understand what private estates from that region were really like."

"I've visited quite a few of these estates," Long Zhongyong explained, "but what I am now most interested in is how these families accumulated all their wealth and rose to such prominence, and how they eventually fell into decline. If we can understand this process, I think it will help us get a better grasp of the overall development of Chinese architectural history. On the other hand, if we are one day able to understand this cycle of prosperity and decline in architectural history, we will be better able to truly appreciate some of these turning points in Chinese history through these real-life imprints of the past."

"Whoa!" Qinglin laughed. "There you go getting all philosophical on me! You're starting to scare me away!"

The three students all laughed, and one of them said, "Professor Long always gets like that in the classroom! Once he gets going, he goes deeper and deeper! He's good at confusing us!"

Long Zhongyong grew even more serious than before. "Architecture is not just an art. It has a practical application for people. But these villa estates take things to another level by cementing the relationship between the family, nature, and society. The reasons behind the establishment, rise, and eventual decline of these estates are intimately intertwined with various forces of social change. If we want to truly understand the architecture of these estates, it is essential that we internalize the true history playing out behind these events. Even if what we discover contradicts the history described in the textbooks, we have the obligation to confirm our historical findings on the basis of the data we find at these architectural sites."

Qinglin couldn't help but laugh again. "You just can't help going into lecture mode around your students, can you?"

The students again all broke out in laughter. Even Long Zhongyong had to laugh at himself.

THE STORY OF A FAMILY

That afternoon one of their friends introduced them to a nearby family. It was said that the head of the household was an old man who had worked as a servant at Great Water Well estate. He now lived at the foot of a mountain not far away. As soon as the team learned about his connection with the villa, they knew they wanted to visit him. That was especially the case for Long Zhongyong, who kept saying how vitally important oral history accounts from those with firsthand knowledge were.

The old man's last name was Xiang. He was a bit too old, though. For him the past was composed not so much of concrete memories as of an endless flow of words he said to himself. He got quite excited by the sight of visitors and took out his long pipe, insisting that each guest take a few puffs. Qinglin noticed that the pipe was carved out of bamboo; it was so old that it had lost its original color and now shone a glossy black. The end of the pipe pointed slightly upward and had a metal coating engraved with fish scales; the pipe was clearly a precious and refined object. The mouth of the pipe was inlaid with light green jade that had not faded at all with the passage of time and still emitted a soft warm glow. Old Man Xiang explained that he had asked the team leader for this pipe when they were divvying up the property of those rich families. He explained that it was so precious that he normally dared not smoke it and took it out only when special guests visited the house. "This thing is probably worth around one thousand yuan by now!" he bragged.

"If it came from a rich landlord's family, it is probably worth ten times that!" Long Zhongyong commented.

Old Man Xiang quickly turned to his son. "Listen to what the professor just said! This thing here is precious. Be sure to take good care of it!"

Old Man Xiang had a heavy country accent, and the way he spoke was somewhat hard to follow. But Long Zhongyong was from Guizhou and had frequent dealings with people who spoke with this type of thick southwestern accent; it was no problem for him to understand the old man. And since Qinglin was raised in Wuhan, he was also able to understand most of what was said. But Long Zhongyong's three graduate students were lost. One was from Shandong, the other from Liaoning, and the third from Fujian. Their poor professor ended up practically serving as their interpreter. That also greatly extended the amount of time needed to interview the old man.

According to Old Man Xiang, if they wanted to hear about the Li family, it was a story that spanned three centuries. "There were originally two Li brothers who came to the region from Hunan. This area used to be referred to as Eastern Sichuan and was administered by the Fengjie municipality. When they first arrived, the brothers worked for the Huang family, who were big landowners at the time. The older brother was extremely bright and hardworking, so he was able to gradually work his way up to become their bookkeeper; meanwhile he also did some business of his own on the side. Over time, he was able to build up his business so that it became even more profitable than that of his employer; eventually *he* became the boss. So the oldest building on the estate was actually the former residence of the Huang family.

"After those two brothers started to rake in the cash, they made sure their kids got a good education. Once they were educated, they could get jobs as government officials—that was the way people did things back then. Once they had a few of their kids in office, the money really started to flow and their family enterprise got even bigger. As the family grew, there were more mouths to feed. Those rich folks take multiple wives and have tons of kids; in the end there are crowds of them! When they held family meetings and they all showed up with their kids, there would be more than a hundred of them! Once the family expanded, they realized they didn't have enough houses for everyone. But that's the thing: none of that is a problem when you've got money. They just built more houses. Generation after generation, they built more and more until they ended up with an entire estate compound! The Li family became powerful players in Eastern Sichuan. They also owned all the farmland for miles around their compound.

"Why do they call the place Great Water Well? Well, back then people were poor and there were lots of bandits. Every year bandits would come through this Eastern Sichuan region. They would pass through and attack any family that appeared wealthy. But our old boss was never worried about bandits. Did you see their ancestral hall? Did you notice how thick the walls were? Did you see how tall that structure was? There were 108 embrasures built into the walls for muskets; and the Lis hired 108 armed men—one to man each embrasure. Can you imagine any bandit being able to survive that in one piece? After the bandits tried their luck a few times, they quickly learned their lesson: they knew this wasn't a place to mess with.

"There was one occasion much later when a man named He came here with an army to attack us—that was back during the Republican era. I was still a little boy back then, and my dad was manning one of the muskets. I heard him say that after being surrounded for several days, they still failed to drive them off. After they started to run out of water inside the ancestral hall, the clan leader, Li Gaiwu, had no choice but to venture out by himself to negotiate with the enemy. Li made an offering of silver, and since the bandit leader was a man of reason, he took the silver and left. It was after that incident with He and his bandits that members of the Li clan decided to dig a well. They knew that no matter how great the army, they would have nothing to fear as long as they had their own water supply. Did you see the words engraved there? 'Great Water Well'—those characters were written in the hand of Li Gaiwu. Those characters are quite something; they really have an air of power and authority about them.

"What Li Gaiwu didn't realize was that once liberation came in 1949, it didn't matter how thick his walls were or how high his tower stood—none of that mattered anymore. The entire Li family, from the old to the young, were labeled landlords, and they were all persecuted in terrible ways. That compound you visited was once owned by the old Li family patriarch Li Liangqing. Since he was the boss of the family, they executed him and his wife. The third brother of the Li family took his own life by leaping from a building. At the time, I was around twenty years old and a tenant farmer on their land. I may have been poor, but I wasn't one of those political activists. The Li family always treated me well, so my mother forbade me from attending the denunciation meetings against them. But I did participate when we burned the deeds to all their land and property. My mom said burning the deeds was a good thing. From then on, the land on which we toiled would be our own.

"The old Li family clan leader, Li Gaiwu, had a good head on his shoulders. He took an active role in suppressing the bandits during the Qing dynasty, and I heard that he later even served as a team leader during the land reform movement in Wan County. He really thought he would be able to escape this calamity, but people from the Agricultural Association dragged him out to be struggled against. Someone from the county level stepped in to protect him by forbidding anyone from beating him or executing him. The agricultural association was forced to respect the orders that had come down from the county level, but so many people despised him that they locked his family up in their compound and wouldn't permit them to leave. They may not have been allowed to beat him or shoot him, but nobody from the county said anything about not depriving him and his family of food. After all, there was no prohibition against starving them. But with all the food and grain cut off, that is exactly what happened. Everyone in the compound starved to death, including two small children. It is hard to imagine what sins one must commit in a past life to deserve such wretched punishment."

Old Man Xiang told the story in starts and stops, and by the time he finished telling us about the Li family, night had already fallen.

The last thing he said was, "That's how the Li family met their demise."

After that, all we heard was the sound of his puffing on his pipe.

Hearing the story filled Qinglin with a deep sense of sorrow. He wondered how the world could be so cruel. He thought back to those two large characters he had seen displayed at the compound: *ren* and *nai*, "tolerance" and "restraint." Over the course of life's vicissitudes, do those words mean anything anymore?

The three graduate students were so moved by the old man's story that they were all quietly sobbing. Long Zhongyong told them, "There are a lot of people who feel that when in times of major historical turmoil there is a transition of political power, this is a necessary process we must go through to stabilize the country. But I think we can all ask ourselves, Was it really necessary for them to use such brutality?"

Qinglin was thinking the same thing. *That's right. Why did they have to be so cruel? I'm sure there must have been a better way for them to carry things out, a more reasonable approach. Perhaps they hadn't encountered anything like this previously and were completely ignorant about how historical progress usually takes place.*

The story of this family struck a chord with the group that was in many ways much more profound than what they actually saw firsthand when they visited the Li family compound. They all remained silent on the car ride back. It was as if they were each lost in thought; at the same time, it seemed as if they were all in a daze.

They stopped in a small town for dinner, and Long Zhongyong decided he would stay there starting the following day. He explained, "There are actually very few southern estates of this size and scale—perhaps 'southern estates' is too broad a category. What I really mean are those estates in the south along the central Yangtze region. They are really nothing when you compare them with the estates in Shanxi and the Jiangnan region. But here in these backwaters, sometimes even hidden deep in a forest, you occasionally discover a massive compound that seems to come out of nowhere. It is really unbelievable when you first encounter these places. But the true history and identity of these estates often leaves one at a loss. The source of the building materials they used is also a detail that has elicited much debate. Whenever I spend time wandering around these places in the south, I'm always struck by a sense of mystery. It's as if there are countless secrets hidden in these places. Look at what we saw today: I used to think that Enshi and Lichuan were really off the beaten path, but who could have imagined that here in this even more secluded place called Cypress Village there would be a compound as expansive and impressive as Great Water Well? The whole thing is a bit hard to wrap your head around. Did you see that single column supporting nine separate roof beams? The way it was so perfectly constructed was the work of a true master craftsman!"

During dinner they continued to discuss the architecture of the buildings in the compound.

One of the students asked, "Professor, you described the 'sense of mystery' you felt. Were you referring to the unpredictable nature of the way of the world?"

"The world is indeed unpredictable," replied Long Zhongyong, "but I think it is also quite accurate to describe it as mysterious. I once visited the Chen family compound in Eastern Sichuan; it was massive in scale—but even that place cannot compare with Great Water Well. We could find no trace of a drainage system there, and yet for the last hundred years they never once had to deal with flooding, even when there were big rainstorms.

Whenever I see places like that, I am indeed filled with a sense of mystery."

Qinglin was about to say something when his cell phone rang. It was his boss, Liu Xiaochuan.

Liu Xiaochuan explained that he was in Chongqing with his father, but an emergency came up at work that required him to make a quick trip to the United States. His brother and sister-in-law were still on vacation in Europe and wouldn't be back for another three days. Knowing that Qinglin was in Enshi, Xiaochuan wanted to know whether he might be able to come down to Chongqing to take care of his father for a few days. He said, "It really takes a lot of effort to get my father out of the house. Now that we are here, it would be a shame for him to have to go right back. I was originally going to hire someone locally to show him around, but my father insisted I ask if you might be available. He's really fond of you. Then I realized that you were actually not too far away. So what do you say? Can you make it here?"

Qinglin told Xiaochuan that he was actually in Lichuan. "I'm not sure what the schedule is for flights from Xujiaping Airport to Chongqing, but if I go back to Wuhan first, I'm afraid it would take me at least two days to get there."

"There is no need for you to make such a big detour," responded Liu Xiaochuan. "It will be much more convenient if you just come directly from Lichuan. My father was planning on visiting Eastern Sichuan anyway. I'll have my driver take him to Wanzhou tomorrow. If you don't mind, you can drive there; it is less than a few hundred kilometers from where you are, so you should be able to make it there by midday. My brother and sister-in-law should be there in three days, and then you can go back to Lichuan."

Qinglin thought about the plan for a moment. "Okay . . ." He then quickly told Long Zhongyong about this new development.

"No problem," said Long Zhongyong. "Take your time and tend to your business. We'll be spending a few more days here in town anyway. We'll be working on the compound maps. After all these years as a big boss, you probably don't have the patience for drawing up those kinds of detailed maps and blueprints anyway!"

Qinglin laughed. "Since when am I a 'big boss'? Look, one phone call from my real boss and I'm forced to rush off like a good little employee!"

GRILLED FISH IN WANZHOU

The next afternoon Qinglin met up with Liu Jinyuan in the lobby of the Chongqing Wanzhou International Hotel.

Liu Jinyuan's usual flushed complexion seemed to be even more red than usual; perhaps that reflected his exhaustion from all his travels, or perhaps he was just excited to see Qinglin. Qinglin greeted him with a handshake and could immediately feel that Liu Jinyuan still had quite a grip.

"Qinglin," Liu Jinyuan said, "I especially requested you! I told Xiaochuan that if he was going to get someone to show me around, I hoped it would be you. Xiaochuan is always good to me and promised he would convince you to come. But I never imagined you would get here so quickly. No matter. I know that your having to spend time with an old man like me is a big hassle. I hope I haven't disturbed your own plans too much."

"Don't be silly," Qinglin responded. "It's my honor to get a chance to spend some time with you."

"I heard from Xiaochuan that your mother hasn't been feeling well. I hope she is doing okay."

"There's not much that can be done." Qinglin sighed. "She is stuck in a vegetative state. But she seems to be at peace. I have a nanny looking after her."

"I see . . ." Liu Jinyuan continued. "Xiaochuan told me that your father passed away when you were still young and your mother raised you. I'm sure it wasn't easy for her. Be sure to take good care of her."

Qinglin's mood grew a bit somber. "I'm afraid that trying to do right by her may be what caused her to get sick in the first place."

Liu Jinyuan tried to console him. "Don't think like that. Parents can sense their children's filial intentions. Although your mother may be in a state where she doesn't recognize people, I'm sure that deep in her heart she appreciates everything you are doing for her."

"I hope so," replied Qinglin. "Your son told me that you once fought in the war here?"

"That's right. We encircled the bandits, and the ensuing battle was quite fierce. At the time, Deng Xiaoping described it as being just as brutal as the Battle of Huaihai. I'll tell you all about it later."

Qinglin smiled. "That's right, you must be exhausted from the trip. You should get some rest. I'll come by later to take you to dinner. The grilled fish here is amazing. It'll be my treat!"

"Just mentioning it is making my stomach growl!" said Liu Jinyuan. "My wife was originally from Wuxi County, and she made the best grilled fish. Later she taught our housekeeper the recipe too. Our housekeeper was also from these parts. She was smart and attentive; in the end, she took that recipe and made even better grilled fish than my wife!"

Liu Jinyuan closed his eyes and gently rocked his head as he spoke, as if he were imagining the heavenly smell of grilled fish. Qinglin laughed at the sight; he also loved grilled fish. His mother used to grill fish all the time; as she was cooking, she would always complain that the quality of the Sichuan pepper they sell at the market these days wasn't so good as what she used in the old days.

He missed his mother. He wondered if she would ever snap out of her current state. What he wouldn't give for her to be back to normal and be able to make that grilled fish again!

It was growing dark outside, and Qinglin figured that Liu Jinyuan had had ample time to rest, so he picked him up to take him to dinner. As they left the hotel, they saw numerous restaurants in the neighborhood. Even though the Three Gorges Dam had recently swallowed up half of Wanzhou and the entire city was somewhat chaotic, none of that seemed to affect the restaurants, where business was still booming.

Liu Jinyuan sighed. "The world is indeed different now. In the old days there were never this many restaurants. I still remember the name of this street, but the sights and scenery have completely changed. I don't recognize anything here anymore."

"These days cities undergo radical changes every ten years and smaller changes every five years," Qinglin explained. "How many years has it been since you were last here?"

"Forty years," replied Liu Jinyuan.

Qinglin laughed. "That's four cycles of radical changes and eight cycles of smaller changes!"

"Wow, that's a lot of changes! About the same frequency as a baby goes through diaper changes," joked Liu Jinyuan.

Qinglin laughed. "Uncle Liu, you've got quite the sense of humor."

Liu Jinyuan also laughed. He had been quite serious and reserved for his entire life but now that he was retired and had so much free time, his personality seemed to gradually change. He wondered if it was because now that he was no longer of use to the world, he was starting to giving up on himself.

They arrived at an intersection, and Liu Jinyuan suddenly stopped to look up at one of the buildings. Pointing to the building, he said, "That used to be the military hospital. Xiaochuan was born right there in that building. To think that he is now in his fifties . . . how could I not feel old?"

"Wow, so this is where Mr. Liu was born!" exclaimed Qinglin. "Uncle Liu, while you're here, please feel free to relive the past. Perhaps then I'll get to know all the deep dark secrets about my boss. When I get back to the office, I'll have something to brag about!"

Liu Jinyuan giggled. "What kind of deep dark secret could a bare-assed baby have! The doctor pulled him out by his feet and gave him a good pat on the butt just like all the other babies!"

With that, Qinglin and Liu Jinyuan simultaneously broke out in raucous laughter. They laughed so hard that a few pedestrians on the street turned their heads to see what all the commotion was about.

Qinglin spied a small restaurant specializing in grilled fish. After taking a quick look around inside, he came out to tell Liu Jinyuan, "This place looks pretty clean. Shall we give it a try?"

"You sound just like my wife," observed Liu Jinyuan. "Throughout her life she talked about the importance of cleanliness more than anything else!"

Qinglin laughed. "That's how my mom and my wife are too."

"That's all how *all* women are!" Liu Jinyuan chuckled. "They get annoying because they're always nagging about the same things, but without them life would be tough."

"That's right, I think you have a deeper understanding about these matters than I do," replied Qinglin.

The grilled fish restaurant was quite small and was filled with the fragrance of spicy Sichuan pepper. The restaurant owner had a faint but shrill voice and spoke with a typical Wanzhou accent. He warmly ushered them in. "Please, have a seat by the window," he said. Then gesturing to Liu Jinyuan, he suggested, "Sir, why don't you sit here. This seat has more legroom; you'll be more comfortable here. You can also look at the scenery outside as you eat."

Qinglin and Liu Jinyuan sat down where the restaurant owner had suggested. Liu Jinyuan sighed. "Everything has indeed changed. But there is still something warm and familiar about the atmosphere here. The people here are still as friendly and considerate as they ever were."

"How many years did you live here?" asked Qinglin.

"Almost a decade," replied Liu Jinyuan. "Those were the best years of my life. New China had just been established, the war was over, the bandits had all been suppressed, society was stable and peaceful, and I had a steady salary that covered all my basic expenses. We had three healthy and active kids: two boys and a girl. Including my wife and our housekeeper, there were six of us. My biggest struggle back then was dealing with those naughty boys; they were quite a handful, especially Xiaochuan. That was exactly the life I had been dreaming about all those years during the war. When I first joined the army, I remember our squad leader telling us, *Do you know what communism is? It's being curled in bed together with your wife and kids.* There wasn't a single one of us in our squadron who didn't crave that kind of a life."

Qinglin smiled. "So . . . that was your dream back then?"

Liu Jinyuan also cracked a smile. "It really was. The main thing driving me in those days was the hope that I might be able to return home and live a decent life with my family. You really think we fought to liberate all humankind? Perhaps that is what those intellectuals in the cities were thinking, but we were just peasants. We left our villages and went straight to the front lines. We joined the revolution to live a better life. We didn't want to be exploited by the landlords anymore. When I went off to join the army, I told my parents I was going to drive out the Japanese and come home to live the good life. Later

I told them the same thing about the Nationalists: 'Once we beat the KMT, I'm coming home to live the good life.' And then it was the bandits: 'Once we wipe out the bandits, I'm coming home to live the good life.' This continued until the Korean War when I told them, 'Once we drive out those damn Americans, I'll be coming home to live the good life.' But it wasn't long after those 'good days' arrived that my dad passed. My mom died too. Once my parents were gone, I didn't particularly want to return home anymore."

The story somehow elicited a chuckle from Qinglin, which angered Liu Jinyuan. "You young people think that's funny? My platoon was the primary military force leading the campaign to exterminate the bandits in Eastern Sichuan. Once that campaign was over, I was sent to North Korea. I returned wounded a year later, but the party bigwigs didn't send me home to my parents; instead, they arranged a job for me here. I had no choice but to stay here. I was transferred back to Wuhan only in the late 1950s."

"That's a long time," said Qinglin. "No wonder you have such a deep connection to this place. But did it really take a major military campaign to deal with a handful of pathetic bandits?"

Liu Jinyuan explained, "Hey, don't underestimate what happened. Look around. Don't you see the layers of mountains? Those bandits had been operating in these parts for more than a hundred years; it was no easy feat to engage with them. Back when we fought the Japanese and the Nationalists, the enemy was always out in the open while we were in the shadows. That gave us a strategic advantage; we could call the shots. But all that was reversed when we had to fight the bandits. Now we were the ones out in the open and they were the ones in the shadows. They knew the lay of the land, and they also were able to draw in stray troops from the Nationalists. And then there were private brigades sponsored by the local gentry class. That was one damn tough battle to fight. We didn't have any experience in the beginning and suffered quite a few losses."

Qinglin was getting more and more drawn in to the old man's story. "So how did you fight them?"

"We had to go back to the old method of mobilizing the masses," explained Liu Jinyuan. "We sent out word to everyone to persuade friends and relatives who had joined the bandits to return home, and we promised not to go after them if they did so. We were, after all, a proper army. We had defeated millions of Nationalist soldiers, so how could this band of ragtag bandits possibly pose a threat to us? Once these bandits were eliminated, we would all be able to enjoy a peaceful life. When the people heard this, they all thought it made sense and agreed to help. Everyone is the same, you see: Who doesn't want to live a good, peaceful life? Right after the establishment of New China, people were gravitating toward the Chinese Communist Party. So although the bandits were running rampant, they couldn't stop all the people who were slipping us secret information, like the people close to the bandits who gave us tips on when and where to strike. There is an old saying that even a fierce dragon is no match for a serpent fighting on its home turf. If we were the fierce dragon, they were the local serpent. Yet somehow it took us only a few months to cut the head off that serpent. Ever since the days of the Qing dynasty there have been local bandits accosting the people of Eastern Sichuan. But take a look. Were there any more bandits in China after that? They were all eradicated in the 1950s, and from then on, the average person was able to live a peaceful life. Who is responsible for bringing them that peace? The people know damn well who that was!"

Qinglin felt a deep respect for Liu Jinyuan. "Uncle Liu, would you like something to drink? I'd like to make a toast to you. If it hadn't been for your sacrifice, people from my generation would never have been able to have the kind of life we now enjoy."

Liu Jinyuan could not have been happier. He loved talking about the old days, but normally no one was interested in listening. Qinglin not only had the patience to listen but also even seemed to agree with everything he said. That was truly something quite special for Liu Jinyuan. "I've got high blood pressure, so my doctor won't let me drink. But hearing your words is enough to make me feel that I have drunk my fill. Young people today just don't understand what my generation endured. That was what you call a soul-stirring era! Do you know how many of my soldier buddies made it through a full decade of constant warfare only to die here at the hands of those bandits? The People's Republic had already been established, and suddenly they were gone before they had the chance to enjoy a single day of peace. Back when we fought the Japanese, we were all mentally prepared to sacrifice ourselves for our country; so when we saw so many of our brothers-in-arms dying all around us, we were never that sad. We knew they were heroes in the struggle against Japan, and their sacrifice meant something.

"But what happened here in this place was completely different. Some of my brothers were taken out by snipers out of the blue; others were ambushed while on the road and ended up being tortured to death by the bandits. I shed more tears during my time here than I did during the entire war against the Japanese. Why? Because we had already made it to the other side; we were on the brink of a new, peaceful era . . . but just as my brothers were about to step over the threshold, they got cut down. They never made it home. Seeing so many people die like that was too painful to bear. That's why I despised those bandits. When we captured them, I so wanted to put a bullet in the heads of every one of them!"

Qinglin felt a cold shiver go through his body. "Did you ever kill anyone?"

Liu Jinyuan retorted with an air of pride. "Of course! I won't mention all the men I killed during the war. But even when I was here, I killed quite a few men. There was a group of bandits that ambushed our team responsible for collecting grain taxes, killing a lot of our men. In fact, my wife almost died during that attack. Once we captured the bandits responsible, I personally executed their leader. My wife was transported from the mountain valley where the attack happened to the battlefield hospital, and she was lucky that a young soldier with a background in medicine happened to be there. He was able to save her just in time; indeed, if it hadn't been for him, Xiaochuan would never have been born! As it so happens, I had actually met this young man deep in the mountains up north, and I was the one who helped him sign up for the army. An old man at the time said this was karma repaying me for my good deeds."

Qinglin was completely ignorant about the battle to suppress the bandits in Eastern Sichuan. His superficial knowledge of past wars mostly came from movies, television, and books. But what he was hearing from Liu Jinyuan left him with a completely different impression. The old man's feelings of resentment, his lament, and his sorrow were emotions you would be able to feel only by sitting beside him and hearing his actual voice. Qinglin did his best to imagine what it must have been like on the battlefield and how close Liu Jinyuan must have been to his brothers-in-arms; but it remained a reality that was difficult for him to fathom. It was also hard for him to truly appreciate the emotions Liu Jinyuan must have experienced. All he could do was quietly listen to these strange stories as if they were a legend from another time.

They continued their conversation as they enjoyed their meal. At one point Liu Xiaochuan called to check in on his father.

When he heard that they were eating grilled fish and talking about his father's military escapades, Liu Xiaochuan burst out laughing. "I knew that Qinglin would take better care of you than I would! He's got more patience to listen to your old war stories!"

Liu Jinyuan felt frustrated. "How come you never have the patience to listen to my stories?"

Liu Xiaochuan laughed even harder. "Dad, from the time I was a young boy until now, do you have any idea how many times I've heard those stories? I must have heard them dozens of times! C'mon, even the best stories get boring after a while!"

Liu Xiaochuan's voice was so loud that even from the other side of the table Qinglin could hear him laughing over the phone.

During his trip to Wanzhou, Liu Jinyuan had plans to visit a man named Li Dongshui, a local who was a few years older than he. Liu Jinyuan said that Old Li had once been his landlord; but when he was younger, he had been a member of a famous secret society active in Sichuan before the revolution. Everyone used to call him Third Brother Li. He was recruited by underground Communist workers just before the liberation of China and became an underground messenger working for the guerrilla forces in Eastern Sichuan. During the campaign against the bandits, Liu Jinyuan had stayed at his house. Since Old Li was so familiar with the strategies employed by all the local bandits, he was able to provide lots of good ideas. A brigade leader named Han had been planning to recommend Old Li for party membership, but that very day Han was struck down by a sniper's bullet. After that campaign against the bandits Liu Jinyuan and Old Li fell out of touch. It was only recently that Old Li's grandson was able to track him down. The grandson wanted Liu Jinyuan to attest to the fact that his grandfather had indeed contributed to the Communist campaign to wipe out the bandits. That was his grandfather's last wish in life. Only then did Liu Jinyuan realize how much Old Li had suffered during the land reform movement and the Cultural Revolution. His history as a member of that secret society as a young man had been a stain that haunted him throughout his life. Liu Jinyuan immediately agreed and even wrote a formal handwritten certificate to attest to Old Li's contributions. The county government had already received these materials to reappraise his status, but the process was quite slow.

"This is one favor I can help with," said Liu Jinyuan. "We are old now, and the minions of Yama are all hovering at the gates waiting for us. I can almost see them waving me on. I told them, 'You guys have let me go several times before. Please give me a little more time. Yama's court of hell isn't short of people. I'll go with you after I take care of a few final errands.' I figured that if I didn't help out Old Li, he would continue to have this injustice hanging over him forever. He's in his nineties now. He has been treated unjustly for his entire life; now that he has only a few years left, this must be weighing heavily on him. Xiaochuan said that what I was doing was a great deed and insisted on accompanying me here to show his support. If that emergency at work hadn't come up, I'm sure he would have been here with me for this."

Qinglin felt that something strange had touched him deeply. When people get to that age, things like fame and fortune no longer matter. Perhaps when it comes down to it, the only thing that is important is the goodwill and relationships you have with other people.

SOMETHING CHANGED IN QINGLIN'S HEART

When Qinglin went down to the hotel cafeteria to meet Liu Jinyuan for breakfast the next morning as they had arranged, he was surprised to discover that Liu Jinyuan had gone out earlier that morning. He had risen at the crack of dawn and had the driver take him around the city; they'd even gone to Taibai Cliff. Liu Jinyuan reflected, "Half of this city was submerged by the Three Gorges Dam. It's a good thing that Taibai Cliff could be preserved."

"What's Taibai Cliff?" asked Qinglin.

Liu Jinyuan explained, "It used to be called West Cliff. But after the poet Li Bai spent time there drinking and playing chess, subsequent generations somehow started referring to West Cliff as Taibai Cliff in Li Bai's honor."

"Wow, I never realized that," said Qinglin. "I guess those old literati really did have a lot of influence!"

Liu Jinyuan sighed. "We lost so many soldiers fighting the bandits here just so we could restore peace and stability, yet no one ever suggested one of the mountains be renamed Hero Mountain. But some literati wrote a few poems thousands of years ago, and his name resonates so much louder than that of any of the heroes we lost."

Qinglin laughed. "No reason to fuss about that. Wherever those literati go, they are always trying to make a name for themselves. You and your old comrades are different: you guys never cared about getting famous and never worried about making a profit. That's why people like you are the true heroes."

Liu Jinyuan flashed Qinglin a thumb's up sign. "That's the perfect response, much better than my son's! Xiaochuan just says, 'It has to do with culture! Culture is what passes down and stands the test of time. You have no choice but to submit to its power!' That's what he always says. But I'm not submitting to anything! I will tip my hat to what you just said, though. I think you hit the nail on the head: heroes are after different things than those literati. Everything we did was really just to serve the people. We didn't give a damn if we got any recognition or not."

"You guys are the true heroes because your minds were on a different level. Nobody thinks like that today. There are many government officials today who certainly lack that sense of humility and dedication."

Liu Jinyuan heaved a deep sigh. "Society has changed. We're old now..."

After breakfast they went to a place called White Horse Slope. Liu Jinyuan said that many of his former war buddies had died and been buried there; he wanted to pay his respects to them. The driver had obtained directions on how to get there ahead of time, but they still ended up driving around in circles unable to find the place. They pulled over to ask a group of pedestrians for help and were told that White Horse Slope was demolished a long time ago. "They dynamited that whole area to build a highway," explained one of the pedestrians. "But I heard from a few old-timers that they would never have blown up the area around the martyrs' tombs. The people all know that the soldiers buried there were our saviors, and we owe a great debt to them. There used to be villagers and students who would come to light incense and pay their respects every year. They relocated the martyrs' remains before construction began, but I have no idea where they moved them to. I'm sure no matter where they ended up, there must be a lot of people who still come to pay their respects."

This news upset Liu Jinyuan, and he wanted to find someone else he could ask. But Qinglin explained, "We're actually a bit tight on time. Didn't you hear what those villagers said? They understand that those who died were their saviors. Every year there are people who visit their graves. Your old comrades live on in the people's hearts."

Liu Jinyuan could tell that Qinglin was trying to cheer him up. Even though Liu Jinyuan wanted to keep looking, he realized that everything Qinglin said made sense. Liu Jinyuan fell silent and decided not to keep pushing. Instead, he just stood there staring quietly at the mountains surrounding them. He silently bowed in the direction of the mountains and, after a long pause, said, "Old Han, Little Dai, my brothers: For the final time, I have come to White Horse Slope to express my gratitude. I thank this place for taking you in and providing you with a final resting place. This place has now been transformed into a mountain highway; the road is smooth and wide, which makes it easier for the villagers to come to visit you. Isn't that what you once wished for? Even though I'm unable to find you, I know that you will like this new change. We will be together again before too long. I remember you guys saying that after we had successfully vanquished the bandits, we would find a place like Taibai Cliff to drink and play chess. I haven't forgotten, and when I arrive I'll be sure to bring a few bottles of the best Luzhou wine."

Qinglin could feel the tears streaming down his face. He felt completely helpless and didn't know what to do. He had never really had any particular feelings about old soldiers like Liu Jinyuan: he'd never had any special admiration for them, but nor did he despise them. He just looked at them as he did any other old-timers. Although before he seemed to be brimming with respect for Liu Jinyuan, that was mostly because he was his boss's father. Qinglin's behavior had primarily been based on courtesy rather than genuine respect. Having witnessed so much superficiality and hypocrisy in the world, he felt there wasn't much that could move him anymore. But in that moment he suddenly saw something real. Something genuine emerged from his heart: it was true emotion. In that moment Qinglin could feel that something inside him had changed.

This old man had aroused in Qinglin a feeling of deep respect and admiration. He wondered if he should delve deeper and try even harder to truly understand him.

DUST TO DUST

They did not arrive at Xiangshui until the afternoon, and they had still to take a long mountain road before they could get to where Li Dongshui lived. Originally Qinglin had hoped to request a car from the military zone to bring Li Dongshui to their hotel. Or maybe someone could drive the old man to a hotel in town. But Liu Jinyuan shot down all these ideas. It had been so many years since he had been in active service that he thought it inappropriate to ask the military to help out with logistics. Besides, because Li Dongshui was his senior and had suffered so much during his life, Liu Jinyuan insisted that he be the one to personally call on him. Unable to convince Liu Jinyuan otherwise, Qinglin and the driver had no choice but to go along with his plan.

Li Dongshui's grandson met them in town to guide them to his grandfather's house. He said that his grandfather could no longer walk and his father had a back injury that also limited his mobility. The grandson was working in Chongqing but had taken off work just to come back home for this meeting. He was the one who had gone to an internet bar to track Liu Jinyuan down online. Li Dongshui was fortunate to have four generations living under one roof; his grandson was already around Qinglin's age.

The road stopped about a hundred meters from the house, so Liu Jinyuan had to get out of the car and walk the final distance. Although the road was narrow, it was smooth. Liu Jinyuan took a few steps and said, "It feels good to be able to set foot on this kind of dirt road again."

Qinglin chuckled. "There you go, getting nostalgic again. I grew up in an area where all we had were big paved roads, so I have never had an attachment to dirt roads."

"You're just like Xiaochuan; neither one of you understands the therapeutic effect that walking on a dirt road has on your feet."

Li Dongshui lived in a red brick house located at the foot of a mountain and surrounded by a thick blanket of green trees, which really made the red house stand out. From far off they could see a feeble old man leaning against the front door gazing toward them.

Li Dongshui's grandson pointed to the old man. "That's my grandfather. He's been standing there by the front door waiting for you since this morning."

Liu Jinyuan unconsciously began to quicken his pace so that by the time he made it to the front door, he was practically jogging. Qinglin feared he might fall and made sure to stay by his side. When the two old men finally stood face to face, they didn't say a word but just embraced in a strong hug. They could all hear the sound of Li Dongshui crying. Through his tears, his speech was not very clear, but he managed to say, "Commissar Liu, I never imagined you would come to see me . . . I never thought you would come . . ."

Liu Jinyuan was likewise choked up. "My brother, I also never imagined I would be able to see you again. You've changed so much. You were really something back then when we used to call you Third Brother Li!"

"I'm old now . . ." Li Dongshui sighed. "But Commissar Liu, you've still got that same energy about you!"

"Not really . . . I too am old," replied Liu Jinyuan.

The Lis' house was filled with quite a few people, young and old, and there wasn't a single one of them who was not moved to tears by the unfolding reunion. Qinglin and Li Dongshui's grandson each supported the two elders inside and helped them settle into a pair of rattan chairs. Li Dongshui's grandson introduced their guests to everyone present, which included the village party secretary.

Another elderly man hobbled over to serve them tea. As he put the tea set down, he said, "Commissar Liu, do you still remember me? It's me, Hairy. I was forty years old the last time we met; you even helped teach me how to read."

After a momentary shock, Liu Jinyuan seemed to remember. "Oh my, Hairy. If you hadn't introduced yourself, I would have completely forgotten! I can't believe how old you are! I remember your father sent you to find me just before the assault on the bandits at Horse Mouth Cave. Isn't that right?"

The old man known as Hairy said, "Exactly right. We won that battle, but it was a brutal sight. We captured several hundred of those bandits hiding out in the cave and didn't suffer a single casualty on our side."

"All thanks to your father's wise suggestion!" responded Liu Jinyuan.

Li Dongshui's grandson pointed to Hairy and said, "Commissar Liu, this is my father. He's almost seventy."

Liu Jinyuan was rather surprised to see Hairy's current condition. "You were such a fast runner back then. I remember you used to deliver letters for us; you used to be able to make it over several mountains in a single night. What happened to you?"

Hairy explained, "The roads around here used to be really bad. I was driving a tractor and got injured when it flipped over."

Qinglin started to worry that they would go on with their nostalgic chit-chat forever, and so he tried to focus the conversation by addressing the village party secretary. "Do you have everything you need for Mr. Li? Commissar Liu has already provided a written affidavit. And now he has made a personal visit. I suppose everything should be settled now?"

The village party secretary hurriedly responded, "Of course, it's all settled. Commissar Liu is quite famous in these parts for his contributions that led to the suppression of the bandits in Eastern Sichuan. With his written affidavit, there should be no problem. Besides overturning the case against Mr. Li, the district also plans on awarding him a special certificate of merit. The local party leaders said they are planning on providing a monthly stipend for Mr. Li, but I'm still not sure exactly how much they will allocate. Mr. Li is judged innocent of all crimes; we were the ones who committed a terrible mistake."

Li Dongshui interrupted, "You didn't do anything wrong. You weren't involved in any of this. You were all too young to be involved; there is no way you could have known anything about what happened. Back then . . . it's hard to explain what exactly happened back then. Better not to talk about it."

Liu Jinyuan asked, "How come you didn't seek me out all those years ago? I was right there in Wan County during that time."

"I did," replied Hairy. "They said you still hadn't returned from the Korean War. Later I tried a second time, but they said you'd been seriously injured and they didn't allow visitors. I went back again after that but couldn't find you. They wouldn't even let me into the facility, and I couldn't find anyone else to vouch for my father. Back then the road conditions were very poor and it was extremely difficult to make a trip out of the mountains. Later, after I injured my back and had trouble walking, my dad said to just forget it."

Liu Jinyuan heaved a deep sigh. "I had no idea that your father would ever have to suffer like that. It never crossed my mind. Everyone around here knows Dongshui as the famous Third Brother Li! Even back then I knew he was also an underground messenger working for the Chinese Communist Party. He was so reliable that we stayed at his house during the campaign to eradicate the bandits. He was not only not a bandit but also a true hero in our effort to wipe them out! Without his help, our campaign would never have gone as smoothly as it did. We were able to capture Horse Mouth Cave so easily and take several hundred prisoners all because we followed Third Brother

Li's plan. I led that campaign, so I can attest to this. And then there was Hairy, who delivered messages for me in the middle of the night after running across several mountains. Those messages he delivered helped prevent our supply team from being attacked. Do you realize how many lives those messages saved? From now on the village should take good care of these two heroes! They should never again be made to face any kind of suffering or humiliation."

Several of the village cadres nodded their heads in agreement.

Li Dongshui began to choke up again. "Commissar Liu, those words you just spoke make everything I have suffered worth it. To hear a man like you describe me as a hero means that I haven't lived this life in vain."

Li Dongshui's family members were again moved to tears.

Qinglin, though, had a difficult time sitting through this scene; he had to leave the room and go outside. As he walked along the dirt road outside, all he saw were mountains, layer after layer of peaks rising up in the distance. Standing against that scenery, a human being seemed as insignificant as a speck of dust. All told, Li Dongshui had been unjustly persecuted for fifty long years. His children and grandchildren also suffered for his crimes and were denied countless opportunities. But now it took only some words of comfort and acknowledgment that he was in fact a hero, and the pain of all those years of suffering seemed to disappear into thin air.

The driver was taking a stroll outside, and Qinglin approached him for a cigarette. The driver asked how the meeting between the old men was going. Qinglin heaved a deep sigh as he described what had happened. The driver commented, "At the end of the day, he's just an average citizen. What is he supposed to do? Sue the government? Seek some big payout to compensate him for his suffering? But how is he ever going to get those fifty years back? You can never make up for that lost time."

Qinglin smiled. "You're right. You can never get it back."

Qinglin was also struck by a sense of helplessness. That's right, from dust to dust. There are some things that are best forgotten.

QIERENLU?

The Li family hosted a huge banquet that day. They set up five big tables in their courtyard, and quite a few of the local villagers in high standing attended. It was considered a happy occasion of the utmost importance. Qinglin was invited to sit at the head table. He sat there eating in silence as he listened to the many conversations. Three or four men present were also in their eighties, and all had stories about the campaign against the bandits in Eastern Sichuan. Liu Jinyuan was quite pleased to discover that he was the main character in almost all the stories the old-timers shared from that era. He drank more glasses of spirits than he had in years.

Qinglin felt a heavy responsibility not to let Liu Jinyuan drink too much. He had to step in to force the hosts not to toast him anymore. Qinglin half-jokingly explained, "My boss asked me to take good care of Mr. Liu. I could lose my job if I don't look out for him!"

Although the villagers realized that losing one's job was a big deal, they still tried to toast Liu Jinyuan; they said it was a rare chance for them to drink with a true hero. As soon as Liu Jinyuan heard the villagers describe him as a hero, he insisted on returning the compliment by drinking another cup. With several dozen people seated at those five tables in the courtyard, even if he took only one sip for each guest, it was still bound to add up. As an emergency tactic, Qinglin resorted to a trick people sometimes play in the city: he swapped the old man's cup of clear heavy liquor for mineral water. Liu Jinyuan was so drunk that he didn't realize what Qinglin had done.

As they went on with their toasts, Liu Jinyuan suddenly interjected, "There is someone I have been wondering about. Why has nobody mentioned Hu Lingyun? He used to pass out after one cup of alcohol, so all the young guys would give him a hard time."

Everyone at the table fell silent. They all just awkwardly stared at one other.

It was Hairy who spoke up first. "Oh, I remember him; he was that college student from Chongqing. He wrote some reports for you, didn't he? He stayed at our house for several days. He even slept in the same room with me. I also remember his giving me a reading textbook."

"Right! That's him!" exclaimed Liu Jinyuan. "He said that his father had studied abroad and had a great fondness for painting and calligraphy. He also talked about the library he had at home. I even said that one day I would bring a friend who loved to read to visit him at his house to check out all his books. But I never got a chance to see him again after I returned from Korea. I also got busy with work and forgot to look him up. But sitting here drinking with all of you is bringing back all those old memories. He was a beautiful writer; I told him that he could be a famous author one day. But everyone always made fun of him; they kept insisting on teaching him how to hold his liquor. A few of them said they were going to take him up a mountain to drink and play chess and that mountain would later be known as Lingyun Mountain! That sounds even better than Taibai Cliff!"

Hairy suddenly interrupted. "He died young . . ."

Liu Jinyuan was shocked. "What? How did he die? He was a young guy!"

Hairy explained, "After the campaign against the bandits, he stayed here to serve as a cadre on the county level. But then when the land reform movement began, his family was labeled as landlords, and that's when things started to go bad. As things tensed up, his sister had someone deliver an oral message urging him to quickly get their parents to safety in the city. He immediately set out that night to his parents' house, but he never made it there—the villagers found him and beat him to death right there beside the road."

Liu Jinyuan couldn't believe his ears. "Huh? What are you talking about? How could such a thing have happened?!"

One of the old men sitting at the table said, "Oh, I heard about that incident. I'm afraid that kid was the eldest son of the landlord from Hu Shuidang. One of the comrades from the work team was on his way back to Chongqing for the Chinese New Year, but as he was passing through our village it began to snow. The roads were not safe for him to drive on, so he ended up staying at my place for a few nights until the weather cleared up. The strange thing was that the only things he had in his luggage were books. I was perplexed as to why someone leaving from the mountains would be traveling with so many books. But then he told me the books all came from landlord Hu's house. The landlord had been an avid book collector and reserved several rooms in his home to house his library. It took the villagers several days just to burn all those books. There was so much ash that the famers used it as fertilizer. But this guy was an intellectual and couldn't bear to see all those books being burned, so he stole a bunch and packed them up in his luggage. He showed a few of the books to me; they were all stamped with a strange name that was something like Qierenlu."

Qinglin suddenly felt his heart skip a beat. Qierenlu was a name he had heard before, but where? He couldn't remember at that moment, but something didn't feel right, and his forehead broke into a sweat. He wondered what connection he could possibly have with that name. Why did it seem to strike a chord inside him? Why did just hearing that name make his heart race?

Qinglin interrupted the old man. "Excuse me, what did you just say? You just mentioned something about a something-something-lu?"

The old man replied, "It's been several decades . . . At the time, I didn't understand what he said either, so I asked him. I thought the *lu* he was referring to was some kind of an oven. I asked him if it was used to start a fire. That comrade explained that all the elders in the Hu family were quite cultured, and they had a family motto to exercise forbearance in times of difficulty, and that's where Qierenlu, "Cottage of Tolerance," comes from. It has nothing to do with an oven; it was actually the inscription carved on the tablet hanging over the Hu family's main house."

Qinglin wanted to follow up with more questions, but there were so many people sitting at the table that the conversation ended up going in another direction.

It was dark out by the time they finally left. Qinglin could tell that Liu Jinyuan was exhausted and urged him to use a cushion as a pillow so that he could lie down in the back seat of the car. No one spoke on the way back, and it was nearly ten o'clock in the evening by the time they made it back to the hotel.

Once Liu Jinyuan was comfortably settled in his room, Qinglin called Liu Xiaochuan to update him on what had happened that day. He even told Xiaochuan about how he had swapped the hard liquor for water. Liu Xiaochuan laughed. "You think my old man didn't notice? He's been a drinker for decades; he knew exactly what you were doing! I suspect he also realized that he shouldn't drink too much at his age, which is why he didn't expose you! But if someone had tried to do that to him when he was younger, he would have cursed them to hell!"

"I'd rather he yell at me than have to worry about something bad happening to him from drinking too much. I was so anxious when he started drinking like that!"

"Well, you did the right thing," said Liu Xiaochuan. "If he secretly allowed you to swap out his liquor, that means he realized he was in over his head but couldn't stand to lose face. That's just the kind of person he is. Tomorrow you should just let him rest at the hotel; don't take him anywhere. If some of his old subordinates from his days in the army want to visit him, have them come to the hotel. Just charge any expenses to his room. The company will cover all the costs upon checkout."

Liu Xiaochuan also said that his big brother, Liu Xiao'an, was already on his way home from abroad. He would take a day in Wuhan to adjust to the time difference and should be on a plane to Wanzhou the day after tomorrow. Qinglin thought that was a good plan for the old man. "Don't worry," said Qinglin. "I'll take care of everything until your brother gets here."

After that Qinglin called his wife to briefly update her on everything that had happened. She didn't have much patience to listen to the details but just urged him to come home soon. She told him she was still thinking about what they had done a few days earlier. Qinglin laughed. "If we did it like that every day, this man of yours would probably have a stroke!" He then called Donghong to check in on how his mother was doing. But her report was exactly the same as it had been: his mother still didn't recognize anyone or respond to anything—there was absolutely no change in her condition.

That's what Qinglin expected.

After having been on the road all day, Qinglin was exhausted. He took a shower and lay down in bed, but just as he was drifting off to sleep, that name Qierenlu popped into his head again. At the same time, he remembered the words he had seen written on that decorative wall at Great Water Well—*ren* and *nai*, "tolerance" and "restraint." Those words reflecting a philosophy of life that hinted at so much helplessness.

In the middle of the night Qinglin unexpectedly found himself dreaming of his mother. In the dream his mother was pointing to a large gate and saying, "This gate is different from the one at Qierenlu." And then he woke up with a start.

Could it be? Qinglin wondered if he had heard right . . . Were those really the same words his mother had uttered? And then there was that other word—something-tang. Did she mention that too?

Qinglin couldn't get back to sleep after that; instead, all the strange things that occurred when his mother first fell ill flashed through his mind. There were so many details that he now recalled: the main gate, that poem by Xie Tiao, that vase with the image from "Guiguzi Descends the Mountain," that time she mentioned how much her father liked painting, and that purple silk comforter.

What was really lurking behind these fragmented words that she kept mentioning? That's right, Mother was scared; she was scared that someone was going to take away her property. What did she experience to trigger this? It was an odd coincidence that there really was a building named Qierenlu. But the strangest thing of all was that Mother's accent seemed to be virtually identical to the local dialect here.

It was a rough night for Qinglin, but he managed to hang in there until sunrise.

He started to worry when Liu Jinyuan failed to show up on time for breakfast at the hotel cafeteria, and so he went up to the room to check on him. Outside the door to Liu Jinyuan's room Qinglin ran into the driver, who said, "I'm afraid that the old man is still exhausted from yesterday, so he didn't go out this morning and he doesn't even want to get out of bed. I brought some breakfast to his room and told him to just relax and take a good rest. I'm going to call his old buddies from the army who are supposed to visit today and tell them not to come until the afternoon."

"That's a good idea," replied Qinglin. "Even I am exhausted from yesterday. We should rest too. Oh, by the way, do you happen to have the phone number for Li Dongshui's grandson?"

"Sure," replied the driver. "You need to get in touch with him?"

"Yeah, there's something I want to ask him," explained Qinglin.

When Qinglin called, Li Dongshui's grandson was on his way back to Chongqing. He said that he wasn't sure about where the term "Qierenlu" came from; he had never heard anyone mention it when he was growing up. But he promised he would see what he could find out. Qinglin thanked him profusely for his help and half an hour later got a call back. Li Dongshui's grandson said that the old man who had mentioned Qierenlu also didn't have any additional information. All he knew was what he'd heard from that traveler on that stormy winter night. Moreover, the former residence at Hu Shuidang was demolished back in the 1950s when a nearby reservoir was being built, and that area had long been submerged. No one in the village had any other leads.

That news left Qinglin feeling rather disappointed.

PEOPLE ALWAYS OVERCOMPENSATE FOR THEIR MISTAKES

The entire afternoon was taken up by three successive groups of visitors who came to call on Liu Jinyuan. The two latter groups overlapped, and it seemed as if they all knew each other. Qinglin accompanied them the entire time; he also helped out by pouring them tea and seeing each guest off. They were all old-timers and had spent most of their time reminiscing together about the past. Qinglin gradually learned a few details that seemed they might be relevant to him, and he would occasionally follow up with a few questions.

There was one elderly man there named Ma who had once worked under Liu Jinyuan in the army. He later transferred to the local government and assumed a leadership position. But he too was persecuted during the Anti-Rightist Campaign and pushed out of power. As soon as he laid eyes on Liu Jinyuan, Old Ma immediately teared up and kept repeating, "Commander, if I had only listened to your advice and stayed in the army, I would never have suffered like I did . . ."

Liu Jinyuan responded, "Hey there, didn't I reprimand you back then for being more interested in girls than in your comrades? Your falling in love with that girl student really screwed up your entire future! Do you see what happened? All you got was trouble, and that girl broke up with you! At the end of the day, you married the woman originally betrothed to you anyway!"

Old Ma shamefully admitted, "I saw that you fell in love with an educated girl, and so did Old Wu. I wanted to be like you guys . . ."

Liu Jinyuan sighed. "Neither Old Wu nor I was already married! But what about you? You were already the father of two children, and then you went after another woman! You got what you deserved!"

Old Ma spoke through his tears. "You're right. I deserved everything that happened. It was my fault."

"It's a good thing you turned over a new leaf," said Liu Jinyuan. "You eventually got your rank restored, so there's nothing to complain about. At least you survived, which is more than we can say for many of our old comrades who died at the hands of those bandits. In that sense, you're pretty lucky compared with Old Wu."

Old Ma philosophized, "When you think about it like that, you are right. I may not have done as well as those on top, but I did a lot better than those below . . ."

"I suggest you don't compare yourself with others," commented Liu Jinyuan. "I may have had a higher rank than you when we were in the military, but none of that matters anymore. We are all just ordinary citizens now. If there is anything left to compare . . . it is which one of us outlives the others."

With that, the two of them broke out into hearty laughter.

They talked mainly about their memories of former friends and past experiences. Most of the people they discussed had already passed away, and so occasional sobs and sighs punctuated their conversation.

As the old men were chatting about the past, Qinglin received a phone call from Long Zhongyong. He said they needed only one more day to finish their maps, and he was wondering if Qinglin would be joining them for the rest of the trip. He said they had gotten much more out of the trip so far than they had expected, and he wanted to know if Qinglin was coming back to Cypress Dam and, when he might arrive. Long Zhongyong needed to start making arrangements for the second half of their trip.

A literature professor from their university who was originally from Eastern Sichuan had sent a text to one of the graduate students about a unique historical estate in his hometown. Apparently the estate had managed to avoid destruction over the decades even though the government never took any special steps to preserve the site. The only reason it managed to escape unscathed was because it had a dark and foreboding atmosphere that led all the locals to believe it was haunted. Nobody dared to go near the place, which the student referred to as the Mansion of Lost Souls. Since the estate was well off the beaten path, no one from the government had ever stepped in to take care of it, and it was just left to languish. The woodwork and carvings on the main structure were said to be unique and really captured the local Eastern Sichuan style. It was not that far by car, and they should be able to make it there in less than a day. All the students were lovers of literature, and as soon as they heard the estate described as the "mansion of lost souls," they all wanted to go. Long Zhongyong also felt that since they were already in the area, it wouldn't hurt to make the extra trip out there. But they would need Qinglin's car to get there.

Also intrigued by this place of "lost souls," Qinglin immediately agreed to rush back. He said he'd confirm the exact time of arrival later that night. Qinglin also figured that he might be able to use this opportunity to ask around to see if any locals had ever heard of Qierenlu.

Qinglin arranged for Liu Jinyuan and his mates to have dinner that night at the hotel. He explained to all Liu Jinyuan's old buddies, "As the local hosts, I know you have all expressed an interest in treating Mr. Liu, but my boss already gave me clear instructions that he will be covering dinner. Unless you want me to get in trouble with my boss, I must insist that you allow my boss to treat everyone tonight!" Once they heard that, the old men all stopped arguing about who was going to pay.

Liu Jinyuan added, "All of you came all the way here to see me. Let's not haggle over this little bit of money! If you hadn't followed me through hell and high water during the revolution, I wouldn't even be here today!" He continued, "Actually, allowing my son to treat us is a way for him to express his filial devotion.

You all know my son Xiaochuan. Back during the Cultural Revolution he smashed up all your homes and broke your windows. I hope you can look at this meal as his way of repaying the debt he owes you."

Those words made everyone laugh uproariously. Qinglin laughed too. "I never knew that my boss had a dark side in his younger days!"

Liu Jinyuan explained, "When Xiaochuan was seventeen he thought he was the leader of the pack! He was such a troublemaker that everyone wanted to whip his ass!"

All the other old men chimed in. One of them responded by quoting the old saying "The more trouble you make when you are young, the more money you make when you grow up!"

But Liu Jinyuan sighed. "But that wasn't really the case. His mother really doted on him when he was young. She always said that he'd grow up to be successful. His mother was always more insightful than me!"

One of the old-timers said, "Sister Peng had it hard back then. When we were fighting the bandits, Commissar Liu didn't come home for long stretches of time. Xiao'an was only two years old at the time, and she had to leave him with her parents in the countryside while she was busy collecting grain taxes, teaching basic literacy classes, running a night school, and lecturing about New China. All the villagers loved hearing her lectures; she even helped to reform a lot of those old bandits!"

Another old man chimed in. "Back then there was that violent uprising in Anping, and a lot of our men were killed. Sister Peng and I were there in Anping to collect grain taxes just as the bandits were planning a second uprising. It was only thanks to Li Gaiwu delivering that message to Minister Wang that the entire battalion was able to be redirected to Qiyue Mountain in time to crush the uprising. I had only just started working at that time and was terrified by what I saw. Sister Peng was the one who kept our spirits up on the way."

As soon as Qinglin heard the name Li Gaiwu, he quickly asked, "Are you talking about the same Li Gaiwu from Great Water Well?"

Liu Jinyuan was a bit taken aback that Qinglin would ever have heard of him, "How do you know Li Gaiwu?"

Qinglin told them about his trip with Long Zhongyong to Lichuan to survey the private estates in the south and their visit to Great Water Well. He also told them a bit about what they'd learned regarding the Li family. All the old men listened intently, occasionally interrupting Qinglin with questions. Qinglin told them, "I just came back from there a few days ago. The Li family compound is still preserved, but no descendants of the family are living there anymore. I heard that Li Gaiwu later suffered a terrible death. But the whole thing seemed strange: If he was one of the good guys, how come no one let him off?"

None of the old men present uttered a word.

After a long silence, Liu Jinyuan spoke up. "I didn't participate in the Land Reform Campaign in Eastern Sichuan, but I'm familiar with what happened. I also heard that it got out of control; a lot of people died who should never have died. I knew some of the victims. Many of them had helped us during our campaign against the bandits. There was also a man named Lu Ziqiao—he shouldn't have been killed either. They all had stood with the Chinese Communist Party and supported the new government."

"That's right," Old Ma added. "Both Lu Ziqiao and Li Gaiwu distinguished themselves during the revolution. When they were educating people about the need to pay grain taxes, Li Gaiwu traveled all over delivering speeches about the importance of supporting the nation through grain taxes. Lu Ziqiao even donated half the grain in his family's granary to the country. At the time, we all thought the party should protect him. We never imagined he would still end up dead. Lu Ziqiao actually killed himself, which in some way was even worse."

Qinglin asked, "So why did you allow those below you to stir up such chaos?"

The men all sighed.

Old Ma tried to explain. "The majority of peasants got extremely worked up during that movement, and things suddenly got out of hand. The working group sent to oversee things was asleep at the wheel and didn't know how to control the situation. In the end, the leaders just followed the will of the peasants, and the whole thing went off the tracks."

Another elderly man jumped in to say, "Actually, there used to be quite a few powerful families in Eastern Sichuan. If the land reform hadn't gotten out of hand, I suspect this region wouldn't be as poor as it is now."

But Liu Jinyuan didn't entirely agree. "People always overcompensate for their mistakes. Otherwise, how would we have ever been able to get control of the landowning class? The situation was actually quite complicated back then!"

"I still don't understand," said Qinglin. "Didn't you all think that all landlords needed to be struggled against? Were all the landlords back then really so evil?"

Old Ma explained, "We weren't the ones leading this. It was the local peasants. We bear the blame for not stopping them when things got out of hand. Of course, looking back, we see all kinds of things that weren't right; after all, hindsight is always 20/20. But you've got to remember that society back then was both dangerous and unstable. Before we arrived in Eastern Sichuan, almost all the towns in the region had already been occupied by bandits. The country was ours, and yet we somehow found ourselves in the defensive position and they were in the offensive position. Do you have any idea how many of our men were killed? And who was really supporting them? What's more, we had been at war for so many years, but none of us had ever participated in a land reform campaign. Nobody understood what the rule of law meant, and there was certainly no one there to tell us that everything we did should be carried out according to the letter of the law. People would just hold a meeting and say so-and-so deserves to be killed, and we'd kill the person. Or in some cases the head of the local land reform committee would receive feedback saying that somebody was evil and should be killed, and so they'd decide to execute the person. Those people on the ground calling the shots really didn't understand anything about what was actually going on. Things were not being run according to real policies; people just wanted to speak up for the lower classes and take some concrete actions to turn things around for them. But nobody gave much thought to the implications of what was happening, and no one questioned whether what was being done was right or wrong."

Liu Jinyuan added, "This isn't the kind of thing that we can go back to and replay. Back then no one was analyzing the root cause of why so many people were so poor, nor did anyone ask whether any local thugs were included among the poor. And there was certainly nobody trying to differentiate which rich people were good and which ones were bad! We were all figuring things out along the way. And you have to remember that we had just finished the campaign against the bandits, so a lot of the people involved still had that bloodlust in their system; they just used the method they thought was the most straightforward and effective.

"It was nothing like today. You might think that the villagers all had a big meeting to discuss who they should kill, but things weren't that simple. These days society has made a lot of progress, but back then nobody understood how things like this should work. That made it really easy for things to get out of hand. And once the situation was out of control, there was no way to stop it. Everything became chaotic. By the time the higher-ups issued an order forbidding the random killing that was taking place, it was already too late for a lot of people. You've seen those big mansions, no? You should have a good sense of just how rich those people were. But you have no idea just how poor the most destitute people really were. Do you have any idea how many people didn't have enough money even for basic food and clothing? It doesn't matter what society you live in, if you were to allow the poor to freely take the wealth from the rich, if you allowed them to claim the property of those landlords as their own—who wouldn't take you up on that offer? Everyone in the world is the same when it comes to things like this."

Several of the old men nodded their heads in agreement. They said that by that time, without such extreme tactics there would have been no way to control the wealthy class. Those rich people had money, guns, and private brigades—it was like having their own private army. And there were also Nationalists hiding out among them. Even after they defeated the bandits, a lot of disruptors were still lying in wait to sabotage things. Thanks to the land reform movement, they were finally about to destroy all their supporters and send them running. The price for social stability may have been high, but the most important thing was achieving that stability. Since when was the region of Eastern Sichuan ever free from bandits? Even after the successful campaign to eradicate the bandits, a few stragglers managed to hang on. Some of them even planned to wait until the army formally retreated before moving into the mountains to regroup. But after the Land Reform Campaign none of them was left. Those who weren't killed may as well have been dead because the new government made sure they were no longer a threat. From then on the people were able to live free from the threat of bandits for the next fifty years.

Qinglin listened intently to their chatter, but he didn't interrupt. He just sat there quietly, though he knew that what they were saying was very different from how he viewed the situation.

Having majored in architecture, Qinglin always tried to look at situations from a human perspective. He was always thinking about what was most convenient and comfortable for people, how people could maintain their privacy and independence, achieve freedom, and feel at home in their own skin. He also pondered what kind of overall environment could allow people to experience beauty, what else people might seek in life besides a comfortable home, and how to create a synthesis between indoor and outdoor space. But he never spent time thinking about the fate of his country. That was a topic so large and far removed from him that it seemed almost an illusion, and he lacked the energy to understand the nuances involved. That is partly why he couldn't find the words to refute what Liu Jinyuan and the other old-timers were saying.

But Liu Jinyuan seemed to sense what Qinglin was thinking and turned to him. "People like you who grew up during peaceful times can't possibly understand our feelings on this. You don't know what it's like to fight for your country. The life you are living today is built on the foundation of all those battles we fought; people sacrificed their lives so you could have what you have today. Back then, every time we went out the door, we never knew if we would come back alive."

Qinglin nodded. "You're absolutely right. There is no way for us to understand. But . . ."

Just as the word "but" left his mouth, he realized he'd better not finish his sentence. Sometimes when you are trying to really communicate with someone, you just end up creating an even greater rift.

Qinglin quickly changed the subject. "The food here is really great. You really can't go wrong with Sichuan food!" But he secretly thought about Lu Xun's old saying "When you can't think of anything substantial to say, you just talk about the weather."

7

HELL IV: THE WESTERN WALL UNDER THE CANNA TREE

Ding Zitao was already completely exhausted. She clearly saw herself ascending to the fourth level. Compared with where she was earlier, there seemed to be at least a faint light here.

She could suddenly see clearly. It took only one glance for her to recognize what she was seeing—it was the western wall.

It was the western wall of the garden in Sanzhitang. She was so very familiar with that tall, long wall. The entire wall zigzagged along in the same direction as the mountains for several hundred meters. The wall was constructed from large and heavy stones, the cracks between them filled with green moss. Halfway up you could see the small openings for guns to shoot out from. The watchtower attached to the far side of the wall gradually entered her field of vision. Her grandfather had put special effort into building a square pavilion on the top of the watchtower; the horns of the rooftop pointed upward in a way that gave people the impression it was a place of leisure to enjoy the scenery. But she knew that there was actually a small cannon hidden inside the watchtower. Back when they needed to protect themselves from bandits, this cannon was most imposing.

Beneath the western wall everything was enveloped in a dark shadow. The Japanese ivy that covered the entire wall was withered and dead. The canna tree at the edge of the wall had a crown of bright flaming-red flowers, but that too was in the process of dying—it was as if they were all on the verge of suffocating after having survived the cold winter.

She couldn't remember what year it was when she first entered the Lu family's Sanzhitang.

It was as if she had known about Sanzhitang from birth. That was because of her father. Although Sanzhitang nestled deep in the mountains, her father would go there every year. He said that even from far away you could see it towering overhead, as the western wall seemed to surround the mountains. The garden was just beyond that wall.

The nearby villagers liked to point to the watchtower and tell stories. They spoke of an incident a long time ago when a powerful bandit by the name of Tan pillaged the entire village; he was unstoppable. But when he arrived at Sanzhitang, the cannon fire from the watchtower kept him at bay. In the end, the cannon not only prevented Tan's advance but also blew his chief general to pieces. No one really knew how many wells and rooms were hiding behind the high walls of Sanzhitang. Even after she married into the Lu family, she still couldn't say for sure how many there were.

Her father used to bring her there when she was a girl. Her father, Hu Ruyun, and the master of the house at Sanzhitang, Lu Ziqiao, had studied in Japan. As soon as he returned to China, Lu Ziqiao participated in the Revolution of 1911. Later he took a government job, which he held until he retired and moved back to his ancestral village. Once back home, her father carried on the family business mining salt. At the same time, he helped manage the family's several hundred acres of farmland. In his free time he liked to recite poetry with his friends, collect books and paintings, and mingle with other men of culture.

While on the road, her father told her that Sanzhitang was built by Grandpa Lu. He had served as an official in the Qing court. *Sanzhi* (三知), meaning "The Three Who Know," referred to a quote from the upright official of the Eastern Han dynasty Yang Zhen, who wrote, "Heaven knows, the gods know, I know, you know." He wanted his descendants to know that during his entire career as an official, he was always fair and just. But he removed "you know," leaving behind the three who know: heaven, the gods, and I. She asked her father why he took out the part "you know." Her father sighed and explained that his grandfather had first earned his fortune selling opium, and he knew how damaging rumors could be. So he reasoned that if heaven and the gods know, and I know, that's enough; there is no reason for you to know. With that, her father sighed and said, "In this world of today, what kind of person can stand by 'the four who know'?"

In that moment Ding Zitao could see her father's exact expression as he sighed.

It was also during that trip that the young master of the Lu household, Lu Zhongwen, took her on a walk around the garden to show her the area around the western wall. Bluestone steps lined the path beneath their feet where the western wall ascended as it ran along the mountain. They could make out gunpowder marks around the embrasures in the wall. When they looked down from one of the embrasures, they could see all the fields and sheds in the valley below.

In one corner beside the wall was a grove of canna trees, their red flowers in full bloom.

She said, "I heard my grandaunt say that canna trees are like the blood flowing from the Buddha's feet; that is why their red color is unique."

Lu Zhongwen gazed at her with a smile. "'The feeble roots of the canna, so difficult to even support themselves; for whom do you release your fragrance? Though your branches are unable to withstand the winter cold, your red heart forever preserves itself.' While you were thinking of blood, I was thinking of poetry. Do you know who wrote that poem?"

"No, I don't know," she replied.

"The Southern Song dynasty master Zhu Xi. He also wrote the famous line 'I ask the pond how it can be so ever clear, it comes from being continually replenished by fresh living water.'"

"I haven't heard that one either," she sulked. "I must have gone to middle school in vain!"

Lu Zhongwen chuckled at her comment. There was something about the sound of his laughter that moved her.

That was probably when they started to develop feelings for each other. From that point forward, the garden area around the western wall became a place where they would frequently spend time together. They would often sit in the pavilion atop the watchtower at the end of the wall. The old cannons from long ago were still there, and the two of them would either sit on the cannon or lean against the pavilion railing. There they would enjoy the cool breeze and recite poetry together, and she would listen to Lu Zhongwen play the harmonica.

But where was Lu Zhongwen now?

Ding Zitao instinctively called out, "Zhongwen, where are you?"

But the sound of her voice seemed be sucked into the embrasures, and except for the sound of the wind, all around was consumed in a perfect silence.

That was when she saw herself. She herself, this woman named Daiyun, kneeling before that grove of canna trees.

She was facing a pit in the ground beside a mound of freshly dug earth.

Lying inside the pit were two bodies. One of them was Little Tea, the servant girl who had followed Daiyun after she married into the Lu family. The other body was that of Ziping. Ziping had originally been in charge of taking care of the old Lu family matriarch, but after Daiyun's arrival, she was reassigned to Daiyun. Now these two young women lay shoulder to shoulder in an earthen ditch. The opening was actually too small for two bodies, so they were placed on their sides. It was unbearable to see Little Tea like that; instead, Daiyun pulled Little Tea out, rearranged Ziping's body so that it could lie flat, and then placed Little Tea on top of her.

Dusk was falling quickly, and she hastily pushed the piled dirt, one clump at a time, into the pit. The earth first covered Little Tea's feet, then the rest of her body. Just as her face was about to be obscured by the dirt, Daiyun couldn't help reaching out to caress Little Tea's face one final time. Suddenly in that moment she thought that Little Tea was still breathing. She cried out, "Little Tea! Little Tea! Wake up! We've got to go! Huiyuan's not coming, but we need to leave. Little Tea, I can't leave you alone here!"

But Little Tea, who had been with her family since the age of eleven, did not respond. She was Daiyun's servant, but more importantly she was her companion. When Daiyun married into the Lu family, Little Tea came along as part of the dowry. For so many years Daiyun could always count on hearing Little Tea's cheerful voice respond every time she called her name. But now Little Tea was no longer able to respond. No matter how loudly Daiyun cried or screamed, Little Tea remained silent, breathless.

And now all she could give to repay Little Tea for her loyalty and companionship were these handfuls of dirt. As she sprinkled the earth over Little Tea's body, she kept complaining, "Little Tea, you should have secretly run away with me. Ritchie is waiting for you by the river. There's room for you . . ."

Daiyun had been drinking when Little Tea came to say goodbye. Little Tea approached her and said, "Misstress, I'm sorry but I cannot go with you." Her only response was to hold Little Tea close and cry uncontrollably. Little Tea cried too, and they remained locked in an embrace until they heard Ziping calling, "Little Tea . . . it's time for us to go . . ." Only then did Little Tea pull off Daiyun's hands and walk out alone.

The next time Daiyun saw them, Little Tea and Ziping would be lying shoulder to shoulder in a pit of earth at the foot of the grove of canna trees.

She took the final clump of dirt and sprinkled it evenly over Little Tea's face. The earth gradually covered Little Tea until Daiyun could no longer see the expression on her face or her disheveled hair. She shed no tears. In fact, she didn't feel sad.

This was the last grave she filled in the Lu family garden. She knew she had to leave. She put Ding Zi into a wicker carrier and covered him with a blanket before putting the carrier on her back. That was when she caught sight of a bracelet beside the bed. She had given that bracelet to Little Tea as a birthday gift. Now she wanted to quietly return it to her before Little Tea embarked on her journey. She quickly picked up the bracelet and went back to the garden.

The garden was covered with mounds of dirt. And there in the dark night the garden was enveloped in a deathly silence. You couldn't even hear insects chirping or birds singing. It was as if they had all died along with the plants and trees. *This place was now a garden of death.*

She walked over to the canna grove near the western wall, kneeled down, and began to dig. She placed the bracelet on Little Tea's wrist. The moon wasn't shining that night, and yet she was able to clearly see all the new mounds of dirt throughout the garden. She turned and bowed deeply toward those mounds of dirt before entering the watchtower. *How can I ever possibly return to this place? Little Tea, I'm so sorry. I'm going to forget that Sanzhitang ever existed. I will never come back to this place.*

She went into the basement of the watchtower and ten minutes later emerged from that secret tunnel, which led to a tea garden. Its exit was hidden by thick foliage from the tea trees and random grasses and weeds and was completely overgrown. A few minutes later she saw that camphor tree. She climbed over the bamboo fence, walked a few dozen steps, and saw the path in front of her. And then she began to run.

HELL V: A SOFT BURIAL IN THE GARDEN

That's right, Ding Zitao knew all too clearly that she had already made it up to the fifth floor.

She knew that she was now back on the road from where she once came. She could now see more and more things. Everything now seemed to be so clear: every detail of every incident, the atmosphere of every scene, the expressions on people's faces, and the sound of their voices.

Her father-in-law, Lu Ziqiao, once said that when a person is born, his soul is rich and full. But as the person lives his life, he gradually loses pieces of his soul. Once it is extinguished, that person is without a soul. People around them all think he is dead, but actually he isn't. He is actually in the process of turning himself around, retrieving those lost bits of his soul, one piece at a time. If he is able to retrieve all the bits of his soul, he will attain the *Dao*. And when he is reborn he will be a good person. But if he doesn't retrieve all those pieces . . . it is hard to predict what he will come. He might even end up as a dog or a pig in his next life.

She decided that she would do what she had to in order to put her soul back together. *I want to be a good person in my next life. I can't bear to live a life of suffering any longer.*

But now she could see that garden again. She could see Daiyun there wailing in anguish. She gazed off in the direction that Daiyun was facing, and what she saw was so horrific that she felt that her soul was going to leave her body.

The garden was enveloped in a deathly silence. All around were freshly dug pits and mounds of dirt. Those were the graves the members of the Lu family had dug for themselves. Once they had dug their own graves and piled up the earth, they were all silent. None of them said goodbye; they simply flung their heads back, drinking the solution of arsenic they had prepared, and then lay down in their graves to die.

Grandma and Grandpa lay in the pit beneath the jujube tree; not far from them was the rose garden, and there too was a pit, where Master Lu's Third Aunt lay. The pit in the bamboo forest near the eastern wall was quite shallow; Master Lu's eldest son, Bowen, who had long suffered from chronic illness, had dug it himself. He was so weak that he was unable to dig a proper hole and just laid himself down in the dirt. He said that although he didn't have a coffin, being buried with the bamboo to keep him company was still an elegant way to die. Auntie, his father's oldest sister, dug her grave right next to Bowen's. Auntie said that since she didn't have any children of her own, Bowen would carry out the filial duties of a son for her in the next life. So she wanted to be next to him.

The pit beside the pond was especially deep; it was for the property caretaker, Old Wei. Amah Wu was not far from him; her job had been to take care of Grandma and the elders. She said there was no point going on living after the Lu family was gone, so she decided to go with them.

There were pits in every corner of the garden, and lying in each were people she had known so well. The entire family clan was buried there. They decided to die together. Grandpa told her to be sure to cover their bodies with earth quickly so that the morning light wouldn't shine on their faces.

That was a night devoid of clouds and moonlight. All the lights inside the house were off. The color of the soil and the shadows of the trees combined into one massive blanket of darkness. The garden was devoid of even the faintest breeze. Spring might have come, but traces of winter lingered. All the wild animals and vegetation in the garden seemed to be curled in fear. It had become a garden devoid of sound, color, and life.

She began to fill all the pits in with those piles of earth. There was already a shovel beside each pit, so she had no need to find tools. As if possessed by madness, she quickly shoveled the dirt into each cavity. Grandma, Grandpa, and the other family elders had the deepest pits—that's because Old Wei helped them dig. Old Wei even managed to force a smile as he dug. "Master Lu," he said, "it is a great blessing for me to be able to die together with you and be buried in the same manner. My parents never had that good fortune." (Old Wei's mother had been beaten to death by bandits while on the road home to visit her parents. His father was on his way back home with a delivery from Henan when the Japanese captured him; he ended up dying in prison. Both of Old Wei's parents died without anyone ever knowing what happened to their bodies.) Old Wei dug an especially deep hole for the family elder not far from his own pit. As he helped him lie down inside, he said, "Please don't be frightened. I'll be right behind you and I'll be sure to protect you."

Grandma kept crying. She was continually repeating, "I don't want a soft burial. My mother told me that you can't be reincarnated if you get a soft burial."

Grandpa drank the arsenic, and as he lay down in the grave he cursed, "If you want to live, then go off and sleep with that old crippled village head! Didn't he say a long time ago that the only thing he wanted was our family's mahogany bed? Why don't you go run off to him! And what's all this talk about reincarnation? That's all you think about! Where the hell are you going to reincarnate to?" Grandma shuddered and downed the arsenic in one gulp. She lay down in the pit beside Grandpa and covered her face with a handkerchief.

The task of covering all the bodies with dirt had originally been assigned to Daiyun and her husband's youngest sister, Huiyuan. But when she called Huiyuan to come help, she discovered her passed out in her bedroom, already foaming at the mouth from the poison. Daiyun screamed and tried to shake her awake while calling her name. Huiyuan faintly opened her eyes and said, "My parents are dead . . . I don't want to go on living. It's all my fault. Although I didn't say anything to Jindian . . . his hatred of the Lu family all started with me. I can't bear to live alone. My dear Sister-in-Law, please bury me beside my parents. I'll look after them and my other family members in the underworld."

Daiyun was rendered speechless. She wanted to say something but came up empty. Instead, all she could do was take a deep gulp to suppress her sorrow.

She carried Huiyuan into the garden. A few meters from where Grandpa and Grandma were buried was the moon-shaped gate that Huiyuan had always adored. She would often perform short opera sketches there with her classmates. That gate had always been Huiyuan's favorite place to make her entrance or strike a pose.

Huiyuan was still breathing as Daiyun began to dig a grave for her. Huiyuan whispered, "Thank you, Sister-in-Law, for digging a grave for me."

Daiyun didn't respond but instead used all her energy to dig that hole. She didn't know where she got the strength, but she somehow dug several graves quite quickly. By the time she placed Huiyuan into that pit, her body had already grown icy cold. Daiyun removed the scarf around her own neck and gently placed it over Huiyuan's face.

She lost track of how many graves she covered with earth that night. All the sights and sounds that normally filled the compound during normal times had vanished. All those faces that had once been animated with smiles or depressed looks, grimaces, hardened expressions, and gloomy appearances now somehow looked the same.

After experiencing what she had that night, Daiyun wondered if she could go on living.

She finally made it over to the area of the garden near the western wall.

She had yet to bury Ziping and Little Tea. Ziping's last words to her tore at her heart: "Bury them first; save me until the end. Don't worry about me if you run out of time. I'm not afraid of my corpse being exposed to the elements. Once I'm dead, none of that matters anyway. Who cares if my body is left out in the open?"

Ziping's little sister, Ziyan, was a servant for Master Chen's mother over in Poding Village on the south side of the mountains. Once the villagers had divided up the Chen family's property, they executed the entire Chen family. The villagers then divvied up the Chen's staff of female servants. The head of the village team wanted Ziyan; he forced her to marry his mentally handicapped second son. One day Ziping went up the mountain to visit her sister, and when she returned she said, "I'd rather die than have to live like that."

Daiyun understood what Ziping meant. She knew that for someone like Ziping, death was the only way out. Not long before that her second mother had said the same thing. This is how her second mother put it: "Our only path forward in this life is to die; otherwise, to go on living will be even more painful than death."

The decision to commit suicide was not an easy one. The discussion began in the morning as soon as the family heard the news that they were all to be taken to the ancestral hall to be struggled against by the villagers. But once they had settled on their decision, carrying out the plan was not so difficult. They all calmly and quietly took the necessary actions to see things through.

Daiyun respected Ziping's sense of loyalty and self-sacrifice and also felt an affection for Little Tea. So although the time was running short, she knew that no matter what, she had to make sure they were both properly buried in the earth before she left. A soft burial was already a terrible insult to the memory of the deceased, but if she were unable to cover their bodies with earth, that would be too great of an injustice to the lives they had lived.

She had already completed all the other burials according to Grandpa's instructions, and her entire body was utterly devoid of energy. When she finally saw the bodies of Ziping and Little Tea together in that pit, her legs gave way and she collapsed, kneeling to the ground.

Little Tea, the girl she had grown up with and grown accustomed to always being by her side, was now lying in a pit of dirt on this moonless night, and Daiyun now had to personally cover her body with earth. From then on there would no longer be anyone to answer her calls.

HELL VI: THE LAST SUPPER

As Ding Zitao ascended to the sixth level, she found it more difficult to continue ahead. By this point she began to feel as though she deserved to be in hell. How come she didn't dig herself a grave there in that garden? Why did it fall on her to bury the others?

The light seemed to glow brighter, but she couldn't tell if that meant she was getting closer to heaven or about to return to the human world. Whatever the case, her eyes could now recognize more and more things.

The shadowy forms of human figures entered her field of vision. One by one, she counted them. There were nine or ten of them. Their faces gradually came into focus. Expressionless, they gazed at her. And then she saw herself.

This was that dining room that she was all too familiar with. The dining room was not far from the granary. And just across the way was the kitchen. The compound behind the kitchen was where all the servants lived. This dining room was where she usually took her meals after marrying into the Lu family. There would usually be two separate tables set up: one for the family elders and one for the younger generation. But during the Chinese New Year when all the family members came home, the dining room wasn't large enough for everyone, so they would move to the larger dining hall. The dining hall could accommodate eight large tables, but the big meals there were always quite formal and reserved; it was as if they were all attending an opera.

It was now after the Chinese New Year. Of the four Lu children, only the eldest son, his wife, and their daughter were still at home. The second son and third son were both out of town. The old family matriarch was sitting in the place of honor, flanked by Grandma and Grandpa on either side. Beside them were Auntie and Third Aunt. The eldest son, Lu Bowen, who was sickly and weak, sat close up against his wife. The arrangement of those six seats never changed because the six of them never left the compound, whereas everyone else came and went as they pleased.

The big table had been set up in the small dining room. Everyone at home was now there in that room with their dull, idle faces. But something terrible had happened; a great catastrophe had befallen their family.

Grandpa's long beard kept trembling. When Grandpa came back home after leaving his official post, his beard was all white. She knew that whenever Grandpa got angry, his white beard would tremble uncontrollably. Whenever she saw that trembling, she thought that even his cheekbones must have been upset.

Sitting beside him and wearing a sorrowful expression was Grandma; she was a weak woman who had spent her entire life following whatever arrangements her husband had made for her. She would always say, "Once you marry a man, your life belongs to him." The grand matriarch was actually Grandpa's stepmother. She was so old that the only thing she really did was continue breathing. She behaved just as she always did, sitting there wearing her black velveteen cap and uttering not a single word. Third Aunt looked absolutely miserable; she really didn't want to die, but she also knew there was no other way. Auntie always had a calm expression on her face. One month after she got married, her husband left Sichuan to fight the Japanese and died on the front lines; she returned home and had been here ever since. For her, whether she lived one extra day really didn't matter anymore. Bowen, the eldest son, just sat there, his sickly appearance making him look as wretched as always. The only one in the room who appeared visibly distraught was Huiyuan, whose long ponytail appeared disheveled. The longtime caretaker Old Wei was also sitting there, although it was rare to see him at the table. The household used to employ several dozen servants, but as soon as China was liberated, most were released. The only ones who stayed behind were a few who were essential and those who had nowhere else to go. The only servants still around were Wu Amah, Ziping, and Little Tea. But for the time being there were no chores for them; they too just stood off to one side wearing expressions of sadness.

Sitting there with his long beard, Grandpa appeared stern as he lowered his voice and said, "You've all seen what is happening. After being insulted and tortured, most of the wealthy families on both sides of the mountain have been killed. Those that have managed to survive are in a wretched state. And then there is Daiyun's family: we all know what happened to them. All her father did was carry on his family business; he ran a shop and enjoyed collecting books and liked to practice calligraphy and paint. He treated people with respect and always emphasized the importance of tolerance. Daiyun's brother worked for the new government; he collected grain taxes for them and even made my family pay their fair share. And look what happened to them! Lingyun rushed home to save his parents and ended up getting shot on the road. He not only was unable to save his parents but also lost his life in the process. Don't cry, Daiyun. Tears won't bring them back. We, the Lu family, have tried to bring honor to our ancestors for several generations, but now there is nowhere for me to set down these old bones of mine, I cannot bear to let us lose our dignity, and I certainly cannot just sit here and wait for them to come and beat me. We are better off just ending it ourselves."

Grandma was the first to break out in tears. "What about our grandson, Ding Zi? He's not even two years old! How could we ever do that to Zhongwen?"

Grandpa responded, "Ding Zi must not die. Daiyun will escape tonight with Ding Zi and Huiyuan. I'll give her instructions on how to get away. I've already made arrangements for Ritchie to wait for them by the river. But it is a small boat that can carry only three people. The current is too strong and treacherous right now for larger boats. As for everyone else, if you are willing to die, we will go out together. If you do not want to die, you can try to find your own way to escape."

Old Wei added, "There are already people outside the compound keeping an eye on the place. I'm afraid it won't be easy for anyone to get away. But once they discover a few dead bodies inside the compound, I'm afraid they won't treat survivors very kindly . . ."

Third Aunt wiped her tears and said, "And you think we can preserve our dignity if we die? And what if they drag our bodies out to Luan Ridge to feed the dogs?"

Grandpa responded, "Once we leave Sanzhitang, we won't get anywhere without a boat. I've already thought the matter through: for those who want to follow me, we will go out to the garden and dig ourselves graves. Daiyun and Huiyuan will stay to make sure we are all buried before they leave. Once our bodies are in the ground, there is no way they will dig us up—doing that would violate a great taboo. I suspect that not one of the villagers would ever dare to dig us up. If you are unwilling to follow my plan, it will be up to you to find a way to save yourselves."

Huiyuan moaned, "Now that my parents will be gone, what's the point of living anyway?"

But Grandpa just ignored her and instead addressed Daiyun. "Take Huiyuan with you; bring her to Zhongwen's Second Uncle's house. From there they'll find a way to get you to Shanghai. When you get there, look up your cousin; he was always close with Zhongwen. I'm sure he'll help you find a way to get to Hong Kong, where you can be reunited with Zhongwen. Tell him to take you to England, where his uncle is. Zhongwen can find a job when you get there, any kind of job; just tell him to never come back here. There is nothing left of this family. If you can one day find Huiyuan a good man to marry, you will have done well by the Lu family."

The old matriarch suddenly spoke. "Put me in the ground."

Third Aunt said, "We still haven't prepared the coffins. How could we just put you in the ground?"

But Grandpa responded with a steely expression when he growled, "A soft burial!"

Grandma's cries became more pronounced. "I don't want a soft burial. You can't be reincarnated if you get a soft burial."

Grandpa admonished her, "You're still worried about your next life? Then what the hell did you come into *this* life for?"

Grandma's whimpering became even more pronounced. All the while, Bowen hadn't said a word, but he finally opened his mouth. "Mom, what Dad said is right. Those people in the villages around us were not even as well off as those of us here in Sanzhitang, but even they were unable to survive—all of them met brutal deaths. For many generations now, the Lu family has upheld their dignity and respect; Dad is someone with an especially strong sense of self-respect. There is no way he can stand to be insulted like this. I feel bad that, with all my ailments, there isn't much I can do to help the family. The only constructive thing I can do is accompany Dad on his journey to the other side. We can't allow anyone to ridicule the Lu family."

Grandpa praised his son. "Bowen is setting a good example. So let it be decided. For those of you who want to take this journey with us, please go and change into something appropriate for what is coming."

All the servants began to cry. Grandpa just waved at them. "If you want to leave, go. Those people outside are waiting for you."

Wu Amah spoke through her tears. "I've been serving the Lu family for many years. I don't think they would ever let me go anyway. Instead, I will stay with Madame Lu; it will be my honor to take care of her in the underworld."

Ziping was also crying as she declared to the old family matriarch, "I'll go with you. I know that Dun Zi, the head of East Village, wants to marry me. There is nothing physically wrong with him and he seems to be decent, but I saw what he did to Grandpa Yue over in the West Village when they were holding a struggle session against him. Dun Zi beat that old man quite viciously, and I know I could never be with a man like that."

Third Aunt turned to Little Tea. "Little Tea, they want you to marry Baldy. Are you willing to do that?"

Little Tea shook her head, crying as she answered, "I refuse to marry him. I hate that man!"

Third Aunt then said, "If you were to marry him, Ritchie would be sure to go after him once he returned. Do you think Ritchie is a match for him? Baldy is considered one of the more politically active people in the village. If you don't kill yourself with us, Ritchie is bound to die for you later."

Third Aunt's words infuriated Daiyun, who retorted angrily, "How could you say such a thing? Little Tea is just a servant. Why should she have to die?"

Little Tea was sobbing so hard that it was difficult for her to speak clearly, but she said, "No, Third Aunt is right. Ritchie will surely fight Baldy if I marry the man. But without the political backing that Baldy has, Ritchie wouldn't stand a chance. I have decided to go with all of you. If I'm dead, there won't be anyone for the two of them to fight over."

The expression on Grandpa's face grew more stern. "Since you all want to accompany me on this journey, so be it! There is nothing for us to cry about. This is our fate. There are some people who so badly want to live that they are willing to sacrifice their dignity; but the Lu family has always placed the value of dignity above all else, including life itself."

At that moment Daiyun felt so dazed and distraught that she really wasn't sure what she should do. She raised her head and on impulse addressed Grandpa. "I'll go with you too . . ."

But Grandpa resolutely shot down her suggestion. "I'll hear nothing of it! You will bury us and then escape with Ding Zi and Huiyuan. Saving you will allow me to face your parents in the underworld with a clear conscience. And by saving Ding Zi, you will be able to preserve the family line for the Lu family."

Ding Zitao began to shudder uncontrollably. Suddenly the pain in her back felt much worse. She had tried to run away that day when the villagers came to struggle against her family, but one of them hit her on the back with the buttstock of a rifle. "I'm so afraid," she said aloud. "I'm not afraid of dying . . . I'm afraid of having to go on living."

Grandpa ordered, "Old Wei, bring me a bottle of spirits."

Old Wei brought over a bottle of Luzhou wine. Grandpa said, "Drink up, Daiyun. After three glasses of this, you'll have the courage to see through what needs to be done. After you drink, take Ding Zi back to your room. You can come out once you no longer hear the sound of digging and the garden is quiet again. By burying us, you will be performing a great charitable deed that will not be forgotten."

She dared not go against Grandpa's orders, so she took the bottle of spirits, opened the cap, and gulped down a massive swig. After taking such a big swig, she involuntarily released a belch. Little Tea approached to gently massage her back. She belched a few more times before taking a few more sips.

She burped after each sip until Old Wei took the bottle out of her hands. "That's enough. If you drink too much, you'll get drunk. And if you pass out, the whole plan will be ruined."

That's when Grandpa pointed to the food on the table and said, "Let's eat. We should have a full stomach for the journey ahead."

This was the Lu family's last supper. Wu Amah had cooked up practically everything the Wu family had in their kitchen for this sumptuous meal. As if they knew they would all be making this journey together, the division between master and servant seemed to disappear, and everyone just sat together in a circle eating in silence. Since no one spoke, the sound of their chewing seemed particularly pronounced.

A stifling sense of uneasiness pervaded the dining room. Among the gentle clatter of chopsticks and clanking chinaware was heard the faint sound of crying. Whenever the crying got too loud, Grandpa would flash a stern look at the sorrowing person, who would immediately try to suppress the sobs.

HELL VII: THE MESSAGE

In her terror-stricken state, Ding Zitao somehow managed to climb up to the seventh level. By the time she got there, that painful anxiety that had been haunting her had begun to dissipate. Replacing it was utter numbness. The numbness was so great that even things she once recognized started to feel strange and distant; what she had once participated in and been a part of now felt so very far away.

The message came at dawn. The messenger frantically knocked on the main gate.

The knocking sound woke up her baby, Ding Zi, who began to cry. She quickly got up and tended to the baby as he peed. That was when she heard the creaking sound of the main gate opening. The Lu family gate was actually quite small; from the high walls it looked like a tiny hole. Only two people walking shoulder to shoulder could fit through at the same time, but once through the gate, they would enter a broad and expansive courtyard. People on the street outside would never imagine that such a magnificent compound lay hidden behind that inconspicuous gate. The Lu family ancestors had once specialized in the sale of opium, handling everything from planting and cultivation of the poppies to production and sales. Once upon a time those mountaintop tea gardens were all filled with opium poppies. Since the family had built their fortune on the sale of opium, the Lu elders had learned to conduct their business carefully and quietly, without attracting too much attention. It was only after Lu Ziqiao's grandfather took up a government post that the family began to turn their poppy fields into a series of tea farms. By the time of Lu Ziqiao's generation, the Lu family had already washed away the stains from their earlier opium trade days and were regarded as a legitimate and distinguished family.

It was a single-leaf door, painted with vermilion lacquer, and it lacked a door knocker. A protruding piece of wood, worn smooth and shiny from so many years of use, served as the door handle. The door panel was quite thick, and it made a deep loud sound when it opened. Lu Ziqiao said that this was the kind of sound the main gate to a big family compound should make. He said you didn't necessarily need a big gate, but the sound the gate made should have a certain weight to it. When visitors arrive and walk through that gate, the sound alone should tell them what kind of place they are walking into.

Ding Zitao thought about how different it was from that of her parents' house. Her childhood home at Qierenlu had a front gate that was much larger than this one, and its double doors opened to a rather ordinary-looking courtyard. The gates were painted black and affixed with a large circular knocker. Daiyun once asked her father why the gate to their house opened so differently from that of the Lu family. Her father explained, "Our ancestors were all scholars, so there was no reason to hide who we were. There was never anything for us to be afraid of, and therefore there was no reason for our family to be different from anyone else. Actually, the people who attract the least attention in this world are those who appear to be just like everyone else. That's how you detract attention from yourself and stay safe."

Just thinking of those words made Ding Zitao well up with a bitter smile. She thought, *No matter what methods you used to downplay your status, in the end you all met a brutal end.*

The caretaker Old Wei went to open the door. She opened her window just wide enough to peek out in order to see what was going on.

Old Wei said, "Who knocks on people's doors so early in the morning?"

The visitor was Chen Bosan, a young man from the neighboring village. He answered, "My mom told me I had to get here early. My name's Chen Bosan. Master Wei, I'm sure you remember: three years ago it was Master Lu who saved my mom when a rock fell on her head; he took her into town to get treated. If it hadn't been for Master Lu's generosity, I would be an orphan today."

Old Wei responded, "I do remember that incident. But don't tell me you came all the way out here at the crack of dawn just to say thank you?"

"No, there is something urgent," Chen Bosan explained. "There's some important news I need to share. My mom told me to make sure to personally deliver the message to Master Lu."

Old Wei said, "Master Lu is still in bed. Why don't you tell me first, and then I'll decide if it is something I need to wake up Master Lu for."

Chen Bosan responded anxiously, "It's really important. Originally my mom wanted me to come last night. But later she said it was better to let Master Lu get one more good night's sleep, because in the future he might not have many more chances for that..."

Old Wei was confused. "What are you talking about?"

Chen Bosan said, "That's what my mom said. She kept repeating how important it was for me to deliver the message personally to Master Lu. She wanted to repay the kindness that Master Lu had once extended to her."

Old Wei looked Chen Bosan over and finally replied, "You look like a decent guy. Wait here."

A few minutes later Old Wei invited Chen Bosan into the compound.

Daiyun didn't go over to get a closer look; after all, she wasn't really the nosy type. At the same time, she knew the Lu family rule: *Those things that you should know about, you will learn in good time; but for matters you shouldn't know about, there is no reason for you to ever ask about them.* Moreover, she had hardly had a single good night's rest in more than a month and felt totally exhausted. Each night she could almost hear her parents' terrible screams, Second Mother's curses, and the sound of the bullets that had ended her brother's life.

Little Tea woke her just before dawn. Little Tea had a terrified look on her face as she told her that Grandpa had summoned everyone to meet in his library. She knew that something terrible must be afoot for him to call a family meeting so early.

She hurriedly brushed her hair and handed the baby over to Little Tea before they went off to the meeting.

There was an oppressive atmosphere hanging over the library. The cause of that dark atmosphere came from the stern look on Grandpa Lu Ziqiao's face; his beard was twitching so violently that it looked as if someone were tugging on it with a string. He was anxiously pacing back and forth but didn't say a word. Grandma was just sitting there in tears with a look of utter sadness on her face.

Daiyun's heart began to race. She was immediately gripped by the fear that something had happened to her husband, Lu Zhongwen. Lu Zhongwen had set out for Hong Kong a few months earlier; he'd sent a letter home last month, but there had been no news from him since. Not knowing if he was safe, everyone in the family was worried about him.

Her sister-in-law Huiyuan was the last person to enter the room; as she strolled into the library she complained, "Dad, what are you thinking calling a meeting so early on such a cold day?"

Daiyun gently tugged on Huiyuan's shirt and whispered, "Do you think something's happened to Zhongwen?"

Huiyuan responded, "Relax, my brother's got a good head on his shoulders; he knows how to stay out of trouble."

That was the kind of response she needed to hear; those words set her at ease.

Grandpa finally stopped his pacing and, looking over everyone in the room, lowered his voice and spoke. "You must already have guessed that something terrible has befallen our family. Early this morning someone came here with a message; he said that tomorrow or the day after tomorrow people from the village would be coming here to begin a purge directed against our family. Because the Lu family is the largest clan in these parts and I also served as an official under the Nationalists, they are saying that struggling against us is the only way to quell the anger of the people. They plan to carry out this denunciation over the course of the next week, and all our family members will be implicated. All the peasants from the nearby villages have been called in to participate."

The room immediately fell silent. It was an unusual silence. You could not only hear everyone's hearts beating but also even identify which heartbeat belonged to which person.

Daiyun felt her body suddenly grow weak. She had witnessed a scene like this before. When you are standing there on that platform facing the villagers' insults and attacks, the only thing you hope for is death. It is difficult to imagine the degree to which you need to harden your heart in order to get to a place where you still want to go on living.

Time seemed to stand still, yet though it remained frozen, you could feel it gradually slipping away. At last, it was Wu Amah who spoke. Her voiced trembled. "Why don't we eat first. The food is getting cold."

Their discussion began over breakfast. Huiyuan was the first to speak up. She said, "Dad, I don't want to light the sky lanterns for more lost souls."

With that, she turned to look at Daiyun, who was sitting beside her. Everyone in the room also looked at Daiyun. Daiyun immediately broke down, her tears falling like rain. There had been rumors that sky lanterns had been set off for both her second mother and her sister-in-law. They were tortured for three days and three nights, and no one really knew what happened to them after that. Someone said their bodies were dumped on Luan Ridge. Someone else said they drowned themselves in the river.

"I won't ask you to light any sky lanterns," Grandpa reassured her. "But what are you going to do if they come to struggle against you?"

Huiyuan's response was firm. "I'd rather die."

Her words hit everyone in the room with a jolt.

Grandpa responded, "There's some truth in that. Right now what we need to discuss is whether there is any way we will be able to come out of this purge alive. If it doesn't look possible, we need to figure out which method we want to use to end our lives. Do we want to be tortured to death by them? Or . . ."

He hesitated, then flashed a look at Old Wei as if signaling for him to take over.

Old Wei lowered his head and stammered, "What the master means is . . . what he is trying to say is . . . are you all willing to die at their hands, or would you rather find . . . an alternative method to end our lives?"

Grandpa continued, "That's the crux of the issue. We should be thankful that someone sent a message to warn us of what is coming. That has bought us some time to figure out whether we will be able to come out of this alive. Of course, it would be best if we are able to survive the coming purge. But if we cannot, we will need to come to our own decision about how we want to die."

Daiyun asked, "Didn't everyone in the village sign a letter attesting to Father's great merits? He was recognized for his role in overthrowing the Qing dynasty; he helped deliver medicine to the guerrilla soldiers fighting in the mountains; and during the campaign against the bandits, he led the People's Liberation Army into the mountains so that they could break up the Blade Society. He also donated more grain to the government than anyone else! And didn't the new government leaders already agree not to come after the Lu family?"

Old Wei responded, "The problem is that the new team leader doesn't recognize any of that. It's all worthless."

"How come the new team leader doesn't listen to what the people are saying?" asked Huiyuan.

Grandpa flashed her a hard look. "Because he's Wang Si's son, that's why!"

Everyone in the room gasped in shock, then they all turned to Huiyuan.

Daiyun could feel her heart violently pounding. She exchanged glances with Little Tea. Little Tea discreetly shook her head as if discouraging Daiyun from saying something. Daiyun got the message and nodded her head.

Huiyuan screamed at them all, "What are you all staring at me for? That's *his* business! I didn't do anything!"

Third Aunt said, "If you hadn't told Jindian how his father died, do you think he would ever have left? Well, good job! Now he's back for revenge!"

Old Wei exclaimed, "He's an ungrateful bastard. No matter how you look at it, it was the Lu family that raised that boy!"

Grandpa's face tightened as he yelled sternly, "It has nothing to do with anything anyone did. This is fate!"

The image of this man named Wang Si, whom everyone in the family had forgotten about, suddenly appeared before them, and they recollected his story.

This was something that had occurred many years before.

Back then Lu Ziqiao was still young; so was the caretaker Old Wei. At the time, the Lu family wanted to rebuild their ancestral hall. The family elders entrusted this job to Lu Ziqiao and Old Wei. They in turn hired a feng shui expert to look over the site. After spending an entire day examining the area, the feng shui master told them which plot of land was most ideal for the ancestral hall. That plot of land belonged to Wang Si's family. Wang Si's grandfather used to serve as a bodyguard for the Lu family and followed the Lus when they moved here. Those eighteen acres of land were given to Wang Si as a token of thanks for his having protected the Lu family elders.

Lu Ziqiao thought he would be able to work things out with the Wangs. He sent Old Wei to talk things over with Wang Si; the Lu family offered to either exchange their plot of land for an even larger twenty-acre plot or simply purchase the land from them at a premium price. But Wang Si refused. He explained that before they died, both his father and his grandfather had told him that this land was given in exchange for his grandfather's life; it represented the Wang family's roots. Wang Si also relied on the crops he cultivated on that land to survive. They discussed things over and over for several days but couldn't come to an agreement. Lu Ziqiao even paid a personal visit to Wang Si's house to persuade him, but Wang Si wouldn't budge. At the time, Lu Ziqiao actually held an outside post in government; he took the refusal as a personal affront and lost his temper. But Wang Si was also a stubborn man; he too lost his temper. The entire affair blew up and ended in a stalemate.

Lu Ziqiao and Old Wei were trying to figure out a better resolution when something terrible happened.

Wang Si had two little daughters—the older girl was five and the younger one was three—and his wife was pregnant with their third child. The night she went into labor there was a downpour that triggered a flash flood from the mountains. The midwife rushed to their house in the rain only to discover Wang Si's wife was at high risk for a miscarriage; the midwife didn't dare go through with the delivery and instead urged Wang Si to rush her to the hospital in town to see a Western doctor. The streams running along the road into the city were all flooded, and the only way for them to get to the hospital would be by using the Lu family's horse-drawn wagon, which even had a tent that could protect the laboring woman from the wind and rain. Without any other options, Wang Si rushed into Sanzhitang to find Old Wei. Old Wei immediately agreed to help him, but only on condition that Wang Si agree to sell the Lu family his land. Wang Si refused and stamped off. He rushed back home, hoping by then that the midwife had reconsidered her stance and was willing to help them, but she insisted the risk was too high.

The midwife then admonished him, "What are you waiting for? Saving them is the most important thing right now! We are talking about two human lives at risk!"

The midwife's words made Wang Si cringe, and he rushed back to the Lu house and quickly signed his name to the deed. Old Wei was a man of his word; he immediately ordered their driver to take Wang Si and his wife to the hospital. But no one could have imagined what would happen: after screaming the whole way to the hospital, Wang Si's wife was delivered of a healthy baby boy, but the doctors couldn't save her. The doctor said, "She would have been fine if you had gotten her here half an hour earlier."

His wife was dead and he had given up the plot of land left to him by his ancestors: Wang Si nearly went mad. He took the money he received from selling the land and moved away with his three children. No one knew where he went. Although the Lu family finally got their hands on that land, because of the death of Wang Si's wife that plot was stained with the inauspicious shadow of her death, and the Lu family was no longer willing to build their ancestral hall there.

Two or three years later someone showed up at the Lu compound with a small boy; he said that a man named Wang Si had asked him to deliver the child. A note tucked into the boy's shirt read, "If you raise this boy for me, we will call things even." Old Wei immediately asked the man what happened to Wang Si. The man replied, "He's dead. He got sick and died." Old Wei was shocked to hear this news and asked about Wang Si's two daughters. The man responded, "I never met his daughters. Perhaps he sold them off?" This news sent shock waves through the Lu family. Old Wei was assaulted by the pangs of deep regret. Since things had already come to this, Lu Ziqiao decided to take the child in and raise him. He even promised to give those eighteen acres of land back to the child when he got older.

That child's name was Wang Jindian. Jindian grew up in the Lu compound. Old Wei and Wu Amah were the ones responsible for raising him. Old Wei carried a deep sense of guilt for what happened to Wang Si and made sure to treat his son well. When the Lu family children went to private school, Jindian went too. But when the Lu children went off to attend middle school in town, Jindian started working around the compound with the other long-term help. Initially everyone seemed to live in peace with one another. But then one day two years ago Jindian suddenly left the Lu compound without saying a word. No one knew where he went. Third Aunt said he left because Huiyuan told him about what transpired between their families. Huiyuan learned what happened only when Madame Lu told her the story to illustrate why she should stay away from him. But it was just a few days later that Jindian ran off. Huiyuan refused to admit that she had told him. Lu Ziqiao didn't place the blame on anyone, but he forbade anyone in the household from speaking about the issue. All he said was that they would hold those eighteen acres of land for Jindian until he returned.

But now Jindian had returned on his own terms.

The silence lasted too long.

Huiyuan was growing impatient and suddenly yelled out, "I'm going to go find Wang Jindian. He should know damn well how good the Lu family treated him!"

Grandpa berated her. "Shut your mouth and sit down! Don't you dare take one step outside this house! Do you think the Lu family needs you to go out and take care of this? Since when has the Lu family ever had to ask the Wang family for a favor?"

Third Aunt muttered, "Even as he's gazing down death's door, he still holds on to his haughty attitude!"

Grandpa raised his voice even louder to yell, "You shut your mouth too!"

The sound of Grandpa's barking voice made everyone at the table shudder.

Breakfast that morning went on for a long time. Even after everyone was finished eating, no one left the table. They all sat there the entire day discussing what to do. They were trying to figure out if there was any possible way for them to survive what was coming. And if not, they needed to figure out a plan.

Over in West Village there was the Fan family, who had been driven out of their mansion and forced to live in a cowshed. Their home was turned into a warehouse. The Liu family compound over on the north slope had been taken over by seven or eight families. These outsiders moved into all the main rooms, and the Liu family were forced to live in the servants' quarters. Not only that, but they had to bear constant insults every time they went in or out. Those same people who used to smile and bow to them were now literally stepping on them every chance they got. The Chens, who lived on the south side of the mountain in Poding Village, had been a large family of four generations; they were all killed with the exception of a few of the old family elders, who ended up living in the tiny temple housing the village god at the edge of town. They were forced to beg for food. Several of the village troublemakers divvied up their house and female servants. And then there were their own relatives by marriage: Hu Ruyun's family from Hu Shuidang— what happened to them was too terrible to mention. Except for Daiyun, no one in their family survived. Their family home and store were of course taken over by others; their collection of books and paintings took several days to burn. The villagers used the ashes as fertilizer for the fields.

After taking into consideration the fate of other wealthy families in neighboring villages, all agreed that there was no real chance for them to survive the coming struggle. And if perchance a few of them should make it, the life waiting them would be even worse than death.

Grandpa Lu Ziqiao concluded by saying, "If we cannot survive the purge, we may as well die. In any case, choosing death by our own hands is better than being beaten to death by theirs."

The moment he announced his decision, all the women in the room began to sob. But after sitting in that tense atmosphere all day, the women somehow felt a sense of release and their sobbing subsided.

Dusk was falling. Although winter was over, spring was taking its time to arrive. The light from the sunset appeared frozen by the early spring cold; there was no warmth, and that night felt particularly cold.

8

WHY DOES HIS SILHOUETTE LOOK SO FAMILIAR?

Liu Jinyuan was now standing on the deck of a tour boat going through the Three Gorges.

Beside him was his older son, Liu Xiao'an. Meanwhile, Liu Xiao'an's wife was still in her cabin. The warm river breeze felt so good as it blew up against their faces. The wind was as it ever was, but this was a very different boat from the kind he once took long ago. There was no deck or railing; there was only a long passage in the middle of the boat flanked by rows of cabins on either side. At least the bow area was open; otherwise, Liu Jinyuan thought, this wouldn't even feel like a boat. Being stuck inside wasn't much different than being in a submarine.

Liu Jinyuan looked out at Qinglin's silhouette as it gradually retreated into the distance. The longer Liu Jinyuan gazed at him, the stronger the sense that there was something so familiar about him. That familiarity seemed to go far back; it was a familiarity that he had long forgotten and yet now had suddenly returned. Liu Jinyuan wondered what it was about Qinglin that was triggering this reaction.

"Dad," Liu Xiao'an asked, "shall we go into the cabin?"

"I'd like to get one more good look at Wanzhou," Liu Jinyuan responded. "This will probably be the last time I see this place. I don't think I'll ever have another opportunity to come back."

"Don't say such depressing things, Dad! We can come back anytime you want. Travel is quite convenient these days."

Liu Jinyuan didn't respond. But he knew that this was goodbye.

By the time Liu Xiao'an and his wife reached Wanzhou, Liu Jinyuan had already been there for four days.

Liu Xiao'an spent several years in Wanzhou during his elementary school years, back when it was still called Wan County. He thought that going back would trigger all kinds of emotions, and he was actually quite excited on the plane after he started thinking about all those childhood memories. He didn't expect to discover he'd been making a big fuss out of nothing. For as soon as he saw the place, he realized there was nothing left that he still recognized. It didn't at all feel like a place where he had once lived. He took his wife out for a drive around the city in a rental car. When they got back to the hotel after driving around for half the day, he told her that few remnants from the old city did actually bring back a handful of memories. But all those emotions about this place that he had saved up inside himself over the years had been completely destroyed by a deep sense of unfamiliarity.

While they were still in Wanzhou, Liu Xiao'an rambled on about his memories as his father flashed him a cool gaze. Meanwhile, Qinglin stood beside them smiling.

Qinglin's original plan had been to leave Wanzhou the day after Liu Xiao'an arrived so that he could rush back to Great Water Well, where he would meet up with Long Zhongyong and his students before heading with them to Eastern Sichuan. It came as a surprise when Qinglin received a phone call from Long Zhongyong telling him that he needed to cancel the trip.

Zhongyong's father had fallen ill, and Long Zhongyong needed to rush home. He had to get back so quickly that he couldn't even wait for Qinglin to drive out; instead, he and his students had already boarded a bus to the airport.

"Since your friends had this change of plans, I guess there is no rush for you to leave, then?" queried Liu Jinyuan.

"That's right," replied Qinglin.

"In that case, why don't you spend some more time with us old folks? I'm sure my old man has more heroic stories from the war he wants to share with you! If you're not here, I'll have to listen to them all!"

Qinglin laughed. "I'm quite happy to listen to Uncle Liu's old stories; they're actually really interesting. He was telling me all about the campaign to suppress the bandits in Eastern Sichuan; that's a part of history that I knew nothing about before this trip. Hearing him share those stories has also helped me understand why people from his generation see things so differently than we do."

Liu Xiao'an smirked before saying, "Those stories may be interesting the first time around . . . but I've been hearing those same stories for fifty years! As far as I can remember, it's always been those same stories about fighting the Japanese, the civil war, and later the campaign against the bandits. I've heard them so many times that I feel like I've practically become one of those characters! When Dad tells his stories, he always says back then Xiao'an was doing so-and-so or Xiaochuan was doing so-and-so. Isn't that right, Dad?"

That made even Liu Jinyuan laugh. He was indeed always making reference to his sons when he told his stories.

Liu Xiao'an added, "Then again, as Dad got older his temper greatly improved. When he was young, I would never have dared to joke about things like that. He has become kinder with age.

To refer to him as a 'kind old man' is the perfect description of him now!"

Liu Xiao'an was the type of person who always took shortcuts when it came to real work, but he was actually a lot of fun to be around. When Qinglin was first hired, Liu Xiao'an was still the office manager. Qinglin was responsible for running various errands for him and he ended up cleaning up all kinds of messes that his boss had created. He did such a good job that most people never knew there had been a problem. That helped Qinglin win Xiao'an's respect. Eventually Qinglin was promoted to the projects division, and not long after that Liu Xiaochuan arranged for his brother to spend all his time taking care of their parents.

Liu Jinyuan had always been disappointed by Liu Xiao'an. He felt that as the eldest son, he should have done more with his life. But Liu Xiao'an was a person who never gave much thought to things like career advancement. When classes shut down during the Cultural Revolution, he never went to the countryside with the other kids who took part in the rustication movement; instead, he just signed up for the army because he felt bored staying home. During that time anyone in the army with a high school education was considered quite cultured, so he was easily offered a promotion. But Liu Xiao'an met a girl and ended up turning the promotion down in the name of love. He dropped out of the military and changed his career track; this was something that infuriated his parents. Liu Xiaochuan secretly said that he could have understood his brother's decision had the girl been some great beauty, but the woman who ended up becoming his sister-in-law not only was ugly but also lacked an ounce of talent. All she knew how to do was eat, drink, and have fun; the only thing she seemed to want out of life was a good time. If it hadn't been for her, Liu Xiao'an could have stayed in the army and would probably have been a general by now.

Qinglin thought what Liu Xiaochuan said made sense. One year he had gone on a business trip with Liu Xiao'an, and the two of them found themselves drinking beer at a small restaurant on the streets of Beijing. Qinglin was in a great mood and asked Liu Xiao'an about why he had left the army. Liu Xiao'an was pretty straightforward in his response: "All I want in life is to be comfortable and be able to be myself. There are a lot different ways to live your life: Do I really have to spend my whole life like my father, vying to climb the bureaucratic ladder? Or like my brother, constantly obsessed with making more money? My wife is someone with the same worldview as me. It feels really good to be with someone who shares the same values. After all these years, I think time has proven me correct. Sure, my wife sometimes gets a bit greedy when it comes to financial matters, but she would never force me to sacrifice my way of life to get some promotion or make more money. Just take a look at Liu Xiaochuan's wife: if he hadn't put away a few hundred million yuan in the bank for her, she would probably treat him like shit. Now look at my wife: she makes things so easy for me. As long as we have enough money to eat decent food and have a good time, she's happy. When it comes right down to it, we all live our lives like everyone else; most of our time is spent on everyday things. So it's only when our big life goals match up with our little daily tasks that we will get the greatest comfort and enjoyment out of life."

Qinglin was still a bachelor then, and Liu Xiao'an's words about finding the right partner in life really left a deep impression on him. At the same time, he thought that as someone who had grown up as a poor kid, he could in no way ever have had the same kind of confidence as Liu Xiao'an. He knew he had to work hard and fight for whatever was coming to him. But there was one thing he understood: once he had put in the work to set up his family economically, he would take a step back to enjoy life.

There was ultimately nothing in Wanzhou to keep Liu Xiao'an and his wife engaged enough to stay there. Wanzhou couldn't hold a candle to those elegant, pristine, beautiful little towns they had seen during their recent trip to Europe. That was especially true for Liu Xiao'an's wife, who kept complaining about how backward this place was and how there was nothing to see here. Liu Jinyuan's frustration with her was written all over his face. But Qinglin had the good sense to say, "We're not here for a vacation, we're here for nostalgia. Nostalgia for the past is one of the most important elements of our modern lifestyle. Those small European towns that don't change for hundreds of years are actually there to serve people's sense of nostalgia."

"That's right," Liu Jinyuan chimed in.

Liu Xiao'an actually agreed with his father and added, "Just ignore her. She has no connection to this place."

Even Liu Xiao'an, who *did* have a connection to Wanzhou, wasn't qualified to be a local tour guide. At the most, he could say he was revisiting a place where he had once lived. Yet he recognized almost nothing left from the old days. Moreover, Liu Xiao'an lacked the emotional connections required to rekindle attachments to the people here. When Liu Xiao'an left Wanzhou, he was just a third-grade student in elementary school. As the saying goes, "Attachments fade when people move away." He was simply too young; there wasn't much of a connection established by the time he left. He had not kept in touch with any of his classmates from Wanzhou and now couldn't even remember their names. So after just one night in the hotel there, he was suggesting they cut their trip short and go home.

Qinglin thought that was a good idea. He felt that Liu Jinyuan must already have had ample time to see everyone he wanted to see in Wanzhou. There seemed little point in hanging around any longer. It was really time to get home. But Liu Jinyuan wanted to stay a few more days. He felt satisfied even if he was just lingering around the hotel, going for walks, and breathing in the air here. Actually, he had something else on his mind, but he wouldn't say what. After several days of running around the city and talking to many, many people, he was physically exhausted and really needed to rest. But Liu Jinyuan was never willing to let anyone see his vulnerable side.

Qinglin made a suggestion: since they had wanted to do some sightseeing, there was no need for them to return the way they came; there was also no point in just hanging around the hotel. He thought the best option would be for them to take a Three Gorges tour boat from Wanzhou back to Wuhan. They could rest on the boat while checking out what the Three Gorges looked like now that the dam had been built. The scenery was apparently no less spectacular than what it had been before.

Actually, Qinglin had his own plans. He really didn't want to spend any more time there. Liu Jinyuan's initial excitement had waned a bit, and Qinglin could clearly see how exhausted he was. He thought it best to give the old man a chance to rest. Qinglin was afraid Liu Jinyuan might get sick if he had to do another long-distance car ride and then get on a plane. Even though his boss had told him his only job was to hand his father over to his brother, Qinglin worried that something might go wrong and he would be held responsible. There was another thing that Qinglin was also concerned about: if he were to leave as soon as Liu Xiao'an arrived, it would look as if he had had been spending time with Liu Jinyuan only because it was his job. He didn't want to hurt the old man's feelings. But if they were to take a tour boat home, everything would be different. That's because they would be able to get some real quality rest on the boat.

Liu Jinyuan immediately embraced the idea of the tour boat. If his son had been the one to suggest the tour, Liu Jinyuan would certainly have thought it was something he had planned from the beginning. That would have undoubtably led him to resist the plan out of spite for his son. But since Qinglin made the suggestion, Liu Jinyuan could tell he had his best interests at heart. Moreover, it was clearly a spur-of-the-moment suggestion that he hadn't discussed in advance with Liu Xiao'an. All that led the old man to immediately embrace the suggestion. Deep down, in fact, he really loved the idea; he could rest while comfortably returning home and even see the Three Gorges.

And as for Liu Xiao'an, he couldn't have been happier. He had actually used the Yangtze boat tour as a way to entice his wife to come on the trip even though she was still complaining about her jet lag. But once they arrived, he didn't dare bring up the idea with his father right away. He was afraid his father and his brother would both accuse him of coming only because he wanted to get a free tour of the Three Gorges. Liu Xiao'an had actually used that only as an excuse to convince his wife to come. He knew he would have plenty of opportunities to visit the Three Gorges. But he also knew that was not how Liu Jinyuan and Liu Xiaochuan would see things. That's why even though his wife had been nagging him about the boat tour the whole time, he hadn't yet brought it up with his father.

The way Qinglin had so naturally suggested the tour and his father had been so quick to agree fit perfectly with Liu Xiao'an and his wife's plans. Liu Xiao'an thought that Qinglin must have been able to read his mind; he really knew exactly what to say. Back when they worked together, Liu Xiao'an felt it was always a pleasure to collaborate with Qinglin, but now that feeling was even stronger.

Qinglin made all the arrangements and saw them off on their cruise. He stood on the dock waving, and only after he watched the boat retreat into the distance did he and the driver finally started walking toward their cars.

Liu Jinyuan and Liu Xiao'an stood on the deck gazing back at Qinglin as the boat pulled away from the dock. Qinglin's silhouette and the way he walked felt so very familiar to Liu Jinyuan, but he couldn't figure out why he would be struck with such a feeling.

Liu Jinyuan turned to his son. "This young guy from your company is really something. He always leaves people with a good feeling. For some reason he also reminds me of someone I once knew . . . but I can't remember who."

"He's not such a young guy, Dad." Liu Xiao'an responded. "He's got to be in his early forties. He used to work for me when we first hired him; he was really young back then. But he's the kind of guy who knows how to get things done. Otherwise, how do you explain how quickly Xiaochuan promoted him."

"He knows what it means to be considerate of other people—that's a rare quality these days," said Liu Jinyuan.

"I should say that most kids who come from poor families learn how to read people better than others," Liu Xiao'an explained. "By the time they are Qinglin's age, it becomes second nature for them. When it comes to taking the right steps to change their fate, they work a lot harder than people like me."

Liu Jinyuan followed up with a somewhat disdainful tone. "I suppose your reason for not working hard is that your parents spoiled you, is that it?"

"Well, that's certainly one reason," Liu Xiao'an responded. "We can reap the benefits of others' hard work, right? So there is no need for us to work so hard. But more importantly, we don't know what it is like to be looked down on. Dad, you should actually thank *me* for choosing this path in life. That's because

I'm not trying to use your good name to climb the social ladder. I'm making things easy for you. Otherwise you'd have to go around calling in all kinds of favors on my behalf."

Liu Xiao'an smirked as he helped his father back to his cabin. Then the second Liu Jinyuan stepped into his cabin, it was as if he suddenly figured something out. He quickly asked, "What is Qinglin's last name? I kept forgetting to ask him."

"Wu," Liu Xiao'an responded. "I heard his father died a long time ago."

Liu Jinyuan felt as if something had struck him in the chest. He hastily asked, "His last name's Wu? What was his father's name? What did his father do?"

Liu Xiao'an laughed. "How would I know? I just heard that he was raised by his widowed mother. Now his mother is quite ill and doesn't even recognize people anymore. Anyway, you can ask him yourself next time you see him."

Liu Jinyuan didn't say anything further. He just thought, *So, his name is Wu. No wonder he looked so familiar. Could he be . . .* As he lay in bed, Liu Jinyuan searched his memories and became increasingly convinced that Qinglin was the person he thought he was; the way he walked, the way he talked, and even the feeling he gave people around him were so similar. But most importantly, when he was with Qinglin he had that same warm feeling he got when he was with that other person from his past. Could Qinglin really be his son?

Liu Jinyuan decided that once he got back home to Wuhan, he would find an opportunity to ask him face to face.

ARE YOU SURE YOU MET HIS FATHER?

Liu Jinyuan was in high spirits after returning home from his trip to Wanzhou.

It had been a long time since he retired, and for all that time hardly anyone paid him much attention. He often wondered if the sacrifices he had made were all in vain; no one seemed to care. But this trip to Wanzhou seemed to untangle that knot in his heart. He came to the deep realization that the choices he had made in life were indeed the right ones. Those things he had done early in life not only were still remembered but also had become, in the eyes of so many people, the stuff of legends. The people not only remembered but also continued to pass those stories down to their children and grandchildren. Even more important was that as he traveled through those mountain villages, he witnessed the peace and stability that he and his comrades had one day hoped to see. Almost everyone he met told him that since ancient times this region had been plagued by bandits, who year after year brought calamities down on them. Thanks to their efforts in suppressing the bandits, the people here had been able to live in peace for more than fifty years without having to worry about bandit attacks.

It was all worth it, Liu Jinyuan thought. *What do I have to complain about? Thinking about my old comrades who tragically sacrificed their lives there, and here I am in my eighties, still able to return to this place. I have no excuse to complain about anything. I should consider myself the luckiest person in the world.*

It was in this rather joyful state of mind that he began taking his morning walks again. After his walk each day he would go over to the shaved noodle shop for a bowl of Shanxi noodles. And he returned to his quiet and simple life.

The weather began to gradually grow cooler. Liu Xiaochuan called his father to invite him down south for the winter; it was already late autumn, and Wuhan was getting cold. Liu Jinyuan immediately replied, "Can you ask your friend Qinglin to accompany me? I have something I want to ask him."

Liu Xiaochuan laughed. "I don't see any problem. You can tell him more of your war stories. He can't get enough of them!"

Liu Jinyuan thought, *What the hell do you know!*

There was a chill in the air that morning. Liu Jinyuan put on a thin wool sweater and went out to the park, where he spent about ten minutes doing stretching exercises before starting for home. He was spending less and less time exercising. He used to spend at least half an hour at the park before going home, but lately he would just go through a few perfunctory exercises before heading back. He started to secretly mock himself—that it was as if the only reason he was going to the park was so that he could reward himself with a bowl of shaved noodles. Those noodles went a long way toward deepening his nostalgia for home. He even began to think about when he might go back to visit.

Then one day he unexpectedly ran into Old Qi again. The two of them were ecstatic to see each other.

Old Qi explained that he had gone back home to Shanxi for a while but returned as soon as it started to get too cold there. Liu Jinyuan responded, "It's cold here too."

"But there is still a lot of greenery here, so it doesn't feel that cold," explained Old Qi. "It's still warm enough here to go out for walks. My daughter also installed a heater in her apartment, so it's quite warm inside. Back in Shanxi it's too cold to even step outside."

Liu Jinyuan laughed. "These days us retired folks are like migratory birds: we all go south to spend the winters!"

Old Qi retorted, "I wouldn't say that . . ."

"But it's a luxury that our parents' generation certainly never got to enjoy," said Liu Jinyuan.

"Just think of the kind of society they lived in compared with us," said Old Qi. "Back then my parents had to wait a month for a letter to be delivered; today it takes only one second for an email to be sent, not to mention that we all have cell phones today. Back then there wasn't a single phone in our entire village; these days there isn't a young person around who doesn't have a cell phone. People back then could never have imagined any of this. Your son has his own car; my daughter-in-law told me they are also getting ready to buy a car in a few years. Just thinking about all these changes makes me nervous. In the old days, not even those rich landlords were able to enjoy such luxuries!"

"I was once telling my grandson about how we risked our lives to deliver intelligence messages during the war. Can you believe that my grandson responded by asking why we didn't just send a text? He even called me an idiot for not texting!" Liu Jinyuan complained.

Liu Jinyuan had told Old Qi that story before; it nevertheless cracked Old Qi up as if this were the first time he'd heard it. The shop boss came over with their noodles just as Liu Jinyuan was telling his story, and he laughed too. They all felt that kids today were too protected and immature. All three of them had started working real jobs like an adult around the age of ten.

The boss added, "You don't even have to talk about those fancy things like cell phones. Just sitting here in the big city enjoying a bowl of shaved noodles is a luxury we could never have imagined back then."

The three of them got so much pleasure from sitting together talking in their native dialect, laughing, and enjoying food from their hometown. Liu Jinyuan thought, *This is the definition of a happy life.* It was a happiness he could not have imagined back during the war years, but it had long surpassed his expectations. He ended up living a life that turned out damn well.

A light breeze was beginning to pick up just as they left the restaurant.

"Here in the south, it always starts to rain as soon as autumn comes," said Old Qi.

Liu Jinyuan saw a bicycle approaching and stepped aside to let it past them as he replied, "The best season here is always autumn. Like the saying goes, the autumn sky is clear and the . . ."

He was still in the middle of his sentence when that bicycle suddenly veered off course to avoid getting hit by a car. The bicycle sped straight toward Liu Jinyuan. He quickly jumped behind a tree to protect himself, and the bike zipped away.

Old Qi was shaken by the close call and quickly asked, "Brother Liu, are you okay?"

Liu Jinyuan was supporting his lower back with his hand. "That kid was really out of control! I barely had time to react. I think I pulled a muscle in my back."

Old Qi scooted over to help support Liu Jinyuan as he said, "See if you are able to walk. Or . . . should I just call a taxi for you?"

Liu Jinyuan tried to walk, and while it seemed okay at first, after a few steps he realized something was wrong. Old Qi continued to support him and asked, "Shall I take you to the hospital?"

"Let's not make a big deal about it," said Liu Jinyuan. "I'll be fine after I get some rest. Anyway, I don't live too far from here."

Old Qi suggested, "If you think you can make it home, we can walk slowly and I'll help you there. If you need to rest, we can find a place to sit down along the way. What do you say?"

Liu Jinyuan laughed. "It's no problem. I can make it home. No need to worry about me, but if you want to walk with me, I can show you where I live."

Old Qi helped support Liu Jinyuan all the way home, but by the time they arrived, Liu Xiao'an and his wife still hadn't returned from their morning community dance group. Liu Jinyuan lay down on the sofa as soon as they got inside and said, "I'll be fine after I get some rest."

Old Qi offered, "Shall I get you some tea?"

Liu Jinyuan nodded. "That would be great. Sorry to have to trouble you."

Old Qi brushed it off. "It's nothing! After all, we're from the same hometown."

After he poured Liu Jinyuan some tea, Old Qi sat down and said, "If you don't mind, I'll stay for a little while to keep you company until I'm sure you're okay."

"That would be great," replied Liu Jinyuan. "We can chat a bit. To tell you the truth, sometimes it's damn lonely being by myself all the time."

Some old photos were out on the table. Old Qi picked up a few of them to take a look. "Wearing your military uniform in these photos, you have quite the imposing look."

"Once upon a time I had my days where I was indeed quite imposing! But now that I'm old, what do I amount to? I can barely walk after trying to dodge a bicycle. I'm really useless," lamented Liu Jinyuan.

Looking at all the old photos, Old Qi asked, "Are you writing a memoir?"

"No . . . I have nothing better to do, so I started organizing those photos," replied Liu Jinyuan. "I actually just came back from Eastern Sichuan, which was where I once fought many battles."

A group photo on the table caught Old Qi's attention. Impulsively, he picked it up for a closer look.

"That's a photo of my old military buddies I served with when we were in Eastern Sichuan to suppress the bandits," explained Liu Jinyuan.

Old Qi suddenly pointed to one of the men in the photo, "Is this guy a doctor?"

Liu Jinyuan looked at him with a strange expression. "Not when that photo was taken, but he later started working at the hospital. Years later he became a great doctor."

Old Qi's voice quivered as he asked, "Was his surname Dong?"

Liu Jinyuan shook his head, "No, his last name was Wu. He was also from Shanxi like us. I met him in a village tucked away deep in the mountains and brought him with me."

Old Qi seemed a bit disappointed. "Hmm, his last name is Wu? And not Dong?"

"Why?" asked Liu Jinyuan. "Do you know him?"

"He really looks like my cousin," replied Old Qi. "The resemblance is stunning."

Liu Jinyuan laughed. "There are lots of people out there who resemble each other."

"Do you know anything about his family?" Old Qi asked. "Where does he work? Do you have his phone number?"

Liu Jinyuan responded, "Back when I first met him, his mother was already dead; he lived with his father, who collected medicinal herbs in the mountains. He learned a bit about traditional Chinese medicine from his father. That was just after the liberation of China. Later..."

Old Qi interrupted him. "Did you meet his father? Are you sure that was really his father?"

"That's right. I had a run-in with some bandits in the mountains. I ended up lost and wounded. I was lying on the ground when the father and son found me. They saved my life and I ended up staying with them for around two weeks while I recovered. Because I was still not fully healed when I left, the father insisted that his son accompany me out of the mountains. That's how I ended up bringing Wu Jiaming into the army. All that happened right after the liberation of China in 1949."

Old Qi looked even more disappointed. "Oh . . ."

"So what exactly happened to your cousin?" Liu Jinyuan asked.

"We lost touch during the war years. All the way until today, I still haven't been able to track him down," explained Old Qi.

"What year did you last see him?" Liu Jinyuan asked.

"That would have been 1948," replied Old Qi. "He was a medical school graduate. He spent many years in Shanghai and was a highly skilled doctor. He originally planned on coming home to open his own clinic. But I managed to intercept him on the road just before he got home and convinced him to turn back. Something terrible had happened. He came from a family of landlords. His parents were both killed; but just before his father died, he managed to utter the words 'Stop him.' I knew what he meant: he wanted me to stop my cousin from coming home."

Liu Jinyuan sighed. "That must have been difficult. But it's been so many years since you were separated. Things were also extremely chaotic back then. I'm afraid he must not have made it. Just think about how many years it's been since liberation: If he had survived, how could he not have attempted to find you or visit your family home? If he never returned, that pretty much says that he wasn't able to."

"No, what his family went through was a difficult situation. Even today nobody considers the deaths his family suffered as being unjust. With everyone in his family gone, how could he dare to return? By the way, what did you say the guy's name in the photo was?"

"His name was Wu Jiaming; *Jia* as in 'family' and *ming* as in 'name,'" responded Liu Jinyuan.

Old Qi leaned forward in shock. "Wait a second, the surname Wu is a homophone for 'without' . . . If we take a moment to put this all together, doesn't his name mean 'without a family, without a name'?"

Liu Jinyuan was taken aback, he had known Wu Jiaming for so many years, yet never once had he interpreted the meaning of his name like that. It took him a while to finally respond. Heaving a long sigh, he said, "Anyway, it's been many years since Jiaming died. He died in a bus accident. It was such a terrible loss."

Old Qi was visibly shaken by what he heard. He mumbled, "He's dead? He's really dead?"

As he spoke, Old Qi quickly got up to leave. He said that he'd come back in a few days with a photo of his cousin; he wanted to see whether Liu Jinyuan would be able to confirm that it was the same person he knew from the army.

Liu Jinyuan had a dream that night.

He dreamed of himself lying there in the mountains, being crushed by some heavy object and unable to move. Then from a vast white blanket of mist two people appeared to lift him up and carry him to a small wooden hut. Eventually he was able to see them clearly: one was Grandpa Wu and the other was his son, Wu Jiaming. He said, "So you saved me again." They didn't respond but instead just gazed intently at him with strange smiles. Those faces were different from each other. In fact, it was hard to find any similarities at all in their features. An explosive voice suddenly rang out in his ears, "Are you sure that was really his father?"

And then he woke up with a start from his dream.

That's when he began to really search his memory, carefully thinking back. As he tried to piece things together, he began to make connections.

He remembered being chased; then after being wounded he found himself lost; and finally, after losing a lot of blood, he passed out on the ground. When he awoke he was already inside a wooden hut. A father and son who lived deep in the mountain forest had saved him. They told him they grew medicinal herbs in the mountains and had lived there for many years. He stayed with them for almost half a month. Although he hadn't recovered, he was anxious to get back to his brigade and said he wanted to leave. Seeing that he was still not fully healed, the father told his son to accompany him out of the mountains to make sure he arrived safely. When he asked the son his name, the son hesitated momentarily before saying his name was Wu Jiaming. The expression on his face when he spoke his name suddenly reappeared before Liu Jinyuan.

He also remembered that once they left the mountain, Wu Jiaming almost never mentioned his father and never went back to visit him. Although Wu Jiaming knew something about Chinese medicine, he was actually much more knowledgeable when it came to Western medicine. With very little training he was able to perform surgeries in the army. When Liu Jinyuan later ran into the head of the hospital, the head even thanked him for bringing him such a great talent. Wu Jiaming was always so professional. Liu Jinyuan never gave any of this much thought back then; but thinking back now, he realized there were a lot of questions surrounding what happened. He wondered, *Were they really father and son?* So many details about Wu Jiaming's life now appeared quite suspicious.

As Liu Jinyuan mulled all this over, he decided he had better give Old Qi a call.

Just as Liu Jinyuan picked up the phone to call Old Qi, he discovered it was actually still dark outside. He didn't want to disturb Old Qi by calling too early and hung up the phone before dialing. That's when he felt that he needed to urinate. On his way to the bathroom he soiled himself. He got mad at himself, thinking, *After being a war hero my entire life, now I can't even hold my own piss?* He clasped the side of his bed to support himself but lost his footing, and his whole body went tumbling to the floor.

AND SO A LIFE COMES TO ITS END

Liu Xiao'an woke up to discover that his father's bedroom door was still closed. He wondered why his father hadn't gone out for his morning walk. He thought that perhaps his back was still sore, so he went in to check on him. As soon as he opened the door, he was shocked to find his father lying on the floor at the foot of his bed, his legs still partially propped up on the bed.

Liu Xiao'an cried out and frantically called for an ambulance.

When Liu Jinyuan arrived at the hospital, he was still unconscious. Everyone in the family rushed to the hospital to be by his side. Liu Jinyuan knew that this was one trench he would not be able to crawl out of. One look at the expression on the doctor's face, and the family also knew that Liu Jinyuan wasn't going to recover. One of the older family members sighed and cited the old superstition "If Yama doesn't come for you at the age of seventy-three or eighty-four, then it is time for you to take yourself to hell's gates."

One week later Liu Jinyuan took his final breath. It all happened so quickly. His three children were especially upset because they had always thought their father was in excellent health. They even thought he might make it to one hundred. As Liu Xiao'an wailed tearfully, all the grandchildren gave him a funny look. They thought death was natural for someone Liu Jinyuan's age. Why get so upset when death was just a necessary result of getting old? Liu Xiao'an regretted not taking his father to the doctor as soon as he learned that he had twisted his back. If Liu Jinyuan had been in the hospital, he probably never would have fallen out of bed. Liu Xiao'an also regretted that he had slept so soundly that night and hadn't bothered checking on his father even though he heard no noise coming from his room.

Liu Xiaochuan shed a few tears and patted his brother Xiao'an on the back. "We all know that you did your best. But some things can't be avoided." He went on, "Dad's apartment was a public housing unit provided by the army for his service; now that he's gone, we will have to return it. I'm sorry to have to trouble you and your wife to take care of all the details. Once this is taken care of, you can move into the house I bought for Dad down in Shenzhen."

The funeral service was held two days later, and family members came from all over to attend. Although they didn't have much time to prepare for the service, it was a rather impressive affair.

Not many of Liu Jinyuan's former comrades from his military days were still around, and of the few still alive, most of them weren't all that mobile. And yet they still came to his funeral—two of them even arrived in their wheelchairs. Liu Xiao'an and his siblings clearly knew them all and had informed them about what happened. One of the old men in a wheelchair said, "Your dad made out good. I've been confined to this wheelchair for thirty years, while your dad was still able to run around all over the place. There must have been at least three times where he made it out of death's door by the skin of his teeth. He had better luck than anybody, but I guess old Yama has turned the tables for this round . . ."

He probably never expected Liu Jinyuan's little grandson to jump in and say, "Who cares about turning the tables! My grandpa is now totally out of the game!"

Who could have imagined that without anything to do all day, that old man in the wheelchair actually learned to play video games from his grandson? He suddenly blurted out, "Well, he probably had a few more health bars in his program than most people!"

That joke almost made Liu Xiao'an go from crying to laughing. But after thinking about it, he conceded that the old man was right. Liu Xiao'an and his siblings had been consumed with sadness, and it was only then that they were able to lighten their mood.

Qinglin was in Shenzhen when he heard the news and was also shocked. He rushed back to Wuhan to attend the funeral. He never imagined that Liu Jinyuan would pass away so quickly. He approached Liu Xiaochuan with two bottles of Luzhou wine. "He must have sensed he was close to the end. How else do you explain his wanting to go on that recent trip to Eastern Sichuan?"

He then repeated to Xiaochuan what Liu Jinyuan had said to his old war buddies at White Horse Slope. Qinglin then handed Xiaochuan the two bottles of wine and said he hoped that Liu Jinyuan would be able to take these two bottles with him on his journey; it was a promise he had made to his old comrades.

"Thank you, Qinglin," said Liu Xiaochuan. "Thank you for being so considerate. If you hadn't told me, I would never have known that my father had expressed such a wish. Maybe he really did sense that this was coming . . . But I'm very happy that I was able to send him on that trip before he passed."

"I'm also very happy that I had the privilege to spend those final days with him on that journey," Qinglin added. "I learned a lot from him on that trip. And I'm not just trying to be polite by saying that."

Li Dongshui's grandson also came all the way from Eastern Sichuan to attend the funeral. He said that his father and grandfather were both unable to travel, but he was there to pay his respects and express his condolences on their behalf. As soon as Qinglin saw him, he was immediately reminded of Qierenlu, so he asked him to poke around to see what he could learn about the place when he went home for the Chinese New Year.

And so a life comes to its end.

As Qinglin was leaving the funeral parlor, he noticed Liu Jinyuan's youngest grandson talking excitedly about video games with the old man in a wheelchair. There was no trace of sadness on their faces. It was as if the person who died had absolutely nothing to do with them. It was almost as if death itself was just some inconsequential affair. *Life is indeed quite interesting*, Qinglin thought.

There was someone else at the funeral. He had a photograph in his pocket and was bawling as he bid farewell to Liu Jinyuan. "My brother, how could you have left us so soon? I never expected this. I was hoping to have another bowl of shaved noodles with you, and I wanted to show you that photo of my cousin. I wanted to find out whether my cousin was the same person as your former comrade from the military."

That was Old Qi. No one at the funeral knew him. He arrived quietly and left all alone.

9

HELL VIII: LET ME DIE!

Ding Zitao finally made it up to the eighth level. She had already been mentally and physically exhausted, but now she passed the point of exhaustion.

She was still surrounded by a thick blanket of darkness that extended in all directions and seemed to go on forever. Faint glitters of light appeared and disappeared. She couldn't refrain from sitting down, which is when she finally saw herself: there was Daiyun crying.

Daiyun's voice was like a sharp needle, piercing Ding Zitao's ears. Through her tears she screamed, "Let me die! Let me die!"

Old Wei and Ritchie were restraining Daiyun, trying their best to get her to calm down. But Daiyun continued to struggle; she thrashed around as if trying to throw herself against the wall.

Amid her screams another set of cries cut through the air even more distinctly. They were the sound of Ding Zi crying. He was in Huiyuan's arms, crying and kicking his little feet as he reached out toward Daiyun.

Little Tea's eyes were all red, as if she too had just been crying. She began to walk in circles around Daiyun, all the while repeating, "Miss, please don't, please don't do that. Ding Zi is still so young. How can he be without his mother? Miss, please don't . . ."

Meanwhile, Daiyun acted as if she were possessed, her voiced increasingly crazed. Old Wei and Ritchie could barely restrain her any longer.

There was commotion outside, and Lu Ziqiao entered. Little Tea quickly yelled, "Miss, the master is here! Miss, please try to calm down! Listen to what the master says."

But Daiyun didn't listen to anyone. She just went on screaming and crying as if possessed by a mad demon. Grandpa Lu Ziqiao walked right up to her and gave her two hard slaps across the face, triggering a sharp scream.

Then Daiyun stopped crying. She gazed at Grandpa Lu with a look of intense anger. Grandpa Lu admonished her, "You think you deserve to die? You're the only survivor left in the Hu family. Do you have any idea what your parents endured to save you? And now you want to die? Even if everyone in this room dies, you must carry on!"

"And what if I don't want to live?" blurted out Daiyun.

"I don't care if you don't want to live. You must go on living!" insisted Grandpa. "I don't care if you have to live like a wretched animal. You must do whatever it takes to survive. That is your fate!"

Through her tears, Daiyun insisted, "I'll kill myself then! You just watch!"

Grandpa responded, "They're not even interested in watching. Your death means nothing more to them than the death of a mangy dog. Your entire family is already dead. Do you really think anyone cares about you?"

Daiyun continued to struggle, but she barely had any energy left.

Grandpa maintained his stern expression. Gazing at her coldly, he said, "Old Wei, Ritchie, let her go. If she wants to die, let her die. Let's see if she can really pull it off."

Old Wei and Ritchie released their grip. Daiyun looked up at Grandpa; her eyes filled with desperation and anger as she slammed her head into the wall. Old Wei reached out to restrain her but instead only succeeded in ripping her shirt as her head again bashed into the wall.

The room filled with piercing shrieks. Little Tea screamed as she rushed over. Through her cries, she pleaded, "Master, please don't let her do that to herself."

Grandpa didn't bother going over to check on her; instead, he just coldly ordered Old Wei to find the doctor: "The doctor is still out back. Call him over and have him apply some Yunnan medicinal powder to her head wound."

Once Grandpa Lu left the room, the atmosphere immediately quieted down. Even Ding Zi stopped crying. The baby had no idea what had been taking place and just looked around the room curiously, grabbed Huiyuan's hairpin, and started cooing.

Ding Zitao was shocked by the scene she just witnessed. She couldn't help reaching up to touch her own forehead. She could feel that thin scar on her forehead and thought, *That's right, that was the day I got that scar.*

HELL IX: WHAT'S THE POINT OF THIS LIFE?

She was already at the ninth level. Ding Zitao silently counted to herself and was even happy that she was now halfway there. She had only to make it through another nine levels and she would be free. Would she then be able to see the sunlight again? The sunlight suddenly became so very important to her. She wondered, *How long has it been since I have seen the sun?*

And then she saw Old Wei.

Dusk was falling and the weather was cold and overcast. The sky was devoid of sunlight, and the north wind was howling. The sky began to turn gray early in the afternoon. Old Wei was walking at a brisk pace as he anxiously opened the gate. The caretaker was still wearing that same old gray cloth jacket that he had before. Ding Zitao remembered that he had a patch on the shoulder of that jacket. When she had asked him about it, Old Wei had laughed and explained that one of the bandits had made that hole with his knife, but thankfully he was uninjured. Later when the old master paid the bandits' ransom, securing his release, Old Wei always looked at that as his lucky jacket. Old Wei's laughter suddenly rang out in her ears.

Old Wei approached the door to Daiyun's room. He was about to knock but pulled his hand back. After a momentary hesitation, he turned and quickly walked toward another part of the compound where he stood before another door.

Ding Zitao could clearly make out the door to Grandpa Lu Ziqiao's study.

Grandpa Lu Ziqiao was inside practicing his calligraphy. Every winter he would prepare a whole series of couplets; then he would invite the villagers to pick the ones they liked most. Ding Zitao even noticed that the inkstone and brush he was using were the ones given to him by her father, Hu Ruyun. Hu Ruyun and Lu Ziqiao were old classmates, and now they were related thanks to their children's marriage. Whenever it was Grandpa Lu's birthday, her father would present him with paintings or a calligraphy set. Grandpa Lu Ziqiao even joked, "Since you moved out to the mountains, I suppose I'm the only one you know who would be interested in this stuff!" Her father laughed. "That's more or less the case."

Old Wei rushed into the room; the loud sound of the door slamming open made Lu Ziqiao's brushstroke waver. As soon as

Old Wei entered, he immediately prostrated himself, touching his head to the floor. His voice quivered as he spoke. "Master, something terrible has happened. Something so very terrible . . ."

Lu Ziqiao dropped his brush, but he didn't move a muscle. Without even turning to look at Old Wei, he asked, "What happened?" His voice was already shaking.

Old Wei responded, "Master, Daiyun's parents and everyone in her family are dead. They all died yesterday."

Lu Ziqiao stood to his feet and turned to look at Old Wei, who was practically crawling on the floor. There was a look of shock on Lu Ziqiao's face. Then he asked sharply, "How did they die?"

"I dare not say it," Old Wei said. "Master, there is no need for you to know the details. All you need to know is that they are no longer with us. Master, no matter what happens, you must protect Daiyun; if something happens to her, it will be the end of the Hu family line."

Lu Ziqiao collapsed into his chair. Then in a despondent voice he said, "Let's not tell anyone about it for now."

But the news nevertheless spread quickly. By nightfall everyone in the family knew what had happened.

Daiyun's mother lost her embroidery room back when the villagers first came to divvy up their property among themselves; by that time she had already handed over all her embroideries. The last embroidery workers to leave the property came to tell the Lu family what had happened: As soon as Daiyun's mother got the news that her son, Lingyun, had been beaten to death on the road, she lost the will to live. She kept saying it was all her fault that her son was dead. She tried to kill herself on two separate occasions. The first time she tried to hang herself, but Uncle's wife found her just in time and called the servants over to help save her. The second time she tried to jump down a well, but they were able to stop her. After all that, they still came for her and forced her to the struggle session. Who could ever have imagined that after the session went on for a while they would drag her off to be shot in the head? During the meeting someone said that from the beginning their names had been on the list of criminals to be executed. Daiyun's uncle's wife and sister-in-law were not on the list of those to be killed, but then they started acting up . . . no one could control them, so in the end the villagers just threw them into the river. By the time they disposed of them in the river, they were both already close to death.

The news absolutely crushed Daiyun. She cried so hard that she passed out. When she came to, she broke down again and continued crying until she fainted a second time. Lu Ziqiao predicted that Daiyun would have difficulty accepting what had happened, so it was a good thing that he'd had Old Wei call a doctor over to the house to take care of her. It was as if he knew this was coming.

Everyone in the family was crying along with Daiyun. Little Tea's throat grew hoarse from crying so much. Daiyun's mother had brought Little Tea's mother with her from Sichuan. She married here in Eastern Sichuan, but one year when she and her family were on their way home to visit her parents, there was a terrible flood. Their boat capsized, and Little Tea's parents both drowned. Little Tea managed to be saved, but she was now an orphan. Daiyun's mother could never stand to see Little Tea suffer at the hands of her grandparents and instead kept her with her own family, and Little Tea became Daiyun's little companion. At the time, Little Tea was only three years old; from then onward she would grow up with the Hu family. She practically looked at Daiyun's parents as her own mother and father. Originally Daiyun's mother had wanted to train Little Tea in embroidery so that she could be an embroidery worker, but Little Tea didn't want to leave Daiyun—they were inseparable. When

Daiyun married, Little Tea insisted on following her to the Lu household. Ultimately, Daiyun's parents had no choice but to accommodate Little Tea's request.

Little Ding Zi was, of course, too small to understand what was happening; he just continued fussing for his mother and Little Tea as usual. Little Tea did her best to hold him in one arm while consoling Daiyun with her other arm; meanwhile, she herself was so upset that she could no longer hold in the tears.

The entire household was thrown into a state of chaos. Old Wei was busy all night long taking care of various matters; by the next morning his face looked dark and ashen.

Lu Ziqiao was also unable to sleep that night. He spent much of the time pacing back and forth in his study, only occasionally sitting down to fiddle with his brushes and inkstones. All the brushes and inkstones on his desk were gifts from Hu Ruyun. He never imagined that his old friend would all of a sudden be labeled a criminal and then, just as suddenly, die a tragic death.

Daiyun didn't come out for breakfast that morning. According to Old Wei, the doctor suggested that she take some medicine and stay in bed. He was afraid she might have a nervous breakdown. After spending the previous day in a constant state of agitation and delirium, she had no physical strength left. The best thing for her at that moment was getting plenty of rest.

"If things continue on like this, who knows what will happen next," said Lu Ziqiao. "If they don't stop, they'll end up coming here to attack Daiyun. If it comes down to that, I'm afraid the situation will be difficult to resolve. Whether or not Daiyun wakes up, we need to find a way to get her out of here. We should have the driver take her into town in the horse cart. Hardly anyone there knows about our house. Huiyuan should go with her. Little Tea can take care of the baby and help get them set up there. If the situation continues to deteriorate, we'll have to find a way to get them to Shanghai. From there they can go to Hong Kong to find Zhongwen. Once the situation eases, they can all come back home. Ritchie should also go with them; he can rotate shifts with the caretaker Old Yang—but day and night, there should always be someone awake to keep guard."

Third Aunt demanded, "I want to go with them. I don't want to stay here in the countryside. You originally bought that house in town for me anyway. I'm familiar with the layout there. I can even help Little Tea care for Ding Zi."

"Are you kidding me?" Lu Ziqiao lost his temper. "What the hell are you proposing at a time like this?"

"I'll stay here," Huiyuan insisted. "I want to stay with my parents. Moreover, my family are revolutionaries. My dad's contributions to the revolution were recognized by the party, and they already promised not to lay a hand on him. It should be perfectly safe for me to stay at home. I don't want to go into town."

Lu Ziqiao flashed her a stern, admonishing gaze. "It's not your decision to make."

Third Aunt continued pressing, "If Huiyuan isn't going, I'll go in her place. What's more, if something should really happen, I'll be much better able to deal with it than her. Don't you think?"

Lu Ziqiao insisted, "Huiyuan must leave this place. She can return once everything has settled down."

But Huiyuan was also insistent. "Unless my parents are also going to be there, I'm not going. No matter what happens, I'm staying with my parents. As long as they are safe, I'll be fine. But I would be the most heartless daughter in the world if I were to abandon them when they needed me most."

Lu Ziqiao took a long hard look at Huiyuan and heaved a deep sigh. That's when Old Pan spoke up. "Master, but what will happen if we bring Daiyun into town now and she starts screaming and making a scene again when she wakes up? They also have the baby to deal with . . . I'm afraid that Little Tea and Ritchie wouldn't be able to handle all that."

Hearing that made Lu Ziqiao finally back down a bit. He took a moment to think before responding, "Okay, then let's put this off for a few days. We'll revisit this once Daiyun is behaving more like herself. But you all better listen: Daiyun is now the sole survivor from the Hu family. I, Lu Ziqiao, vow to do everything in my power to protect her life. You all need to keep a close eye on her to make sure she is safe."

All at the table nodded their heads, but no one spoke. There was a tension in the air that felt as if it would explode at any moment.

Ding Zitao had no memories of anything that transpired that day. Her heart was filled with such terrible pain. There was no way for her to describe what she was going through. She thought, *You all wanted me to stay alive and I did. But how is a life like this any different from death? And what does the fact that I am still alive have to do with the Hu family or the Lu family? They are all gone. Who even cares anymore if I am part of the Hu family or the Lu family? You all insisted on saving my life, but what's the point of that life when I don't even know who I am anymore?*

At this point Ding Zitao didn't have any more tears to cry. After all, tears are the most useless thing in the world.

HELL X: WHERE IS MY BROTHER?

Ding Zitao has now arrived at the tenth level. She had finally gotten a glimpse of hope, yet filling this hope was something that left her in despair. She now knew who she was and what she had been through. At the same time, she had forgotten who she was and why she was forced to go on living after experiencing all those things. She thought, *No wonder why Grandpa didn't hesitate when it came to ending his own life. Death was actually the easy way out.*

As Ding Zitao could see more, her feeling of pain receded. All those familiar faces and names began to jump out. But none of that shocked her anymore. When she heard the name Lingyun, she knew that was her brother. His full name was Hu Lingyun. That's right, Big Brother Lingyun, as she used to call him. But she still couldn't remember what he looked like.

Then everything started to come back to her with perfect clarity.

Ritchie walked all night. The first person he saw when he arrived from town was Little Tea. He told her that he had seen Brother Lingyun. Ritchie addressed him as Young Master as he always had, but Lingyun insisted he immediately stop calling him that; from now on he should just call him Brother Lingyun. Brother Lingyun was on his way to Zhong County to participate in a land reform meeting. But he was shocked to learn that his own parents were being targeted. He instead decided he had better rush home to bring his parents to town. He said to tell Daiyun not to worry. He would make sure their parents were safe. He also said that if Young Master Zhongwen didn't return, Daiyun should go to town to spend the Chinese New Year with her parents.

Hearing that made Little Tea a little less anxious. She immediately passed the message on to Daiyun.

The sky was dark and overcast when Old Wei said, "If the weather continues on like this, it will probably snow. This year there will be a lot of heavy snow. We should prepare all the supplies we need for the Lunar New Year before the snow comes. We don't want to run out of food after all the guests arrive."

Third Aunt explained that everyone was consumed with the land reform movement. People were in a state of constant anxiety.

No one was in the mood to celebrate or call on old friends as they would have done during normal times. Daiyun agreed with her. But Old Wei replied, "It doesn't matter if anyone comes or not. The Lu family still needs to prepare properly. The Lu family should never cut corners when it comes to the proper rites. This is a rule set by Master Lu."

In the middle of the night the old man responsible for feeding the Lus' stable of horses came looking for Old Wei. He said there was someone outside who yelled through the gate to tell Daiyun that her brother had been beaten to death the previous night. The old man threw on a jacket and rushed outside the horse stable to see who was there, but there was no trace of anyone outside. He felt scared and rushed over to deliver the message to Old Wei.

The news shocked Old Wei. He was the one who arranged a horse cart to take Ritchie into town so that Lingyun could pick up his parents and bring them there, where they would be safer. Ritchie came back to say that Lingyun had promised to immediately go home to pick up his parents. But he could have . . .

At the crack of dawn, Old Wei sought out Master Lu to tell him what had happened.

Lu Ziqiao was deeply disturbed by what he heard; Lingyun was the Hu family's only son. If something happened to him, his parents might not be able to recover from such a blow. Lu Ziqiao said, "I want you and Ritchie to immediately go out and ask around to see what you can learn. If something really did happen to Lingyun, keep quiet about it. Just come back and report to me first, and we'll figure out what to do next." Old Wei agreed and immediately set out with Ritchie.

Old Wei returned that afternoon with the news. He said, "Hu Lingyun had his dinner and then with one of his classmates rushed back to his parents' house in the countryside. He was still twenty *li* from home when he was ambushed on the road at the foot of the mountain. Lingyun and his classmate were both killed. Whoever killed them didn't want to leave any witnesses. We still don't know who killed them. But his family already knows that he was killed on his way home to them. No one brought their bodies home to Hu Shuidang; instead, they were just temporarily placed in the local temple. Should we tell Daiyun what happened?"

Lu Ziqiao heaved a long sigh. "Even his parents know what happened, so how could we not tell Daiyun? She will blame me if I don't tell her. Why don't you tell Little Tea and let her be the one to break the news to her. Don't tell her that I already know."

Little Tea learned what happened just before dinner. She waited until Daiyun finished her meal before sharing the horrific news about her brother. Daiyun immediately shut down. She ran into Grandma's room to find out if what Little Tea said was really true. There was a long silent pause before Grandpa Lu Ziqiao responded, "I also just heard the news from Old Wei. I never imagined such a thing could happen. According to Old Wei, your parents also know what happened."

That's when Daiyun's tears began to flow freely. Without a word, she just turned and left the room.

Lu Ziqiao called out, "Where are you going?"

Daiyun didn't respond. She just walked toward the front gate of the compound. Old Wei rushed over to stop her. "You can't go . . ." he insisted. "You can't go out at this hour."

Daiyun shrieked, "I want to see my brother!"

The sound of her scream startled everyone in the compound; they all ran into the courtyard to see what happened. They helped Old Wei to restrain her. Old Wei explained, "Young Master Lingyun was ambushed; we still haven't figured out who was responsible. But right now it isn't safe out there for us. Why don't we go tomorrow when it's light out?"

But Daiyun insisted, "I'm going tonight. I want to see my brother tonight."

The last one to come out into the courtyard was Lu Ziqiao. He sternly ordered, "Old Wei, close the gate. No one is permitted to leave the compound tonight." With that, he turned and went back inside.

Daiyun collapsed to the ground. She cried out, "Brother Lingyun, where are you? It's all my fault that you got killed. If I hadn't told you to go home to our parents, you would still be alive. My brother . . . Oh, heavens . . ."

That night, against the backdrop of Daiyun's heartbreak and tears, Lu Ziqiao wrote a letter instructing his son Lu Zhongwen to stay in Hong Kong for the time being and not to return home. He also instructed his younger son, Lu Shuwen, to quickly go to England to pursue his studies. He told them both that unless they received a handwritten letter from him instructing them otherwise, they should under no circumstances return.

10

QINGLIN BEGINS TO READ HIS FATHER'S JOURNALS

When the Lunar New Year arrived, Qinglin decided not to return to Shenzhen. His mother had been in a semicatatonic state for more than two years. Qinglin felt there was something increasingly mysterious about the way she just carried on in that vegetative state. Although she wore a blank look and you could barely tell if she was alive or dead, her heart kept on beating and she was still able to maintain her normal eating habits. The only abnormal thing was her breathing, which would occasionally seem strained. It was as if she were living in a world of her own creation; all her actions were such that only someone from that world of hers could possibly understand. Even though her dear son, Qinglin, was the most beloved person in her life, even he existed outside that world she created for herself.

Qinglin would sometimes think that perhaps this was all a necessary stage in his mother's life journey. Perhaps her destination was somewhere that other people were unable to go. She was simply living a different type of life. Maybe even now she was living a life that most common people would never be able to understand. But the most important thing was that as long as she kept breathing, his mother was still alive. Qinglin was at peace.

Thinking about it like that, Qinglin sometimes thought his mother wasn't sick at all; she was just existing in a kind of secret state. Whenever he spoke to his son on the phone, he would tell him that Grandma was like an alien: everything she did was filled with mystery. His son didn't believe him and wanted to fly out there to see for himself what was so strange and mysterious about his grandma. But Qinglin's wife immediately shot that idea down; she insisted that school was number one. She even made her son spend most of his vacation time studying.

Qinglin kept thinking that he should spend as much free time as possible with his mother. Perhaps she would suddenly recover. If she should one day snap out of her daze, he wanted to be the first person she saw. Qinglin knew that he would be the most powerful force to jog his mother's memory.

Donghong left on New Year's Eve to go back home to visit her parents for the Lunar New Year holiday. Before she left, she made a New Year's Eve dinner and prepared all the food for the coming holiday. She explained to Qinglin how important it was for her to visit her parents this holiday; she had been so busy taking care of Qinglin's mother that she hadn't been home for Lunar New Year in two years, which upset her parents. Yet she still felt guilty about leaving. Just before she left, she kept promising that she would be back right after the Lantern Festival on the fifteenth day of the new year.

Qinglin reassured her, "Don't worry. Just enjoy your time with your parents. I can handle things here. My friend will come over to visit on the third day of the new year. And my friend's nanny will stop by every night to help out with my mom. Everything will be okay."

Although it was winter and was chilly out, the weather actually wasn't too bad. The window in Qinglin's mother's room faced south, and the sunlight came in at an angle; and since the heat was also on, her room got very toasty. That afternoon Qinglin led his mother to sit over by the window and gently placed a wool blanket over her shoulders to keep her warm. His wife had bought that blanket as a Lunar New Year present. Although his wife refused to live under the same roof as her mother-in-law, she often made these little gestures to stay on Qinglin's good side. In most families, wives and mothers-in-law are natural enemies, but that tension is elevated when the mother-in-law worked her whole life as a nanny without any real social status. Qinglin had a good understanding of how selfish women could sometimes be. So he knew better than to raise objections about his wife's attitude toward his mother. That she was willing to occasionally make some kind gestures and allow her husband to spend the Lunar New Year with his mother was already a lot to ask for a woman like her. Qinglin figured it was unreasonable to expect anyone in this world to be completely devoid of selfishness.

Qinglin grabbed a book to read as he sat beside his mother. The trees and vegetation visible outside the window were already starting to shed their leaves. That empty plot of land that Qinglin had set aside for his mother to garden had been filled by Donghong with assorted vegetable plants. But now that winter had arrived, the vegetables were gone and Donghong had already turned up the soil. Qinglin looked down thinking about how wonderful it would be if his mother snapped out of her daze by spring and could finally tend to the garden herself. He even told her, "Mom, once you're better, perhaps you can plant some tomatoes in the garden. You know how much I love stir-fried tomatoes with scrambled eggs!"

Actually, Qinglin was a bigger fan of the scrambled eggs than of the tomatoes. He never really liked the sour taste of tomatoes. But his father used to force him to eat tomatoes for their nutritional value. When his father wasn't paying attention, his mother would always help him by secretly gobbling down his tomatoes for him. As his mind wandered back to those happy days, Qinglin thought about what a shame it was that his father was no longer with them. Had he still been alive, he would have been living with them in this big house and their life would have been perfect.

As he reminisced about the old days, Qinglin's thoughts wandered off to those notebooks his father kept. He went up to his bedroom and dragged that old trunk into his mother's room. He picked it up in front of his mother to show her and asked, "Mom, take a look. Do you remember this old leather trunk? It used to belong to Dad. I remember how much you loved Dad. You must remember this, don't you?"

His mother didn't respond. He figured that no matter what happened, he needed to understand his parents. Even if those journals contained things that might be difficult to face, he knew that would never change the love he felt for them.

And so that is how, on that mild winter's day during the Lunar New Year holiday, Qinglin came to start reading his father's old journals.

WAS FATHER'S REAL LAST NAME REALLY DONG?

Qinglin opened the first notebook.

It was a journal that began in summer 1948. The ink on the page was already beginning to fade, and the handwriting was not entirely clear. Qinglin wasn't used to reading his father's handwriting; he had previously seen only around a dozen or so handwritten messages his father had written to his mother. Somehow in the characters written on those pages of that journal, he was able to sense his father's presence. He knew that these were his father's words.

His father's entries were all quite short; some had dates, others did not. But most of them just recorded the year or the season along with some records he'd jotted down. Many of the entries seemed to have been written in haste. Qinglin figured that since his father was a doctor, writing long-form essays was probably not his strong point.

July 15, 1948

Going home. Crossed the Yellow River. Just thinking about seeing my parents again makes me so happy. Mom's eyesight isn't good; she always reaches out to caress my face. Her hands are coarse, but there is something special about her touch. Dad sent a letter encouraging me to open a clinic in town. He suggested it be the type of clinic that is equipped for surgery, like the ones those Western doctors run. They have already found the perfect building for me to use for the clinic. My cousin Little Qi can be my assistant. He grew up in his uncle's pharmacy and knows a lot about herbal medicine; he will be a good person to help out.

Chaos is all around us these days; it is hard for people to make a living everywhere. I should listen to my father. He said that our family, the Dong clan, has been fortunate to receive much help from people in the village over the years. If I were to come home and open a clinic, it would be a proper way to repay their kindness.

The local priest once arranged for my mom to be treated by a Western doctor, and ever since Mom's condition improved, my father started to have faith in Western medicine. Dad was right.

Chaos is all around us; it is difficult wherever you go. Perhaps it is indeed best to go home and be with my family.

The Dong clan? Qinglin was taken aback by that first entry. Could Dad's surname really have been Dong? How could that be?

Qinglin was confused. It was hard for him wrap his head around what he was reading, but he continued.

July 21

Terrible news came out of nowhere today! I don't want to go on living!

I ran into Little Qi at the foot of the mountain a few days ago. He said he had come especially to prevent me from going home. He was crying as he told me that my parents, sister, and grandparents were all dead. I can't go home. Going back would mean death. The last thing my father said before he died was "Stop him." No one understood what he meant, but Little Qi knew that Dad wanted him to stop me from going home.

My God! My God! My God! Why, why, why? Why did they all have to die? How can I go on alone now that they are all gone? Little Qi cried out through his tears; he told me that for the sake of my parents, I had to survive. He told me to go as far away as I could. The Dong family must preserve its family line.

He is right. But what does this mean? From now on I'll be someone without a family?

I'm so confused inside. I'm not sure how I got through these past few days. I'm staying at an inn tonight, but where will I stay tomorrow? Where else can I go?

This entry was quite short and the penmanship very sloppy. The sentences and paragraphs were choppy and fragmentary. In several spots on the page it looked as if the pen had actually penetrated the paper; there was also what looked like tear stains on the paper. Right there on the page you could see the pain and all the complex emotions the writer was going through.

Qinglin was stunned by what he had just read.

The entry was only a few lines of text, and yet it contained so much information. What could have happened that would result in the death of his father's entire family? Not only that, but whatever happened also prevented him from ever returning home for fear of death. Did it have to do with the bandits? Or the war? Perhaps someone in his family had a sworn enemy who was intent on carrying out a vendetta against them and decided to wipe out their entire family? Qinglin felt that his brain was about to short-circuit. And who was this person named Little Qi? His father's cousin? If so, why did his father never mentioned this person?

Qinglin grew scared. He stood up and began to pace around the room. He seemed to be struggling with whether he should keep reading. It was getting dark. Qinglin took his mother to the bathroom and then sat her on the rattan chair in her room. Qinglin asked her, "Mom, did you know that Dad's last name was really Dong? Did you know that?"

His mother didn't respond.

For their New Year's Eve dinner, it was just Qinglin and his mother. In addition to the food that Donghong had prepared before she left, Qinglin made his mother steamed eggs with garlic silver fish; he wanted to make sure his mother got enough nutrition. He was hoping a solid diet would help keep her immune system up and prevent her from coming down with any other illnesses. Perhaps one day she might even snap out of this trance she has been in for the last two years. When Qinglin had asked her doctor if that were a possibility, the doctor said they shouldn't rule anything out.

As Qinglin fed his mother the steamed eggs, he couldn't help feeling sad when he saw the way she robotically chewed the food. He tried talking to her. "Mom, I hope you don't make things so hard for me next year when we celebrate the New Year! You've got to get better. Didn't you promise me you'd prepare meat and fish for me every day? It's been so long since I've been able to enjoy your cooking."

As he spoke, tears flowed down Qinglin's face. But he didn't wipe them away; he just let them stream down.

During their New Year's Eve dinner that year, the taste that left the deepest impression on him was that of his own tears.

After dinner Qinglin turned on the television in the living room and sat his mother on the sofa so that she could watch. The New Year's Gala television special was on, and just as in years past, it filled the screen with a kaleidoscope of colors and sounds. But no matter how much laughter and how many joyful songs filled the air, nothing was able to capture even an ounce of his mother's attention. After sitting with his mother for a while, Qinglin, quite bored, self-mockingly said, "Well Mom, I guess your taste in television shows has improved! You're not even interested in the New Year's Gala anymore. Just like me . . . I always hated that show!"

As he mumbled to himself, he got up to turn the television off and helped his mother back to her bedroom.

Afterward he sat down, and as he picked up his father's diary to continue reading, he discovered that the next entry had been written when it jumped ahead to autumn.

Autumn 1948

I don't know what day it is. I'm now living deep in the mountains. It is late autumn.

There is a local hunter named Grandpa Wu who is a good man. He said that he found me lying on the rocks on his way back from collecting herbs. He couldn't tell if I was alive or dead. He tried to wake me up, but I didn't respond. Then he touched my forehead and discovered I had a high fever. Eventually I began to mutter nonsensical words and call out for my parents. So he carried me to his hut.

That's where I am now. Grandpa Wu said I was unconscious for at least five days. Once I woke up, I just lay there in bed for a few more days. I was fortunate that after collecting herbs for so many years, Grandpa Wu knew something about their medicinal properties. He said I would surely have died if he hadn't discovered me. In reality that is exactly what I wanted . . .

Grandpa Wu seemed to understand that. He said that living here in the mountains was pretty much like being dead.

Those words got to me. Since fate didn't kill you, you may as well stay alive.

Grandpa Wu suggested that I leave the mountain soon because once it got colder, the snow would block off all the roads and I would end up being stuck here. You had to get through five mountains to make it to the border of Henan.

But where could I go? When Grandpa Wu noticed I wasn't responding, he said I could stay here if I didn't have a place to go. Here in the mountains there wasn't anyone else around for miles. He was old and said he could use the company. Grandpa Wu asked me what my last name was. What last name? I just told him to call me whatever he wanted.

Grandpa Wu looked at me and said okay; then you can take my surname. I saved your life and gained a son. I'll take it as heaven's way of repaying me for my good deed.

That's it. I'm living like a dead man. Since I'm already dead, there shouldn't be anything I can't endure.

Still Late Autumn 1948

It must be November by now. I finally went outside today. Grandpa Wu's hut is actually inside a cave. Just outside the cave entrance are several small gardens surrounded by stones, and there are all kinds of vegetables and plants I have never seen before; they must be medicinal herbs. The gardens are all at the base of a cliff, so there is a natural water source that drips down from the mountain above. A bamboo tube catches some of the water trickling down from the mountain and redirects it to a stone mortar beside the entrance to the cave. Grandpa Wu has said that here in the mountains you will never starve as long as you live close to a water source. A few meters away from the cave entrance is a cliff. To enter the forest you need to follow the eighty-six stone steps that descend from the face of the mountain. Grandpa Wu has gone out hunting with his rifle. Winters here in the mountains last for a long time, so you need to prepare ample rations to get through the cold months. Since I just recovered, Grandpa Wu will not let me go with him. He says my legs still aren't strong enough to climb down the cliff.

* * *

There is a bit of sunlight this afternoon, so I sat down on a rock outside to get some sun; it felt so warm. I dare not think of what happened. As soon any of that crosses my mind, I feel numb, as if I am dead inside.

My pen is almost out of ink. I'll just record as much as I can.

* * *

It's raining today. These days are filled with boredom and helplessness. I miss my parents so much that my insides hurt. I never want to get out of bed in the morning. Perhaps just going to sleep forever is a good option for me.

Today Grandpa Wu told me it is already November. I'm not sure if he's right. He can't be sure either . . . but none of that is important anymore. It is already extremely cold here. According to Grandpa Wu, it will start snowing in a few days.

Winter 1948

It is probably December. Or perhaps we are already in the new year? Grandpa Wu asked, "What's the point of recording the date? What's really important is following the weather, staying well fed, and keeping warm." He's right.

* * *

It is snowing. Grandpa Wu and I shoveled all the snow outside the cave entrance and dumped it over the cliff. If we left it there to freeze, we could end up being stuck inside.

* * *

Bored. Grandpa Wu is teaching me how to identify different medical herbs. I recently told him that I have studied medicine. I also opened up to him about my family: I told him my parents are dead, so I don't want to go on living. He said that he had suspected something bad had happened to my family.

* * *

Today Grandpa Wu told me that he came out here to live in the mountains when he was forty-two years old. His parents were also persecuted to death. He killed the people responsible for murdering his parents and ran off with his wife and children. His children died on the road trying to escape. His wife stayed by his side during those first few years; back then they would often go into town to exchange furs, herbs, and other mountain products for various household items. But after his wife died, he didn't feel like going into town anymore. Instead, he would just ask those people who came up to the mountains each spring to pick medicinal herbs to bring him some salt and a few of the most basic necessities. He said he was used to living in the mountains. It was a quiet and peaceful way of life.

Now that I know his story, I think I could also get used to this way of life.

* * *

The snow on the ground is getting deep. When I look down from the top of the slope, the only thing I see is my trail of footprints in the snow. I caught a pheasant; as I was bringing it back to the cave, I caught a glimpse of the sadness in its eyes. I wanted to let it go but didn't want to return to Grandpa Wu empty-handed. In the end, I brought it back to the cave.

January 1949

I'm not sure, but I think it must be the new year already. Actually, no need to guess. Who cares what year it is, anyway? Time doesn't matter. That's just how it is.

* * *

The snow is heavy. We are practically snowed in, curled inside our hut. Just before he went to bed, Grandpa Wu told me it's good to take long rests when you have nothing better to do. What's a long rest? It's how we learn to gradually die.

Grandpa Wu was just trying to make a joke, but there was a resigned helplessness in his words. If you need to gradually practice to achieve a good death, then what about what happened to my parents?

They had worked hard their entire lives to do good, and yet they died horrible deaths.

I don't want to even think about it. Just thinking about it is too painful.

It was clear that Qinglin's father ran out of ink just as he got to this point. You could tell by the fact that the last few strokes in the word "painful" were barely visible.

Qinglin's tears were rushing down. He was wondering how this sad and lonely man could really be his father. How was it that as his son, he never knew anything about the deep pain his father had suffered? Qinglin had just started elementary school when his father died. His impression was always of that strong man lifting him up under his arms and tossing him into the air. They would both giggle and laugh. In Qinglin's mind's eye, his father always wore a joyful smile. So how could he have ever imagined the terrible things his father had experienced?

Qinglin was assaulted with a heart-wrenching pain unlike anything he had ever known; it was even worse than the pain he felt when his mother first fell ill.

He closed the diary and tried to calm down.

LIFE BEGINS AGAIN

The nanny of Qinglin's friend came over to help out. She was able to give his mother a bath, help her dress, and get her into bed. His mother was quite docile and went along with whatever the nanny told her to do. Once in bed, she immediately closed her eyes and went to sleep. She didn't make a sound.

Qinglin also took the opportunity to take a shower himself. Ever since he was a child, his mother made sure he washed himself on New Year's Eve to get ready for the new year. Back then there weren't great bathing facilities available to them; it was nothing like today, when Qinglin could take a shower every day. Their bathroom back then consisted of a tiny squat toilet. If you wanted to wash, you had to fill up a basin with hot water and bring it to your room. When it was cold out, his mother would even prepare a plastic bath screen to keep the heat from escaping. When Qinglin was growing up, they could wash only once per week.

Qinglin put on his bathrobe and went back into his mother's bedroom. He placed all his father's diaries back into the trunk and walked over to the bed. "Mom, did you know about Dad's background? Did you know that he had lived through such terrible things? How come you never told me? Don't tell me you didn't know either? Did he not even tell you?"

Although Qinglin kept asking his mother questions, he might as well have been talking to himself. Ding Zitao's eyes were closed, and her face showed not the slightest reaction to his words. Qinglin wasn't going to get any answers from her.

Qinglin heaved a deep sigh and picked up all the diaries and took them to his room.

It had already been dark for some time now. Outside, countless houses had their lights on, and you could occasionally hear music coming from the neighbors' homes, the sounds filling the night with a festive atmosphere. There was something warm and comfortable about the feeling in the air. Qinglin stood quietly in front of the window, but his heart was torn. He kept wondering what exactly had happened to his father.

He returned to the diaries.

Tucked between the pages at the end of one of the diaries were a few leaves. Qinglin didn't know anything about trees and wondered why his father had saved these leaves in his diary; perhaps there was something special about them. He picked up one of the leaves and held it up to the light. He carefully examined each leaf. But except for the veins of each leaf, he noticed nothing special.

On the last page of the diary was a rough sketch that was obviously drawn with a different pen. The lines seemed to be a map pointing out a route somewhere. But Qinglin had no idea what it was.

On the other side of that page were three words: "Life Begins Again!"

Right after committing that exclamation mark to paper, his father had gone over it a few more times with his pen to accentuate it in boldface. It was clear that his father had had a change of heart: he was no longer ready to give up on life. Seeing that affected Qinglin's mood. He wondered what could have happened that turned his father around. *Could that have been when he met my mother? Was it love that pulled him out of that dark place?*

Qinglin went through the notebooks until he found the second diary; it was dated 1950.

Counting on his fingers, Qinglin figured out that this was written a year and a half after his father's first diary entry. Could his father have been living in the mountains cut off from society for all that time? Had he now left the mountains?

1950

New Year's Eve of the Lunar New Year. I miss my family even more during the holidays.

I decided to continue writing my diary. Keeping a diary is something my father required me to do as soon as I was able to write. He told me to write down what I did each day and what I was feeling. He said that when I got old I'd be able to look back and see what I did. My father is now so very far away from me; the only thing he left me with is this habit of keeping a diary. So I decided to keep it up. Although I'm quite busy and unable to write every day, I can always make up for things I missed when I get some free time.

When did my rebirth begin?

It must have been from the day that I was up in the mountains and came upon Commissar Liu. I didn't even know he was a person at first—I actually thought he was a rock! He was lying on the ground when I tripped over him on a steep slope. I rolled several meters downhill. There was already snow on the ground, and he was buried under the snow. But Grandpa Wu recognized that what I tripped over was no rock. He yelled, "It's a person!"

The man was seriously injured and unconscious. As we were trying to revive him, Grandpa Wu said, "He's been shot! He must have been either a bandit or a soldier. Getting involved might bring us trouble." I said that we had to try to save him; otherwise, he wouldn't survive the night.

Grandpa Wu left it up to me. So we carried him back to our hut. He didn't wake up for several days. When he came to, he gazed at us suspiciously. Grandpa Wu told him to relax. He said, "You're here in the mountains, and we are the only ones around. We figure you must be a bandit or a soldier; since we saved your life, we are begging you not to cause us any trouble once you recover." The man didn't have enough strength to respond; he just lay there listening.

Over the next few days his condition began to turn around. He asked us if we had always been living here in the mountains. Grandpa Wu responded with an "Uh huh, been here for several decades." The man then asked, "Then you don't know that the world has changed?" Grandpa Wu said, "Why should I care about any of that? No matter what changes come, you still have to survive." The man told us that the Republic of China had fallen and old Chiang Kai-shek ran off to the small island of Taiwan. "This is now the era of the People's Republic of China. The Chinese Communist Party is in control, and Chairman Mao is the new leader. New China was established more than a month ago. I'm a political commissar with the People's Liberation Army. I was returning to my hometown to attend a funeral when bandits attacked me. They shot me, and I ended up lost in the mountains. Saving me is an act of merit that the new government will certainly thank you for."

I was shocked by the news. I quickly learned that there is indeed some truth to the old saying "Three days in a cave and the outside world already undergoes a thousand years of changes."

Grandpa Wu said that it didn't matter which party or army was in control. None of that affected our family.

I, on the other hand, was interested in hearing the man speak more about what was going on in the outside world. He obviously knew all about what had been happening. He asked me, "You're still so young. Is it really worth it to spend your whole life here in these mountains?" I told him that it was all worth it if I could stay alive. And if not, it didn't really matter anyway.

He didn't say anything else, but that night when we were getting ready to go to sleep, he suddenly said, "You've gone to school. I can tell from the refined way in which you hold yourself." I didn't know quite how to respond. That was when Grandpa Wu cut in to say, "Of course my kid went to school. He joined me here in the mountains only after his mother died."

He didn't respond to what Grandpa Wu said, but over the next several days he kept telling me what a waste it was for an educated person like me to live in the mountains. He said he wanted to take me away so that I could contribute to the construction of New China. According to him, it would be a democratic and peaceful society without war, hunger, or the rich exploiting the poor. Everyone would have access to an education and a job, and all would enjoy freedom and equality.

What he said made my heart race with excitement. He was describing everything I had ever hoped for my country to achieve one day.

When we were alone, Grandpa Wu encouraged me to leave with him. He thought the man was sincere and seemed to be speaking the truth. "Staying with me isn't a long-term solution,"

Grandpa Wu said. "If you are able to find a path forward for your future, you'll be doing something that would have made your parents proud."

The commissar stayed with us in the mountains for more than ten days, and even though he hadn't fully recovered, he was getting ready to leave. He asked me again if I would go with him. Grandpa Wu said, "Son, why don't you see him off. He's still recovering and will need someone to take care of him on the way. While you are there, you should check out what's happening in the world. If things look good, stay there. Otherwise, you can always come back here."

I was actually convinced that it was best for me to leave, but I was still torn about leaving Grandpa Wu all alone. He is quite old, and I didn't want to abandon him. Commissar Liu tried to convince Grandpa Wu to come with us. "You can settle down in town and let the government take care of you," he said. But Grandpa Wu insisted on staying; he said that he had grown accustomed to living in the mountains.

That's how I ended up leaving the mountain with Commissar Liu. He took me to his detachment, where I signed up for training and eventually became a member of the People's Liberation Army. I told everyone that my name was Wu Jiaming and that my father was a hermit living in the mountains collecting medicinal herbs and that my mother had passed away. Commissar Liu authenticated my story.

I am the only one who knows about the pain lurking beneath this name. I will never be able to go back to my real home, and I will never be able to ever utter my real name again. More important is that I must never let my future children know what happened in that place.

Tomorrow is the Chinese New Year. I'm going to swear to my parents that as they rest, I will do my best to make them proud.

So that's how my father got his name! And given the meaning of Wu Jiaming, it seemed that all along that name had contained a cryptic hint that he was a man without a family and without a name. Qinglin thought about how terrible it must have been for his father to live with that pain throughout his life.

No dates were included in that long passage. But from the handwriting and the color of the ink, Qinglin could tell that his father had written it in several different sittings. He must have written those entries under incredibly tense circumstances and just jotted what he could when he had time.

Going from being a mountain hermit to a soldier was a radical transition to make overnight. Qinglin wondered how his father adapted.

As he pondered that, Qinglin realized he had just vicariously experienced this transformation over the course of several hours, but for his father it actually spanned several years. Sometimes by extending the time frame you are able to see extremely complicated things from a more simple and natural perspective. Time has the great ability to clear things up; it can make the strongest emotions grow weak and transform great feats of determination into weak expressions of helplessness. This was something that Qinglin understood well.

> Spring 1950 (makeup entry)
> Heading south, heading south . . .
> My battalion received orders to go to Eastern Sichuan to suppress the bandits there; we have been furiously moving south ever since. We are not permitted to bring any personal items that weigh more than ten kilograms. It's a good thing that I don't really have any belongings. The mountains in the south are very different from those in the north. They are humid and clammy; it never stops raining, often going on for days. Even my blanket is wet.

***

Throughout our journey we have been staying at different villages, and the people have all been very welcoming; they have also been telling us all about the terrible things the bandits have done. I'm quite moved by their hospitality. We are careful not to disturb the local residents, and we always clean up after ourselves before we leave. I never realized the People's Liberation Army behaved like this. But now I understand that I made the right decision by leaving with Commissar Liu. I need to let everything that happened remain in the past and start a new life. This new life will have nothing to do with my previous life. I will never go back. I need to bury my past forever.

***

The bandits in Eastern Sichuan are extremely fierce. Before we left, our superior sent a mobilization order stating that among the three areas overrun by bandits in Hubei, Sichuan, and Guizhou, this part of Eastern Sichuan is the worst. There are also large numbers of rogue troops from the Nationalist army that have mingled with them. But no matter how fierce they may be, they will be no match for our army. We will be able to achieve true peace only after the forces of New China destroy them. Many of our troops have already fought in other wars. According to them, suppressing these thieves and bandits shouldn't even count as a real battle. But in reality, this is going to be a very difficult campaign because the bandits have a strategic advantage.

I should write about Commissar Liu, who led me out of the mountains.

Political Commissar Liu was in the military division. He arranged for me to join the same company that he had led during the Battle of Huaihai. He even gave the company leader special instructions to look after me. He said to him, "I've got a little gift for you—Little Wu is a doctor. He knows how to treat all kinds of minor illnesses and injuries, like snake bites or poison insect bites." The company commander was ecstatic and let me join the company; my fellow soldiers also welcomed me. Everyone in my company feels rather uneasy about what awaits them in those southern mountain forests.

On our way south I kept my eyes open for various medicinal plants and would pick them along the way. There were some herbs that I would boil on rainy days to help remove the various toxins that come with excessive humidity. That is something that Grandpa Wu had taught me. Very few of us got sick on the way there. The company commander even appointed two soldiers to help me carry all the herbal medicines I had collected. He said we would need them later.

Commissar Liu has a lot of experience when it comes to how to attack the mountain strongholds where the bandits have their bases. So we all follow his lead. One day we were launching an attack on Horse Mouth Cave. The opening to the cave was high up on a cliff, and the rock walls were extremely thick. With the added support from former Nationalist soldiers, the bandits appeared to have the entrance well guarded. We expended a lot of time and effort trying to capture the cave, but nothing worked. That's when Commissar Liu came to inspect the situation. He started off by getting as close as he could to the cave's entrance to survey the area, then he went to the fortified village nearby to ask the locals a few questions. That night he ordered us to pile up a stack of straw just under the cave's entrance and set the straw ablaze at dawn. At first I thought it was a faulty plan because the fire would never be able to penetrate the thick stone walls. I suspect the bandits guarding the cave entrance thought the same thing; they saw us piling up the straw and just laughed at us. But come morning we lit the fire and the wind also picked up. The wind blew the thick smoke and scattered flames directly into the mouth of the cave. It took only a few minutes before we started hearing people coughing and screaming inside the cave. Half an hour later Commissar Liu had his men put out the fire; then we all covered our faces with damp handkerchiefs and launched a full frontal attack. The smoke had rendered the soldiers inside the cave unable to fight, and we quickly overcame them. We were able to capture all the bandits inside the cave alive. As it turns out, Commissar Liu had discovered several patches of dried peppers near the mouth of the cave. Once a patch of the peppers caught fire, all the other patches quickly burned. The local villagers had told Commissar Liu that the morning wind usually blows toward the cave. Commissar Liu said that even if those Sichuan bandits had an appetite for spicy food, they certainly wouldn't be able to take the burning sensation when the pungent scent of those same hot peppers assaulted their noses and eyes. It was truly a stroke of genius that was hard not to admire.

The entries in the diary continued in starts and stops, and most of them still did not list the date. The handwriting was sloppy, as if the entries had been written in a hurry. Some sections were even written in pencil, and the characters were so faded that they were barely discernable.

And yet Qinglin was so excited that his hands were trembling.

The campaign to suppress the bandits in Eastern Sichuan? He had just heard about that battle during his recent trip to Eastern Sichuan. And this Commissar Liu—that is exactly how all the locals in Eastern Sichuan referred to Liu Jinyuan. Could it really be . . . was Liu Jinyuan really Commissar Liu? He had clearly heard the name Horse Mouth Cave before. And burning hot peppers? My God, was that the trick that Li Dongshui taught Liu Jinyuan? They had talked about that when they reunited, and they actually got a good laugh out of that.

This discovery came as such a shock. Could his father really have been one of Liu Jinyuan's subordinates?

Qinglin immediately called Liu Xiaochuan, but his phone was turned off. His boss must have turned off his phone to avoid calls during the holiday. Instead, Qinglin tried to call Liu Xiao'an, but his phone was off too. That's when Qinglin remembered that this was the first Chinese New Year since the Liu brothers had lost their father; perhaps they both needed some peace and quiet to mourn. Qinglin also realized that this probably wasn't the kind of thing he should discuss with them over the phone. It would be best to wait a few days to tell them in person.

> Late Summer 1950 (makeup entry)
>
> We never imagined that the bandits would be such fierce opponents. We recently used a comblike formation, which almost succeeded in eliminating them. But then the U.S. imperialists' invasion of North Korea broke out, inspiring a new wave of rumors. People were saying that we were on the verge of World War III and that the Nationalists' return was imminent. All those rumors worked in the bandits' favor, and they were able to gain strength.
>
> * * *
>
> A few days ago a team charged with collecting grain taxes was attacked by the bandits and we were ordered to save them. The team leader was tragically killed, and two female comrades were seriously injured. There were no doctors anywhere in the area, so the company commander ordered me to go help them. I did my best to administer emergency care: I employed Western medical treatment methods but also used Chinese medicinal herbs. I even personally accompanied the injured to the field hospital set up in the military district. I provided the attending doctor with a full summary of their injuries before going off to get some rest. I had

been on the road with them all night and was so exhausted that I could barely keep my eyes open.

I never expected to be awakened by Commissar Liu. One of the injured female comrades happened to be his wife. Commissar Liu told me, "You saved me, and now you saved my wife. My entire family owes you a great debt."

* * *

The head of the field hospital told Commissar Liu that I took exactly the right steps and that if I hadn't been there to provide emergency care during that crucial period shortly after the commissioner's wife was injured, she probably wouldn't have survived. I told no one that I had actually studied to be a surgeon in Shanghai. The surgeons at Jen Chi Hospital where I did my residency always used to compliment me on my skills. Commissar Liu said I was his company's self-trained medical specialist, but the head of the hospital could tell I had received formal training. He pulled me aside and said, "I know that you know more about medicine than simple herbal remedies. Right now our field hospital is extremely short staffed; might you be willing to stay here and work with us at the hospital?" I hesitated for a moment, but I also thought it would be a shame to waste all that specialized training I had received. So I told him I would stay. The head of the hospital immediately requested Commissar Liu's permission to requisition me. Commissar Liu agreed on the spot. Later the head had to send multiple requests to his superiors to complete the transfer, for which I was always grateful.

* * *

Fate is a strange thing. Somehow, just like that, I became a doctor. And, just like that, I returned to the field I had originally been trained in. My life underwent such a massive change, and it all happened over the course of just three days. I returned to my company to collect my luggage and then showed up for work at the field hospital. Everyone in the entire company saw me off when I left. They even started to address me as "Dr. Wu." What a moving scene! I had served with them for less than six months, and yet we had established a bond that would last a lifetime.

Since I was familiar with the condition of the two female patients I had brought to the hospital, I was assigned to help with their treatment. The head of the hospital had studied medicine in the West and was an excellent doctor. There is much I can still learn from him. He asked if I was a member of the Chinese Communist Party, and I told him not yet. But when Commissar Liu brought me into the army, he advised me to work hard so that I could one day join the party. He told me he was a member (he had joined during the War of Resistance against Japan). He also promised to help me advance.

* * *

Working in the hospital proved to be more difficult than being a soldier. Soldiers have a lot of down time when not engaged in fighting, whereas here we are busy all the time. But staying busy like this suits me; somehow it gives me a sense of inner peace.

* * *

It took around ten days for the two female patients to begin their recovery. Commissar Liu's wife has a no-nonsense personality; she told me to call her Sister Peng. That is what everyone calls her, she said. The other woman was Little Yan, a graduate of a teaching college. She was generous and easygoing. Perhaps because I saved them, we three became quite close over a very short period of time; I am much closer to the two of them than to most other people. Once they get back to normal, I'm sure we'll be even better friends. What we have is a special bond, a kind of life-death friendship.

* * *

Little Yan's injury was much worse than that of Sister Peng. She was shot three times: one bullet went through a lung, another pierced her shoulder, and the third went through her leg and damaged the bone.

By the time Sister Peng was discharged from the hospital, Little Yan was still unable to stand up by herself. I offered to carry her on my back so that she could go to the door to see Sister Peng off, but even the slightest movement causes her great pain. Besides, Sister Peng insisted that Little Yan stay in bed. They both cried profusely as they said goodbye.

* * *

Little Yan is the kind of person who can't bear being idle. As soon as she was able to get out of bed, she started hobbling around the hospital doing various chores. Sometimes she would teach wounded soldiers how to read and write. There is something quite adorable about her.

* * *

I've been struck with a strange feeling these days. Whenever I go to the sick ward and don't see Little Yan, I'm left feeling utterly lost. Is this love?

* * *

We truly are in love. Thank God! I thought I was incapable of love, but the sound of her laughing and singing still manages to melt my heart. She's four years younger than I am and originally from Chengdu. I also sense that she fell for me before I even realized I was in love with her.

* * *

I kept thinking that I would never again experience true happiness in this life. But when Little Yan appeared in my life, I realized there is still a chance for me.

* * *

Tonight I held her in my arms. I kissed her. My feeling of joy somehow made me scared. She told me how content she felt with me. Is God trying to make up for all the suffering I was forced to endure?

* * *

The bandits continue to retreat. The army continues to advance toward the border with Guizhou.

* * *

By November the bandits in Eastern Sichuan have been almost entirely eliminated. Life is finally more peaceful. I am staying with the hospital director at the field hospital in the military zone; meanwhile, Commissar Liu is leading his company north to Korea. I'm not sure when I will see him again. Little Yan and I saw the commissar off, and just before he left he asked us to be sure to look after Sister Peng. He also made us promise to be there for her and his son if he should be killed on the front lines. His son is already around three years old.

I fought to hold back the tears, but Little Yan broke down and cried. Commissar Liu is the greatest and most selfless member of the Communist Party that I have ever met.

Seeing the two of us so broken up, Commissar Liu immediately began laughing and tried to reassure us. "Don't worry," he said. "I'm a tough one. They can't kill me! I've got to come back to serve as the master of ceremonies at your wedding!" "That's a promise," we replied. We told him we would be waiting for him to return to officiate our wedding.

Reading these diary entries was an extremely moving experience for Qinglin. At the same time, he was disappointed to learn that his father's first love was not his mother. But then he seemed to remember his mother once telling him that they had married in the early 1960s. His father was such a talented man and had a good job as a doctor. Without his parents around, he didn't need anyone to approve his relationship. So what would have brought him to marry a woman like Qinglin's mother? She could barely read and wasn't very cultured... there was something strange about it.

This long string of entries was without dates, but Qinglin could tell the entries were written on and off at different times. In some cases, there seemed to be long gaps of time between entries.

THE WOMAN WITH NO NAME

It was already late in the night. Qinglin was about to go to sleep, intending to continue reading the next morning; but just as he was about to close the diary, he caught sight of his name. In that sloppy mix of paragraphs written alternately in pen and pencil, the characters "Qinglin" jumped out like a pair of nails shooting into his eyes. The exhaustion he had felt just moments earlier immediately disappeared. *What does this mean?* Qinglin wondered. *After all, that diary entry predates my birth by more than ten years... How could my name appear there?*

> Spring 1952
>
> Today is the first day of spring, but the weather remains cold. Little Yan went to Chengdu to visit her parents and hasn't returned yet. Before she left, she promised she would tell her parents about our relationship. I suggested we get engaged as soon as her parents agreed. She laughed and said I was being too anxious, but she accepted my proposal. My God! I wish we could fly off together into the heavens!
>
> I really had a stabbing sensation in my chest when I saw her off. And ever since she left, missing her has become the only thing I think about every day!

***

I miss Little Yan more and more each day. Being unable to see her is really a form of torture for me.

***

Several doctors and I have spent the past few days in the countryside seeing patients. The villagers here have been extremely welcoming and are happy we are here. They have been letting us stay in the nicest homes of each village we visit. Today it was raining, and a few villagers came by around dusk carrying a patient. She was barely breathing. The villagers said they had fished her out of the Eternal Valley River. They didn't know who she was, but they thought she might still be alive. They were afraid she wouldn't make it to the hospital in town, so they just brought her to us.

I immediately began to administer emergency treatment. Her body was covered in bruises, and in multiple parts of her body the skin had peeled away. I suspect these injuries were the result of her body getting tossed against the rocks in the river. She also had a fractured leg. She was unconscious but would occasionally mutter the words "Ding Zi." After treating her with basic first aid, I decided her injuries were too severe and unless she was quickly transferred to a real hospital, she didn't have a great chance of pulling through. My colleagues agreed with my assessment, so that night we called the hospital director, found a car, and drove all night to get her to the hospital.

We didn't know who she was or where she was from, so we just referred to her as Wu Mingshi, or "Woman with No Name." As soon as I committed the characters to paper, I was taken aback to realize that Wu Mingshi sounded quite similar to my name, Wu Jiaming.

***

Little Yan finally returned with the news that her parents had agreed to let us marry. I am mad with joy. From now on I will finally have a family again. We decided to get officially engaged on National Day.

Such a wonderful future awaits! And I'll have my own family. I've already decided what to name my future children: if it's a girl, I'll call her Puzhen; and if a boy, Qinglin. Those names come from combining the characters in my parents' names: My father's name was Puqing, and my mother's name was Zhenlin. This is the only way I know how to commemorate them.

Qinglin finally understood the origin of his name. All his life his parents never explained the meaning of his name to him. Since Qinglin had been quite small when his father was still alive, the topic never came up. Later when he asked his mother, she just said that the name was chosen by his father. Qinglin always liked his name, as it had a certain poetic flavor about it. But he never dug any deeper into its meaning.

Now he finally understood that his grandparents were in some way living on through his life; that he was part of his father's deepest and most profound commemoration of his parents. *My grandfather's name was Dong Puqing; my grandmother's name was Zhenlin.* In that moment, Qinglin, who had never before had a real conception about what a family meant, could feel the deep connection he had with a group of people from a specific place in a dark history. He felt as if an artery now connected him to a massive family network that he was unable to touch and unable to see. His bloodline was now connected, and blood was beginning to flow.

Qinglin could actually feel the blood in his body surging. He skipped ahead to the last page in the diary.

The entry was still under the heading from spring 1952. His mother's name appeared as well. And Qinglin felt that he was getting closer to unraveling the mystery.

I asked Dr. Jiang to cover my shift so that Little Yan and I could go call on Sister Peng. We had to walk nearly fifteen kilometers to get there.

We informed Sister Peng that we hoped to get engaged in autumn and hold the wedding as soon as Commissar Liu returned to China. Sister Peng was ecstatic and promised to arrange a proper ceremony for us. Commissar Liu had been my mentor, and Little Yan and Sister Peng had an unusual bond after enduring a traumatic experience together. In some ways, they were like our family.

Sister Peng said that a comrade who had just returned from North Korea brought her a letter from Commissar Liu. He said that everything was going okay. Life there was difficult, but he had managed to avoid getting injured.

We were all so happy and relieved to hear that news.

Sister Peng asked me if I planned to go up to the mountains to invite my father to attend the wedding. Her suggestion took me off guard—she was referring to Grandpa Wu. I just told her that the mountain region where he lived was too remote and I couldn't afford the time to get away from the hospital to pick him up in person; nor would I feel good about his making the trip alone. It would be better to take Little Yan up to the mountain to meet him sometime after the wedding. Sister Peng thought what I said made sense.

Where was Grandpa Wu? Was he still up in the mountains? I also miss him, but he doesn't have a proper address, and we don't have any common acquaintances, so there is no way for me to even write him a letter. But after the wedding I should really make time to visit him. If it hadn't been for him, I would never have been able to achieve all this. I should really go visit the old man. I should take care of him and give him a proper funeral one day when he passes away.

* * *

Yesterday when I got back to the hospital from our visit to Sister Peng, I saw a few villagers place a wooden stretcher on a horse-drawn cart. I went over to ask what they were doing; they said that the woman without a name that they had saved had died, and they were here to collect the body.

The hospital director had told me that he didn't think she would make it, so the news didn't come as a surprise. But I couldn't refrain from going over to examine her body. That was when I noticed that one of her fingers was twitching. That faint twitch was the only sign of life I needed to see. I immediately stopped them.

"You can't take her away," I said. "She's still alive."

* * *

The woman managed to pull through. This is really something to celebrate! One of our nurses, Miss He, told me that she heard the patient sighing in the middle of the night; the next morning she saw her eyelids fluttering. It has been nearly two weeks since the villagers first brought her to the hospital.

All her flesh wounds have scabbed over, but her fractured leg remains in a plaster cast. Whenever she is awake, she seems completely terrified. No matter who speaks to her, she always responds to our questions with a confused look. Miss He asked her basic questions such as Which village are you from? How old are you? and What's your name?; but the patient just says she doesn't know.

She seems to be suffering from a case of amnesia. Based on her accent, we suspect she is from this area.

* * *

There was quite a lot of commotion at the hospital today. As it turns out, all the noise was coming from the sick ward where the woman with no name was staying. It seems that the other patients in her room discovered that she had amnesia and told her she had been pulled out of the Eternal Valley River. They asked her to recall what happened at the river to see if she could remember anything. She concentrated on trying to remember, but after a few minutes she broke down. Her hysterical screams terrified everyone around her. I injected her with a sedative and asked the others not to press her anymore. I told them she would need more time before trying to remember what happened.

* * *

This afternoon I needed to fill out a medical history for the woman with no name. When I asked her what her name was, she had absolutely no idea. Then I followed up by asking her, "Are you sure you can't remember anything?" and for some reason that immediately filled her with terror. It was terrible to see her in such a state.

No matter what, I need to find a name for her. I remember that she would repeatedly call out the name Ding Zi when she was delirious; that name must be extremely important to her. It must be connected with her past. I suggested to her that we use that as part of her name, and she nodded in agreement. The peach tree outside her window was in full bloom, so I wrote down the name Ding Zitao, adding the word *tao* for "peach." I told her, "As you try to remember your name, let's use this one for the time being, okay?" She nodded in agreement.

She doesn't speak much, but there is this strange sad look in her eyes—it runs very deep. Her amnesia seems to be the result of a terrible shock. Perhaps the shock was so powerful that she is instinctively refusing to remember the past? If that is really the case, I'm in some way jealous of her.

* * *

Little Yan has to work tonight, so I took an extra shift at the hospital. As I was studying Ding Zitao's chart, a strange idea suddenly came to me. Looking at her hands, feet, and overall complexion, I'm having an increasingly difficult time believing that she came from a poor family. I could even tell that her fingernails had once been nicely manicured. So just who is she?

I know that land reform policies are being carried out in these parts. Could what happened to her be related to that?

Just thinking about that look in her eyes wounds me like a sharp dagger stabbing me in the heart and dredging up all the pain I have hidden inside. Could she be like me, another lost soul in this world?

Qinglin was shocked by how his mother first appeared in the diary. So that is how she and his father first met. She had been saved from the brink of death and ended up with amnesia. No wonder his father always used to tell him, "Be sure to take good care of your mother when you grow up. She has had a hard life. She is a very special person."

But when he wrote, "Could what happened to her be related to that?" what exactly did his father mean?

What could have occurred in this world to have driven both his parents to such a terrible place? Not only that, but consciously or unconsciously both of them buried the truth about what happened so deep that no one around them even knew.

That's when the name Qierenlu stubbornly jumped back into his head. According to what his father had written, his mother clearly came from somewhere in Eastern Sichuan. So what was the significance of Qierenlu to her? Was that where she grew up? Qierenlu, or "Cottage of Tolerance," was owned by the Hu family. Hu was a landlord who collected paintings and calligraphy, and Qinglin's mother had said her father used to enjoy painting "Guiguzi Descends the Mountain" patterns. Could all this just be a coincidence?

Qinglin leapt out of his chair.

QINGLIN'S SHOCK

Qinglin truly felt as if in a state of shock. His father's experience had left him utterly stunned. He could never have imagined that his parents had experienced such difficulties in their lives. Even more difficult to comprehend was the extent they went to bury the past, a past buried so deep that no one in the world knew what had happened to them. It was as if they had completely buried the first half of their lives, neatly tucking it away behind the mundane events of daily life. But the way they hid their past also spoke to a deep mistrust they must have harbored toward everyone around them.

They must have felt so lonely and vulnerable living as individuals in an age when everything around them was constantly changing. Just one gentle wind from the era might completely capsize the little boat that was their life.

Qinglin couldn't wait to finish reading his father's diary.

> Summer 1952
>
> Commissar Liu ended up getting injured in Korea and was sent home. Thank goodness that although it was a serious injury, at no point was his life in jeopardy. However, these new wounds combined with some of his older injuries have really taken a toll on his health. For an extended period he needed to spend most of his time resting and trying to recover. I boiled him a medicinal brew that included ginseng, milk vetch root, and various mountain herbs to help bolster his energy. He said the brew really helped improve both his physical and his mental state. His words also gave me some comfort.
>
> * * *
>
> Little Yan came to the hospital this morning, but I was busy with patients in the sick ward. A soldier had just been admitted

with extreme stomach pain; I suspected it was appendicitis. After the hospital director concurred with my diagnosis, we decided to operate that afternoon. Meanwhile, Little Yan was reading a book in my office as she was waiting for me. When I was finished, we went out to lunch. She told me that one of her colleagues was going to give us a new set of sheets for a wedding present, so we didn't have to buy any. She looked a bit embarrassed as she spoke; I always love it when she makes that expression.

When Little Yan left, she forgot to take her beloved copy of *Dream of the Red Chamber*, left in my office.

Once I got out of surgery later that afternoon, I returned to my office to discover Ding Zitao inside. She was standing in front of my desk reading that copy of *Dream of the Red Chamber*. I even heard her faintly utter the name of one of the characters, Daiyu. I was quite surprised. How was she able to read a difficult book like this?

She hurriedly put the book down as soon as she saw me walk in.

I thought for a second before carefully warning her, "Don't let anyone know you can read. I think it will probably be better for you if they don't know." She looked at me in confusion; at first she nodded, and then she shook her head. I tried to clarify: "I don't want to make you uncomfortable; I'm just concerned that people in the hospital will talk and spread rumors. No one knows anything about your background, which makes it easy for people to make assumptions."

This time she intently nodded her head.

I asked her why she had come to my office, and she explained that now that she was better, she was hoping to get a job working here in the hospital.

I promised to help her. But after she left, I felt my heart pounding.

Just who was this woman who could read *Dream of the Red Chamber*? Just today the hospital director came to see me to emphasize the importance of getting to the bottom of who she really was. If we can't figure it out, we should probably send her to a government institution to take her in. I'm wondering if I should share my suspicions with the director. What might be the consequences if I tell him?

I'm perplexed. For some reason I have a strange feeling that she and I both underwent something similar.

* * *

I arranged for Ding Zitao to help out with various odds and ends around the hospital. The nurses all said she was extremely hardworking and detail oriented. But she wasn't much of a talker and didn't interact much with others. She seemed to be consumed with her own thoughts and showed no real ambition. She was, in short, an odd woman. With her having such a mysterious background, I think it better not to keep her here in the hospital long term.

Hearing what the nurses said about her also made me uneasy.

I saw Sister Peng this afternoon. She brought her son to the hospital for a checkup and looked exhausted. She mentioned how they were looking to hire a new nanny to replace the last one. Commissar Liu is still recovering from his injuries, and she has to take care of both her son and her husband. It is a lot for her.

* * *

I suddenly came up with an idea today: instead of having Ding Zitao help out around the hospital, I should recommend her for the nanny job with Commissar Liu's family. It will probably be much better for her to be with the Liu family than here at the hospital. I went straight to the office and called Commissar Liu. I told him I had seen Sister Peng at the hospital and explained how hard things were for her. "How can you manage without a nanny?" I asked. Commissar Liu said that he was also anxious about finding a new nanny. He explained they had recently hired one, but she lasted only two days. Sister Peng didn't like how much she talked. She was telling everyone all about their business, so they let her go. I told him, "I've got a woman here looking for a job. She is quite meticulous, extremely neat, and not a big talker." Commissar Liu responded, "That sounds like exactly the kind of person we need, especially if she isn't talking all the time!" I suggested, "Why don't I send her over so that you can see if she works out? If she isn't a good fit, you can look for someone else." Commissar Liu agreed.

* * *

In the afternoon I told Ding Zitao about the nanny job at Commissar Liu's house. I earnestly explained to her how her life would be more simple if she could get a job there. No one there would be scrutinizing her background. She looked at me with a perplexed expression, as if thinking about what I said. I just told her, "If you do a good job, you can stay with them long term. Commissar Liu and Sister Peng will be able to protect you." She gazed at me suspiciously, but in the end she ultimately nodded in agreement. "I'll take your advice," she said.

I heaved a deep sigh of relief. If my guess is correct, this will be the best way to ensure her safety.

Qinglin was speechless.

It was now clear, Commissar Liu was indeed Liu Jinyuan. That would also mean that Liu Xiao'an and Liu Xiaochuan must also know his mother. He couldn't believe that his mother had been working for the Liu family for all those years.

The fact that his mother had to work as a housekeeper and a nanny was always something that made Qinglin feel bad. At the same time, he realized that without his father's income and given his mother's lack of education and training, if she hadn't worked as a nanny, they would have had no other source of income. But he had thought that his mother started working as a nanny only after his father died. He had never realized that she had started when she was still young. Qinglin now knew that his mother had been a nanny for most of her adult life.

He remembered his father having someone he used to work under with the last name of Liu. When Qinglin was a child, his father would occasionally take him to his house. The Liu family lived close to Hongshan Park. The tomb of the martyr Shi Yang in Hongshan Park left quite an impression on young Qinglin. Sitting on the steps in the park, his father would tell him stories about Shi Yang and Lin Xiangqian. That was also the first time that Qinglin learned that there are people in this world called lawyers. They help both good people and bad people. They speak from the perspective of the other side.

After his father's death, Qinglin and his mother had no further contact with the Liu family. He never knew that his mother had been their nanny, and he certainly never drew any connections between his father and Liu Jinyuan or the Liu sons.

He now finally had someone he could ask about his parents' past, but that person had just passed away.

Qinglin was struck with the pangs of painful regret; in particular he regretted not having read his father's diaries earlier. He had just let those diaries sit there for two full years without reading them. If he had read them earlier, he could have understood so much more when he went to Eastern Sichuan with Liu Jinyuan. But now he realized he had been so close to one of the most important people in his father's life and never even realized it.

I WANT TO MARRY DING ZITAO

Qinglin continued reading his father's hastily composed diary. There were lots of passages about medicine and his relationship with patients; there were also long sections about various political movements and things related to his first wife, Little Yan; but Qinglin quickly skimmed through those sections. Qinglin learned that his father's first wife died during the winter of 1960. She had a cold that developed into pneumonia. Her condition was further complicated by her previous lung injury, and the doctors were ultimately unable to save her. They never had any children together.

It was in spring 1963 that Qinglin's father was transferred to Wuhan. He started out at the Institute for Chinese Medicine but later applied for a job at the hospital. All the while, a few people attempted to set him up with a girlfriend; in all, he met with three different women, but none was to his liking. Only when he went to call on his former superior, Liu Jinyuan, did he finally became reunited with Qinglin's mother.

Qinglin went back to reading the diary.

Summer 1963

It's been hard to get any free time, so I made sure to take some time off to visit Commissar Liu and Sister Peng. I never imagined I'd find myself living in the same city with them. I feel as if I have a family again.

I also saw her again—Ding Zitao. She is the woman saved from drowning in the Eternal Valley River. She has been working as a nanny for Commissar Liu's family for more than a decade. My heart began to pound the moment I laid eyes on her. When I saw how peaceful her life was—all this time no one ever asked about her past—I feel that I made the right decision all those years ago. She must be well into her thirties by now.

Commissar Liu and Sister Peng felt terrible when they heard about what happened to Little Yan, but they were also concerned about how I have been getting on by myself. Commissar Liu seems to think it would be a good idea for Ding Zitao and me to start a new family together. While he was clearly jumping the gun by insinuating that we would be a good couple, the suggestion actually made my heart race. I'm not sure why, but I always felt as if I had some strange connection with this woman. For some reason, I know that I'm the only one in the world who remembers what happened to her. I'm the only one who senses her mysterious past and understands that there is something quite complicated about where she came from.

***

As I tried to get to sleep, Ding Zitao's face kept to appearing before me. I recollected how I thought we were a pair of lost souls in this world. And we are. She is all alone. But aren't I too? I called Commissar Liu the next day and told him how much I had been wanting to start a family; I really want to marry Ding Zitao.

Autumn 1963

We married on National Day. It was a simple ceremony, which basically consisted of a dinner with the Liu family. When we left, Ding Zitao seemed quite comfortable and content. I could tell that deep down she really liked me. That made me happy. But for me the most important thing is being able to love and protect her.

When we arrived home, she asked me why I wanted to marry her. I told her I would never have been able to rest at ease had she married anyone else. She seemed to understand what I was implying. Then after thinking about it for a while, she said that she too wouldn't have been able to rest easy had I married someone else. That let me know just how smart she was. I told her that from now on, together both of us would have a family again.

But then an inexplicable fear gripped her. I have no idea where that sense of terror came from. No matter how I tried to console her, she just couldn't shake it. This is something I never experienced with Little Yan. But I entered this relationship fully prepared. No matter who she is, I am committed to fully embracing every part of her, treasuring her, and protecting her.

* * *

The morning after we married, Zitao got up to make me breakfast—she is a great cook. I told her that our new life has begun. Everything is wonderful now, and it will only get better in the future.

That look of terror from the night before has largely dissipated. Could she have been worried that I would discover she wasn't a virgin? That was something I had actually anticipated. Although she may have fallen into the river by accident, I am sure there must be a reason for her to resist remembering what happened. Her doctor said that she must have suffered a terrible trauma that triggered her memory loss. Whenever she starts to remember, her mind dredges up all kinds of terrible pain. Her natural instinct is always to resist the past. But what exactly was it that happened to her? No one knows. Perhaps she tried to drown herself in the river after someone tried to rape her. Or she may have had an affair, and members of her clan threw her in the river as punishment. Or perhaps there is another reason: Was it that like me, she just couldn't bear to go on living after her family was killed?

I don't know . . .

Spring 1964

Zitao told me she is pregnant. My God, this is such important news for me. Mom and Dad, the Dong family line finally has a successor. But I need to apologize to you because this child will not bear the surname Dong. The blood that will run through his veins will be that of the Dong family, but he will have no connection to the Dongs. No matter what happens, even after the child grows up, I will never tell him where his real ancestral home is located. Nor will I let him use my real surname. I hope he never learns about any of this. He will be a native of Wuhan; his surname will be Wu; that should be enough. Things will be easier for him if I am able to keep everything simple.

* * *

Zitao's pregnancy is starting to show. But the anxiety she has been fighting is getting worse. She is suspicious of everything around her and thinks there are demons trying to hurt her. My only recourse has been to take her to a psychologist. The doctor has said the anxiety is possibly the result of trauma she experienced before losing her memory. Something about that trauma is continuing to cause her pain. Perhaps if she can remember what happened, she might be treatable. But Zitao resists any attempt to remember. I'm careful not to force her for fear that if she were to remember, the shock of what happened would prove too much for her to bear. So I think a more natural approach is better.

* * *

Every day I take Zitao on walks by the church. One time as we stood before the statue of Our Lady of Lourdes, Zitao asked me who the figure was. I told her that's what people used to ask the figure. They would all ask, "Who are you?" Our Lady would respond, "I am the Immaculate Conception." Zitao didn't understand what that meant, so I explained the whole story to her. I even used my finger to draw some of the characters on the palm of her hand. She asked what "Immaculate Conception" meant. I told her it meant there was no such thing as original sin. I then told her that here in this world both she and I are the Immaculate Conception. She seemed to partially understand what I was saying, and she remembered it. The following day she told me that as she gazed at the statue of Our Lady of Lourdes, she quietly recited the words "I am the Immaculate Conception" and felt at peace.

That's great. I need her to be at peace.

***

Zitao's due date is getting close, and she is eating a lot more these days. I've been making sure she doesn't do any housework. I want her to know how much I appreciate everything she does and how much I love her. I'm almost forty and now finally about to become a father. I told Zitao that it doesn't matter if the baby is a boy or a girl; I will love the child with all my heart. I told her I want to name the baby Qinglin if a boy and Puzhen if a girl. Zitao agrees. But that sense of anxiety and terror troubles her and has grown steadily worse as she gets closer to giving birth. She is now constantly in an abnormal state. I'm really worried. I used to be able to calm her down a bit by gently consoling her. But these days that doesn't work. I don't know what she is afraid of, but I'm also quite depressed these days.

***

Zitao started to go into labor. I immediately rushed her to the hospital. Her whole body was trembling. There is simply no way to describe the terror that has taken control of her. No matter what I say to console her, she is simply unable to control herself. When her obstetrician, Dr. Li, a trusted colleague of mine, saw how terrified she was, he allowed me to stay by her side during the delivery. I never imagined that would lead to her getting even more upset. She started to yell and insisted that I leave the room.

Thank goodness the delivery went smoothly. It was a boy, and I was so excited by the news. Qinglin, my dear Qinglin, from now on that's what Daddy will call you.

***

As we were leaving the hospital, Dr. Li pulled me aside to tell me that Qinglin wasn't her first child. She had clearly given birth to a baby before. He asked me if I knew that. I quickly responded, "I know. She was previously married. So was I."

In reality, though, I was absolutely floored by this news. My first thought was, Where is her child? Could Zitao have been thrown into the river for getting pregnant out of wedlock? Or perhaps her husband was the target of a political purge? I just can't figure it out. Could her fear be the result of her being worried that I might discover that she already had a child? Could she be unconsciously worried that others would discover something about her past?

I spent a lot of time with her that night. I told her that no matter what happens, no matter who she is, I will always love her and protect her. She is now the mother of my son.

As I spoke to her, she just continued to stare at me. I have no idea if that was a look of trust or a look of guarded caution.

Zitao didn't want to remember the past, and I also started to hope that she wouldn't remember. That's also how I feel about my own past. I just want time to gradually bury the past. We now have each other, and a son; my salary is enough to support the three of us. It will be fine if we can just live a quiet simple life together.

Winter 1965

Qinglin is growing fast. He is now running around all over the place. Seeing him learning to talk and say basic words like "baba" and "mama" is such a joy. Ever since we married, Zitao would have paralyzing spells of fear and anxiety, but since Qinglin's birth she seems to be much better. She has been behaving like a normal wife and mother. She seems very happy just taking care of the baby and maintaining the household. It's now been a long time since I've seen any trace of her anxiety.

I wonder if our son gets the credit for turning her around. The power of motherly love is indeed incredible. Perhaps motherhood is the only thing that can cure everything.

Summer 1966

The political movements are growing increasingly intense. When I was first transferred, Commissar Liu wrote an affidavit for me. The document certified that my father had collected medicinal herbs in the mountains and that we were classified as poor peasants; it also stated that we had contributed to the revolution. My experience in the army also helped protect me. In the end, I was able to easily avoid trouble; in fact, I have become one of the more politically progressive people in the courtyard complex where we live.

I must protect myself. Protecting myself is the only way to protect Zitao and Qinglin.

Spring 1967

Things seem to be getting more chaotic here in Wuhan. I'm getting increasingly worried.

I can't continue keeping records in my diary. I had better find a place to hide all my notebooks.

New Year's Day 1968

Qinglin, my son, I'm writing this for you. By the time you read this, I will certainly be dead. There are some secrets contained here. I have written them down only out of habit as I recorded details from my everyday life, but I didn't do so with the intention of letting you know everything. Understand that keeping all this from you is in some way in your best interest. Right now I don't want to destroy these notebooks. I just hope that by the time you read them, you will be an adult. Perhaps by then the world will have changed. I hope by then you won't need to feel scared by the words contained in these diaries.

What I want to tell you is this: I hope you never investigate what happened to our family. There is no reason for you to know where our real home is located. There is no one else left in our family, so leaving all that out is actually a good thing. Never go back, and never let our descendants know about that place. This is the decision I have made. Your surname is Wu, you were born in Wuhan and grew up there—that's all you need to know.

As for your mother's past, I'm afraid how to approach that is something you will need to decide for yourself. She was pulled out of the Eternal Valley River in Eastern Sichuan. Perhaps she still has living relatives (you might even have a big brother or a big sister). I don't want you to be all alone after your mother and I are gone. If you are able to locate your mother's relatives, you will at least have someone to rely on and provide you with the kind of warmth you can get only from family.

Of course, if you decide to seek them out, you should do so only after your mother has passed away. I'm afraid if you really do find her relatives or uncover things about her past, you might stir up your mother's memories. It is very possible that she won't be able to withstand the shock of that. So as long as she is alive, I ask you not to do anything that might trigger her memories.

My son, I also want to implore you, if you start digging into the past and begin to uncover horrific stories, please just give up. There are many unknowns in this world. It's okay to leave some questions unanswered.

Being able to forget the past is a coping mechanism that we use to get through life. It is something that has enabled your mother and me to live a peaceful life for so many years. Forgetting can help relieve the burden you might feel and make things easier as you look toward the future.

My hope for you is that you will be able to live a happy, carefree life. By the time we get to your children's generation, all this will be in the distant past and there won't be the slightest trace that any of this ever happened.

The diaries stopped after spring 1967. It was only on New Year's Day, in 1968, that Qinglin's father recorded this passage, which was addressed directly to Qinglin. The only thing contained in his remaining diaries were his research notes about various case studies regarding different diseases and illnesses.

By then it was nearly dawn. Yet Qinglin didn't feel at all tired. The facts regarding his mother's background were left dangling, and his father's final message left him deeply confused.

CONJECTURES AND SUSPICIONS

Qinglin couldn't contain his own curiosity.

He still felt that he needed to know what happened to his parents. He was afraid he might forget all the fleeting thoughts running through his mind and decided to turn on his computer and there jot down what he was thinking. He then cataloged the most important content from his father's diary, thus keeping an electronic record. As he made his notes, he also compiled a list of his own conjectures and suspicions.

CONJECTURES

1. Commissar Liu, who led my father from the mountain, is the same person as Liu Jinyuan.
2. Father attended medical school in Shanghai. He studied Western medicine. As a result of some kind of family misfortune (What exactly happened? Was it related to the land reform movement?), he was forced to run away and escape to somewhere deep in the mountains. While there he saved Commissar Liu's life and, after heeding his advice, joined the army. He then followed the army to Eastern Sichuan, where he joined

the campaign to eliminate the bandits. While in Eastern Sichuan he was transferred to the army's field hospital.
3. Mother was originally from Eastern Sichuan. She was saved when people pulled her body out of the Eternal Valley River in Eastern Sichuan. She was later saved again by Father. The day they discovered her in the river is recorded as her birthday. Her name was given to her by my father. Ding Zi is a name she called out when she was unconscious.
4. Mother suffered from amnesia, and no one knows anything about her past. It doesn't seem as if she came from a poor family, since she was literate and had read *Dream of the Red Chamber*. (Note: She also has knowledge of things like the poetry of Xie Tiao and artworks on the theme "Guiguzi Descends the Mountain.")
5. She got a job as a nanny with the Liu family after Father recommended her. According to Father's diary, he made this arrangement as a way of protecting her.

SUSPICIONS

1. Mother once mentioned the word "Qierenlu," which is the name of a building in the village of Hu Shuidang in Eastern Sichuan. Qierenlu contained many rare books. Could this place be related to mother?
2. The Hu family had a son named Hu Lingyun. He attended university in Chongqing. He was killed. He had a younger sister.
3. Mother's name Ding Zitao was given to her by my father, which means her original surname was likely not Ding. Could her real surname be Hu?
4. Before my mother lost her memory, there was a person or place in her life named Ding Zi that she must have had an intimate relationship with.

5. Perhaps Mother's father was an artist. At the very least he knew how to paint "Guiguzi Descends the Mountain."
6. Mother likely did not come from a poor family. She said that the lining of her comforter was deep red and not purple. Did she go to school?
7. She has a talent for embroidery. She was once hit on the back by a buttstock.
8. She had someone from her parents' house who stayed with her named Little Tea (perhaps a servant?).

As Qinglin wrote and organized these clues, he became increasingly convinced that a more complicated story lay behind all this. This story had been buried by his mother's broken memories and his father's vague assumptions and intentional efforts to cover up the past.

Qinglin wondered whether he should try to answer all these questions. Even though his father had hoped he would leave the past alone, Qinglin thought this was something he should know. He had the right to figure out what had happened to both his father and his mother.

After repeatedly reviewing everything, he realized there were very few clues to go on for his father's side. His surname was Dong. His grandparents' names were Dong Puqing and Dong Zhenlin. His father also had a cousin named Little Qi. All the other details seemed extremely murky. The entire area north of the Yellow River was so vast that Qinglin had no idea where to even start looking. His father had intentionally tried to prevent himself from remembering what happened and was also intent on not letting others know what happened. Indeed, he completely cut himself off from the life he had once lived.

In contrast, there seemed to be quite a few obvious clues concerning his mother's situation. The most important thing was that his mother was still alive. He thought that if he were able to understand more about his mother's past and even find some of her relatives, perhaps that might provide the key to wake her up. Because his mother had always been a strong woman, Qinglin was confident she would be able to handle whatever details might emerge about her past. *After all, what year is it now? We should be able to brush off all those things that happened so far back in the past*—at least that is what Qinglin thought.

He gradually became clear about what he needed to investigate:

1. The Eternal Valley River is a site I should be able to find.
2. I must attempt to locate anyone who once lived at Hu Shuidang.
3. What is the geographic relationship between the Eternal Valley River and Hu Shuidang?
4. Could there be anything that Liu Xiao'an or Liu Xiaochuan knows about my mother's situation? For instance, did anyone ever show up at the Liu house looking for her? Or did she ever accidentally reveal anything that might be a clue? (Since it was so many years ago and they were both little kids back then, I suspect they won't remember anything.)
5. The most important thing is to find someone who knows something about Qierenlu.

As soon as he typed all that on his computer, Qinglin heaved a deep sigh.

11

HELL XI: I HAVE TO FIND MY BROTHER

Ding Zitao now knew that no one from her family survived and that most of the people in her husband's family were also killed. Of everyone from Sanzhitang, she was the sole survivor. She wondered what the point was for her to go on living. *They are all dead; even Ding Zi is dead. How can I ever face Lu Zhongwen?*

Just thinking about that made her back ache; it hurt so much. The person who hit her with his buttstock had used so much force. She actually knew who it was that hit her; in fact, she knew him very well.

His image appeared for a moment.

That's right, she knew him well. He lived in one of the rear buildings on their property. They even used to play together when they were young. His family hated her family. The reason for that hatred stemmed from the fact that his family had once been very rich, but after the death of his grandfather, the next generation couldn't agree on how to divvy up his property; they fought bitterly, which brought about the family's decline. Almost all his family's land ended up sold off, as were all their houses. In the end, all the remaining family members were forced to squeeze into the small house in the rear courtyard where their servants used to live.

Ding Zitao remembered that her father was not the one who bought their land. Her father had said, "I don't care how cheap their land is, I don't want it. There is a deep enmity between our two families that goes back several generations. I refuse to carry on that cycle of hatred and enmity." But Ding Zitao thought her father was wrong: as long as her family was better off than theirs, the cycle of enmity was certain to carry on.

As she thought about these things, her back pain got even worse. She had no choice but to lie down.

As Ding Zitao lay down, she saw Daiyun lying there on the bed. She was bawling uncontrollably.

Little Tea ran over to say, "Miss, please do your best to bear it just a little longer. The doctor is almost here."

Daiyun continued to cry loudly. Little Tea asked, "Miss, what happened? Are the master and his wife okay?"

Through her tears Daiyun managed to answer, "How could they be okay? What happened to them was terrible. They didn't do anything wrong. Why did they have to be treated like that?"

Little Tea grew anxious. "Miss, I'm not following what you're saying. Can you explain what happened? I owe a great debt of gratitude to your parents for raising me. What happened to them?"

Daiyun refused to explain. It was then that Old Wei arrived with a doctor. Little Tea gently pulled open Daiyun's shirt to reveal her back; she couldn't help but cry out, "Heavens! Miss, what happened?"

Daiyun's entire back appeared red and swollen to the point that it was almost purple; the bruise extended all the way up her back and across her shoulder blades. The doctor asked, "What did he hit you with?"

"A rifle," she replied, "the buttstock of a rifle."

"How could he have hit you so hard?" the doctor asked.

"I don't know..." As Daiyun responded, she once again broke down in tears.

Grandpa Lu Ziqiao, standing outside the door, asked, "Do we need to take her to the doctor in town?"

The doctor answered, "I don't think that is necessary. I'll apply medicine to her injury, and it should heal up in a few days."

Little Tea used a blanket to cover Daiyun's chest as the doctor applied the medicine to her back. As it was a bit chilly, Little Tea said she would prepare the brazier.

That night Old Wei brought Grandpa Lu Ziqiao and his wife over to check on her. Daiyun said, "I have to go into town first thing tomorrow morning. I'll need the horse cart to take me there."

Grandma was upset. "You're going into town? Who is going to take care of my grandson, Ding Zi?"

Daiyun responded, "I'll take him with me. Little Tea will go too."

"What are you planning to do there in town?" Grandpa asked.

"I'm going to find my brother, Lingyun," replied Daiyun. "I need to tell him to fetch our parents and bring them to town. They can't take many more of those beatings from the struggle sessions against them."

"What's the point of his going back?" asked Grandpa. "If he goes, won't he just be causing trouble for himself?"

"My dad will find a way to get through this. After all, Lingyun is a cadre now," replied Daiyun.

"I first met your father when we were still young," said Grandpa. "He was still a student then and looked at everything from the perspective of how it could benefit him, but he had terrible judgment. I don't think you should leave this compound. It is much safer if you stay here. And let's not forget that you are injured."

"And what about my parents?" Daiyun asked. "They're the only reason I was able to escape. They came up with the idea of having me publicly sever my relationship with them at the denunciation meeting. Otherwise, I wouldn't have gotten away."

Shocked, Little Tea yelled at Daiyun, "Miss, you've gone mad!"

Daiyun began to cry. "I even hit them. Second Mother gave me a terrible tongue-lashing for that."

Little Tea was even more taken aback by what she was hearing. "Miss, how could you do that?"

"I was just doing what my parents told me to do," Daiyun tearfully explained.

Grandpa Lu Ziqiao remained silent for a spell before he said, "This has all been very hard on your parents. They came up with a strategy that involved sacrificing themselves in order to save you. Being cursed by their very own daughter in front of those crowds of people was worth it to them if it could protect you. I owe them a great debt of gratitude. If you absolutely insist on finding your brother, you shouldn't be the one to go. You are injured and he is far away; if you get there too late, your efforts will have been in vain. Why don't we send Ritchie to warn him? Old Wei, it is cold these days and the sun rises late; tell Ritchie to head out first thing in the morning. If he leaves before dawn, he should be able to make it back by tomorrow evening."

"Of course, I'll do as you instruct," replied Old Wei.

Grandpa turned to Daiyun and continued, "As to what message you want Ritchie to deliver to your brother, you can tell him yourself."

Daiyun responded, "I don't have much to say. He just needs to know that our parents cannot take many more of the attacks against them. My brother should pick them up and bring them into town, where they will be safer."

Grandpa said, "Old Wei, go inform Ritchie. If Lingyun says he is too busy with work to go to the countryside to fetch his parents, don't press the matter."

"My brother is the most filial son. I'm sure he will rush to save them."

Grandpa Lu Ziqiao just heaved a deep sigh and followed Old Wei out of the room.

A cold, damp wind slipped into the room from a small opening in the window, so Little Tea added some coal to the brazier. Daiyun's back started to ache again. She crawled into bed and began to sob.

Winter that year seemed to go on forever. A thin layer of snow covered the mountaintops, and the weather was constantly cold and clammy. Even when the sun came out, there lingered a cold chill in the air that cut to the bone. Ding Zitao suddenly thought about her hometown; she thought about the winter there. The weather was just like this. It was the kind of cold that penetrates your flesh.

At that moment she felt as if the cold were a series of thorns, sharply stabbing her.

HELL XII: PANIC-RIDDLED STEPS

Ding Zitao was walking slowly, but from time to time she felt as if she were not walking but crawling. She was already on the twelfth level.

As her back throbbed in pain, Ding Zitao thought back to what had happened the day she ran away.

The struggle session was held in her family's ancestral hall. People had hung up posters with political slogans on either side of the door. One side read "Bring down the landlords! Stop paying rent!" and the other side read "Never again will peasants shed their blood and sweat."

She kept softly pleading with the comrades working there. She said her father-in-law was a man named Lu Ziqiao; he had fought in the Revolution of 1911 and later won merit for his part in suppressing the bandits. They had even published stories about him in the newspaper. And now she had already participated in the struggle session against her own parents and even gone so far as to publicly cut off relations with them. She even displayed all her family's rent contracts. She fully supported the new Chinese government. But her child was still a baby, and she needed to go home to take care of him.

She repeatedly pleaded with them until one of the comrades looked at her and, after thinking about it, finally said, "I know Lu Ziqiao; he really stepped up during the campaign against the bandits. Since you're his daughter-in-law, I'll let you leave."

Daiyun immediately took to her feet and ran home. Her heart was racing; she didn't even turn back to get a final glimpse of her family members who were still being struggled against.

As she reached the edge of the village, she ran into two men with rifles. She stopped as one of them yelled, "Are you trying to sneak away?"

Daiyun was so scared that her legs went weak and she almost collapsed to the ground. But she recognized the person yelling at her as Hu Xiaosi. That was the same Xiaosi who was actually a distant relative living on the property behind her family's house. His family and her family had a long-standing disagreement about a plot of land. Once his family fell on hard times, one of their children joined up with the bandits, while a few others ended up working as hired laborers for other families. But Daiyun's family never hired any of them. That's because Daiyun's father said he wanted to avoid any further disagreements with their family.

"No," responded Daiyun. "One of the comrades allowed me to leave. I have a child at home that I have to get back to."

Hu Xiaosi continued yelling at her. "The struggle session isn't over yet. You're not allowed to leave!"

Daiyun tried to explain, telling him, "My father-in-law Lu Ziqiao is a politically advanced landlord; he's even been featured in the newspaper. My son is his grandson. Please, my son is only a year old; he needs his mother."

Hu Xiaosi roared back, "The Lu family are even bigger landlords than your parents. Sooner or later we'll be coming to struggle against you too! You can't stand seeing us poor people in control now, can you?"

"Actually, your family originally owned a lot more land than my family!"

Hu Xiaosi angrily raised his rifle. "How dare you speak back to me!"

His friend tried to calm him down by tugging his arm. "The comrade from the working committee already agreed to let her go. Just let her go. Why are you bothering to argue with a woman like her?"

Hu Xiaosi thought for a second about what his friend said and lowered his rifle. "Get lost!" he barked at Daiyun.

She didn't say anything else to him and immediately set off. But she took only a few steps before she felt a vicious blow come crashing down on her back. She stumbled and immediately fell to the ground.

Before she could get up she felt a second blow to her back; this time she could tell it was the buttstock. She managed to turned around and, through her tears, yelled at Xiaosi, "What right do you have to hit me? If you've got the guts, why don't you just shoot me?"

Xiaosi's friend pulled him in the direction of the ancestral hall. As they walked off, Hu Xiaosi turned around to say, "Don't worry, we'll be coming to execute your entire family in good time. We'll shoot every one of you. Actually, my grandfather wanted to execute your family a long time ago!"

Daiyun got to her feet and stumbled down the village road. She cried along the way, occasionally screaming out toward the mountains in the distance. Her screams were filled with anguish and terror.

The pale yellow winter scenery seemed to match Daiyun's panic-riddled steps. She had walked that road countless times, but never before did it feel as long as it felt that day.

Ding Zitao saw everything clearly. She knew that from this point forward there would be no going back.

HELL XIII: EVERYTHING TURNS TO ASH

This was the memory that Ding Zitao found most difficult to face.

It was this scene that filled her heart with such a deep sense of self-loathing. But now this scene was laying itself bare before her eyes. Her heart was trembling and her hands were shaking. She used her left hand to grab hold of her right hand, yet she still couldn't control the shaking.

She understood that her hands would forever remember the terrible sins she committed.

The political slogans hanging outside the ancestral hall were immediately visible; posters with slogans were also hanging from the rafters inside the hall. All the posters contained slogans written in black calligraphy on red paper: *If you have suffered, speak of your suffering! Down with the landlords! If you have faced injustice, demand justice! Return our land!*

All members of the three landlord families from Hu Shuidang, no matter how young or old, were lined up on the stage, where they stood with their heads lowered. Daiyun was also among them. It was a denunciation meeting. One after another, everyone went up to the stage to accuse these three families of various crimes.

When it was time to denounce Daiyun's family, Daiyun suddenly raised her head and addressed the team leader in charge of the meeting. "Can I say a few words?"

The comrade in charge gazed at Daiyun with a somewhat confused look. Daiyun quickly began, "When the campaign against the bandits was raging, I was in town attending school. I even volunteered to teach literacy courses. I was considered a progressive revolutionary youth. I returned to my family home only when I became pregnant."

The comrade in charge was puzzled. "What exactly are you trying to say?"

Daiyun gestured toward one of her family's former servants, who dragged three wooden chests to the stage.

Daiyun continued, "I support the abolition of all the exploitative systems of land ownership that have been put in place by the feudal landlord class. I also support all land being returned to the peasants. I hereby cut all ties with my parents and renounce my relationship with this landlord family. From this moment forward I shall have nothing more to do with them! I'm taking action to show my support for the people!"

The audience broke into applause. Perhaps it was the clapping that emboldened Daiyun. She raised her voice and continued, "Contained in these chests are all the deeds and lease agreements in my family's possession. Here in front of you I shall burn every one of them! From this day forward, all the land once owned by Hu Ruyun will be returned to those who tend the land. Everyone in Hu Ruyun's family will get down in the fields and do manual labor just like the other peasants!"

Everyone listening was shocked by what they were hearing, but then someone suddenly began to clap, which was quickly followed by cries of happiness and excited screams. It was during these chaotic cries that she began to burn the papers. The fire lit up the entire room. Following the glow of the flames was a thick fragrant smell, which assaulted the noses of everyone present. But that is when the entire room unexpectedly reached a new boiling point.

Someone suddenly yelled out, "Why is there such a strong smell coming from the fire? Is it poison? Maybe it's a trick and they are trying to poison us?"

Someone else responded by frantically trying to extinguish the fire. Daiyun was taken off guard. She too didn't know where that fragrant smell was coming from. She gazed at her father. Hu Ruyun mumbled, "It's not poison. It's not. All those documents are stamped with official government seals. The ink used contains fragments of pearls and scented tea; that is what is emitting that fragrance."

But he spoke so softly that none of the onlookers could understand what he said.

Daiyun repeated what her father said in a loud voice so everyone could hear. "It's not poison! Government documents are stamped with seals. The ink contains scented tea—that's why the smoke has a strong fragrance when they burn."

How many years of contracts and deeds were included there? How many people did they affect? Daiyun had no idea. She had never read them. There were probably contracts and deeds that her grandfather or even great-grandfather had signed. But from now on those things would be gone forever.

Everyone present exchanged confidential whispers to each other for a while before breaking out in another round of applause. Some of the onlookers started shouting slogans. The faces of the comrades in change all lit up with smiles.

Daiyun continued, "This landlord named Hu Ruyun knows nothing but eating, drinking, and enjoying himself. He spends all day practicing calligraphy and painting. He even keeps a concubine! I hope all the revolutionary comrades here can send his concubine back to her family. Hu Ruyun should be forbidden from living a decadent life of the landowning class; he should be forced to live like the peasants!"

That earned even more applause from those present. But then Second Mother rushed over to Daiyun and yelled, "I married into the Hu family more than twenty years ago! And now you want to send me back? Where are you going to send me? How can you be so heartless? And now you want to cut ties with your family? You don't deserve to even call yourself a human being! Your parents raised you in vain!"

Daiyun didn't say a word and turned away, but then she suddenly raised her hand and slapped Second Mother across the face. Everyone watching fell silent for a moment. Then someone yelled, "Good job! She deserves it!"

Those words encouraged many others to join the chorus. "She deserves it! Keep hitting her!"

Daiyun didn't heed their chants; instead, she addressed Second Mother. "You've been a concubine in my family for so many years and all you did was take, take, take without doing any work! You enjoyed fancy food and wine long enough! Do you think you can continue on like that now under the new society? I can't wait to send you back to where you came from!"

Second Mother stared at Daiyun in shock. She abruptly started yelling at her. "You deserve to be stabbed a thousand times! You're going to hell! Yama will teach you a lesson!" As she cried she turned to Daiyun's parents and asked, "Is this that precious daughter you raised? She's even betraying her own parents!"

Daiyun's father lowered his head and let Second Wife go on. But Daiyun rushed over to push her out of the way and viciously knocked her father to the ground. She then knocked down Second Wife too. Daiyun bent over and grabbed hold of her father's collar and screamed, "Stand up! You must accept the judgment of the people!"

Hu Ruyun got to his feet, his head hung low and his entire body trembling.

Daiyun arrogantly stood before him and continued her attack. "Before today I had already asked the landlord Hu Ruyun to release all the long-term laborers from his employment. I also asked the landlord and his wife to move into the workers' quarters so that the main house could be given over to the village government. Our family has a lot of books, and so I suggested that we open a school here so that poor children might have the opportunity to be educated."

The comrades in charge clapped in approval, triggering another round of applause. That was when Daiyun raised her fist in the air and yelled, "Down with the landlords! Return the land to the peasants!"

Daiyun's parents along with everyone standing on stage followed her gesture and repeated her slogans. The only exception was Second Mother, who just sat on the ground rolling her eyes and muttering something inaudible.

The contracts and leases had all burned to ash. But the fragrance from the ink still lingered throughout the hall. Someone went outside, and as the door opened, a bolt of wind sent the remnants of black ash twirling through the air. Small particles of black ash landed on the heads and shoulders of everyone on stage.

The comrade in charge asked Daiyun to come down from the stage. "You've done a good job here today," he said. "Your revolutionary attitude is warmly welcomed. No need for you to continue standing up there on stage."

As Daiyun came down from the stage, she turned to look at her parents, who were both trembling with fear. Her mother's hairpin had loosened revealing her white hair, which was hanging down over her neck. At some point her father's gray cotton jacket had developed a hole in the right corner, and a thread of cotton fiber was coming out. A cold draft made her father shudder . . . and she shuddered with him. They all stood there with their heads down; none of them dared to look up. They just stood there shuddering as wave after wave of curses and angry screams rained down upon them.

That was the last image of her parents she was left with.

HELL XIV: MOM AND DAD ARE RELYING ON YOU

Ding Zitao began to see the light.

The light flickered, becoming suddenly bright and then dark again. One minute it looked like sheets of darkness dancing through the air, and the next minute it looked like flakes of snow. She thought, *God in heaven, am I really about to finally make it? What will it be like once I am out? Will Father be wearing a new cotton jacket? Will Mother still be upset with me? I'm especially worried about Second Mother. I wonder if she'll slap me back when she sees me.* But then she suddenly remembered that her parents were already dead. Second Mother was dead. Once she got out, who would she be able to share these things with? Wasn't talking about what happened what she really wanted?

It was raining that day. Autumn had passed and winter was here. The cold descended on the mountains earlier this year than most, and every corner was enveloped in an icy cold.

Although their family was in decline, they still wanted to celebrate her mother's birthday. Daiyun made a special trip back to

Qierenlu just for the occasion. The house was especially quiet; all the servants had been sent home, and it was a bit strange to see all the courtyards devoid of people walking about.

Daiyun asked her father, "Isn't Brother Lingyun coming back for the party?"

Father replied, "He sent a message saying he needed to attend a multiday conference. He won't be able to make it back."

Mother said, "It's okay. He should focus on his work. Affairs of state are important business."

Second Mother and Sister-in-Law prepared longevity noodles for the birthday. Before they could sit down to eat, someone unexpectedly came to the house—it was a former long-term worked named Xiao Er. Xiao Er said, "The comrades from the working team want me to inform you that they will be coming tomorrow to hold a struggle session against your family. No one is permitted to leave."

Daiyun immediately responded, "How could they come after our family? My brother is a cadre in town."

Xiao Er explained, "According to the work team, all landlords need to be struggled against. Everyone in the family must show up. It will be held in the ancestral hall."

Daiyun's father said, "My daughter came home only to celebrate her mother's birthday. She'll be leaving first thing tomorrow morning."

"Well then, your daughter came home at just the right moment," responded Xiao Er. "Didn't she go straight from being the precious young lady of your household to the young mistress of another? She's here just in time to also participate in the struggle session!"

Xiao Er spoke with an arrogance none of them had ever seen in him before; everyone in the family was shocked by not only what he said but also how he said it. Xiao Er had worked for the Hu family for well over a decade and had always been an honest, hardworking man. It had been only one month since he had left them, and they were shocked to see how much he had changed.

"Xiao Er, how dare you talk to us like that!" said Daiyun.

"I'm a peasant who has turned himself around; you are all landlords," explained Xiao Er. "We walk two different paths, and we don't speak the same language. But I will be kind enough to give you a little warning: be sure to eat well today because the struggle session is slated to go on for several days."

"Do you know Lu Ziqiao from Sanzhitang? He's my father-in-law; the Hu family and the Lu family are related. Lu Ziqiao is an important person in the county," Daiyun explained.

"Is he a landlord too?" asked Xiao Er.

"That's right . . . But he contributed to the revolution. He also earned merit during the campaign against the bandits. His family contributed more to the grain tax fund than anyone else," said Daiyun.

"Even more than your family?" asked Xiao Er.

"Of course," replied Daiyun. "The Lu family collect several thousand *shi* of grain each year as land rental fees."

"Well, let's wait and see then," said Xiao Er. "Later the struggle sessions are sure to get even more brutal. But none of you are permitted to leave tomorrow!"

Xiao Er strutted off. Daiyun's father said, "He's just a servant; there's no use trying to reason with him."

Everyone ate the longevity noodles under a cloud of desolate silence.

That night Daiyun was so upset that she couldn't sleep. She regretted having come home. Although she still didn't know what the scene would be like when they were all on stage being struggled against, she was extremely worried about what was coming. She didn't even know if she would be able to return to her husband's house. For the first time she felt completely helpless.

That was when she suddenly heard a knock at her door. She swiftly got out of bed and threw on a robe. She opened the door to discover her parents standing there. As they entered her room, they looked around as if worried someone had been following them. There was something secretive about their expression. Daiyun felt uneasy. "Mom, Dad, what's wrong?"

Daiyun's parents closed the door and had their daughter sit down beside them. Her father said, "Daiyun, the situation right now doesn't look very good for us. Your mother and I both feel it will be much safer for you if you are able to get into town."

Daiyun responded, "Of course. Don't we have a place with several rooms near the town gate? You could both stay there, and Brother Lingyun would be able to check on you regularly."

"We had originally planned on waiting until after the Chinese New Year, and then we would all move there," explained Daiyun's father. "But now with your mother and me slated to be struggled against, I'm afraid we won't be able to handle what's coming. We had better move to town sooner."

"That would be best," agreed Daiyun.

"Your mother and I have been thinking about this all day," her father continued. "Tomorrow you need to find a way to get out of this. You should have your father-in-law send someone into town to find your brother. Your brother is a cadre; tell him to come and get us right away. Otherwise . . . I'm afraid we will never be able to get away."

Daiyun's mother looked extremely distressed. "I'm not sure what this struggle will be like. . . . but I'm so afraid . . ."

"Do you think they'll let me leave?" Daiyun asked.

"That's what your mother and I have been discussing," her father explained. "Tomorrow you should go on stage to speak out against us. You must also take all our deeds and contracts and burn them in public."

Daiyun was shocked by her father's suggestion. "How could I ever do that? If our family were to give up all our land, how would we get by?"

"There is no point in keeping it anymore," her father explained. "Last time your brother came home to visit, he told us that from now on there would be no more landlords; all the land was to be returned to the peasants. Right now the most important thing is trying to stay alive. You should burn the contracts and give our house over to the state; tell them it can be used to open a village school. And one more thing . . . you must publicly break off your relationship with us. You must make them believe you; otherwise, they'll never let you go."

Daiyun broke down crying. "Father . . . Mother . . . how could you ever ask such things of me?"

But Daiyun's father was firm. "If you want to save us, you must find a way to say those things. By the way, we also need you to save your second mother. You should suggest she be sent back to her parents' home. There is no way your brother will be able to take your second mother in, and she certainly can't stay here. So we need to find a way to send her back. Later we can figure out a way for her to meet us in town. I can't tell her any of this right now, but I'll explain everything to her later once things settle down and we are all together again. You know her: she can't keep a secret and isn't a very good actor. I'm afraid she'll ruin our plan if we tell her now."

Daiyun continued to cry. "I'm afraid I won't be able to bring myself to do it. Second Mother will hate me."

"In a situation where we have no options, this is the only way," her father explained. "Once Zhongwen returns, you should go into town together with him. You can't stay here in the countryside; there is no way to stay here anymore."

Daiyun's mother said, "There is no other way. Just do your best to get out of here quickly and tell your brother to come get us. I won't be able to take much of this. If it's not safe in town, then we'll go to my parents' house in Chengdu. Daiyun, we are all relying on you."

"Are you really ready to give up our house?" Daiyun asked.

"We can worry about all that later," Daiyun's father explained. "Right now, we need to worry about staying alive. Daiyun, we have to remind you, when the time calls for it tomorrow, you are going to need to appear ruthless. If you need to hit us, just do it. We won't blame you. The only important thing is your getting out. We should be able to hold out for a few days, but you must hurry to find your brother, Lingyun, and tell him to come for us. And tell him not to come alone. It will be best if he comes with a few other cadres; otherwise, they'll never let us go."

Daiyun promised to do as they instructed.

All night long she thought about how to face the struggle session coming the following day and about how she would be able to get away. She never imagined she would ever be in such a position. And now she was being forced to raise these accusations against her family and cut off her relationship with her own parents. Just thinking about what was coming caused tears to pour down her cheeks.

At that moment Ding Zitao was unusually calm. She was wondering, *How did her parents manage to live for all those years? How could they have been so simple-minded? They could just have had a proper goodbye, but instead they came up with this stupid plan that not only failed to save their lives but ended up costing their son his life as well.* And even though Ding Zitao managed to survive, she was left with a sense of immeasurable hatred for herself and what she had done.

HELL XV: YOU ARE A MEMBER OF THE LU FAMILY

Ding Zitao had no tears left to cry. Those horrific events that had occurred had long ago left her numb inside. She had buried her in-laws, her parents were dead, her brother and his wife were also gone. Why was she still alive? How could she possibly continue living? Why didn't she die like the others? These were all questions that haunted her.

By the time she realized she had reached the fifteenth level, she felt that nothing mattered anymore.

Whom could she ever tell about what happened? Did she even know who was left? She couldn't even figure out if it would have been better to have died like the others or to go on living as she did.

The moon gate from the Sanzhitang garden appeared before her eyes.

Back when she and Lu Zhongwen were just starting to fall in love with each other, they used to talk to each other while standing on either side of that moon gate. It was as if they were each sitting on opposite sides of the moon's rim, chatting about everything that was happening in the universe around them. On one occasion Lu Zhongwen gave her a silk scarf that he had asked a friend to purchase for him in Hong Kong. She leaned against the moon gate with that silk scarf wrapped around her neck, all the while talking and laughing with Lu Zhongwen. When the wind picked up, the scarf's dancing in the air caused Lu Zhongwen to comment, "I love the way the scarf looks around your neck as it blows in the wind."

On some days when she really missed Lu Zhongwen, she would bring Ding Zi and Little Tea along the long corridor to the moon gate to play. She would tell Ding Zi, "Be sure to remember, this is one of your daddy's favorite spots."

That day right around sunset, she brought Ding Zi out near the moon gate to play. Meanwhile she was discussing with Little Tea whether she should go home. Grandpa Lu Ziqiao happened to be walking in the garden and overheard them. He immediately interrupted. "Tomorrow is your mother's birthday. It is a rare occasion for you to go home to see your family. If you don't go, your parents will think the Lu family doesn't abide by the proper etiquette."

Daiyun responded, "It's not that I don't want to go home. It's just that Ding Zi has been a bit constipated these past few days. I'm afraid . . ."

Grandpa Lu interrupted her. "Leave Ding Zi with us. Little Tea will take care of him. Just come right back. My wife has woven a new pair of cotton shoes for your mother. Please take them along with you."

Daiyun thought momentarily before accepting his suggestion. "I thank you on behalf of my mother."

That night Daiyun packed her things, and first thing the next morning she went to see Old Wei to request the horse cart. Old Wei replied, "Oh no. The village agricultural association needed to transport holiday supplies from town, so they are using our horse cart. Master Lu gave me orders to always let the villagers use anything of ours they need. So we always try to prioritize their needs. What should we do?"

Daiyun was disappointed, but there was nothing she could do. "I guess I'll just have to walk. At least it isn't that far away."

"Stay on the main roads and avoid those smaller paths. Even if it ends up taking you an extra hour or two. Safety is most important."

As she left, Daiyun said goodbye to Ding Zi. That's when Grandpa Lu Ziqiao ran outside to tell her, "Daiyun, if anyone tries to give you trouble, just tell them that you are related to the

Lu family. If anyone hassles you on the road, just tell them that you are Lu Ziqiao's daughter-in-law."

Daiyun hesitated. "Will that work?"

Grandpa flashed a cool smile. "Our family owns several hundred acres of land around here—that still means something. I know virtually all the cadres on the county level."

"But do you realize we are now living in a new era? All that was before . . ."

Grandpa insisted, "I've done a lot for them over the years; I'm sure they will still give me some face. Just do as I say and you'll be fine."

In that moment Ding Zitao offered a cold smile just like her father-in-law's. She thought, *Just how much face do you really have, Lu Ziqiao? When you have given up your very life, who cares about face? It was your arrogance and tyrannical attitude that forced your entire family to die with you. What was the point of all that arrogance and pride? Let me tell you, it's worth nothing!*

12

MY GOD, IS AMAH DING REALLY YOUR MOTHER?

Qinglin somehow managed to hold out until the fifth day of the Chinese New Year before finally calling Liu Xiao'an.

Liu Xiao'an said that it was best if no one in the family went out this year, since they were still mourning his father's death. All they wanted was a peaceful Lunar New Year and didn't want to do anything that might disturb their father's memory.

Qinglin said, "I wanted to drop by your house for a visit. Is that convenient?"

Liu Xiao'an didn't expect that but answered, "Of course. You are always welcome if you want to come over. Xiaochuan is here too. Are there any issues with your project that you need to discuss with him?"

"No, the project is proceeding really well," Qinglin explained. "It is actually something private that I wanted to talk to the two of you about. It's really important to me."

"No problem then. Come on over," Liu Xiao'an replied.

Qinglin left his mother in the care of his friend's nanny, grabbed a picture of his parents, and hopped in the car. Although there were more pedestrians out in the street because of the holiday, there was actually a lot less traffic than normal. The streets were filled with myriad red banners, and a celebratory atmosphere seemed to be exploding all over the city.

After spending five days stuck at home, Qinglin wasn't really affected by the festive mood outside; he was instead completely fixated on his own sadness.

The brothers had not yet given up Liu Jinyuan's apartment. Liu Xiao'an and Liu Xiaochuan had spread out a set of blueprints in the dining room, where a portrait of Liu Jinyuan was on display. The image of Liu Jinyuan, smiling broadly and glowing, was from a photo taken when he was in Wanzhou. Two burning candles stood on either side of the portrait.

The moment Qinglin stepped inside, he encountered that portrait of Liu Jinyuan; he was so familiar with that smiling face. Qinglin had spent several days together with Liu Jinyuan and yet all the while had no idea that his own father had such a close relationship with him. Qinglin couldn't help breaking down in tears as he stood there, almost paralyzed, in front of Liu Jinyuan's portrait.

Both brothers were home, and Liu Xiao'an came over to pat him on the shoulder. "Have a seat. This marks the beginning of a new year for Father. According to custom, we aren't supposed to leave the house to call on friends, so we are just staying in. We're not even supposed to play mah-jongg, which might disturb Father's rest. Have you ever heard of all these rules?"

"I've also been staying at home," Qinglin replied. "I haven't gone anywhere."

Liu Xiaochuan came over. "You're staying there alone with your mother? What about your wife and son? They didn't come with you?"

"It's just me," Qinglin replied. "My father-in-law is ill, so my wife took our son to visit him. Our regular nanny also went home for the Lunar New Year, so I had to stay home to take care of my mom. Anyway, it's good to have quiet time; besides, it's a good chance for me to spend some quality time with my mom. Did you go out to the cemetery to visit your father? Please let me know next time you go. I'd love to go with you. I'd really like to have a chance to pay my respects to your father."

"We appreciate your sentiments," said Liu Xiao'an. "According to custom, the family isn't supposed to visit the grave site during the first year. They say that the soul of the departed is still wandering around the cemetery during that time. If you disturb his spirit, he'll have a more difficult journey. It's an interesting way of looking at things. We don't really believe any of that, of course, but we still want to respect the rites. So for the time being we are just doing what we can at home to commemorate him."

"I see," said Qinglin. "But those of us who associate with the Chu all place great emphasis on the return of the soul. We saw in the museum that among all those Chu graves one was left open; that was so that the soul of the dead could freely come and go as it pleased. They really had an incredible imagination back then."

"That's interesting," said Liu Xiaochuan. "By the way, you mentioned that you had something you wanted to discuss with us today?"

Qinglin hesitated for a moment. "I wanted to ask you, did you know a doctor named Wu Jiaming?"

"Of course we knew him!" exclaimed Liu Xiao'an. "My dad always used to brag about how he had found Dr. Wu living deep in the mountains and helped him find a new life." He paused suddenly as if struck by a realization. "You're . . . are you related to him?"

"He was my father," replied Qinglin.

Liu Xiaochuan was visibly shocked. "What? So that means . . . your mother is . . ."

"My mother's name is Ding Zitao," said Qinglin.

Qinglin took out the photograph he brought and walked over to hand it to Liu Xiaochuan. "You both recognize the two of them?"

Liu Xiao'an raised his voice in surprise. "My God! Of course I recognize them! I can't believe you are their son!"

Qinglin started to choke up. "That's right."

Liu Xiaochuan jumped to his feet and gave Qinglin a big hug. "My goodness, I would never have imagined that you're Amah Ding's son! Brother, I'm glad I was always good to you; otherwise, I could never have forgiven myself. Your mother was the one who basically raised me."

Liu Xiao'an appeared momentarily lost in thought. "Wait a second . . . Let me think . . . No wonder Dad kept saying there was something so familiar about you. He was convinced you reminded him of somebody, but he just couldn't put his finger on it. When we were on the Yangtze cruise, he even asked me what your surname was. I told him Wu, and he seemed quite surprised. My God, he must have sensed it! Ever since the first time he met you, he just kept repeating how much you reminded him of somebody. He also talked about how comfortable he felt around you. But I never imagined you were Dr. Wu's son, even though now I see you really do resemble your father."

Liu Xiaochuan said, "Now it all makes sense. I was always confused about why Dad seemed to like you so much. I see now that there was a long story behind that. He must have sensed a presence about you that reminded him of your father. I'm not sure if you know this or not, but your father saved not only my dad's life but also my mom's. Both my parents relied heavily on your father. Whenever they got sick, your father was the only doctor they would really listen to. My dad always considered your father more like a member of his family than just a friend. And Mom and Dad were even closer with your mother. When we were little, our parents were always busy with work, so your mother was the one who really raised us and held our family together. My brother, sister, and I spent all our time with her. I remember way back there was even a time that whenever my father would mention Dr. Wu, my sister would get upset and declare, 'I hate him! He took away Amah Ding!'"

Tears welled up in Qinglin's eyes. He took a deep gulp before saying, "After my father died, my mom started working as a live-in nanny, so it wasn't easy for her to go out. She was also self-conscious about her low social status, so she didn't keep in touch with anyone. That's probably why she stopped contacting you. I was just a little boy and didn't understand what was happening."

Liu Xiao'an asked, "So that person that you told me is in a semivegetative state is Amah Ding?"

Qinglin dejectedly responded, "That's right. Physically she seems fairly normal. It's just that she can't seem to snap out of this daze. Originally I had hoped to fulfill my filial duty by saving up all my money to buy her a nice villa. How could I ever have imagined that the very day she moved in, she would suddenly become dazed? I just can't figure out what triggered this."

"This is all so unexpected," said Liu Xiaochuan. "Qinglin, I never imagined such a thing could happen. As soon as the Spring Festival is over, I'll come to your house to pay a visit to Amah Ding. Since our family is still in mourning, the rules prohibit us from visiting other people's homes right now. But as soon as the holiday is over, I'll come to see your mom."

Liu Xiao'an added, "I'll go too."

"Thank you," said Qinglin. "I'm not sure if your showing up will be the kind of happy surprise that might snap her out of her daze. But that would be amazing if it helped her."

Liu Xiaochuan asked, "How did you manage to put all this together?"

Qinglin explained how he had discovered the diaries inside his father's trunk and concisely described what was contained within. But he didn't mention the reason his father went into the mountains in the first place. He figured that his father had probably not wanted anyone to know those secrets. He had wanted to forget that part of his life. So Qinglin made sure to begin the story from the moment his father and Grandpa Wu saved Liu Jinyuan. He told the brothers about how his father followed Liu Jinyuan out of the mountains and joined the army, and he told them all about how his mother was saved and later lost her memory.

Liu Xiao'an and Liu Xiaochuan knew nothing about Ding Zitao's memory loss. Perhaps out of respect for Ding Zitao, their parents had made sure never to mention that in front of the children; then again, it is also possible they were simply too young and just didn't pay attention to any details that might have been related to her memory loss.

The most important clue, according to Qinglin, was that as soon as his mother arrived at the villa, she suddenly started saying strange things. She began mumbling words like "Qierenlu" and something-tang. When she saw the bamboo growing outside the house, she immediately began reciting a poem. (Qinglin noted that he later looked up the poem, which turned out to be written by Xie Tiao, a poet not terribly well known now.) She also started to say things that didn't seem to match her background. At the time Qinglin thought it was all a bit strange but paid little attention to it. But last year when he accompanied Liu Jinyuan to Eastern Sichuan, he overheard some people talking about Qierenlu. That came as a complete shock to him. Now that he had read his father's diary, he knew that his mother had been discovered right around that same area. Even when he was alive, his father had made various conjectures about Ding Zitao's true background. He eventually hypothesized that she didn't come from a poor family; he was quite sure that she was literate. After marriage she began exhibiting abnormal behavior, which he theorized about in his diaries. For many years she was haunted by constant anxiety and fear, but she refused to face those old memories. Her doctor said her amnesia must be the result of a terrible trauma. Qinglin learned about all this over the New Year holiday from reading his father's old diaries.

The Liu brothers listened in silence, shocked by what Qinglin was telling them.

"My goodness," Liu Xiao'an exclaimed, "this whole story is unbelievable!"

Liu Xiaochuan added, "Who could ever have imagined . . . Do you think there is a way to figure out what happened to her before she lost her memory?"

"I'm not sure," replied Qinglin. "But I keep thinking that helping her figure out what happened in the past or locating some of her living relatives might be the key to getting her to snap out of her daze. All I want is for her to wake up."

"You're right. Before she lost her memory, she must have had a family and relatives," agreed Liu Xiao'an. "It has already been fifty years, so her parents are sure to no longer be living, but perhaps she might have siblings who are still alive?"

"According to my dad's diary, she had another child," Qinglin revealed. "That's what the doctor who delivered me told my dad. My dad was completely shocked when he learned this, but my mom didn't seem to remember anything about her first child."

"My God!" exclaimed Liu Xiao'an. "You might even end up finding a long-lost brother or sister! Back then women had children early in life. Maybe she had more than one child. If you can find those lost siblings, I think you really might have a shot at waking her up."

"Anyway, perhaps her waking up is just part of my fanciful thinking," said Qinglin. "As of now, I know that they first found my mother in a place called the Eternal Valley River. I also know about Qierenlu, which I already asked about. It is located in a place called Hu Shuidang. This family seemed to have a lot of books. And I know that they had a son named Hu Lingyun. He went to college in Chongqing, and your father even knew him. But some of the villagers from those parts said he was killed one year while on his way home. Those are all the clues I have managed to piece together. Apparently Hu Shuidang was completely destroyed several decades ago in order to build a dam; there is now nothing left of the place."

"The fact that your mother seems to subconsciously remember Qierenlu means one of two things," Liu Xiaochuan conjectured. "The first seems to indicate that Qierenlu was where she grew up, or perhaps it was where her in-laws lived. Or maybe it was the place where her trauma originated. It is a shame my father is gone; otherwise, I'm sure he would have been able to help us figure this out."

"That's right. I'm sure a lot of the things my father sensed back then were correct. I'll bet your father must also have sensed something strange about my mother. For instance, I recently made the discovery that my mother knows how to embroider and is actually extremely skilled. But throughout my childhood I never once saw her embroider anything!"

Liu Xiao'an and Liu Xiaochuan looked at each other; they both said they had no impression of Amah Ding ever embroidering anything.

Qinglin sighed. "I really missed out on my chance to ask your father about all this. I'm sure there are all kinds of things he could have told me."

"The whole thing feels as if it's right out of a soap opera," said Liu Xiao'an. "What happened to your family is so interesting. You have to wonder what a person's subconscious looks like after the person loses their memory. Does it become the place most long to be in or a place of nightmares?"

Qinglin thought about it for a moment. "I'm not sure . . ."

Liu Xiaochuan chimed in, "I'm sure that for me my subconscious would be my most hated place, a place of nightmares. That is because I'm sure that after suffering such a profound injury, all I would think about would be exacting revenge."

"Well, I'm the exact opposite," said Liu Xiao'an. "I think I would mostly remember those happy places, which is what would give me the drive to go on living." Liu Xiao'an continued until he eventually broke out in laughter and said, "Anyway, I give up. Qinglin, what's your interpretation?"

Qinglin offered a wry smile. "It's hard to say . . ."

"I'm afraid you are going to have to do some investigating to figure things out," suggested Liu Xiaochuan. "You need to find some closure for your mother and yourself. I can let you take an extended vacation with pay until you get to the bottom of this. If she really does have living relatives out there, perhaps they might be able to help snap her out of this state she is in. Frankly speaking, your mother's business is also my business. From the time I was just a few days old, I slept side by side with her in the same bed every night; she slept with me for five years. Every night she would calm me to sleep. Then when I was six years old she started putting my little sister to bed every night, so I started sleeping on the other side of the bed with my head down by her feet. And every day I ate the food she cooked. That went on for more than a decade. She's responsible for the kinds of food I like. But I was so little back then that I never knew anything about her experience."

Liu Xiao'an added, "Qinglin, I never imagined anything like this could happen. When your mother first came to work for us, Xiaochuan wasn't even born yet and I was only three years old. My mother had been injured and wasn't in the best of health; she also was busy with work. So we all ended up growing up with your mother. I remember being in middle school when she left. I remember coming home from school and getting upset because I didn't like the new nanny's cooking."

"I still remember you losing your temper about that!" said Liu Xiaochuan. "Mom reprimanded you for that. She even forced you to apologize to the new nanny. You were too stubborn to do it and gave in only after Dad slapped you."

Liu Xiao'an continued, "That's right. Later I ended up in boarding school and gradually forgot about all that. None of those later nannies treated us like family the way your mother did, Qinglin. Your father passed away when you were young, and now your mother is so terribly sick. From now on we are your brothers. I'll be your big brother and Xiaochuan will be your second brother; our little sister is your sister too. If she were here, I'm sure she'd give you a big hug and break down in tears. After your mother left us, my sister made an even bigger scene than I did."

Qinglin had no idea how important his mother had been to their family; he certainly didn't realize how deep ran the emotional bond between the Liu siblings and his mother. He began to tear up again.

QINGWEN WAS A SERVANT GIRL

After the Lantern Festival, Liu Xiao'an and Liu Xiaochuan paid a visit to Qinglin's house just as they had promised.

But no matter how loudly they spoke to get her attention or what they said about the past to jog her memory, nothing they said or did was able to snap Ding Zitao out of her frozen state. Both brothers were upset, but ultimately there was nothing they could do.

"I guess we don't have enough of a connection with her to sway her..." said Liu Xiao'an.

"Well, who might have more sway?" asked Qinglin.

"I suspect it must be someone she had dealings with back then, or someone connected with what happened," suggested Liu Xiaochuan. "You said that she had a child? Perhaps she also had a husband back then? What if her former husband is still alive?"

"If such a person really exists and he is able to wake up my mother, I swear right here and now that I'll take care of him for the rest of his life!" Qinglin exclaimed. "But if we can't find a single relative of hers still living, does that mean she will never wake up?"

The Liu brothers remained silent.

Actually, on the way over the brothers had already discussed this between themselves. They felt that even if Qinglin were to uncover the truth about his mother or locate her relatives, the chance that Amah Ding would ever recover was still very slim. But they weren't yet willing to share their honest opinion with Qinglin; they didn't want him to completely lose hope.

Qinglin showed the Liu brothers around his house. As they approached a large porcelain vessel, Qinglin asked them, "Do you recognize this painting?"

"How would I know? Those classical Chinese paintings all look the same to me," replied Liu Xiao'an.

Liu Xiaochuan took a closer look. "Is it 'Laozi Departs from the City Gate'?"

Qinglin said, "A friend gave this to me. I initially had no idea what the painting was. I never had much interest in the thing.

But the first time my mother saw this vessel, she immediately identified the image as 'Guiguzi Descends the Mountain.' I checked with my friend and confirmed that's what it is. In 'Laozi Departs from the City Gate,' Laozi is always riding on a black ox, but 'Guiguzi Descends the Mountain' always shows a figure riding a cart drawn by a tiger and a panther. My mother also said that her father always used to paint it. When she told me all that, it was almost as if she were speaking through her subconscious. When I followed up to ask her more about it, she became confused and seemed to have no idea what she had just said."

Liu Xiao'an suddenly added, "Now that you mention it, I'm reminded of something that happened when I was in elementary school. I had to memorize Li Bai's poem "The Path to Sichuan Is Difficult," in which there is a line referring to the ancients Can Cong and Yu Fu, but I mistakenly wrote 'Can Cong and Yu Niao.' Amah Ding told me I wrote it incorrectly and it should be Yu Fu, not Yu Niao. At the time I didn't believe her, but later I realized she was correct. So she really must have been completely literate."

Qinglin said, "I always knew that my mother was semiliterate. She said she learned to read and write at one of the night schools set up to eradicate illiteracy. But there is no way she would have learned such things in a basic literacy class."

Liu Xiaochuan also seemed to think of something. "Now I also remember a story. Right after we moved to Wuhan, a friend of the family gave my mom a painting depicting those classic beauties from ancient China; it had a few lines of calligraphy that read, *'The heart is purer than heaven, but the body is vile; To be skilled in romance brings only resentment.'* My mother looked at it and questioned, 'What's the point of such paintings?' Amah Ding was beside her pouring tea and spontaneously said, 'Qingwen was a servant girl. She had a tragic fate.' I remember my mom bursting out, 'Who is Qingwen? What are you talking about?' But Amah Ding just stood there staring blankly at my mom. Finally, she said, 'I'm not sure, but I think that girl in the painting is Qingwen.' My mom ended up keeping that painting. Later when I went to high school and read *Dream of the Red Chamber*, I realized those lines of calligraphy on the painting were referencing a character from the novel named Qingwen. This means that your mother must certainly have read *Dream of the Red Chamber*. Moreover, she knew the book well enough to immediately identify who the painting was referencing."

Qinglin seemed quite happy to learn this. "Really? Is that true? Just think about what level of education someone needs to have to really master *Dream of the Red Chamber*."

As the Liu brothers gradually started to piece together their memories, Ding Zitao's background became an enigma that drew them all in.

Qinglin realized that actually, there had always been such surprising details they had simply failed to see. Somehow they had never paid attention to them. In reality there might very well have been all manner of secrets hidden in plain sight that they had just let slip by.

THOSE BEAUTIFUL POINTED EAVES

Qinglin went back to Eastern Sichuan.

It was early summer, and he was accompanied by Long Zhongyong.

Although Qinglin was a filial son, he was a rather heartless man. After spending so many years in the business world, he was long accustomed to looking at everything from a pragmatic perspective. He had been deeply shaken when he first read his father's diaries and was prepared to take time to really get to the bottom of things. However, after some time had passed, his attitude began to change and the whole thing no longer seemed like such a big deal. It was as if with each passing day those once strong emotions faded until they eventually all disappeared. Qinglin wondered what the real point was for him to expend so much time and energy digging up the past? What would he get out of it? His mother was already so old; what were the real chances of her waking up anyway? Even if he were to find a bunch of relatives, they would all be total strangers. How could he deal with that? Moreover, his father had very clearly stated that there was no need for him to know any of that. If his own parents weren't willing to remember the past, why should he insist on dredging up all those details for himself? He ultimately thought it was better to respect the wishes of his parents.

But time can be a wicked monster. And reality is sometimes even more malicious—it can turn a man brimming with passion and ideals into a shameful opportunist interested only in money and recognition. That also describes Qinglin. He decided the most important thing was to focus on his job and his life at hand. He needed to look toward the future, not back to the past. He needed to follow the trends of the times, not try to turn the clock back. That is actually also what his father had said in his diary.

After making that decision, Qinglin quickly adjusted his mindset and pushed the whole affair into a corner, just as he had done with his father's old trunk.

But then Long Zhongyong became involved, and that led Qinglin to suddenly change his mind again. It all happened quite unexpectedly.

Long Zhongyong had long been planning to write a collection of books about villa estates in southern China. One important part of his projected series was going to be on the estates in the central Yangtze River valley. He had previously approached this subject from the perspective of architecture, but the background surrounding Great Water Well had been something of a revelation to him. He realized that when it comes to these private homes, especially those wealthy estates, it is extremely difficult to offer any new discoveries from a purely architectural perspective. He realized there was actually more scholarly value in exploring the background history of these estates, including their rise, how they changed over time, and their eventual decline. It would be especially important to look at how, over the course of the last fifty years, various societal changes had transformed almost all these once thriving southern estates over a relatively short period of time. Many of them were now abandoned, while others had been turned into schools, storage facilities, or offices; yet others had completely vanished. But since the original families who once owned these estates had gone into decline, many of the estates had been reduced to ruins. To say that they had been abandoned by time would not be as accurate as saying that they had been abandoned by society.

Long Zhongyong realized what a fascinating research topic this would be. Most of the estates hidden deep in the mountains in Eastern Sichuan and in the central Yangtze River valley remained unknown to most people. But how did those estates get established, and what eventually befell them? How did external changes playing out in society affect their architectural style and the eventual fate of those buildings? The fact that many of these buildings had a relatively short lifespan often had little to do with the construction materials used and was more significantly affected by human actions. These were some of the questions guiding Long Zhongyong's research. If he were to pursue this line of thought for his book, he knew that producing diagrams would never be enough. He needed to have a much deeper understanding of those estates. Since he would be exploring the social and human dimensions behind the estates, he knew that he was looking at a great deal of work that would take an extended period of time to carry out.

Shortly after his new semester began, Long Zhongyong called Qinglin to see if his company might be willing to provide a grant to support this research project. He said he would be happy to acknowledge their support in his book, which would be part of a series. He explained that this current volume would be entitled *Private Estates of Eastern Sichuan*.

Listening to Long Zhongyong go on and on about his project on the phone seemed to stir up something inside Qinglin, reigniting his passion to find out what happened to his own parents. He suddenly came up with an idea and said, "The research funding is no problem, and I'll leave it up to you whether or not you decide to acknowledge our support. But I do have one condition . . . I want to go with you."

Surprised by this request, Long Zhongyong blurted out, "Why? Are you even able to take time off work to go?"

"I also need you to help me with some research to track down a place I've been interested in. It is a wealthy home in Eastern Sichuan referred to as Qierenlu. It no longer exists; it was razed to build a dam. But I need to find people who might know something about that place. If you are willing to help out, I can provide a car to take us around Eastern Sichuan."

"I wouldn't call that a condition," said Long Zhongyong. "It's actually an added incentive! With you in tow, all our food, lodging, and transportation are sure to be taken care of. And it's not like you are a layman when it comes to architecture. I'm sure you'll be able to provide a lot of good input. But I'm wondering why you are interested in finding this place?"

"I'll explain all that when I see you," said Qinglin.

It didn't take long at all for them to settle on a date for their departure. They agreed to meet in Chongqing. Liu Xiaochuan also lent his full support; he immediately called his company's branch office in Chongqing and asked them to pick up Qinglin at the airport and provide him with a jeep to use. Liu Xiaochuan also told Qinglin, "If there is anything I can do to help, I'm just a phone call away."

But then just before Qinglin left, Liu Xiao'an called him. "Qinglin," he said, "I'm a generation older than you and have seen more things in my days than you have. I just wanted to tell you, if you end up having trouble making headway in your search, it's okay to give up. There is really no reason to insist on finding out what really happened. You have to understand that there are many things in the world that we will never know the whole truth about. There is something to be said for trying to make your life as simple and uncomplicated as possible; often that is what the true essence of life is about."

That phone call really had an impact on Qinglin. He walked over to the window, lost in thought.

Long Zhongyong's students all had classes and couldn't accompany him on this trip, so he traveled alone. When he met up with Qinglin, he kept saying, "I still can't believe it! All these years after our college graduation and we're finally going on a professional research expedition together! So what was the sudden impulse that made you want to do this? Or are you having marital problems at home and needed an excuse to get away?"

Qinglin laughed. "Not on your life! I just have some private matters I want to take care of on this trip."

That's when Qinglin told his friend all about what his father's diary had revealed about his mother.

Long Zhongyong was utterly spellbound as he listened to Qinglin's story. He commented, "I can't believe how calm you are! It's amazing that you've been sitting with this news ever since the Lunar New Year. I promise to help you find out what we can. This is actually much more important than my book!"

Qinglin laughed. "It's not such a big deal. At first I was also all worked up about it, but once I settled down and started to give the situation careful thought, I started to wonder what the point of the whole thing really was. My father did his best to forget, and my mother refuses to remember; it is as if they used their entire lives to resist all this—I'm sure they had their reasons for doing so."

"But what could those reasons be?" asked Long Zhongyong.

"There must always be some things in the world not worth remembering. Or rather, some people and things that *must* be forgotten," responded Qinglin.

Long Zhongyong remained silent for quite some time. It was only after their car left Chongqing that he finally spoke. "Indeed, there are always going to be people and things that most people will choose to forget, but there must also be people who choose to remember."

Qinglin didn't respond.

This time they didn't stay over in Wanzhou, but Qinglin did take Long Zhongyong to the grilled fish restaurant where he had taken Liu Jinyuan for a quick lunch before they continued to Li Dongshui's house.

The elderly Li Dongshui was bedridden. His son, Hairy, kept saying that he knew of Hu Shuidang but had never heard of Qierenlu. It was indeed quite far away, and since there never used to be good transportation routes in these parts, news didn't really travel.

Hairy took them to the house of the old man who had mentioned Qierenlu last time. He also just kept repeating that he had heard comrades from the work team mention the place but didn't know anything else. Since he thought it had something to do with a furnace of some kind, he'd always thought the name Qierenlu rather strange. He'd even asked the cadre about the name, which is why he remembered it. Otherwise, there was nothing else he knew.

It seemed as if their trail of clues had gone cold.

Long Zhongyong said, "We have to find someone who used to live in Hu Shuidang back then. Somehow we need to figure out where all those people from Hu Shuidang went."

"One option is for us to go back into town to see if we can look up records about where those residents from Hu Shuidang moved," suggested Qinglin.

"But that was fifty years ago. I'm afraid it's unlikely there will be any records."

"Another option is for us to search along the Eternal Valley River," offered Qinglin. "We can follow the river upstream. That's the river where they found my mother. If we follow along the western bank of the river, I wonder if we might find something? That area is basically the hinterland of Eastern Sichuan. If we see any old estates or architectural sites along the way, we can always stop to check them out."

"I like that idea. We can kill two birds with one stone," said Long Zhongyong.

They stayed the night in a town called Xiangshui and by noon the next day had found the Eternal Valley River.

Qinglin's original plan was to follow the river upstream. It sounded good in theory, but it turned out to be difficult in practice. That's because there was no road running alongside the river; instead, they had to travel on several small winding roads that took them through numerous mountains and valleys. They would often see a series of hills stretching out before them, but then a steep wall of strange peaks would appear as if out of nowhere. Each mountain connected to other mountains, and the valleys seemed to be surrounded by even larger valleys. On the way, Qinglin told Long Zhongyong all about the stories that took place here during the campaign to wipe out the bandits.

Long Zhongyong stared out the window toward the mountains and the river and sighed. "No wonder there were so many bandits here. There is lush vegetation, good soil, and a constant water source. It's a great place for farming; it's the perfect place to live off the land and be completely self-sufficient. It's also the kind of place that while ideal for hiding out is also easy to escape from."

"So what you are trying to say is that it was a good life to be a bandit back then?" Qinglin asked.

"I'm sure it was a much better life than being a poor peasant; otherwise, how do you explain the scourge of bandits who overtook this region?"

"You're right, Zhongyong. Anytime you have a phenomenon that deviates from the norm, there is always a deeper context that explains why," said Qinglin.

The two of them continued on their journey, frequently stopping along the way. Whenever they passed a village, they would pull over to ask around to see if they could learn anything. On the way, they were actually able to talk to quite a few elderly people, but all of them just shook their heads when asked about Hu Shuidang or Qierenlu. They spent several days on the road alongside the river and saw a few estates that were more than a hundred years old; none of them were very large, and all had been severely damaged. No one they met had ever heard of Qierenlu. Qinglin was growing ever more puzzled; it was as if this place Qierenlu had never existed. He even started to question himself: *Did I somehow mishear the name?*

The majority of the villages here in the hinterland of Eastern Sichuan were quite desolate. Perhaps it was owing to their sparse papulation that these places all felt as if they were devoid of life. The rapeseed had been harvested, the spring corn had already fallen to the ground, and with the seedlings yet to sprout the turquoise green of the fields appeared somewhat faded. Wherever there was a village there were also rows of dense green trees and vegetation—all promising the tranquility of the rural life hidden within.

Long Zhongyong kept sighing all the way there, but there were more sighs of lamentation than admiration. His sighs of admiration were mostly in response to the natural scenery; his sighs of lamentation were primarily directed at the affairs of the human world. He kept complaining about how ugly all the new construction they saw was and how all the older buildings were dilapidated and in disrepair. Beyond the natural scenery, virtually none of the architecture they encountered on their trip was worth looking at.

Long Zhongyong felt that people used to build homes that were in harmony with nature, evoking the sense of a mutually dependent relationship between architecture and nature. But today, even though there are all these architects and rapid advances in the quality of construction materials and tools, rural homes seemed to just keep getting uglier and uglier. He felt that every building seemed to be intent on going against nature, as if through their very posture the buildings were announcing, I'm not going to cooperate with you! I'm not going to allow you to create anything beautiful! Instead, I'm going to become a rotten tumor to make you ugly beyond belief. I'm determined to be your enemy.

He said, "Just look at that! Look, look, look! Take a look at Chongqing and you will see! It is a city with so much potential: it could be improved in so many ways, and yet they insist on building high-rise buildings on the peaks of mountains. It is as if they are insisting on destroying the aesthetic beauty you get from viewing the different layers of the mountains. When you are walking on the streets of Chongqing, there is nowhere you can look without seeing buildings hanging overhead. It leaves people with such an oppressive feeling. It's a real shame."

Qinglin laughed. "That's what you call 'trying to win a height contest with the God of Heaven!'"

Long Zhongyong said, "People have all been operating as if they actually get pleasure from competing with nature. In the process, they have forgotten how important harmony is as a basic principle. Isn't it foolish?"

The two of them had spent a lot of time driving in circles around the area. They were constantly chatting to kill the time, and they both had much to complain about.

They were also surrounded by mountains, which meant that cell service would frequently go in and out of dead zones as they were driving.

Qinglin received few calls during their trip, but Long Zhongyong continued to get numerous texts and calls. He was chatting the entire way. After a call from one of his students, Long Zhongyong abruptly turned to Qinglin to say, "Hey, do you remember our talking about going to a place called the Mansion of Lost Souls? According to my student, it should be right in this area. Why don't we go check it out? Of course, we'll continue searching for Qierenlu along the way. What do you say?"

"That sounds great," replied Qinglin.

Long Zhongyong's student texted him on how to find the place. He read the directions aloud: "Head toward the town of Lucky and find Pearl Stream Bay. Not far from there you should be able to see a towering building on the mountain. Just head straight for the tower. The villagers there are quite down-to-earth, and the village head is an educated man; I'm sure he'll be able to help you."

Qinglin checked his map and discovered that they had not been taking the most efficient route, but as it turned out, they weren't that far from the place the student had suggested. They got out of the car to ask some local villagers for directions and then veered away from the river in a different direction.

It wasn't too long before they left the main road behind and ended up on a much smaller dirt road; it was so bumpy that they felt as if they were on a ship battling through heavy waves. They were forced to slow down the jeep to a crawl. By the time they arrived at a town called Black Dragon, it was already pitch-black outside. They decided to stay the night in Black Dragon and head out for Lucky first thing the next morning.

Black Dragon and Lucky were small towns tucked away deep in the mountains. Most outsiders didn't even know these places existed. Because of the difficulty getting to these places, non-locals almost never passed through these parts. Although the darkness of night was especially dense and the winds were raging, they could make out layers of shadows projecting down from the mountains.

Qinglin said, "This place reminds me of Great Water Well in the town of Cypress Dam. If this Mansion of Lost Souls turns out to be another large family estate, you have to wonder what kind of person would set up an estate in such a remote location. Just think of the cost of transporting all the construction materials out here!"

"It's hard to imagine, but there are always people willing to do strange things like that," responded Long Zhongyong.

The town was quiet, and there was nothing to see or do there. Since the two of them were exhausted from driving around all day, they found a place to stay and decided to turn in early. The next morning they picked up breakfast at a small store they found along the road; they asked the people there if they knew about the Mansion of Lost Souls. They knew they must be getting close because everyone at the shop knew of the place. The shop owner said to head west for a few dozen *li*; he said there was no reason to stop in Lucky, which would be a detour. But he did warn them to be sure to go during daylight hours—ghosts and spirits took over the place at night. "If you go at night," he claimed, "some of those disturbed spirits might try to take over the bodies of the living." The way he spoke sent shivers along their spines; at the same time, though, it piqued their interest.

They set off on another bumpy road. They felt as if they were driving through rocks and woods, and their jeep had to proceed so slowly that they could have walked faster. They put on Bandari's *Silence with Sound from Nature*. Long Zhongyong unrolled his window, and the music's melodies echoed throughout the mountains. It was as if the notes were suspended on the branches of all the trees, and they both felt a sense of peace and harmony.

"I can't imagine how upset my boss would be if he knew what we were using this jeep for!" Qinglin joked.

"Well, since he already agreed to let you use the car, I wouldn't give it a second thought. We would never make it out of these mountains alive if we didn't have a car, so your boss should be happy!" retorted Long Zhongyong.

They both laughed, and it was while they were laughing that they caught sight of upturned pointed eaves appearing atop the mountain.

Their laughter immediately ceased. Long Zhongyong exclaimed, "Wow, it's gorgeous!"

They continued forward, and their destination became clearer as they got closer. It was a stone tower, and the way it was built on the top of a mountain made the tower itself become the peak. Atop the tower was a pavilion with pointed eaves curved toward the sky; the four corners looked like a set of extended wings preparing to lift the entire tower off the ground.

The sun wasn't terribly strong that day; nonetheless, it was a magnificent sight when it shone directly on the tower. Those aged beams and upturned eaves all had a strange and unique quality about them.

As their jeep got closer, through the foliage they could make out several openings in the tower wall; these were for the cannons. A long wall around the perimeter of the tower stretched from the tower base and extended along the curves of the mountain. The wall was also built from stones, and there were more square-shaped blastholes equally spaced out along the wall. The wall followed the natural rock formations of the mountain and was partially obscured by a section of dense woods.

"You can only imagine how many bandits must have tried to attack this place in order for the defenders to have built a fortification like that," said Long Zhongyong.

"After we left Great Water Well last time, I spent a few days in Eastern Sichuan with my boss's father; he was actually the one who led my father out of the mountains. He was an old revolutionary who had led the campaign against the bandits in this area. He proudly told me that ever since their campaign, this region has been completely free from any trace of bandit activity. From then on and throughout the next half century, the people of Eastern Sichuan have been able to enjoy a peaceful life free from the threat of bandits. According to him, this was an unprecedented achievement."

Long Zhongyong replied, "From what I learned on the way here, people were particularly brutal here when it came to how they implemented the land reform campaign."

Qinglin sighed. "That's right. But that's how revolution works; it's either us or them. There isn't much else that could have been done. At least people in our profession don't need to worry about all that. But looking at the direction they went with those old-style villas and estates and the overall layout of their walls and courtyard; protecting themselves from bandits was indeed an extremely important part of their lives. This estate actually reminds me of the high walls surrounding the Li family's ancestral hall at Great Water Well."

Long Zhongyong noted, "Actually, this place isn't that far from Cypress Dam."

Finally, just before sunset, they found Pearl Stream Bay, and the village was not far away. The village at dusk was so quiet that it might as well have been deserted.

Long Zhongyong suggested, "Why don't we knock on one of the nicer homes to see if they might be willing to take us in for the night. You're in charge of the money, so perhaps you can offer them something for their trouble."

Qinglin laughed. "I'll offer them a few hundred yuan a night for them to put us up and provide a meal. I'm sure for most of the people here that much money will feel like a fortune that just fell from heaven onto their lap!"

Long Zhongyong also laughed. "You should offer a few hundred yuan for each of us! Show some charity—after all, you've got money! Just think about how difficult it is for the people living here in this backwater mountain village! Don't be so cheap!"

Qinglin responded, "Of course!"

A SOFT BURIAL

Qinglin's jeep passed by the Mansion of Lost Souls. The trees and foliage surrounding the estate were so thick that they couldn't find the front gate; they couldn't even see the courtyard walls that clearly.

Qinglin commented, "My goodness, this place is really guarded like a fortress."

Long Zhongyong said, "Didn't they say the place was abandoned? Clearly no one has been maintaining the roads here either."

Pearl Stream Bay was the name of a nearby cove where the river water was shallow and filled with rocks and boulders. It was almost impossible to steer a boat through that area. It was next to an area called Luxiao Village (even the names of these places seemed to be buried here deep in the mountains). Only a few dozen families were living there, all in stone houses; it looked as if they built their homes using rocks that had fallen from the mountain. The village was surrounded by trees, thorny bushes, and reeds so thick that from a distance the entire outline of the village was completely obscured by the foliage.

They were able to identify the village head, and since his house wasn't too bad, they decided to ask him if they could stay the night. They were particularly happy to learn that his newly constructed home even had a working toilet. The village head, who was in his thirties, was named Happy Lu. He said he had spent time as a migrant worker in both Shenzhen and Chongqing. After growing weary of life in the big city, he wanted to return to his hometown. When he was away, he was always working for others and had no real social standing to speak of. But once he returned home, he could be his own boss. And wherever he went, his fellow villagers seemed to respect him. He might not have been making as much money as he had in the cities, but at least he was able carry his head high and had a future to look forward to. In a self-deprecating tone he joked, "People used to treat poor people without dignity and respect; they looked at them as people who deserved to be yelled at and scorned. But as I see it, even poor people should be treated with some amount of dignity and respect."

Quite a few houses in the village turned out to be empty and abandoned. Happy Lu said that a lot of people once lived here. But in the end the village proved to be too far off the beaten path, and over time people gradually moved away. Some of them migrated to Wanzhou, others to Chongqing. A few even moved to Fengjie. Happy Lu said, "Life is much more convenient in the city. As long as you're willing to work hard, you can always find work. Almost any little random job in the city will earn you more money than you can make here in several months."

The village turned out not to be as impoverished as Qinglin and Long Zhongyong had imagined. The villagers had electricity, and several families even had television sets. But there was still no internet service here. And every night just after nine o'clock the electricity would turn off. They had a few extra hours of electricity on the weekends.

Long Zhongyong said, "This place is so close to the Three Gorges Dam. There should be more than ample power for this area."

Happy Lu responded, "We're just happy to have any electricity at all. We all go to bed early and are asleep when they shut it down anyway."

They continued with their small talk for a quite a while before finally asking about the Mansion of Lost Souls.

Happy Lu said, "That mansion must be at least several hundred years old. We all refer to it as the Ghost House. I don't know where the name Mansion of Lost Souls came from, but it was probably from some student who once visited the place. The Ghost House really is haunted—I'm being serious. There are ghosts there. No one in the village ever dares going anywhere near the walls of that property after dark. You can hear the ghosts wandering around the courtyard up there."

Qinglin quickly asked, "What kinds of sounds do you actually hear?"

"All kinds of sounds," replied Happy Lu. "Sometimes you hear crying and laughter; other times you can hear the sound of human voices. I heard that Master Lu, who used to live there, was quite an imposing figure; we often hear him barking orders. Whenever it is windy, you can hear clanking and banging and things flapping in the wind. It sounds as if there are a lot of people inside doing all kinds of things. You also hear people on the mountaintop moaning in tears. And whenever there is thunder, Master Lu follows the thunderclaps with his own thunderous screams; it is as if the thunder god himself is calling out."

Long Zhongyong's curiosity was aroused. "What exactly does he scream?"

Happy Lu lowered his voice. "He speaks in a deep authoritative tone, saying, 'Give them a soft burial! Soft burial!'"

Qinglin was taken aback. "What?"

Happy Lu repeated, "He says, 'Soft burial!'"

Qinglin was bemused. "Hmm, I could swear that I've heard that phrase before."

Long Zhongyong asked, "What does it mean?"

Happy Lu answered, "It is when you bury someone's body directly in the dirt without any casket or wrapping. The local elders say that someone who will die with lingering anger or regret and doesn't want to be reincarnated can decide to have a soft burial."

Qinglin abruptly got to his feet and announced, "I just remembered! When my father died in that traffic accident, my mother cried out, 'Don't give him a soft burial!' It's all coming back to me now. That's what she said!"

Qinglin suddenly felt as if he were on the verge of finally figuring something out. It was as if it were now almost within his reach.

Long Zhongyong said, "First time I've ever heard of such a thing. Why would he call out 'soft burial'? Is that how he was buried?"

"That's right," replied Happy Lu. "You can visit the Ghost House tomorrow when it's light out and you'll see for yourself."

Qinglin could hardly sleep that night.

Every time he came to Eastern Sichuan, a few things always seemed to clash with the isolated information he was able to garner from his mother over the years. What was the connection between this place and what happened here and his mother? He couldn't figure it out. But that night as he drifted back and forth between being asleep and being awake, Qinglin could hear a voice whispering in his ear: "Soft burial! Soft burial!" One moment it was a stern weathered voice, the next moment it was a shrill sharp voice. He couldn't identify that first voice, but he knew that second one—it was the sound of his mother's voice calling.

That night he even saw in his dreams the scene of the bus accident that took his father's life. He could also see his mother's body collapsed on the ground as she cried out—it was all right there playing out before his eyes.

SANZHITANG

First thing the next morning Qinglin and Long Zhongyong ate breakfast at village head Happy Lu's house before following him off to the Ghost House.

Happy Lu said that the Ghost House had been there so many years that they had all grown accustomed to its presence; nobody really gave it a second thought.

"A few years back a middle school student from the village brought a classmate from Fengjie here; that classmate took some photographs. After that we started getting occasional visits from outsiders who think of the place as some kind of marvel. That student referred to the place as the Mansion of Lost Souls; but it is unclear who first coined the term. Everyone in the village still refers to the place as the Ghost House, though. I don't know where that name came from either."

Happy Lu said that no one ever had to tell him; he just grew up always knowing that the place was the Ghost House. There were many courtyards and rooms within the walled compound, but they were all empty. Almost no one from the village ever went in there, and certainly no one dared to live there. Back when they were still children, all the adults instructed them not to go anywhere near that place. In fact, they would probably never have ventured inside had it not been for the occasional visit from a guest or local politician who wanted to see the place.

"These days there is only a crazy old man who lives there," said Happy Lu. "He lives on state welfare and rarely leaves the compound. The village committee has people regularly deliver him rice, salt, and other basic necessities. He grows his own potatoes and vegetables in the garden there."

"Does he know the history of the place?" asked Long Zhongyong.

"He's is his seventies and used to be a caretaker at the house," explained Happy Lu. "He should know all about what happened there. But he's a madman. Even if he knows, I'm afraid he might have trouble articulating things."

The courtyard walls surrounding the Ghost House were particularly long. As Qinglin drove, he said, "This mansion is really huge."

"Are we able to go up to the top of the tower to take a look?" asked Long Zhongyong.

Happy Lu responded, "The madman doesn't allow anyone near it, so I've never been up there. I suspect that no one from our village has ever been to the top of the tower."

"This mansion would be a really strong selling point if you ever wanted to make this village a tourist destination," Qinglin suggested. "I think you could attract a lot of visitors. You could turn all those village homes into bed-and-breakfast venues. All you really need to do is to repair the local roads. You could instantly improve the local economy."

Happy Lu responded, "I also thought about doing something like that, but it won't work."

"Why not?" asked Long Zhongyong. "I could help you draw up a design diagram and shoot a series of photos you could use for promotion and advertising. If the mansion really is several hundred years old, I suspect it should have various architectural traits consistent with Qing dynasty homes. You could even apply for the place to be designated a protected cultural heritage site."

"Unfortunately, there is no way that will work," explained Happy Lu. "The village elders don't want anyone entering the Ghost House. They say it will disturb the spirits of the Lu family and cause a great calamity to befall the village."

"Really?" Qinglin seemed surprised. "How could people believe such a thing?"

"Once you see the place, you will understand," said Happy Lu. "I don't want to talk about it. None of us here in the village are willing to talk about what happened there."

Happy's words left them with an even greater sense of mystery. Qinglin and Long Zhongyong were utterly perplexed.

The Ghost House was not far from the village, but it stood alone in the middle of a forest and up on a mountain. Since it had been so long since anyone went up there, all the paths were covered with wild grasses and overgrown weeds. Just below the courtyard wall were a few structures so badly damaged that they were uninhabitable. Happy Lu pointed to the structures and explained, "That area is where the Lu family's horse stables used to be. In the past they were the only family in the entire village to have a horse cart. If you have a horse cart, you can go straight through the mountains to reach Wanzhou in less than a day. I'm not sure if you know, but Sichuan is famous for its horses."

As their jeep reached the forest surrounding the mansion, they came to where they could proceed no farther. But they could see a series of green paving stones forming a path that cut directly through the forest toward the courtyard wall. As they pulled up closer, they spied a small gate that seemed to be set into the courtyard wall. They all got out of the car and started walking along the stone path toward that gate.

"This must be the rear gate," noted Qinglin.

But Happy Lu corrected him. "Nope, this is the main gate. There is only one entrance into the Ghost House."

Qinglin was surprised. "Only one tiny gate for a mansion compound of this size?"

Long Zhongyong explained, "This seemed to be a feature of many of the buildings here in Eastern Sichuan. I saw a similarly small gate at another mansion estate, owned by the Chen family, in this region.

"The village elders say that a large mansion with a single tiny gate is a sign that the family was once engaged in the opium trade. Since these families were not involved in a proper business, they had no right to have a big official front gate; instead, they just have small gates or side gates."

"Wow, that's really fascinating," said Qinglin. "It is hard to imagine a large powerful family like this still respecting a local rule like that."

Long Zhongyong said, "Actually, here in the Chinese countryside, these types of rules are extremely strict. And just because a given family may have built up a lot of wealth doesn't necessarily mean that they were respected."

"So according to what you are saying, this Lu family must once have been involved in the opium trade?" asked Qinglin.

Happy Lu said, "A few generations back they were. Once they built up enough capital, some members of their family were able to serve as officials for the Qing court. Later they turned all the opium farms on this mountain into tea farms. The family were already engaged in legitimate business pursuits before the Republican period. But since their ancestors had already built the gate like this, later generations never bothered changing it. Later, when the bandits became active in this area, they probably thought having one small gate was safer anyway."

Long Zhongyong laughed. "Keeping bandits at bay is more important than showing off one's wealth. That actually makes sense."

The estate stretched from the foot of the mountain all the way up to its peak. All the structures were built to fit with the terrain of the mountain. Standing at the foot of the mountain, one could see only the main tower; all the other structures were obscured by the high courtyard walls and the many trees.

The gate wasn't much worth mentioning, having only a single-panel door. It was quite shocking to see just how narrow it was. Two people walking shoulder to shoulder would barely get through. The gatepost was constructed from two solid pieces of large stone; carved into the left side were three large Chinese characters.

Long Zhongyong was the first one to notice the characters and immediately read them aloud: "Sanzhitang. Wow, this Ghost House has its own proper name: Sanzhitang, the 'Hall of the Three Who Know'—it's actually quite elegant."

Qinglin was straggling a bit behind the others, but as soon as he heard the word "Sanzhitang" he felt as if he had been struck by a bolt of lightning. He frantically asked, "What did you just say? Did you mention something-tang?"

Long Zhongyong explained, "This Ghost House's formal name is Sanzhitang."

Qinglin took a step forward and saw those three faded characters carved clearly into the stone gatepost: Sanzhitang. He remembered what his mother had said the first time she arrived at the villa he had bought for her: "My house? Is this Qierenlu or Sanzhitang?"

He couldn't help becoming excited. He turned to Long Zhongyong and exclaimed, "This is it. This is the place I've been looking for!"

Long Zhongyong was confused. "Didn't you say you were looking for a place called Qierenlu?"

Qinglin explained, "When I first brought my mother to see the new house I'd bought her, I told her this was our new home. She responded by asking, 'My house? Is this Qierenlu or Sanzhitang?' At the time, I didn't understand what she said. I just heard something-tang. But now I'm sure she said Sanzhitang."

Long Zhongyong was quite surprised. "Really? That's unbelievable! So what you're saying is that this Ghost House is somehow connected with your mother?"

"I'm not exactly sure," said Qinglin. "But isn't the whole thing strange?"

Happy Lu had been intently following their conversation and interrupted with surprise, "Your mother is from here? She mentioned Sanzhitang?"

"I'm not exactly sure," said Qinglin. "She is suffering from amnesia. Fifty years ago some people saved her from drowning; they pulled her out of the Eternal Valley River, and she hasn't been able to remember anything that happened before that. She is now quite ill, but just before she got sick she said some strange things that gave me a few clues."

Happy Lu pointed up to the mountain where the tower was situated. "Behind this mountain is a smaller hill, and beyond that is a body of water that merges with the Eternal Valley River." As he spoke he hesitated for a moment. "But . . . I hope you're not related to the Lu family."

"Why not?" asked Qinglin.

Happy Lu didn't answer; instead, he just pushed the gate open and called out: "Grandpa Ritchie? I'm coming in. It's me, Happy Lu."

A husky voice coarsely responded, "Close the door!"

"I know . . ." Happy Lu said.

Inside was a large open courtyard. The wall was crumbling, but the trees and grass were growing profusely everywhere. On either side of the courtyard stood two massive stone cauldrons, both filled with water with fallen leaves floating on the surface.

Long Zhongyong said, "One look at those cauldrons and you know this was a family with inordinate wealth." Happy Lu didn't understand the meaning of those cauldrons, so Long Zhongyong explained it to him. "These are called *taiping gang*, 'cauldrons for peace and prosperity'; they are required for large courtyards like this and are especially common among large wealthy families. These cauldrons are supposed to bring good luck. The water they collect is a symbol of the family's accumulated wealth. The other use is more practical, as you can use the water in case you need to put out a fire. These stone cauldrons are especially common in Eastern Sichuan, where they usually source the stone locally, and are quite sturdy and able to last a long time."

Happy Lu nodded. "So that's what they are for!"

Happy Lu led Qinglin and Long Zhongyong forward. They passed through several atriums, each separate and yet connected. Although the atriums were all contained within a single large courtyard, each one felt different from the others. The main house was abandoned, its rafters full of dust and cobwebs. Large portions of the beams and columns had been eaten away by moths, and piles of sawdust littered the floor.

Long Zhongyong explained, "This is a typical southern-style estate layout. The structures are quite similar to Great Water Well, but this is on a different scale and has certain stylistic elements inspired by Huizhou homes from this period. I suspect that the generation that built this house came to Sichuan from the south, around Hunan or Guangxi. Wow, you can still see all the intricate carvings on the beams, even if the colors have faded."

Meanwhile, Qinglin had something else on his mind.

THE CRAZY OLD MAN

Qinglin appeared numb as he followed behind Happy Lu.

He had so much on his mind. All at once his mind seemed to be braving an internal storm while at the same time remaining a complete blank. He kept quietly muttering, "Sanzhitang. Sanzhitang. That must have been what my mother said; otherwise, why else would that name sound so familiar?"

They walked down a long wooden passageway, but Happy Lu abruptly stopped just as they arrived at the moon gate. "Once you go through this moon gate," he said, "you will enter the garden of the Ghost House. Take a look around for yourselves. If you want to know about what happened to the Lu family, you need to start here."

Without hesitation, Qinglin and Long Zhongyong stepped over the threshold of the moon gate and headed directly toward the garden. As soon as they walked through the gate, they both felt as if they were struck by a bolt of lightning. They froze in their steps.

The garden before them was littered with graves. The graves were everywhere: under the trees, beside the courtyard walls, beside the dilapidated flower terrace, inside the flower bed, and nestled between the bamboo trees—they seemed to be haphazardly spread out as far as the eye could see. A rock marked each grave. The ground was covered with rotting leaves, and wild grasses were growing all around the burial sites.

Long Zhongyong almost screamed, "What is this?"

Happy Lu wasn't willing to go any closer. He just stood behind them and from a distance replied, "The entire Lu family is here."

"What do you mean?" asked Qinglin.

"I'm not exactly sure of all the details," Happy Lu explained. "But according to the elders around here, the Lu family was one of the most powerful and respected clans in the area. Master Lu was said to have a very strong personality. When the Land Reform Campaign began, word came down that people would be arriving the following day to struggle against them . . . so the night before the entire Lu family committed group suicide."

Long Zhongyong and Qinglin both exclaimed in unison, "My God!"

Happy Lu continued, "The person who insisted on carrying out the struggle session against the Lu family was actually someone who used to work for them. He showed up the next morning with a group of people to start the struggle session but was surprised to discover there was no one at home. Everyone thought it was strange because in order to assure that everything would go smoothly, they had actually sent a few people there the previous day to stand guard outside their compound. Since there was only one entrance, it was a fairly straightforward task and no one was reported trying to leave. They also noted that the courtyard walls were too high for anyone to have climbed over. And so they began to search the premises, one atrium at a time. Once they got to the garden and stepped through the moon gate, they immediately saw all the freshly dug graves. They were all scared out of their wits. Originally their compound had been slated to be divvied up among the poor, but after that no one dared to move in. And they never held that struggle session."

"They all died? Then who dug these graves? Who buried them?" asked Long Zhongyong.

"That's the thing, everyone was confused by that. But no one had an answer," said Happy Lu. "At the time, some people were saying there were ghosts that did it and things like that. It is said that the night it happened, a sudden wind descended from the mountains, roaring through the valley. Then came a terrible thunderstorm and a downpour. A lot of people swore they could hear Master Lu's voice amid the thunder. They heard him screaming, 'Soft burial! Soft burial!' My dad said that his voice was filled with anger and resentment. After that, people were even more afraid of stepping on the property. That's why it has remained empty for all these years. Ever since then, whenever there is a thunderstorm or on stormy nights, everyone in the village can hear myriad sounds coming from the mansion; it's as if all kinds of people are milling around inside and making noise. By the time I was a bit older, everyone already referred to this place as the Ghost House."

Qinglin couldn't help but shudder.

He wondered, *What's my mother's connection with this place? If she's not connected, then why would she have mentioned Sanzhitang? And what does Qierenlu have to do with Sanzhitang? Could my mother be related to that Master Lu he spoke of? Soft burial? Could it be just a coincidence that my mother also spoke those same two words? That isn't a common phrase that normally escapes people's lips.*

Could all this be a coincidence? Qinglin tried to channel his thinking in the direction of coincidence—that this was all just a big coincidence—but no matter how hard he tried, he kept coming up with ideas that pointed him in a different direction. When you have too many coincidences lining up, you start to realize they are not coincidences at all.

Long Zhongyong had no idea what Qinglin was going through in that moment; all he was keen on exploring was that old tower. He asked Happy Lu, "Is it okay with you if we climb up the tower to take a look? If we can get a bird's-eye view, we'll have a much better overall understanding of the entire estate and its layout."

"The crazy old man won't allow it. He'll stop you from going up."

Long Zhongyong was curious. "Who is this guy? Why isn't he afraid of staying here?"

"I heard that he was adopted by the Lu family," said Happy Lu. "He grew up in the Lu compound, and when he got older he stayed on as one of their servants. He wasn't home on the day of the struggle session but returned to discover that the entire family was dead. It drove him insane."

Qinglin suddenly asked, "He grew up with the Lu family?"

"That's what the elders said," affirmed Happy Lu. "They also said that he was in love with one of the Lu family servants. He dug her body out of the ground; miraculously, she somehow still had a pulse. I'm not sure why, but even though she survived she refused to be with him. Later she disappeared. Some say she became a Buddhist nun. The whole story is really complicated. My dad would occasionally talk about that stuff when he was still alive. He said that one of our relatives, named Grandpa Four, wanted to marry another one of the Lu family servants, a girl named Ziping. But she died in the mass suicide too. Grandpa Four didn't understand why she would kill herself: she was young and had nothing to do with the Lu family; there were no plans to struggle against her. Why would she want to die together with a landlord? She would have been much better off leaving them behind and getting married."

"Are there any other village elders who know about the Lu family?" asked Long Zhongyong.

"All that happened more than fifty years ago. There aren't many elders left who remember what happened," replied Happy Lu. "And those who weren't politically active at the time probably wouldn't know much about what happened anyway. Let me think, perhaps I can find one or two people who might know something."

"That would be wonderful. No matter what, we'd really appreciate it if you can help us find a few elders to talk to; even one would be great. As you can see, he might be related to the Lu family." Long Zhongyong pointed to Qinglin and continued, "He's an important businessman from Wuhan. If this mansion is somehow related to his family, it might actually be in your interest. At least he should be able to help fund some better roads for this area."

Happy Lu's face lit up. "Sounds great! I'll do my best. We're not interested in developing tourism here, but we could really use a decent road to get in and out of the area."

Qinglin was lost in thought and wasn't paying attention to what they were talking about, but then he impulsively asked, "Can you find that crazy old man for me? There are some things I'd like to ask him."

"Unfortunately, he always refuses to speak to people," Happy Lu responded. "Actually, for all these years, the only thing he ever says is 'Close the door!'"

"Do you mind if I see him and at least try talking to him?" Qinglin asked.

"There is one option you can try," Happy Lu suggested, "if you walk straight toward the tower. Do you see the canna tree near the western side of the wall? If you walk toward the grave there, he will certainly come out to stop you. But I'm not going to go there with you. It is taboo for those of us who bear the surname Lu to go into that garden."

Qinglin and Long Zhongyong discussed it between themselves and then started to head in the direction of the canna tree.

When they were three or four meters away from the canna tree, an old man with long disheveled hair and a straggly beard suddenly appeared. It was as if he just jumped out of the forest. Although Qinglin and Long Zhongyong both expected him, they were nonetheless startled by his sudden entrance.

The old man extended his hands in an attempt to wave them away. Long Zhongyong pointed toward the tower and said, "Excuse us, sir. Is it okay if we go up to take a look?"

The crazy old man didn't respond; instead, with his arms extended he just glared at them like a tiger stalking its prey. The whites of his eyes seemed particularly pronounced, which gave him a terrifying appearance. Long Zhongyong tried to speak more slowly and to imitate the local dialect, explaining, "We are both teachers, we study architecture, and we build houses. We have no ulterior motives. We just want to check out the tower."

"I don't think talking to him is any use," Qinglin said.

"Well, you're the one who wanted to see him. What do you want to talk to him about?"

Qinglin hesitated for a moment. "Sir, have you heard of a place called Qierenlu? It's located in Hu Shuidang."

The crazy old man seemed surprised. He trained his gaze directly on Qinglin's face. Qinglin reached into his pocket and pulled out a photograph before approaching the old man. He said, "Sir, have you ever seen this person before?"

It was a picture of Qinglin's mother, a photo of her when she was still young. It was originally her wedding photo; but before

Qinglin left on this trip he had the photo scanned, then he cut out his father, enlarged his mother, and had several copies developed.

That's the photo Qinglin showed to the crazy old man.

The old man took a look and appeared visibly shaken. A strange expression appeared on his face; it looked like a combination of shock and fear. He then looked back at Qinglin and studied his face for a long time.

"You recognize her, don't you?" Qinglin grew excited. "She's my mother. I'm her son."

The crazy old man's expression grew even more contorted, and then he suddenly let out a crazed scream and ran off. He continued to cry out as he scurried away.

His reaction made both Qinglin and Long Zhongyong shudder with an uncomfortable fear.

Qinglin was so taken aback that he began to stammer, "He . . . he . . . he . . . he seemed to recognize my mother, didn't he?"

Long Zhongyong was also surprised. "It indeed seems that something is wrong . . ."

Qinglin decided to pursue the crazy old man. Long Zhongyong followed close behind. That's when they heard Happy Lu calling out from the other side of the moon gate. "Hey, What happened? Where is Grandpa Ritchie?"

Qinglin and Long Zhongyong ran over to Happy Lu. Qinglin asked, "Did you see in which direction the old man ran off?"

Happy Lu responded, "He just ran past and went into the house, but I'm not sure which section of the mansion he is in. What happened?"

Qinglin waved the photograph in his hand. "I showed him this picture of my mother, and he seemed to recognize her."

Happy Lu took the photo in his hand and looked at it. "Really? How is such a coincidence possible?"

For the time being, none of them knew what to do next. Gradually they all began to search the residence for the crazy old man. Since they didn't know their way around, their search was completely chaotic and disorganized.

They spent the entire morning looking for him, but they found no trace of the old man.

Eventually Qinglin and Long Zhongyong decided to walk toward the tower, even ascending to the top, but at no point did the crazy old man come out to stop them.

That's how they eventually saw the top of the tower and were able to finally visit the rooftop pavilion.

Leaning against the railing and looking down, they had a bird's-eye view of the entire estate. Long Zhongyong said, "There's actually no need for us to run all over looking for him. We can just stay here and keep an eye out for the old man, and we'll see him as soon as he appears."

Qinglin thought the plan made sense, so he just stared down, scanning the property below. Long Zhongyong took out his camera, put on a long-focus lens, and started taking shots of all the different corners of the estate. They skipped lunch and stayed up there until dusk, but there was still no sign of the crazy old man.

HOW SHOULD WE SPEAK OF THIS HISTORY?

News that two city folk had come to the village—a professor and a businessman, whose mother might be somehow related to the Ghost House—spread quickly, and it wasn't long before everyone in the village knew.

That night quite a few people came to Happy Lu's house to see the new visitors from the city. So many people showed up that there wasn't enough room for everybody inside the house. Happy Lu had to move some chairs outside so that everyone could sit out on the drying field. Once all the people were there, everyone started chatting and the whole thing took on a festive atmosphere. Happy Lu's wife was ecstatic to see so much activity around her house. She busied herself going in and out, boiling water and serving tea.

But the crazy old man never showed up, and Qinglin was getting quite anxious. He was determined to solve the mystery of his mother's past, for he still believed that revealing the truth about the past might be the key to awakening his mother. But what he had seen and heard earlier that day made him fearful. He worried that the secret waiting to be revealed might be too horrific to face; it might even end up hurting both his mother and him.

Long Zhongyong seemed to sense his friend's apprehension. "Are you scared about what you might find?"

"I'm not sure if 'scared' is the right word, but I am feeling anxious," replied Qinglin.

"There must be some terrible story that led everyone to refer to this once luxurious estate as the Ghost House. Not matter what, I think we need to face that. I'm afraid what we discover will be the real, historical truth."

Qinglin got up his courage and said, "Okay, let's hear what the villagers have to say."

Here in the mountains in early summer it could get chilly at night. Some of the older villagers even placed a lined jacket over their shoulders to keep warm. Qinglin was wearing short sleeves, and whenever the cold night wind blew, he would start to sneeze.

Happy Lu's wife was quite considerate and quickly found a blanket to keep him warm. She even joked, "Don't they say sneezing is a sign you miss home? Mr. Wu, you've been here only one day and you're already missing home!"

All the villagers broke out in raucous laughter. Happy Lu also found a coat for Long Zhongyong to put on. He also laughed. "We've got to take good care of our guests! If we send them back sick, no one will come visit us here in Luxiao Village anymore! We're still hoping our two guests will help us fix the roads here!"

Everyone laughed at that joke. Their laughter really stood out against the utter silence of the mountains.

The villagers sat in a circle around the two guests. Occasionally some of the villagers would walk over to Qinglin to get a better look at him; they seemed to really look at him as a member of the Lu clan. One old-timer said, "Many years ago, someone from the Lu family returned here. You resemble him a bit; he also had a fair complexion like you."

Someone immediately interrupted, "Sanba, you're getting confused—that guy who visited was from the United States! How could you confuse him with this guy?"

Someone else chimed in, "Back in 1991, or maybe it was 1992 . . . that's right, it was 1992. I remember, I was teaching third grade at the time and it was quite exciting. Happy's dad was guarding the door and wouldn't let us go in."

Happy Lu said, "Let's not get off the subject. Please let Lu Sanba continue." With that, he turned to Qinglin and Long Zhongyong. "Lu Sanba used to teach middle school in town. He moved back to our village after retirement. He is a very cultured person and knows a lot about many things."

Qinglin and Long Zhongyong offered a few pleasantries and shared their business cards with him. Lu Sanba looked at their business cards and announced to everyone, "Today we have two truly important guests. A professor from Shanghai and a business manager from Wuhan, where he is a big boss. These are the kind of people we'd never be able to get an appointment with if we were to go to the big city."

Qinglin said, "Today we have come here hoping to hear you tell us some stories about the Lu family. We'd really appreciate it if you could share some with us."

Lu Sanba said, "I was still quite young back then. All I knew was that the entire Lu family had died. But I still had no idea what exactly happened to them. So everything I know is all secondhand knowledge. But when the Lu family's two sons returned home, I was part of the welcoming committee, so I saw them both with my own eyes. We all share the same surname of Lu, you see, which means we are all descended from the same ancestor. That's why the county leaders asked me to help out when they visited. Just now Fuwa was correct: that was in 1992. Master Lu's second-born son and youngest son both returned home. They came back for the Tomb-Sweeping Festival forty years after they had left. At the time, Second Young Master was around the same age that I am now. But he had clearly taken good care of himself and looked much younger than his age; he had fair skin and a lot of meat on his bones."

Another villager chimed in, "The rich eat well!"

"They certainly do," continued Lu Sanba. "They came back from the United States to pay their respects to their ancestors. Several cadres from the county accompanied them, but no matter how much those cadres smiled and tried to cajole them, the Lu brothers never smiled once. As soon as they got out of their car, they headed straight for the Ghost House. The two brothers must already have heard about what happened to their family. The second they laid eyes on the main gate, they both burst into tears. Second Young Master said that the family gate looked exactly the same as the day he left, though perhaps a bit worse for wear. When they passed through the moon gate and saw all the graves, the two of them dropped to their knees. They practically crawled their way to the site where their parents were buried.

The sound of their sobbing was enough to shatter the hearts of everyone around them. Even those cadres shed a few tears. No one tried to calm the brothers down; they just let them mourn. Everyone knew this was decades of accumulated tears that they were letting out. After spending so long crying, they finally got up to burn incense and paper money, they kowtowed over and over, and then they cried again. Although quite advanced in age, Second Young Master kowtowed so many times that he even scraped his forehead open. When he finished kowtowing, he stood up and yelled, 'Where is Jindian?'"

"Who is Jindian?" Qinglin asked.

Happy Lu answered, "He was the leader of the group that instigated the struggle against the Lu family. He used to work for them. His full name was Wang Jindian. The Lu family had raised him ever since he was a young boy. The Lu brothers all knew him. A lot of people in the village accused him of being ungrateful and betraying the Lu family."

Lu Sanba continued, "Actually, you can't say that Jindian was being ungrateful. A long time ago Jindian's family was completely shattered, and what happened was very much connected with the Lu family. Almost everyone in the Wang family died—Jindian was the only survivor. At the time, Jindian was still breastfeeding; he was too young to understand anything about what happened. Only after he grew up did he learn the truth. How could he not hate the Lus after learning what happened? After hearing what happened to his family, he immediately packed up and left the Lu household the very next morning. I remember my uncle telling me that Jindian returned here with the sole intention of exacting revenge. Before he came back, however, the county officials had already agreed not to target the Lu family."

"Why would the county ever agree to that in the first place?" asked Long Zhongyong.

"Master Lu was a veteran revolutionary from the Revolution of 1911. But that wasn't the main reason. The main thing was that the Lu family had provided major assistance to the Communist forces in Eastern Sichuan. They gave financial support and even helped hide several wounded Communist soldiers. During the campaign against the bandits, Master Lu went with Second Young Master into the mountains to convince the bandits to surrender."

Another old man spoke up. "I remember when they met with the bandits to persuade them to surrender. Master Lu told the bandit leaders that the forces leading the campaign to suppress them were a proper army; they had defeated several hundred thousand Nationalist troops, so how could a few bandits with rifles possibly stand up to them? If the bandits got killed in the mountains, their bodies would be left there to feed the wolves; not even a trace of their bones would be left. It would be much better if they just surrendered and went home. At the most, maybe they would be locked up for a few days, but then they could go home to be reunited with their wives and children.

"Master Lu also told them that the new government had sent out a notice stating that most of the bandits were poor people who were forced into banditry because they had no other means to make a living. But the new government was intent on putting the poor in charge. As long as you were willing to work, he told them, the government guaranteed you would have food and clothing. There should be no reason for you to ever feel the need to turn to banditry again, he said. 'If you come down off the mountain now and sign a guarantee promising to break ties with the bandits and never to go against the government, we will ensure that you won't even have to go to jail!'"

Lu Sanba added, "That's right. That's exactly what Master Lu said. The Lu family ancestors used to deal in opium. They were considered the most powerful clan in these parts. Even the father of the bandit leader used to work as a hired hand for the Lu family. So after they heard Master Lu out and received assurance from him that they wouldn't be arrested, the bandits all came out of the mountains and surrendered. They were forced to enroll in a reeducation program that lasted a few days, and then they were all released to go home. Not one of them was sent to prison.

"The party recognized Master Lu's contributions, which is why the village signed a joint petition during the land reform movement requesting that the Lu family not be targeted. Everyone in the village signed that petition. The cadres working at the county level also recognized the Lu family's past merits and approved the request. But then Jindian returned from out of town where he had been involved in revolutionary activities. The first thing he did when he got back was to demand that the Lu family be struggled against. He said, 'If we don't struggle against them, how are we supposed to break up their land? Are we supposed to keep paying rent to them? Should we allow them to continue having servants and maids wait on them? Are we supposed to just let them go on living in that massive estate and not let the poor live there?' As he made all these arguments, he gradually swayed people, and they decided that the Lu family should be struggled against after all. That's how my uncle explained it to me. My uncle was quite active politically at the time."

An old lady interrupted. "His uncle's name was Baldy. He was really active during those days. He had a thing for the Lu family's maid. But she would rather die than marry him. Then there was Dunzi—he was Happy's dad—he was also an activist; he had his eye on another one of the Lu family's maids. But she also chose to die rather than marry him!"

Everyone present laughed at that.

Lu Sanba also giggled. "Oh my, all those things that happened in the past were so messy; better not to talk about them. We should get to the main subject at hand. After Second Young Master Lu paid his respects to his parents, he stood up and turned to me and asked, 'Where are my wife and son buried?' He also asked where his brother, sister, and aunt were buried. How would I know? We quickly asked everyone there, but no one knew. They sent someone to ask Ritchie—he is that crazy old man you met—but who knows where he ran off to that day. When the brothers discovered that Ritchie was still alive, they wanted to see him. Later when they found out that he was insane, they even suggested bringing him back with them to America to get treated. But they couldn't find him anywhere. The crazy old man reappeared only after the brothers had already left. That night he sat at the head of Master Lu's grave bawling like a baby."

"How did he know which grave belonged to Master Lu?" asked Qinglin.

"Didn't you notice it when you visited the grave earlier today?" asked Happy Lu. "One of the graves was marked with a memorial tablet. That's where Master Lu and his wife were buried. It is said that the two of them were buried together in a single pit."

Long Zhongyong asked, "Who erected that tablet? How would that person have known it was their grave?"

Lu Sanba explained, "The madman told us. He wasn't at the compound when they all committed suicide, but he returned the next morning and managed to save one of the servants. She was able to tell him where Master Lu and his wife were buried."

"So it was that crazy old man who erected that tablet?" asked Qinglin.

"No," Lu Sanba continued. "According to my uncle, it was Jindian. Jindian entered the garden, and as soon as he saw all those graves he collapsed to the ground. My uncle saw that firsthand.

My uncle said that Jindian never expected the Lu family to be so unwavering as to take such a dark path. But it was too much for Jindian to take. Someone else said that he had grown up with the Lu's daughter and they were very close, but the Lu family prevented them from being together. The Lus' daughter died that night too. So many members of the Lu family died that night, including several of their servants. These were all people who had once been very close to Jindian; they had raised him. The weight of the guilt he felt was too great for him to bear. A few days later he sneaked into the compound and erected a memorial tablet for Master Lu and his wife. After that he completely disappeared. A lot of people said that he died, though I'm not sure he is really dead; but no one ever saw or heard from him again."

Happy Lu commented, "I never heard any of these stories. It sounds like a television drama!"

Qinglin took out the photo of his mother and asked, "Have any of you ever seen this woman before?"

The villagers passed the photo around, but everyone shook their head and said they had never seen her before.

"Could she be one of the Lu family's daughters? Or their daughter-in-law?" Qinglin asked.

"Although we all live in the same village where the Ghost House is located, we are separated by a forest. The women of the Lu family would normally stay hidden behind the gates of their compound and seldom come out. So we rarely ever saw them. I never once laid eyes on their daughter-in-law. I saw their daughter only once or twice when she was on her way to school," said Lu Sanba.

"Indeed, once you close the gate on large mansions like that, you are basically cut off from the world," said Long Zhongyong.

"That's right; that's exactly how it is," echoed Lu Sanba.

Qinglin asked again whether anyone had ever heard of Qierenlu. But all the villagers shook their heads.

"I really never heard of it," said Happy Lu.

That's when Long Zhongyong suddenly asked, "Exactly how many daughters did the Lu family have? And how many daughters-in-law did they have?"

Lu Sanba responded, "I think they had just one daughter. Second Young Master had a wife and a son. And Little Young Master was still going to school, so he hadn't taken a wife yet."

"Is it possible that one of them was able to escape?" asked Qinglin.

They all shook their heads and said that would have been impossible. There was someone guarding the gate, and in order to keep the Ghost House safe from bandits, there was only that single way in or out.

Long Zhongyong turned to Qinglin and said, "According to that, the Lu family had one daughter and one daughter-in-law, and they both died that night in the garden. So I don't see how your mother could be connected to any of this."

Qinglin thought about it and nodded his head. "I guess you're right."

Long Zhongyong asked, "No one from the Lu family ever came back here again? Do you have any way to get in touch with them?" He then turned to Qinglin. "If you can get in touch with any Lu family members who are still alive, they should be able to help you. If that crazy old man recognized your mother, I'm sure they would. If we can find a way to contact them, it should be easy to get to the bottom of this."

Qinglin's eyes lit up. "That's right. Lu Sanba, when the Lu brothers visited from America, did they leave you their business card? Or perhaps someone from the county government has their contact information?"

Lu Sanba shook his head. "The cadres from the county government knew they had money and really wanted them to invest in their hometown. They even said they would pay to relocate Master Lu's grave to a nice location and fix up their old mansion. But the brothers didn't give their consent. Second Young Master declared, 'It was my father's decision to be buried there. If you have a conscience, please do not disturb them.' As he left the village he just shook my hand and said thank you. That's because I am also a part of the Lu family. But he had only cold stares for everyone else. My niece, who in those days was working in the county taking care of foreign guests, came home and told me that Second Young Master tried to visit his in-laws while he was here, but he couldn't even find the village where they used to live. Just before he left, he swore that there was three things he would never do: he would never again come back to this place, he would never again look at this place as his home, and he would never allow his children and grandchildren to know about this place. The way he spoke of this place was quite cruel."

Qinglin felt his heart pounding. He remembered what his father had written in his diary: *I will never be able to go back, and I must never let my future children know what happened in that place.* They shared that same sense of resoluteness.

Long Zhongyong sighed, then said, "They cut off their ties so completely. You can tell the pain they felt went all the way down to the bone."

Lu Sanba suddenly raised his voice. "Everyone always looks at the Ghost House and thinks about how tragic the Lu family's fate was. But we should remember that what happened to the Lu family was something they themselves chose. Why doesn't anyone talk about the tragic fate suffered by Jindian's family? If the Lu family hadn't tried to take away their land, would the Wang family have been torn apart like that? How come no one talks about it when a poor person's family are destroyed, but everyone cries about how tragic it is when a rich family are destroyed? And so you need to look at what happened like this: the Lu family destroyed the Wang family, and then they came back for revenge. It boils down to a blood feud between those two families. And before Jindian even had a chance to strike, the Lu family destroyed itself; they didn't even let the servants go. The Lu family raised Jindian, and he later established a memorial tablet for the parents; I guess you could say that hatred was repaid with hatred and kindness was repaid with kindness.

"Now you grit your teeth and say how much you hate the home from which you came. What's the point of that? If you go further back, where do you think all your family wealth came from? You sold opium and made out like a bandit! Do you have any idea how many people died helping your family get rich? They never grit their teeth. Why can't you just let those things go?"

Lu Sanba got really worked up. Some of the things he said really shocked Qinglin and Long Zhongyong.

The old lady who interrupted earlier said, "Lu Sanba, back then your entire family were all politically active. Your family grabbed up all the best land in the village. You all couldn't wait to see Master Lu's family wiped out."

The old lady spoke sharply with a shrill voice that cut right through the night. No one responded after that. Under the blanket of stars, everyone seemed somewhat confused. Even Qinglin and Long Zhongyong were both struck with a feeling of uncertainty.

By then it was already late at night and the villagers began to disperse.

Qinglin and Long Zhongyong returned to their room, but neither of them could get to sleep.

"Tonight was really interesting," said Long Zhongyong. "How should we speak of this history? Depending on the angle from which you look at it, each side seems to have a point."

"I'm also not sure what to say. When you dig back far enough, you find there are some things that become even more difficult to understand," said Qinglin.

"Actually, I feel that things get easier to understand if you dig back far enough," retorted Long Zhongyong.

"Do you agree that all this boils down to a conflict between two families?" asked Qinglin.

"Somewhat, though not entirely. You can't remove what happened from the historical context," said Long Zhongyong.

"That's right," said Qinglin. "I suddenly feel that there is actually no need for us to understand all history. Life has its own natural rules in terms of what gets forgotten and abandoned. Those things that don't want you to know about them have their own way of making sure you never find out. So perhaps it's better if we simply don't know at all. In this world there will always be more things we don't know than those that we do. Even after our working so hard to understand the past, there is no telling if what we find is an accurate version of what really happened."

"So what you're saying is that since we are already in the dark about the past, there is no reason for us to go digging around just to satisfy our own curiosity?" Long Zhongyong asked.

"This isn't at all what I was thinking when I first arrived," Qinglin explained. "But tonight I suddenly had this strong revelation. It really hit me when I heard about what Second Young Master Lu said about those three things he would never do. The Lu brothers were so clear about wanting to completely forget what happened, and they had no intention of ever letting their descendants know the truth. Their driving philosophy seems to have been to let time wash all this away. Seeing the extent to which they went to make sure this past stays completely buried, I'm starting to question why I keep trying to find out what happened. I have nothing to do with any of this, so why am I so intent on trying to find a connection?"

Long Zhongyong didn't respond but just stared intently at Qinglin. That didn't seem to bother Qinglin, who continued, "At the same time, I'm also starting to wonder whether learning about what happened is really good for my mother and me. My mother suffers from amnesia. Could it be that her subconscious is preventing her from remembering those terrible things that happened? Perhaps something inside her is helping her completely forget the past. If she really is somehow related to the Lu family or is even one of them, what good would it do for her to know all this?"

Long Zhongyong responded, "I think what you are saying is that your mother left you with a bunch of words that are nothing but broken fragments and you would be better off just leaving them in pieces like that. If you take your time to ponder what those pieces are, they might lead you to yearn for something more. But if you take the time to find all the other related pieces and assemble them into their original form, you might not even have a place to put it. That's not to mention that the thing you end up assembling is likely not the true thing anyway. Is that what you're thinking?"

"That's partly it. Actually, when it comes down to it, I'm a coward. The reason I put off reading my father's diary for so long was that I was afraid there might be things in there I would be unable to handle. It would be terrifying to learn that my mother's past life somehow really was connected with the Lu family; it would be too complicated to comprehend. In some ways, I hope she doesn't wake up. Perhaps she is better off just lying there peacefully for the rest of her days."

Long Zhongyong was silent for a moment before saying, "Back when we were at the watchtower, I kept thinking about the expression on that crazy old man's face. There was something horrifying about it. He clearly knew your mother. I'm afraid that this might be too much even for you to take. I'm just your friend, but at times even I feel that it is all too much to handle."

"You're right. I'm really not such a tough guy. It's almost as if I have an instinctive fear when it comes to facing the cruelty of the world. I've got to admit that I'm really a bit scared," said Qinglin.

There followed a long period of silence in which Long Zhongyong didn't say a word.

It was deep into the dead of night. Although the wind blowing through the mountain valley wasn't that strong, it had a certain fierceness to it. From far off, they could indeed hear noises coming from the Ghost House. They composed a cacophony of strange sounds that seemed to have no beginning and no end. Then they suddenly heard a prolonged whistle. They didn't hear anyone calling "Soft burial," as Happy Lu had described, but they did seem to hear someone cry out "Still alive . . ." The voice trailed through the quiet night sky of Luxiao in a way that was alternately prolonged and then marked by short cries. It was terrifying.

Long Zhongyong cracked the window open. "It seems that there really is something going on in that mansion at night. It's as if all those lost souls buried there are unwilling to leave."

"Please close the window. All this is starting to make me really anxious," said Qinglin.

Long Zhongyong closed the window and after a brief pause finally said, "If that's the case, I wonder if it makes more sense for us to leave early? It's not too late to leave if you don't want to know about what happened and want to wash your hands of all this. We can just focus on our survey work and leave all that other stuff aside."

Qinglin heaved a deep sigh. "I think if we do what you suggest, I'll feel much more relaxed psychologically. On the surface our lives seem peaceful and normal, but as soon as you peel back the facade, you see this monster lurking there. It's actually quite terrifying. I guess I'm not the kind of person who has the courage to face reality, and I'm certainly not the kind of person who has the strength to carry the burden of history on his shoulders. Average people like me don't stir up confrontations. I need to learn how to follow the course of nature when it comes to what should be remembered and what should be forgotten. Time is our greatest teacher; I think I need to follow its lead."

"I like the way you said 'average people don't stir up confrontations,'" said Long Zhongyong. "If that's the case, you should just let it go. No need to continue thinking about all this and continually trying to chase down answers. I completely understand where you're coming from."

This was turning out to be one of the most stressful and emotional days of Qinglin's life. But that night he decided to let it all go. As soon as he embraced the idea of walking away, he felt as if a terrible burden had been lifted from his shoulders. He lay down in bed, heaved another deep sigh, and fell asleep.

Meanwhile, the cries coming from outside never ceased.

The sounds were so disturbing that Long Zhongyong didn't sleep a wink all night long.

13

HELL XVI: THE PETITION

Ding Zitao extended her hand. She could clearly see its shape. She could even see that her right hand was blood red. That was the hand she used to slap Second Mother and push her father. Second Mother's face still had the imprint of her fingers on her cheek after being hit. She wondered, was this Second Mother's blood that she was seeing on her hand? She wondered how she had been able to bring herself to raise her hand and actually hit Second Mother like that? That's right, she remembered: she had seen the way her mother cried when Second Mother first married into the family, and from that she moment harbored an instinctive hatred for her. One day she even secretly threw away Second Mother's rouge. When Second Mother discovered what she had done, she punished her by hitting the palm of her hand with a ruler. She also threatened her by saying she would do it again if she ever told her parents. She never told her parents. That's right, this hand that struck Second Mother was the same hand that was once hit by that ruler. Ding Zitao thought, *My brain might not remember the pain anymore, but the palm of my hand still remembers.*

That path became clearer. It was raining, and the rainwater was beginning to wash away this boundless darkness; it rinsed the sky until some hazy forms appeared. She could see Daiyun walking down a corridor toward her. She passed through two separate atriums and entered the main entrance hall.

Two guests were seated in the hall. Grandpa Lu Ziqiao had an excited look on his face. He was holding a letter he was reading as he was speaking with the guests. Daiyun thought both guests looked familiar, but she didn't know who they were.

One of the guests said, "The party leaders from the county all know about your family. They said you made major contributions to the revolution by helping to bring down the Qing and opposing the local bandits. Given your outstanding service, when the comrades from the working group received this petition signed by all the villagers, they decided not to come after the Lu family."

Grandpa Lu replied, "That's excellent news. Lu Da, when you go back, please tell the comrades from the working group that I, Lu Ziqiao, promise that my family will always stand on the side of the government and follow the government leaders. You can also tell the villagers that after the Lunar New Year holiday I will share half of all our grain and divide it among them. And if the village agricultural association ever needs to use my horse cart to purchase goods for the Chinese New Year, they can use it anytime."

The guest named Lu Da said, "Thank you, Master Lu. I understand. Everyone in the village knows how generous the Lu family is."

The other guest chimed in, "Don't worry, Master Lu. Everything will be fine."

"That's good to hear," replied Grandpa Lu. "As long as the Lu family is doing well, the entire village will prosper. From now on, no matter what happens, I'm committed to setting aside half of all my business profits to benefit Luxiao Village. We can use those funds to build a school, provide a medical clinic, and repair the nearby roads and bridges. You know I am a man of my word. I apologize that I didn't do more in the past; I hope the villagers can forgive me."

Lu Da pointed to the letter Grandpa Lu was holding and said, "I need to take that back to the village."

Grandpa Lu put the paper back in its envelope and handed it to him. The two men took the document and bowed deeply before taking their leave.

Daiyun was perplexed as she watched them leave. She then handed Grandpa Lu a letter. "Zhongwen wrote," she said. "He said he might not be able to make it back in time for the Lunar New Year. But he is worried about us. He is already set up there with a house and wants us to join him."

Grandpa Lu took the letter to read it for himself. "Hmm, things are actually starting to look good right now. The new government is doing a lot of positive things to help the people. I'm planning on creating a second gate on the eastern wall of the compound; we'll open up two courtyards there and establish a school. No matter rich or poor, all the children from Luxiao Village will be able to attend and get an education. You and Huiyuan can be their teachers. While Ding Zi is still young, he can learn to read and write right here at home. He'll have time to go to school somewhere else when gets a little older."

Daiyun nodded and headed toward the door, but after a few steps she turned around to say, "I heard the struggle sessions they have been holding against the landlords in Poding Village are quite fierce. They are also holding them in South Mountain Village. Ritchie said they even killed some people there. We are also categorized as landlords, and we own even more property than the do. We are all getting a bit worried."

"Don't worry," assured Grandpa Lu. "I've already found a way to deal with this issue. I had everyone in the village sign a petition. They all attested to the fact that although the Lu family is classified as a landlord family, we have always been good, fair-minded landlords. Whether or not it was when we helped the Communist guerrilla forces or when we aided in the suppression of the bandits, we have always been recognized for our service to the government. We have a lot of land, but that was all left to us by our ancestors. There is no reason to hold a meeting to struggle against me; I've already agreed to divide our land and share it with everyone. I will always stand on the side of the government."

Daiyun was visibly worried. "But . . . will that be enough?"

"Of course," Grandpa Lu confidently replied. "Everyone in the village signed that petition. The government knows all about it. I've done so many things to help them. How could they possibly turn their back on us? That's why the comrades in charge have already agreed not to struggle against our family."

"That's wonderful! They already agreed?" Daiyun was ecstatic. "My parents have also been designated landlords. Do you think you can talk to my father to convince him to do the same thing you did?"

Grandpa Lu hesitated. "Well . . . this is the kind of thing that needs the approval of the village agricultural association. And your father never did anything for them. Instead, he just spent all his time on leisure activities like playing *go* and painting. Instead of donating money or grain to support the cause, he just wasted his time on those worthless hobbies of his. I don't see how they would ever agree."

"Does that mean my family will be struggled against?" Daiyun asked.

"That's hard to say. But you should tell your father to be careful," warned Grandpa Lu.

Daiyun was clearly unhappy. "My father might not be as wise as you, but he is an honest and good person. If you had such a great plan, why didn't you share it with him? I'm sure the people in our village would have signed a petition to support my family. My family always treated the poor people in our village really well. People even refer to my father as Kind Man Hu. If the comrades leading the struggle meetings agree, I'm sure the villagers would agree to spare my family from being targeted."

Grandpa Lu didn't say anything more; he just waved her away. But as she was leaving he said, "You're still young, you don't understand these things. All we can do now is protect ourselves—and we'll be extremely lucky if we are able to do even that! Tell you father to use his head and do whatever he can to survive the coming storm. By the way, when you write back to Zhongwen, tell him not to worry. He should try to make it back for the Lunar New Year if he can."

Daiyun had a long face as she left the room. She was bitterly angry; she felt that Grandpa Lu was being too selfish in not sharing his plan with her father.

But at that moment Ding Zitao was already calm. She thought, *Grandpa Lu was right: they would be extremely lucky to just protect themselves.* Yet in reality the family still proved to be terribly unlucky. Grandpa Lu miscalculated the situation; in the end, he was unable to save himself, and his entire family was sacrificed. The hatred those people felt was not necessarily aimed at a specific family. Rather, their hatred was aimed at all rich people, and dividing the wealth and property of the rich among themselves was something they all wanted.

HELL XVII: THE OTHER SIDE OF THE PEONY

The light was getting brighter.

Ding Zitao instantly realized that everything in front of her was opening wider. The only strange thing was that under the light, she could no longer see the path she had walked, nor could she see what she was wearing; she didn't even know whether she was wearing shoes or not. *What a strange place!*

All she knew was that she had been walking for a long, long time. But was it a stone path or a dirt road? Was she walking on flat ground, or was it a terraced path through the mountains? She couldn't tell. Nonetheless, she just kept moving forward, ascending, and walking, walking.

She reflected on all the levels she had already walked—seventeen so far. She shed no tears and felt no anger or pain. All she thought was that if there were indeed eighteen levels, then she had definitely landed in hell. But what would be beyond those eighteen levels? What place would be waiting there? Who would be there? Would anyone she knew be there?

Ding Zitao was bewildered. And in her bewilderment she saw Daiyun holding Ding Zi. She was standing in her room and appeared to be in a daze. Her bed was a bit messy, but Little Tea was busy straightening it.

Little Tea said, "The village is pressing us hard to start divvying up our property and valuables. Master said you should hand over everything that's not of use."

"What does he mean by everything that's not of use? I use everything I have!" Daiyun protested.

Little Tea explained, "Master said any gold or silver jewelry should be handed over. So I didn't dare hold on to anything; there was just one pair of your silver bracelets that I hid. I remember your telling me that your grandmother gave them to you as a birthday present when you turned ten. But I didn't dare try hiding anything else. Auntie and Huiyuan were both there watching. Miss Huiyuan said that if they searched the house and found any of this, they might kill someone!"

"What business is it of theirs?" scoffed Daiyun.

Little Tea again tried to explain. "Master ordered them to have all the women of the household hand everything over. Just now Auntie and Huiyuan came by again to tell me that you must even give up that embroidered silk comforter you received as a wedding gift. I had no choice; I had to give it to them. I still don't understand what kind of a poor person would want that!"

Daiyun's expression immediately soured. She cried out angrily, "They could never stand the fact that I had that embroidered silk comforter! Auntie complained to me a long time ago about how she never got such a beautiful comforter when she got married! What does she expect—I come from a respectable family! Who does she think she is? She's just a cheap opera singer! The only reason she can live this life is because she was able to seduce Master Lu!"

Little Tea replied, "When Miss Huiyuan marries, Master will probably provide even more items like that."

"Humph, who said anything about her ever getting married!" Daiyun protested. "Don't tell me she is going to wait for her dear Jindian to return? Even if he comes back, I don't think Jindian would want her!"

Little Tea said, "Madame Lu had wanted Miss Huiyuan to marry into the Li family from Poding Village. But Old Wei ruined it with his big mouth! He said that someone had seen Jindian in Chongqing, and he was now a big-shot cadre! When Huiyuan heard that, she refused to marry into the Li family. Master Lu said that if Jindian was really now a cadre, he would approve of her marrying him."

"Jindian is a cadre?" Daiyun was surprised. "Really? If he's really a cadre, why would he still be interested in Huiyuan? There are plenty of educated girls for him to choose from!"

"That's right," Little Tea nodded.

Daiyun was going through the drawers in her dresser when she abruptly asked, "They also took away my red peony quilt?"

Little Tea faced her with a guilty expression. She nodded, "Uh, Huiyuan said we had to turn it over to them."

Daiyun retorted angrily, "My mom went all the way to Chongqing to buy this! Do you mean to tell me that we can't even keep a simple quilt?"

"Miss, please try to just let it go," begged Little Tea. "You can use your cotton quilt. Madame Lu also handed over many of her personal items. Master even forced her to give away her fur-lined gown. Madame Lu has been crying ever since."

"Didn't Zhongwen bring his mother that gown all the way from Shanghai? She had it for less than a year. I remember how much she loved that gown," said Daiyun.

"That's right," said Little Tea. "But Master said we need to divide up our property, so we have to hand it all over. Huiyuan and Auntie already took it away. They donated it to the village agricultural association."

Daiyun was silent. She sat there on the edge of the bed, a look of sadness on her face. Little Tea took Ding Zi out to the garden to play. But Daiyun just sat there alone. She was especially crushed to have to let go of her red peony quilt. Her mother had spent an entire day going store to store to pick it out. She couldn't even hold on to this token of her mother's love?

It was almost dusk when Daiyun went through the compound to look around. Every corner of the house was in chaos. Grandma wore a long face and didn't even say anything when she saw Daiyun. But Huiyuan was bouncing around the compound while humming a song; she actually seemed quite chirpy.

"I handed over all my jewelry," Huiyuan announced proudly. "I also turned over the leather shoes and leather handbag my brother gave me. The only thing I held on to were two cotton outfits. There should be equality between the rich and the poor. If we really want to make sure the people who work the fields own their own land, our family needs to do their part and make a sacrifice. Don't you agree?"

Daiyun replied coldly, "Sure . . . but that doesn't mean you needed to sacrifice my wedding quilt!" She wasn't in the mood to hear Huiyuan's response and walked straight out of the room.

In that moment, Ding Zitao was thinking about how beautiful the quilt had looked when it was spread out on her bed. Everyone was gathering around to see, and they all were complimenting her on how gorgeous it looked. That one quilt seemed to light up her entire bridal chamber.

She marveled at the fact that early in her life she had once experienced such moments of splendor.

HELL XIII: THE GATE OF HELL

The light was growing increasingly bright. Ray after ray of shining light flooded her vision, its radiance almost hurting her eyes. Was this the path that would lead to a way out?

Ding Zitao was astonished.

She could now clearly see that this was a path surrounded by the colors of spring. Bushels of flowers adorned both sides of the road. She couldn't discern the color or shape of the flowers, but she could strongly sense their presence. The rays of bright light in front of her kept hovering from right to left as if they were floating, or perhaps guiding her.

Ding Zitao wondered, *Am I really emerging from the depths of hell? Or perhaps I'm walking toward another hell where you can see bright sunlight shining down just before you enter? If there is sunlight, will I be able to see myself?*

Ding Zitao could no longer remember what she looked like. But then she thought that even if she couldn't see herself, it didn't matter. The most important thing was getting out of hell.

A horse cart was fast approaching.

But it wasn't the usual driver sitting in the cart. As the cart got closer, Ding Zitao could finally see clearly: it was Jindian driving! Sitting in the cart beside him were Daiyun and Little Tea.

Ding Zitao felt as if her heart were going to jump out of her chest. A terrible sense of guilt suddenly assaulted her.

Daiyun sat in the cart chatting with Little Tea. She was wearing a crimson cheongsam and had around her neck a silk scarf that Zhongwen had given her as a gift. Her hand was gently clasping her belly, and her face was flushed with a look of happiness.

Daiyun was returning from the hospital in town; she had just learned that she was pregnant. Lu Zhongwen was still in Shanghai, so she and Little Tea went to the telegraph office to send him a telegram.

"Jindian, slow down!" Little Tea exclaimed. "Don't topple our dear Miss!"

"No problem!" Jindian yelled as he drove the cart.

"I'm sure that Zhongwen will be jumping for joy when he hears the news! I'll bet he'll rush right home to see you," said Little Tea.

Daiyun laughed. She knew that Little Tea was right. "But Zhongwen seems interested only in having a son. I'm afraid he'll be upset if it turns out to be a girl."

"Don't worry, Miss," Jindian assured her. "Master Lu is the one intent on having a grandson, but I'm sure Young Master will be happy either way. I remember when Young Master was still a little boy, he really doted on Huiyuan."

Little Tea laughed. "There is a big difference between having a daughter and a little sister!"

"Well, they're both girls!" said Jindian. "Anyway, I know that the Young Master really has a soft spot in his heart for little girls."

"Jindian, this is the first time you've driven us in the horse cart. We should thank you for giving us the pleasure of riding with you! You're our lucky star!" exclaimed Daiyun.

"Jindian, if you really want to bring Daiyun good luck, you should see to it she has a healthy baby boy!" joked Little Tea.

"Okay then, a boy it is!" Jindian laughed.

Jindian's words made both Daiyun and Little Tea giggle. The crisp sound of their laughter echoed throughout the mountain valley.

Daiyun knew the only reason that Jindian was driving them was that Grandpa Lu Ziqiao had already sent most of the other servants home. He said they no longer needed so much help around the compound; they just kept a few servants on to care for the sick and elderly members of the clan.

Daiyun asked, "Jindian, how come you didn't leave with the others? I heard that you elected to stay with us."

"Ritchie and I both wanted to stay," said Jindian. "Both of us are orphans who were raised by the Lu family; this is the only life we are accustomed to. Also, Ritchie said that he's not going anywhere without Little Tea!"

Little Tea retorted, "Stop that! I'm sure *you're* the one who insisted on staying for Huiyuan's sake!"

"Hey, stop that crazy talk! You'll get me into trouble!" protested Jindian.

Daiyun flashed Little Tea a look and whispered, "Stop with that nonsense! Master Lu and his wife would scold you if they heard you talking like that!"

"Master publicly declared that there should be equality between the rich and the poor. But when it comes to his own family, there is no such thing as equality," said Little Tea.

Daiyun admonished Little Tea, "Do you really think there is such a thing as equality in this world?"

Little Tea meekly muttered, "Well . . . that's what Master said. That's also what Uncle said."

"There will never be true equality between the rich and the poor. Where or when in the world have you ever seen equality between the rich and the poor?" retorted Daiyun.

Little Tea pouted but didn't respond.

That's when Jindian suddenly spoke up. "Both Second Young Master and Huiyuan have said that the new society will be a place where true social equality will be achieved. Masters and servants will all be treated the same; they will just be assigned to do different jobs."

"Is that also what Zhongwen said?" asked Daiyun.

"That's right. The three of them were in the Young Master's room flipping through books together and chatting. Young Master said he agreed with what his siblings said. When I went in to bring him water, Miss Huiyuan even asked, 'Jindian, did you hear what he said? In the future we will all be equal.'"

Daiyun offered a cool smirk. "But remember, the issue between you and Huiyuan has nothing to do with equality. It has to do with the deep enmity between your two families."

"What went on between earlier generations has nothing to do with Jindian," Little Tea said.

"What enmity are you talking about? Are you saying there is some kind of hatred between my family and the Lu family?" Jindian was visibly shocked.

"Oh, you didn't know about that?" Daiyun said with surprise.

"I have never heard anything about that," said Jindian.

Daiyun and Little Tea both fell silent. Their horse cart left the flat land near the embankment and moved on to the small path through the mountains.

The path was surrounded by the mountain on one side and the river on the other. A riotous assortment of pink and golden wildflowers were blooming on both sides of the path. The flowers followed the narrow muddy road as it twisted through the mountains as if it were embracing them.

Daiyun abruptly declared, "This is the same horse cart your mother rode in when she was driven into town to see the Western doctor."

"I know about that," said Jindian. "She was at risk of having a miscarriage. There was a rainstorm that night and the roads weren't in very good condition; the ditch beside the road was flooded. Master Lu lent my father his horse cart to take my mother to the doctor. But they got there too late and there was no way to save her."

Daiyun offered a wry smile. "You know they got there too late, but do you know *why* they got there too late?"

Jindian was again visibly surprised. "Why? Didn't it have to do with the rainstorm?"

Little Tea jumped in to plainly tell the rest of the story. "I heard Amah Wu tell the story. Master wanted your family's property to build an ancestral hall. Your family refused. They argued about this over and over. Then the day your mom went into labor, your father asked the Lu family if he could borrow their horse cart. But the Lu family said they would agree only if your father would sign the contract to sell his land to the Lu family. You dad refused, but after running back and forth, he finally realized he had no other options. In order to save your mother's life, he finally signed the contract. But he was too late; he had already lost too much time. Amah Wu wanted to tell you a long time ago to dissuade you from falling in love with Miss Huiyuan, since there is this bad blood between your families."

The cart bumped around violently as Jindian yelled, "You're lying! That can't be!"

"Zhongwen said that it was Old Wei who made the decision," explained Daiyun. "But do you know what happened later? Anyway, you can ask Amah Wu yourself. The only reason I am telling you all this today is so that you don't get any ideas about Huiyuan. There is no way the two of you can ever be together."

Little Tea continued, "Old Wei and Amah Wu really wanted to tell you a long time ago, but they were afraid you might obsess over what happened, and they thought it wouldn't be good for you to know. Today we were finally able to share this with you on their behalf."

"That's right," said Daiyun. "Your case is different from that of Ritchie. Ritchie and Little Tea actually come from the same class, so they are a perfect match. But you shouldn't set your sights so high. Just take one look at Grandpa Lu—do you really think you could ever marry his daughter?"

Jindian remained silent.

For the rest of the ride home, no matter what Daiyun or Little Tea said, Jindian didn't say another word or laugh at any of their jokes.

The horse cart kept winding through the mountain paths as if entering a labyrinth. Over and over, Jindian took a series of wrong turns and had to go back. It was gradually growing dark, yet the cart continued forward; it felt as though they might never emerge from those mountains.

Daiyun and Little Tea both fell silent. Neither of them blamed Jindian for getting them lost; instead, they just sat there as he kept driving them in circles. Finally they caught sight of a lantern in the distance: it was Old Wei. He had come on horseback to find them.

Old Wei was nearly out of breath. "I was worried at home thinking that since this was Jindian's first time taking the cart into town, he might get lost in the dark on the way back. I see I was right, wasn't I?"

Jindian didn't respond. Instead, Daiyun answered, "That's right. We were completely lost."

"Just follow the light from my horse and I'll lead you back," said Old Wei.

All the wildflowers disappeared in the vast darkness as everything in nature became enveloped by the night. The only thing visible was that lantern dangling from Old Wei's horse; it gently rocked back and forth without rhyme or reason, like a lost soul wandering through the night.

First thing the next morning, Little Tea frantically sought out Daiyun to tell her that Jindian was missing.

Shocked, Daiyun asked anxiously, "Do you think it has to do with what we told him last night? Perhaps we said too much?"

"I'm afraid you're right," replied Little Tea.

Daiyun thought for a moment. "Don't say a word about this to anyone. Just pretend we don't know anything. Otherwise Master Lu will surely scold us."

"Understood," said Little Tea. "But you should realize that even if Master loses his temper, it is only for a little while. But if Miss Huiyuan learns, I'm afraid she will hate us for the rest of her life."

Ding Zitao was struck by a sudden revelation.

She finally understood that the path adorned by wildflowers was actually her road to hell. It was on that path, as she chased that lost soul appearing and disappearing through the night, that she first stepped through the gate of hell.

Now she was back at that very same gate. And as she raised her foot to step over the threshold, a flash of blinding light almost knocked her to the ground.

14

THE SECRET UNDERGROUND TUNNEL

Qinglin and Long Zhongyong spent an entire day at the Ghost House.

That long talk they'd had on the first night there seemed to allow Qinglin to unburden himself of some of the things that had been bothering him. First thing the next morning, Happy Lu went into town for a meeting, and the two of them returned to the Ghost House to go back up the tower. The gate to Sanzhitang was unlocked, so they went right in. They encountered no other people and were able to go straight up the tower.

Once they reached the top, Long Zhongyong kept taking photos of the property from many different angles. Meanwhile, Qinglin was sketching the entire estate, all the while commenting on how rusty his skills had gotten.

That afternoon they then went into each atrium to measure, sketch diagrams, and catalog the many unique characteristics of the property. As in many other wealthy private residences from this period, the beams, pillars, and window lattices in the Ghost House all featured intricate carvings that told all kinds of stories. The window lattices featured images of the four respectable occupations: fisherman, woodcutter, farmer, and scholar; there were also images of magpies announcing their safety. On the beams were carvings from traditional stories like the mouse that married off his daughter and the kylin that saw off his son. The elegance of the imagery inside the compound marked a stark contrast with the embrasures built into the courtyard walls.

"It looks as if life here in the compound was extremely peaceful and comfortable, but I'm sure that was only the case for the women and children who lived here. I suspect the head of the household must have been filled with worries and anxiety," observed Qinglin. "Just take one look at the tower and all the defensive measures he took with the cannon touch holes and you can see that."

"The master of the house needed to make his family feel safe. That tower is actually a sentry post and a turret. The fact that he added a pavilion on top wasn't a sign of his romantic imagination; rather, it was a way of telling people that the main function of the tower wasn't to defend against attackers but to enjoy the scenery and recite poetry," explained Long Zhongyong, before adding, "I think the real tension here lies in the way this structure combines war and peace within its very design."

The two of them laughed at that comment.

Long Zhongyong continued, "The Japanese architect Tadao Ando once said that architecture is something to be experienced with all five senses, not just the eyes. As I stand here today, I am much better able to appreciate the importance of what he said."

They calmly chatted as they carried out their work. It was as if all those other things never happened and they had never even heard the stories. *We're professionals and should focus on the job at hand.* Qinglin repeated that sentence to himself several times; it was as if he were using it to help him dispel all those terrible thoughts about past events.

That afternoon Long Zhongyong said that he wanted to take a few more aerial shots of the entire property at dusk; the lighting during that time would be much softer. And so they again ascended the tower.

It was extremely dark on the lower levels of the tower. During their previous two visits they had never really gotten a good look at the layout down there. But this time, as Long Zhongyong was on the lower stairway, he discovered evidence that something had been moved since last time. He went over to get a closer look. He exclaimed when he saw what looked like a secret door exposed.

Qinglin followed right behind him, and the two of them moved aside the random objects that had been blocking the door. They pushed open the wooden door to reveal a dark tunnel stretching before them. Extremely narrow and dark inside, it was in fact pitch-black and only big enough for one person. Long Zhongyong used the screen light from his cell phone to help him see the way. Without question, this was a secret underground tunnel. The direction it extended suggested the tunnel must lead underground through the mountain and open up somewhere on the other side.

"What does this mean?" asked Qinglin anxiously.

"What it means is that while all the locals have been assuming there is only one entrance into the compound, none of them know there is actually another secret way in," explained Long Zhonglong.

"Do you think it's possible . . . could it really be possible that . . ." Qinglin hesitated. "Happy Lu said the other side of that rear mountain connects to the Eternal Valley River."

"I think it is possible. We never found the crazy old man, but he must know about this tunnel," said Long Zhongyong. "If you want to check out where the tunnel leads, I'll go with you."

Leaning with his back against the wall, Qinglin closed his eyes as if lost in thought. He didn't respond to Long Zhongyong's suggestion. Long Zhongyong took a good look at Qinglin's pained expression before closing the tunnel door. He led Qinglin up the stairs of the tower to the pavilion crowning the tower's four stories. They ascended to the top in complete silence, stopping only when they reached the pavilion.

At that moment, the angular rays of the setting sun bathed the entire compound in warm sunlight. Under the blanket of the fading golden sunlight, the graves overgrown with wild grasses and weeds remained silent and unmoving. For fifty years they had lain thus, battered by wind and rain and giving birth to the wild grasses.

Long Zhongyong took out his camera and with his lens began to carefully document the garden. As his shutter clicked, he commented, "I really can't imagine how they could have made such a decision. Can you imagine the courage it took for them to do that?"

But Qinglin seemed disturbed by something. "Do you think anyone escaped through that secret tunnel? Could my mother have escaped that way? If so, wouldn't that mean that she was either the Lu family's daughter or daughter-in-law?"

"The real question is whether we should come back tomorrow to try to go through that tunnel to see where it leads," interjected Long Zhongyong. "Another question is whether we should tell Happy Lu about it. Besides, you can already guess what is going to be on the other side of that tunnel."

"I'm sure it must just be some abandoned plot of land," replied Qinglin.

"Of course," said Long Zhongyong.

"What I really want to know is whether or not this tunnel might lead to some kind of a resolution. I'm also wondering how the locals will react if they suddenly learn about the existence of this tunnel," said Qinglin.

"Perhaps the spirits here will never again be able to rest peacefully," said Long Zhongyong.

"I'm afraid if the locals find out, people will be coming through here every day making noise and disturbing the spirits," said Qinglin. "But that goes against the Lu family's wishes to let their deceased relatives quietly rest without being disturbed by the outside world. Their bodies should be allowed to become one with the earth. The structures on the property should be allowed to erode naturally over time. And after many, many years, people will gradually forget that there was a family that went by the name of Lu who lived in this place. Then, even further into the future, there will come a time when people won't even know that there was once a compound here—and they will certainly never know about the terrible things that once occurred here. It will eventually be just another one of those abandoned sites of ruin that we pass by and never give a second thought to."

"You really think that is the best outcome for this place?" asked Long Zhongyong.

"I think so," replied Qinglin. "Perhaps we should just pretend this place never existed."

"Are you sure that's the best approach?" Long Zhongyong asked. "You really don't want to know about who your mother really is and what actually happened to her? You don't want to know what kind of connection she has with Sanzhitang?"

"No . . . I don't want to know anymore," asserted Qinglin. "No matter what her relationship to this family may once have been, I don't want to know anymore. Even when she was still lucid, every fiber of her being tried to suppress the memory of what happened. Why should I try to figure it out now?"

Long Zhongyong heaved a deep sigh. "Sanzhitang, 'Hall of the Three Who Know' . . . I guess, in the end, it is heaven knows, the earth knows, and the ghosts know; and both you and I know nothing!"

"I've got a better one: at the end of the day, all meaning is absolutely meaningless," joked Qinglin.

The sky was growing dark and the sun was already setting behind the waves of mountains in the distance. Qinglin and Long Zhongyong descended from the tower. They had spent an entire day there, but never once did that terrifying crazy old man ever show his face.

First thing the next morning, Qinglin and Long Zhongyong got in their jeep and drove away from Luxiao Village. Since they were now more familiar with the lay of the land, they were able to drive much more quickly on the way back. They arrived at Chongqing that afternoon. Once they got to the airport, they each boarded separate flights home, Long Zhongyong to Shanghai and Qinglin to Shenzhen.

Qinglin's plane took off, leaving behind the illuminated city below. There in the clouds he gazed out the window as the sky grew darker. Qinglin suddenly felt as if everything that had happened were another lifetime ago.

THERE ARE SOME THINGS HEAVEN KEEPS HUMANS FROM KNOWING

Qinglin seemed to have finally let go of his obsession with his parents' past.

After taking a few days to rest in Shenzhen, he flew back to Wuhan. When he showed up at his company's headquarters, Liu Xiaochuan asked him how the search was going, but Qinglin just told him that Eastern Sichuan was a huge area and no one had heard of Sanzhitang; in fact, he could find hardly anyone who had heard of Hu Shuidang. Qinglin didn't want to talk about Sanzhitang, and he didn't want anyone else to know about that place. He thought, *Better not to do anything to further disturb the spirits of the Lu family.*

Liu Xiaochuan sighed, then said, "I guess that's the result one would expect. At the heart of most history are those parts that will always remain unknown. And in the end, so many of our conjectures turn out to be unreliable. And so there are many things in the world that we really don't need to know. That's because even if you think you know something, in reality it might be completely different from the actual truth."

"That's right," said Qinglin. "That's the same realization I came to during my trip. There are some things in life that heaven wants to keep humans from knowing. Instead, it just hands them over to time to let the passage of time gradually destroy them, and eventually . . . it gives them a soft burial."

Liu Xiaochuan laughed. "I see that although you didn't find what you were looking for, you did learn something. I think this trip turned you into a philosopher."

"I'm no philosopher. I just figured some things out for myself." Qinglin smiled.

The first day back in Wuhan, Qinglin spent the entire night sitting by his mother's bedside. Her face was peaceful but marked by an emptiness and was devoid of expression and movement.

Qinglin sat there tearfully in silence. He said, "Mom, I don't need to know what happened to you that made you lose your memory. I just want you to wake up and be able to live a peaceful and comfortable life. It would mean so much for me to know that you haven't lived in vain."

As he expected, Ding Zitao didn't have any reaction.

That night Qinglin packed up all his father's diaries and put them back inside that old leather trunk. He wondered where to put the trunk. He wanted to find a place where he would never have to look at those diaries again.

I DON'T WANT A SOFT BURIAL

Eventually things settled back into a normal routine.

On this day there was heavy rain with occasional thunder—the type of weather common during the summers in Wuhan. But besides the rain, everything was quite normal, so normal that there was barely anything worth mentioning.

That's when Qinglin received a phone call from his mother's caretaker, Donghong.

Donghong sounded somewhat flustered, almost frantic. "As I was feeding your mom today, she seemed to be more lucid than usual. Her eyes were moving and she even said, 'You can't go out.'"

Qinglin had been in a meeting, but the news was so exciting that he immediately apologized to his colleagues and told them he needed to rush home. He explained that his mother had been in a vegetative state for several years, but the caretaker just called and said she was able to move and even spoke.

As Qinglin burst into the house, he called out, "Mom! Mom! Are you awake? It's me, Qinglin!"

Ding Zitao could sense the sunlight radiating on everything. The brightness hurt her eyes.

She wondered, *Where am I?* It didn't feel like where she lived. She heard a girl's voice, but it wasn't Little Tea. There was also a male voice, but it wasn't Lu Zhongwen, and it certainly wasn't her baby, Ding Zi. *This isn't Sanzhitang or Qierenlu. Where in the world is this place?*

The voices began to grow chaotic. Then came a crack of thunder. With that sound of thunder came a desolate and heavy voice rolling through the air. It screamed, *Soft burial! Soft burial!*

The screams ignited Ding Zitao's anger. She looked to the sky in the direction of the thunder and yelled, *I don't want a soft burial! I don't want a soft burial!*

Qinglin was going over to open a window to let a little more light in when Donghong called out, "Listen! Your mother is saying something!"

Qinglin was shocked and rushed into her room. He leaned over beside her bed and saw his mother's lips quivering. He raised his voice to make sure she could hear him. "Mom, did you say something? What do you want to say? Take your time, just say it slowly."

Ding Zitao was finally able to make a sound. Her voice was extremely weak, but it couldn't have been clearer. "I don't want a soft burial!"

Donghong was confused. "What does that mean?"

Qinglin collapsed onto the bed. His mood turned sullen as he thought this must mean his mother was getting ready to leave him.

Indeed, it was on that night that Ding Zitao breathed her last. There was no struggle or pain. She just heaved a deep sigh and let go of this world.

SADNESS FLOWS FROM OUR BONES

Nobody knew about the difficulties Ding Zitao faced during her final years, and no one knew how many secrets she took to the grave when she left. Actually, whenever people die, they always take some secrets with them as they leave this world. Perhaps some of those secrets would shake the world if they were ever revealed . . . but if they remain unspoken, they will eventually just disappear into the wind.

Although no one around him noticed, deep down Qinglin was emotionally quite torn. He appeared calm, which set everyone else at ease; after all, Ding Zitao had been ill for so many years, and it seemed a blessing that when she finally passed, it was without pain and actually much more peaceful than anyone had expected.

Qinglin bought a coffin for his mother and wanted to buy a plot of land for her final resting place, but he didn't know where she would have wanted to be buried. The authorities no longer allowed traditional burials to be carried out in urban areas, but Qinglin worried about his mother being all alone if he buried her somewhere in the countryside. Burying her also opened up the question of what to do with his father's ashes. Qinglin wrestled with these different options; he thought about the old saying "Falling leaves all return to their roots," but that is predicated on a person having roots. Both his parents were people who spent their entire lives trying to rip out their own roots. He knew they would never want to go back from where they came.

Qinglin decided that one way to make his mother happy was to buy her a nice casket to rest in, and then he would have her cremated along with the casket. His wife and friends couldn't understand the logic behind that, but Qinglin insisted, "Just listen to me to on this. I have my own reasons for wanting to do this."

Seeing how stubborn her husband was being, his wife stopped nagging him about it. After all, this would be the last thing in life that he could do for Ding Zitao; now that his mother was gone, Qinglin was finally all hers. His friends, though, just assumed this was his way of expressing a final gesture of filial piety.

They held a simple memorial service for his mother. Since they didn't have any relatives, the only family members Qinglin had there were his wife and son. Both his parents had always been alone in this world. When Qinglin's friend asked him about why they didn't have more people in their lives, Qinglin would just say, "My parents were both orphans."

In the end, it was the Liu brothers who came over to bid a final goodbye to Ding Zitao; they also brought a memorial wreath on behalf of their sister, Liu Xiaowu. Both the Liu brothers made statements about how unpredictable the world can be, and they tried to console Qinglin by encouraging him to let things take their own course. After that, they both accompanied Qinglin as he took Ding Zitao on the journey to her final resting place. The care that the Liu brothers expressed moved not only Qinglin but also their other employees, who were all impressed by the level of attention their boss devoted to this funeral.

Qinglin brought along his father's ashes so they could be interred together with his mother's. The plot was actually not far away from where Liu Jinyuan was buried. Liu Xiao'an said, "Dr. Wu, Amah Ding, I hope you are able to rest in peace. My parents are also close by. Since you were all close friends, I hope you get to see each other when you have free time."

Somehow Liu Xiao'an's little speech made the people burning paper money giggle. All the sadness seemed to disperse into the air with the ashes of the paper money and those sounds of laughter.

That night Qinglin decided to sleep in his mother's room.

He lay down in his mother's bed and could smell her lingering presence. Finally, he was so shattered that he broke down in tears. It was as if the sadness he was feeling was flowing from deep in his bones. He cried for his mother, and he cried for his father. Those two lonely souls both lived with a lifetime of secrets. They were so careful never to let anyone know the truth. And even though they were married, neither knew the depth of the other's secrets. Even he as their son knew only one small part of the story. His father told him that there was no need for him to ever know more; that he should just focus on living a carefree life. Qinglin knew that wouldn't be too difficult. But late in the night when he was all alone, was there really any way to feel truly carefree?

Qinglin spent that whole night thinking about his parents. It was nearly sunrise by the time he finally drifted off to sleep.

By the time Qinglin finally woke up, the sun was already high in the sky. He went out to the garden to cut the bushes and water the plants. The air was refreshing, and he gazed up at the French window of his mother's now-empty bedroom; its white curtains seemed to emit a special warmth. Qinglin suddenly felt that he finally had the carefree and relaxed life that his father always wanted for him.

A page had turned. His family—the Wu family—would start anew with him. He would be the earliest ancestor in this new family tree. They would have no connection with the Dong family. Nor would they have any connection to other people who bear the surname Wu. Nonetheless, their family name would remain Wu.

His parents' remains were interred at Stone Gate Peak Mausoleum. Qinglin personally laid the slab stone over their tomb. Just before closing the lid, he quietly placed all his father's diaries, wrapped in a plastic bag, inside the tomb. Qinglin didn't end up leaving a hole in the tomb to allow their souls to go in and out as the people of Chu had done. Instead, his parents, their secrets, and their souls would be eternally buried here under this stone tablet. Qinglin closed everything off, tightly sealing it all away. He whispered, "Mom, Dad, don't worry. I'll be strong and try to live a carefree life."

According to Qinglin's perspective, a way for him to be strong was not to chase after those things he shouldn't know about. Time goes on forever, eventually giving a soft burial to everything that is real. Even if you think you really know something, how can you ever be sure that it is the entire truth?

CODA

SOME CHOOSE TO FORGET, OTHERS CHOOSE TO LEAVE A RECORD

Qinglin finally began living a more carefree life.

His parents were now two smiling portraits hanging on the wall in Qinglin's study. As time went by, Qinglin would often forget to so much as look up at them. But even when he wasn't paying attention, they were always there gazing down on him.

Late autumn had come again. The leaves were all turning yellow. Qinglin's project in Wuhan was coming to its end. Liu Xiaochuan seemed to rely on Qinglin more and more, and Qinglin understood that besides his relationship with his parents, the most important thing for him had been how dedicated he was to his work.

Another big project at work was just about to get started. It was a large development slated for a big plot of land near Liangzi Lake. The rocks and small islands surrounding the shoreline formed what looked like a series of jagged teeth. All the reeds around the lake were blown down by the heavy winds and, under the sunlight, glowed with a faint yellow luster. The scenery around the lake area was incredible.

Qinglin was quite excited as he inspected the area. The contours of the shore around the lake inspired his imagination. He could make his project unique, he realized, if he incorporated this beautiful landscape into his overall design. He decided he should call in Long Zhongyong to get his input.

As it happened, just as Qinglin was thinking of his old friend, Long Zhongyong called. Qinglin spoke excitedly as he picked up the phone: "I was just about to call you! I was going to try to convince you to come here to check out the site for our new project!"

Besides sending a few texts to express his condolences, Long Zhongyong hadn't been in touch since Qinglin's mother died. Long Zhongyong explained that he had actually called to check on how Qinglin had been coping since his mother's passing. From the sound of it, Qinglin was doing just fine.

Qinglin said, "I'm doing well. As soon as I decided to settle on being content with a modest life, everything became easy. Birth, death, sickness, and aging are experiences that we all go through. My mother, after all, was able to live a long life well into her seventies, despite her suffering with illness for so many years. I suppose her death was something to be expected."

"Actually, you don't need to worry about what lifestyle to settle on," explained Long Zhongyong. "We all have lots of choices in life. Some people decide to die a good death, while others decide to live a wretched life. Some people decide to hold on to all their memories, while others decide to forget. You can't say any one of those choices is 100 percent correct. All that matters is which path is best for you. So there's no need for you to think too much about that stuff. Just do what feels most natural for you and you'll be fine."

"I'm really not sure which option is most natural for me. All I know is that this is the only path forward for me," said Qinglin.

"That sounds good," said Long Zhongyong before asking his friend, "Do you know where I am right now?"

Qinglin laughed. "You're always running all over the damn place! How should I know? But if you have some free time, you should take a trip out here to Wuhan. The site for my next project is really amazing, and I could use your input. What do you say? Are you up for a trip?"

But Long Zhongyong responded, "I'm actually in Eastern Sichuan. How am I supposed to find time to fly out to Wuhan? I'm still working on my book."

Qinglin could feel his heart begin to race.

Before Qinglin could say anything, Long Zhongyong continued, "I'm in Luxiao Village. More precisely, I'm at Sanzhitang. Happy Lu helped me track down that crazy old man. His name is Ritchie. I tried all day to get him to talk, but in the end I could get only a few words out of him: 'Little Tea. Yunzhong Temple.'"

Qinglin suddenly felt dizzy. Little Tea, that was the name his mother had mentioned.

Long Zhongyong continued, "Last time we visited we heard the story about how the crazy old man had saved one of the Lu family's servants. This servant girl later took the oath of a Buddhist nun. I suspect that her name was Little Tea. She probably ended up at a place called Yunzhong Temple. Happy Lu told me that there indeed is a nearby temple with that name, and there is also a nunnery. Happy is going to take me there tomorrow."

Qinglin suddenly felt a sharp pain in his chest. He really didn't want to hear any more about any of this. He even felt that his own view of things somehow now aligned with that of the Lu family's Second Young Master—he didn't want anyone to ever know anything about Sanzhitang; he just wanted time to wash all that away.

Noticing the lack of response from Qinglin, Long Zhongyong eased his tone. "I understand how you feel. I know what you are going through. If what I uncover ends up being connected with your family or touches on any privacy issues, I'll be sure to change the names in my book to protect your identity. No need to worry! But I'm committed to seeing this book project through. When it comes to history, someone needs to preserve the truth about what happened."

Qinglin still said nothing. It wasn't that he didn't want to talk, but those words "Little Tea" had rendered him silent. His mother had told him that Little Tea was the servant girl who had accompanied her from her parents' house.

Long Zhongyong ended their conversation with his philosophy: "Some choose to forget, others choose to leave a record. But at the end of the day, we must all choose the kind of life we want to live—that's the way to go."

Qinglin hung up. He felt flustered and deeply upset.

A wind blew over the vast surface of the lake before him, sending a series of small waves rippling toward him.

That's right, he thought, *I've chosen to forget, while you have chosen to leave a record. But once you record what happened, how will I ever be able to forget?* And as for the truth of what happened, all Qinglin could do was offer a wry smile. *Can your one book really portray the truth? In this world, when it comes to what actually happened, there is no real truth.*

Autumn 2015, Wuhan

AFTERWORD

WE DON'T WANT A SOFT BURIAL

Many years ago there was a young lady who went into business for herself. One day when she was on a train going through a most difficult time in her life, she happened to read a novella I wrote entitled *The Scenery*. The novella struck her in a powerful way and gave her a kind of strength. She told herself, *One day I must meet the person who wrote this story.*

She eventually succeeded. She joined the ranks of the new upper class and even became the owner of one of the first villas built during that era in Wuhan, a beautiful single-standing multilevel house. After closing on the house, she brought her mother over to move in. Her mother, who had worked hard all her life, took one step inside the house and immediately started to tremble with fear. She said, "Oh no, what are we going to do? They are coming to divvy up the property!"

By the time her mother spoke those words she had already been suffering from Alzheimer's disease for many years.

I first met this woman back in the 1990s. At the time, I was the editor-in-chief of a magazine entitled *Celebrities Today* and she was an investor in documentary films. One of the partners she had been investing in was a colleague of mine from Hubei Television Station's documentary film division. Thanks to her investment, our division had several films that were awarded major international prizes. One day my colleague introduced us and we went out to dinner together.

Like most friends, we slowly got to know each other better. We started spending more time together, and we had more conversations, which gradually grew deeper. We would go out to dinner, have tea, and even go on a few trips together. I never had a good understanding of her business, but I knew that she was good at what she did. She rarely lost money on her investments and was a brilliant businesswoman.

It was also around this time that I met her mother. She was an elderly woman with fair white skin. Without our realizing it, her mother often became the subject of our conversations. She told me about how her mother had escaped alone from Sichuan; how she had lost her child while trying to get away; how she had taken a job as a nanny as a means of having a quiet, stable life; and how she had suddenly been assaulted with a strange fear and anxiety as soon as she moved into their villa. Her husband also told me how there had been a long time when her mother would wake up in the middle of the night screaming about how much pain she was in. She said her back hurt where she got hit by a buttstock. My friend told me that although her mother was suffering from Alzheimer's, she clearly heard her say, "I don't want a soft burial!"

The parts of my novel that depict the land reform movement are all taken from the historical experience of my friend's mother. But what is presented not only captures what her family went through but also represents what my own parents' families, many of my friends, and many other neighbors went through; this was a collective experience that affected countless people. All these people may lead very different lives, but the tragedies their families experienced are remarkably similar. What happened affected the next generation as well; as if marked from birth, they lived their lives in an abyss of discrimination. When you add up all the people affected, it is difficult to calculate the number. Once you were labeled a landlord, rich peasant, counterrevolutionary, bad element, or Rightist (or even the child of one of these classes), your entire life was destined to be stained by endless struggle and humiliation. The type of humiliation suffered ranged from the physical to the psychological; it was immersive and cut deep, all the way down to the bones. By the time things eventually settled down and one's "class status" (a term that I suspect many young people today don't know even though it was one of the most important determining factors of our youth) was no longer the decisive criterion to determine whether they were a good or a bad person, almost all those people who emerged from the abyss decided to take that era when they were forced to live without dignity and those private experiences filled with scars and trauma and bury them away deep inside their hearts. They never mentioned their experiences, they never looked back, and they had no intention of ever letting their children and grandchildren find out what had happened. It was as if speaking of those things would be like ripping the scars off old wounds, and they couldn't bear to go through that pain again. It was a pain so unbearable that one doesn't want to go on living.

Then two years ago my friend's mother passed away. I ran into my friend at a conference not long after her mother's funeral. She invited me out to dinner and told me about how her mother died. She had bought her mother an expensive coffin for the cremation. Most of her friends couldn't understand why anyone would spend so much money on a coffin just to have it cremated with the body; it didn't make sense. But she insisted on doing it her way. She told me that before her mother died, she had repeated over and over that she didn't want a soft burial. My friend knew she had to fulfill her mother's wish.

It was during that meal that I was struck by those two words: "soft burial." It was as if something had been ignited inside me. I spent the entire day thinking about those two words. It was as if I was given a glimpse of a black hole and I couldn't see the bottom. There had always been those who wanted to explore what was inside, but no one had ever gotten to the bottom of it. In fact, they still hadn't been able to make out even the most basic forms lurking inside. Time is not only silent but also devoid of color, sound, and form; it breaks down countless parts of our human world and turns them to ash. *Soft burial it is*, I thought to myself.

I told my friend that I wanted to write a novel and I was going to name it *Soft Burial*.

That's how it began.

First I started with the title. I put all my other writing assignments aside. And in order to create a focused writing environment, beginning right after the 2014 Lunar New Year, I avoided all my other commitments and even avoided the cold winter in Wuhan by going to a place near the ocean in Shenzhen where I could focus on this novel. The weather in Shenzhen during March was perfect. I stayed at an old friend's house, which had been left vacant for a long time. My friend and her relatives were delighted to let me stay there to work on my novel. The environment was amazing: looking out the window you could see trees, flowers, and even the ocean. Sitting at my computer and gazing out the window, I felt as if the ocean were right outside my door. After dark, the sound of the waves crashing slipped into my dreams each night. Except for my daily morning stretches on the balcony and my evening walks, I barely left the house. Every morning my friend would prepare a simple breakfast, which usually consisted of cereal, eggs, or bread, and I would usually get a boxed meal delivered for lunch. The chef who prepared the box lunches was from Hunan, and his cooking exactly matched my taste. At night I'd have some fruit, a bowl of noodles, or often I'd just skip dinner altogether. It was the environment and lifestyle I had been craving for a long time.

But how should I tackle the subject matter? What kind of structuring device should I employ to express what I wanted to say? What should my angle be? How should I introduce my characters? What tone should I employ in order to create the right atmosphere? I started to tackle these questions one by one, and as I experimented, one by one, I shot down all my own early ideas. I felt as if I kept opening up door after door after door, but they were all leading me to dead ends—until finally I found the door that I wanted to walk through.

There is always an excitement in the process of writing. In that excitement you find a new kind of freedom. You can be with anyone you want; you can say anything you want to say. You are no longer conscious of the passage of time; no longer conscious of your own existence. You never feel bored or lonely, even though you might be all alone for days on end. The sound of your fingers typing away on the keyboard becomes your dialogue with the world. You can freely walk right up to people and hand them a piece of paper that explains your perspective and views on any number of things. And the words on that piece of paper are the same words you just typed on the computer.

This is a kind of freedom that we are unable to experience given the pressures and restrictions of the real world. That's why the joy experienced when writing is able to surpass all else and the magic of writing is able to perpetually extend—that's enough to make me never want to put down my pen.

Once the cold months passed, I returned to Wuhan. Without my realizing it, an assortment of random things in my life collided, requiring my attention. All these had a massive impact on my writing, and I had no choice but to tend to them. It wasn't until July of the following year that I was finally able to take care of everything.

I needed to complete my novel, and so I moved out to the suburbs in the Jiangxia District of Wuhan, shut myself off from the world, and got back to writing. I was able to quickly recapture the same state I was in a year earlier while in Shenzhen. The environment in Jiangxia was extremely peaceful, and the air quality there was great. I would start writing each afternoon and go straight until two o'clock in the morning. I would then sleep in until ten each morning. I think the famous Chinese novelist Lu Yao once said, "The morning starts in the afternoon." I suspect that only writers can fully appreciate what that means.

There was a small garden outside the front door where I planted peppers, tomatoes, and other vegetables, so my meals were extremely simple. Occasionally a colleague might drop by with fresh vegetables or take me out to lunch to discuss some editorial affairs at a magazine I sometimes write for. Another important daily task was taking time to go online to keep up with the various things happening with the literary magazine *Changjiang Literature & Art*, where I have some editorial duties.

I carried on like this for two months. All the while those two words "soft burial" seemed like a ghost that was continually chasing me down. I would constantly hear different voices whispering to me, "Don't give me a soft burial, I don't want a soft burial!" Each day around dusk I would go out for a walk around the nearby lake. As I strolled by the lake and through the forest, I could hear those strange cries, "I don't want a soft burial! We don't want a soft burial!" The voices I heard would send chills down my spine.

In late September I finally finished the first draft of the novel and began a long period of revisions. My schedule became much more flexible, and it was during this time that the Hubei Museum of Culture and History invited me to Chongqing to visit the ancient towns there. Accompanying me on that trip were two of my old friends, Shen Hongguang and Jiang Zuosu. This trip helped pull me out of the fictional world of Eastern Sichuan from my novel and deliver me to the real Eastern Sichuan. Much of the background story in *Soft Burial* takes place in this region. During my trip there I saw quite a few abandoned mansions, which helped me flesh out even more details for this book. And so I continued to tweak, revise, do more tweaking and more revisions; I worked on and off on the novel all the way until the end of the year.

During the long three-year period of writing, the words "soft burial" were like a seed buried deep in my heart. The seed began to take root and grow as I wrote, eventually growing into a tree. As the roots extended, the crown of the tree became increasingly lush; but with that lushness, my heart grew heavier. The shadowy forms of countless people flashed before my eyes. Among them were my parents and their siblings; they kept coming back to me, converging and overlapping with the characters in my novel. I thought back to those family stories that they rarely spoke of while they were alive and those relatives of mine that I rarely ever had contact with. They were all the children of former landlords and government officials. And they all used the method of silence to give a soft burial to their own past. This has resulted in all of us having absolutely no understanding of our grandparents' generation. Except for my paternal grandfather, whom I know a little bit about thanks to an old newspaper article that recorded how he was killed by the Japanese, I have absolutely no knowledge of my relatives from that generation; I don't even know their names. As I wrote this book, I reflected on my own family's past; and as I gradually came to understand those members of my family from that generation, I also came to understand Qinglin and his father. That's right, they too didn't want us to know what had happened. They didn't want to pass on to us the historical burden that they had carried their entire lives. And so, silence became their best option for achieving that goal. As far as I can remember, the one thing my mother would repeatedly express regret about was how tragic her sister's life was. How many other lives are hidden behind the same kind of sighs and regrets my mother had about her sister? Perhaps that will be left for another novel.

And so as I wrote this book, I also reflected on my own past. The images of Ding Zitao's face, my friend's mother's face, and that of my aunt would alternately appear before my eyes. These were all women who walked through life alone; they shouldered the heaviest burden and the deepest pain, and yet, in the end, their lives seemed so inconsequential, as if they had never even existed in this world.

To be put into the earth without a coffin and have your body placed directly into the dirt is one kind of soft burial, but when the living insist on consciously or unconsciously cutting themselves off from what happened, covering up the past, abandoning history, and refusing to remember, this is another form of soft burial committed over the passage of time. And once the past has been committed to a soft burial, it will likely lie there generation after generation, forgotten for all eternity.

And so, what I can do in a situation like this is actually quite simple. I can sit down and diligently commit my knowledge, feelings, confusions, and pain to paper. I can let my writing transform into a kind of memory to express my conflicted and complex feelings. That's enough.

Even when my friend's mother was no longer mentally lucid, she was still able to utter those words: "I don't want a soft burial."

I think she's right. We don't want a soft burial.

May 2016

Printed and bound by CPI Group (UK) Ltd, Croydon, CR0 4YY

01/07/2025

14697017-0004